VEIL Online

VEIL ONLINE

Book 1

An Epic LitRPG Series

Written by John Cressman

ISBN: 978-0-9844087-3-3 (Paperback)
ISBN: 978-0-9844087-1-9 (Hardcover)
ISBN: 978-0-9844087-4-0 (Amazon Kindle)
ISBN: 978-0-9844087-5-7 (Audiobook)

Any references to historical events, real people, or real places are used fictitiously. Names, characters, and places are products of the author's twisted imagination.

Front cover image by Karen Dimmick from ArcaneCovers.com.
Book design by Rebecka Yaeger of Becka's Best Author Services.

Printed by Maverick-Gage Publishing in conjunction with IngramSpark, in the United States of America.

First printing edition 2020.

Maverick-Gage Publishing
Allentown, PA
info@maverick-gage.com
www.maverick-gage.com

John Elijah Cressman
www.johnecressman.com

*To my biggest fan and mother,
Diane Cressman. For all the stories
she read to me at bedtime that helped
me dream big.*

*To my dad, John P. Cressman,
who taught me the value of hard work
and pushing through obstacles to get
the work done.*

*To my wife, Angela, who allowed
me to sequester myself away in my
office to write my books.*

*To my brothers and sisters who
are the only ones who I can exchange
movie quotes with and understand
what I'm talking about.*

*To my nieces and nephews, who
bring laughter and joy into my life
whenever I see them.*

*And to my orange tabby cat Luna,
who allows me to take care of her,
feed her and be her undying servant.*

Chapter 1

Mordred Blacklock's heart skipped a beat as part of the stone he'd been using as a handhold crumbled under his right grip, sending stone tumbling to the moat below. He experienced a moment of vertigo and a sensation of falling and then suddenly he was dangling from only the fingers of his left hand 50 feet above a frozen moat.

Mordred knew it was only a game. At this moment, he was Mordred Blacklock, a level 95 *Vampyre Assassin* in a fully immersive virtual reality game called Virtual Emulation Immersive Landscape, or as most people called it VEIL Online. But back in his apartment, he was just an ordinary human named Jace Burton, who was lying in a virtual reality pod in his living room. But that wasn't his reality right now. Right now, he was in VEIL and he was seconds away from falling to his death in the game.

Dying would mean he'd have a death penalty for days. If that happened, it would lower his skills and experience gain for four days. He'd have to wait until it ended before he could attempt the keep again. Now that the other members of his group knew about the brigand fortress and the named items the boss would drop, they wouldn't wait. They'd either find another rogue or one of them would sell the location to another group. So, he had to get it right the first time if he wanted the last piece of his set gear.

Getting the last piece of the *Assassin's Mantle* set, the *Sash of Kobadera*, would give him the boost he'd need to be considered for the top-level raids.

The top-level raids were by invite only and to be considered they had a minimum standard of gear. The sash would complete the set and he'd finally be eligible to raid. It had taken him months to get the other pieces and tonight he'd finally get the last piece. But not if he fell.

Pulling himself back into the moment, his right hand scrambled around the stonework of the fortress wall trying to find purchase. Finally, his slim vampyre fingers finally closed on a seam in the mortar. After a moment of testing it, he dug his fingers in and took some of the weight off his aching left hand.

"You okay up there pointy-teeth?" came a voice in his head, nearly startling him. It was Krogan, the Dwarf Paladin he'd recruited to help with this adventure. Their warlock had cast a *Far Speak* spell on the group earlier. The high-level spell allowed players in the same group to communicate with each other mentally. The spell was perfect in adventures and raids since players could always hear each other over the sounds of battle. It also allowed group members to communicate up to a mile away.

"Just a little loose mortar," Jace mentally responded to his team, still trying to slow his racing heart.

"Did they hear the rock?" asked a worried voice that Jace recognized as belonging to Dharci, their Rabbit-kin Healer. Rabbit-kin were one of the furry neutral races. And just like a rabbit, Dharci seemed to be a bit skittish.

He wouldn't have invited her but she and Krogan were a package deal.

Tilting his head up towards the parapet, Jace scanned the top of the wall for any signs of movement. He knew some guards patrolled the walls, but they were humans and their hearing shouldn't be acute enough to hear a rock hitting the iced-over moat, all the way down at the bottom of the wall.

"Did they?" she asked again, a little more urgently.

Jace gritted his teeth at the impatient healer and tried to hide his annoyance when he answered. "Give me a second. I'm checking."

Three minutes passed until Jace heard the two guards walk nonchalantly past him. Their casual banter and unhurried steps told him they hadn't heard anything. "We're good. Give me a few minutes to reach the top and then another few to make it to the gate."

"Yeah, yeah," responded the dwarf in a bored tone. "Then come in with axes waving and kick some bandit butt!"

Jace chuckled to himself. He knew Krogan probably said something more vulgar, but his profanity filter was on and the game was translating all vulgarity into more family-friendly language.

He appreciated the enthusiasm from Krogan. The dwarf seemed particularly bloodthirsty which Jace thought was ironic considering dwarves were supposed to be one of the "good" races. Still, a player could play their character any way they wanted. That was one of the great things about VEIL, you could be anything you wanted.

The sound of the guards' footsteps fading into the distance brought Jace's attention back to the game and his purpose. He moved determinedly to the top of the parapet and then peered over. As expected, the guards were on the opposite side of the keep. Just as he had planned.

Moving as silent as the night, Jace slipped over the parapet and shimmied to the edge of the wooden walkway. From his perch, he looked down on the interior of the fortress, his keen eyes soaking in every detail.

"We have three interior buildings," Jace sent to his group. "I think the one to the left is the barracks, the one to the right is probably the mess hall. The center building is got to be where the boss is."

Jace made a quick count of the guards as he swept his eyes back and forth across the courtyard. "I count two roamers on the wall, two at the gate, four by the fire and another two at the boss's door."

"How many do you think are in the barracks?" asked Lucy, their Half-demoness Warlock. Half-demons were one of the "evil" races, just like vampyres. And while Jace played things down the middle, Lucy was utterly ruthless. She wanted what she wanted and anyone who got in her way was an obstacle. He'd made a mental note not to get in her way.

Jace considered the size of the barracks and how many people it could hold. "If they're using bunk beds, it might hold 40 people total, otherwise no more than 20."

"Great," Lucy replied. "There's either 10 more plus the boss or 30 more plus the boss. That's a big difference."

Jace noticed that the wall guards were starting to make their way back his way. "Just stick to the plan and we'll be fine. The guards are almost back, I need to get in position."

With that, he turned his attention to the guards who were getting closer. Jace drew his twin daggers and used some of his mana to activate his assassin ability *Shadow Stalk*. As soon as he did, his body went invisible for the next 60 seconds. He stood and stepped to the edge of the walkway to make room for the two guards who were now only a dozen steps away.

He held his breath as they passed and then stepped silently behind them. In a single fluid motion, he plunged his daggers into the unsuspecting brigands and saw the system message flash across his screen.

You backstab Blackcoat Brigand for 1,269 damage.
Blackcoat Brigand dies.
You gain 450 experience.
You backstab Blackcoat Brigand for 1,401 damage.
Blackcoat Brigand dies.
You gain 450 experience.

Jace caught the brigands' lifeless bodies as they began to collapse and eased them onto the walkway. He retrieved his daggers and wiped the blades on the clothes of the two dead men before replacing them in their sheaths. So far, so good.

"The roamers are down," he told his group. "Moving to the gates now. Get into position."

He didn't wait for the others to acknowledge him and quietly crept towards the ladder that led down to the gates. His *stealth* skill was high enough with his assassin gear, that he didn't really have to worry about being seen unless he walked right in front of a guard.

As if the universe, or game universe in this case, had read his mind, a brigand guard poked his head up from the ladder near the gate. "Hey, Brock, where'd you hide the keg?"

Jace froze as the brigand's head began to swivel towards his position. Even with the triple moons hidden behind the clouds, the man was only ten feet away. There would be no way he could miss Jace's silhouette, even with his poor human eyes.

Not for the first time, Jace wished he had some sort of ranged attack. If he was a dark elf, he would have gotten the ability to use hand crossbows, as a vampyre he had no such option. He was limited to daggers.

Cursing under his breath, he rushed the guard just as the man caught sight of him. It took the brigand a second to process the figure darting at him, and then another second to decide what to do. Unfortunately for the man, that was a second too long. Just as he opened his mouth to raise the alarm, Jace thrust one of his daggers into his eye as he slashed the other one across the man's throat. He activated his *Dark Critical* ability, guaranteeing the strikes would do maximum damage.

You critically hit Blackcoat Brigand for 603 damage.
You critically hit Blackcoat Brigand for 621 damage.

Blackcoat Brigand dies.
You gain 450 experience.

Just as Jace was about to congratulate himself, the man's body went limp. As he died, the corpse slipped from the ladder. Jace watched in horror as the brigand's limp form fell away towards the ground. It crashed noisily into a small table far below where the brigand must have been eating, sending plates and mugs clattering in every direction.

"Frag it!" Jace sent over the link as he moved to the ladder. He slammed his daggers into their sheaths and began descending as quickly as possible. "It looks like we're going in loud."

"Oh shoot," he heard the dwarf mutter over their link.

Jace tuned out the other team members as he focused on the scene below. Two guards from the gate were coming out from the gatehouse to check out the noise.

As they checked on their companion, Jace continued to descend the ladder as quickly as possible.

One of the brigands looked up and Jace immediately kicked off the ladder. His acrobatics skill was so high, he instinctively did a somersault in midair and landed gingerly behind the two men.

The guard who had been looking up was starting to whirl around to face him while reaching for the sword on his hip.

Jace side-stepped towards the second brigand, who still had his back to him and stabbed one his daggers into the man's back.

You backstab Blackcoat Brigand for 1,496 damage.
Blackcoat Brigand dies.
You gain 450 experience.

At the same time, he used more of his mana to activate *Paralyzing Strike* and stabbed his second dagger into the other man's side.

You pierce Blackcoat Brigand with Paralyzing Strike for 127 damage.
Blackcoat Brigand is paralyzed for 10 seconds.

The strike hadn't done much damage, but it served its purpose. The guard wouldn't be able to attack or raise the alarm for 10 seconds and by then it wouldn't matter. Hopefully.

Spinning, Jace dashed into the gatehouse door the two men had emerged from. He quickly found the drawbridge mechanism and yanked the lever to release the chains holding up the drawbridge.

"Drawbridge is coming down!" he mentally shouted over their link over the noise of the thick metal chains lowering the drawbridge.

"Good," he heard the dwarf's voice in his mind. "It's time for some action! Butt kicking for goodness!"

Chapter 2

The drawbridge slammed into the ground with a bone-jarring thud. The sound was immediately followed by the dwarf's war cry and the sound of armor-clad boots clambering across the wooden drawbridge.

Just then, the guard he'd paralyzed stepped into the doorway with his weapon drawn. "You're dead!" he snarled.

The brigand advanced into the cramped gatehouse and slashed at Jace with his sword. Jace danced aside, trusting his dodge skill to help him avoid the strike and then stepped in towards the guard and *Feinted* toward his head while using more of his mana to do a Crippling Strike to his exposed left leg.

You pierce Blackcoat Brigand with Crippling Strike for 119 damage.
Blackcoat Brigand has been Crippled.

The brigand's left leg buckled and the man barely kept himself from falling. Jace took the opportunity to roll to the right as the guard fell to the left and came up behind the man. He stabbed both daggers into the man's back.

You backstab Blackcoat Brigand for 1,421 damage.
You backstab Blackcoat Brigand for 1,371 damage.
Blackcoat Brigand dies.
You gain 450 experience.

The guard dropped noisily to the floor but it no longer mattered. Between the sound of the drawbridge and the dwarf shouting, stealth was no longer an option.

If the enemy hadn't been aware of them before, they would be now. Jogging outside the gatehouse, he joined his companions.

"I thought you were supposed to be stealthy," the dwarf muttered, speaking now instead of using the link.

"Some random brigand looking for a keg," Jace shot back.

"Ah," sighed the dwarf. "A brigand after my own heart!"

Jace shook his head and took in the devolving situation. Brigands were starting to pour out of the mess hall and the barracks.

"Oh shoot! Oh shoot!" Dharci squealed. She was cowering behind the paladin, who in real life was her boyfriend. Her large rabbit ears were down, flattened against her head.

"We'll be fine," Jace said. "As long as Lucy does her job."

The half-demoness glared at him with yellow eyes. She was the tallest one in the group with a sexy, buxom hourglass figure that rivaled that of any of the real-life model. But unlike Earthly models, Lucy had deep red skin, small black horns on her temple, small bat-like wings and a five-foot-long pointy tail. "I can do my job better than you did yours."

Jace flashed her a grin. "I never doubted it for a moment."

Lucy's expression didn't soften but she did begin her incantation. She performed some complicated hand gestures and then pointed a finger at the assembling mob of brigands. "*Pila Immanis Ignis!*"

Lucy Furr casts fireball.

A small glowing sphere appeared at her fingertip and then shot towards the group of brigands near the barracks. When it came in contact with the first brigand, the sphere detonated, and the area exploded in a huge fireball. System messages scrolled across his screen as every brigand in the blast range was damaged but none of them had died.

The brigands made a collective decision not to stand around and become targets for more fireballs and charged his group.

Dharci squealed again, trying to make herself even smaller behind Krogan.

The dwarf looked back at her. "It's okay Dharci. Just cast the buffs."

"Yes," snapped the demoness. "Get that fluffy tail in gear and start doing your job or I'll be eating rabbit stew tonight!"

Both Krogan and Dharci's faces went red, but for different reasons. Krogan turned his head towards the warlock and opened his mouth to say something but Lucy had already begun casting another spell. Dharci seemed to snap out of it as well and began casting protective spells on the group, increasing their armor, attack, damage and skill bonuses.

A second fireball went off at the front of the group of charging brigands, followed by more system messages. More damage messages scrolled by, but he didn't have time to read them. Jace did a quick count. There were twenty brigands less than fifteen feet from them and a few more were still coming out of the barracks and mess hall.

As the motley crew of bandits got within five feet, Krogan let loose a mighty shout. "Come get some!"

Krogan Strongdrink uses Godly Taunt.

The paladin had used his *Taunt* ability and every bandit in range snapped their attention to the dwarf. They'd now be compelled to attack him until the duration of his ability wore off. Even as Jace watched, they were surrounding him, trying to hack him to pieces.

"Okay fang-boy," grunted the dwarf as he took hit after hit from the bandits surrounding him. "You and demon wench start earning your keep! Dharci, keep the healing coming."

Even as the dwarf finished his sentence, the golden glow of healing surrounded him, healing the dwarf up to full health.

Jace wasted no time and began dancing among the bandits who were now engrossed in attacking the dwarf. With their backs to him, they made perfect targets for his backstab ability and he took full advantage of the situation. At the same time, bolts of fire began to strike men around him as Lucy cast *Flame Bolt* spells.

Within a few minutes, they had decimated the bandits in the courtyard. As the last one slid off his dagger, the group took a collective sigh of relief.

"That wasn't so bad," squeaked Dharci.

"Don't jinx…" Lucy started to say but the sound of a door slamming open drowned out her words.

"You dare attack me in my own keep!" bellowed the burly human who had just emerged from the central building.

The man was tall and heavily muscled. His tanned face was pockmarked, and he wore a patch over his left eye. He was garbed in a studded leather jerkin over a green tunic with tan leather pants and high leather boots. From each hip hung battle axes.

Jace examined the man in his heads-up display (HUD) utilizing his monster lore skill.

Ulric Blackcoat
Level 99 Human Brigand
Legendary

Jace read the description and it was exactly what he had expected. Legendary bosses were the greater sort that dropped the best loot a small group like his could acquire. To get better loot, you had to raid mythical or fabled bosses with a group of 24, which he'd be able to do once he got his sash.

"My lieutenants and I will make short work of you!" Ulric finished and stepped out of the way to allow a brunette woman in a forest green robe and a shorter man with a shaved head wearing chain mail and carrying a mace and shield. Jace didn't even have to look at them to realize one was a caster and the other a healer.

"Lieutenants?" growled the dwarf. "You didn't say anything about adds!"

"What the hell Mordred?!" snarled Lucy.

"There was no mention of them!" Jace said defensively. "From any of the villages they attacked!"

This made things much more complicated. The boss alone would have been a challenge. But with the support of a healer and a caster, it just got much more difficult.

"We can do this," Jace told his group. "Take down the healer first, then the mage and then we'll focus on the boss."

His group may have been angry with him, but they were experienced players and they got to work. But he had no doubt that once this was over, they'd have words with him.

Ulric charged forward towards Jace since he was the closest but as soon as he was in range, Krogan called out a *Taunt* and the boss ran by him straight towards the dwarf. The boss chopped down with both axes and the paladin barely got his shield up in time to deflect them.

Instinctively, Jace took the opportunity to backstab the boss but no sooner had he removed the daggers than golden light surrounded the boss and the wounds healed. He hated healers when they weren't on his side!

Jace spun and started to rush the healer but stumbled back as a fiery bolt struck him in the chest.

Jaiyana Stormdragon burns YOU with Flame Bolt for 359 fire damage.

Jace staggered back, glad his sensory feedback was set at 15% of normal otherwise he would have felt that blast as if it were real. It still stung but he ignored the stinging sensation and activated his *Shadow Stalk* ability and disappeared.

He dodged to the left and then ran forward towards the healer. The man was caught in the chest by a flaming bolt from Lucy. He started casting a spell to heal himself and Jace rolled between the two lieutenants and came behind the healer. He immediately stabbed both his daggers into the man's back.

You backstab Gerett Fistspirit for 1,111 damage.
You backstab Gerett Fistspirit for 1,103 damage.

While the damage would have easily brought down a normal bandit, these were mini-bosses and had 10 times the normal health and mana. As it was, it did ruin his spell.

Gerett staggered forward, turning to get his shield up and face his unseen attacker. Another flame arrow slammed into the bandit healer's back just as Jace turned visible.

Jaiyana saw him and began casting a spell at the same time Gerett began casting his own spell.

Using double mana, Jace activated *Paralyzing Strike* for each hand and struck out at both Gerett and Jaiyana.

You pierce Gerett Fistspirit with Paralyzing Strike for 111 damage.

Gerett Fistspirit is paralyzed for 10 seconds.

You pierce Jaiyana Stormdragon with Paralyzing Strike for 110 damage.
Jaiyana Stormdragon is paralyzed for 10 seconds.

With both the mini-bosses paralyzed, Jace rolled between them once more and came up behind Gerett. He stabbed his daggers into the healer over and over again as many times as he could for the extra backstab damage before the paralyzation ran out. Just as the last second of paralyzation ticked off, Jace saw the message he was looking for.

You backstab Gerett Fistspirit for 1,101 damage.
Gerett Fistspirit dies.
You gain 4500 experience.

The bandit healer collapsed in a lifeless heap as Jaiyana began casting another spell. Jace didn't have enough time to interrupt her and was suddenly flying backwards across the courtyard.

Jaiyana Stormdragon hits YOU with Tornado Blast for 679 damage.
YOU are stunned for 10 seconds.

Slamming into the wall, Jace felt the air explode from his lungs. His vision clouded and he saw stars even as he slid to the ground.

Even though his body was stunned, Jace could still do mental activity. He activated his *Slippery Grasp* ability to break the stun. He saw his mana drain and suddenly he could move. Retrieving his daggers from where they had fallen, he sprinted at the brigand spellcaster.

She saw him coming and began casting a spell. He spared a glance at his health and saw he only had 12 health left. If it weren't for the boost from his armor and the buffs Dharci had cast earlier, he'd be dead. He couldn't let the mage land another spell on him.

He looked at his mana and stamina. Both were almost gone. Jace didn't have enough for another *Shadow Stalk* nor one of his spell dodging abilities. He barely had enough stamina for a few attacks. His only chance was his racial ability, *Form of Bats*. It cost no mana but was only usable once a day. He had no choice if he wanted to live. He activated the ability.

You have activated Form of Bats.
You are immune to direct damage effects for 30 seconds.
You now possess the characteristics of a Medium Bat Swarm.
Cooldown timer: 23:59:59

A *Flame Bolt* hurled towards him but right before it hit, his body burst apart into a swarm of dozens of bats. The bolt struck one the bats and vaporized it, but he took no damage. He swarmed around Jaiyana, using the bat swarm confusion ability. As long as he swarmed around her, she couldn't take any actions that took concentration - like spellcasting.

Luckily, Lucy saw the opportunity and cast *Flame Bolt* after *Flame Bolt* until Jaiyana finally died. As she did, Jace ended the ability and returned to his humanoid body. Jace breathed a sigh of relief that he managed to stay alive when a frantic voice came over their link.

"I'm almost out of mana!" Dharci squealed hysterically. "Help him! Help him!"

Chapter 3

Jace could see that the dwarf had taken a beating from the boss. His armor and shield were dented, and blood flowed from several cuts that hadn't been healed completely. Krogan wore a mask of concentration on his face as he desperately tried to parry and duck Ulric's deadly blows. If the dwarf went down, they would fail.

Reaching into a pouch at his waist, Jace retrieved the one potion he hadn't wanted to use. It was an incandescent potion. Incandescent potions were rare and expensive because they restored mana, health and stamina. It would cost him every penny he'd make from his share of the loot today to replace it. But he had no choice. He popped the stopper and gulped down the contents.

You use Supreme Incandescent Potion.
Supreme Incandescent Potion restores 1000 health.
Supreme Incandescent Potion restores 1000 stamina.
Supreme Incandescent Potion restores 1000 mana.

The potion burned as it went down his throat, but he instantly felt better as new energy surged throughout his body. His stamina and mana were back at maximum and his health was nearly there.

With his newly restored attributes, he rushed at Ulric's back and began backstabbing the boss. To his side, Lucy was doing the same. She was hurling firebolts as fast as she could cast, and their combined attacks were dropping the boss's health steadily.

The boss continued to hammer the dwarf with relentless blows from his axe and after every few blows, the golden glow of healing would surround the dwarf as Dharci cast her healing magic on him.

"Dharci, how are you doing on mana?" Jace asked the rabbit-kin over their link.

"Down to 25% and I'm out of potions," she responded. "I only brought 3 potions with me. I thought that would be enough."

Jace was angry with himself. The potions she had brought would have been enough if they'd only had Ulric to contend with and not the two mini-bosses. He eased off his backstabs to check his inventory. He had one mana potion. Damn. This was going to be an expensive fight.

"I'm bringing one back to you," he told her.

Just then, Ulric's health hit 75% and the boss stopped hitting Korgan and crossed his axes in front of his chest and twisted his body slightly. Jace had seen this before. It was a special attack called a *Whirlwind Attack*.

"Special attack! Back up! Back up!" he shouted over their link as he backpedaled to get out of range. To their credit, his group listened and did as he said. They all moved back, and it saved their lives.

Ulric Blackcoat uses Whirlwind Attack.

The boss jumped into the air and began spinning around in a circle. As he did, he extended his arms and let go of axes. The axes flew a good three feet from him, still attached to his wrists by leather cords. This extended his range by a good six feet. He spun around like a deadly top with his axes whistling through the air.

Luckily, all of his group were out of range and Jace took the opportunity to rush around the spinning brigand of death and hand Dharci a potion. She took it gratefully and hurriedly drank it down.

"Do you have any mana potions you could give Dharci?" Jace asked Lucy as he made his way back to his previous spot.

The demoness gave him a disdainful look. "I have one, but she'll need to pay me back for it."

Frustrated, Jace shook his head. "Just give it to her. If she can't pay you, I will."

The boss stopped spinning and yanked the axes back into his hands. Krogan shouted his *Taunt* and Ulric resumed his attacks on the dwarf.

Jace resumed his own attacks and was joined by Lucy after she gave Dharci one of her potions. "That's 10,000 gold vamp-boy."

"Sure," Jace said in between backstabs. "Once we kill this guy."

Once again, the boss's health bar began to decline until it hit the 50% mark. Jace knew he'd probably do another special attack at 50% but he wasn't prepared for what happened.

Ulric Blackcoat goes Berserk.

Suddenly Ulric let loose a primal scream and seemed to grow in size. He stopped attacking the dwarf and looked from group member to group member before settling his gaze on Lucy. He began stalking towards her, slashing the air in front of him with his axes.

"Come get some!" shouted the dwarf, trying to draw the boss back with his *Taunt*.

"Help!" she screamed as the boss got closer. "Get him away from me dwarf!"

"I'm trying!" Krogan yelled back to her. He used another *Taunt*. "Come get some!"

Ulric reached the warlock and began to hack her with a frenzy. Unlike the dwarf, she had no armor to protect her. After only two hits, she collapsed to the ground dead.

Lucy Furr has died.

"Dammit!" Jace swore as he saw the warlock's dead body. "Dharci, can you raise her?"

Ulric Blackcoat is no longer Berserk.

The boss was turning toward Jace when its *Beserk* ability must have run out. Jace cursed himself for not timing it. These abilities might be triggered by low health, but they generally only lasted a certain duration. In the excitement, he'd neglected to time it.

"Uh," the healer sounded dubious. "I could, but I don't think I'd have enough mana for the rest of the fight."

He knew the warlock would hate him, but he made the call. "Leave her until the end."

Jace resumed his attacks on the boss, slowly getting him down towards 25%. As soon as Ulric's health reached 25%, he stopped and prepared to do another *Whirlwind Attack.*

"Whirlwind!" he shouted over the link. "Back up!"

Dharci and Krogan did so and the three of them waited out of range for the boss to finish and then resumed his normal attacks.

Jace resumed his backstabs until the boss reached 15%. As soon as Ulric's health dipped below 15%, Jace used the last of his mana to activate *Shadow Stalk* and then his special once a day class ability, *Assassinate.*

Assassinate could only be used on targets at less than 15% health and only from stealth. If both the conditions were met, it killed the target instantly. Like his race ability, it used no mana, but could only be used once per day.

Activating the special ability, Jace drove his dagger in the brigand's back, between his ribs and into his heart.

You have activated Assassinate.
Ulric Blackcoat has been assassinated by Mordred Blacklock.
Ulric Blackcoat dies.
You gain 9000 experience.
Cooldown timer: 23:59:59

"Ha!" bellowed the paladin. "Good job pointy-teeth!"

"Thank god that's over," squeaked Dharci.

"Can you raise Lucy?" Jace asked the healer.

Dharci checked her mana level. "Yes, barely!"

The rabbit-kin cast *Raise Dead*, a spell that could raise a recently fallen companion, but could only be cast outside of combat. It's sister spell, resurrection did the same thing but could be cast during combat. It also cost four times as much mana. *"Immanis suscitavit mortuis!"*

The demoness' body was bathed in golden light as her body was healed and life was restored to it. After only a second, she sucked in air and her eyes popped open. "You son of bitch!"

The half-demoness got unsteadily to her feet and turned to Jace. "What the hell? Waiting until after the combat to raise me?"

Even though Lucy was addressing Jace, Dharci shrank back behind Krogan.

"I made the call to save the group," Jace told her defensively. "If we'd raised you during the fight, Dharci wouldn't have had enough mana to keep Krogan up. And then we'd all be dead."

The demoness continued to seethe and glare at Jace until Krogan cleared his throat. "If you two are going to glare at each other all day, Dharci and I will just take our share of the loot and leave."

"Fine," the demoness snapped, turning away from Jace. "Let's just get our loot and get out of here."

The four of them walked over to Ulric's body. The first thing to divide was always the money. In this case, since he was a high level boss, it was probably in the form of gems. Jace grabbed the money pouch from the bandit's belt. Opening it, he dumped the contents into his hand.

In his hand he now held a dozen sparkling gemstones, all worth at least 20,000 gold each. He used his *Appraise* skill and got the exact values, then divided them as equally as possible, taking the lowest portion for himself to avoid arguments.

When no one argued with their cut of the money, he moved on to the items. The first item was the slightly glowing weapon on the ground next to the leader's body. His *Appraise* skill showed it as the *Axe of the Burning Sun*. Looking at the stats, Jace imagined Mordred's eyes were bulging.

The thing not only penetrated 10 points of Defense, it also did a huge amount of fire damage and once per day could call down a *Firestorm*.

"Krogan, I assume you are interested in the axe?" Jace asked, still looking at its impressive stats. As party leader, only he could release items to be looted. It was one of the things that broke immersion, but before they implemented it, looting had been a nightmare that caused all sorts of problems.

"Anyone else?" Jace asked. He knew no one else would, but it was courtesy to ask.

"It's all yours," Jace told the dwarf and assigned the axe to Krogan.

The dwarf bent down and lovingly picked up the axe. "Come to papa!"

"The ring next," Lucy demanded.

Jace examined the ring the bandit leader was wearing. It was called the *Ring of the Serpent's Eye*. Jace took the opportunity to examine and and whistled. The ring not only increased mana by 10%, it also acted as a mana battery, allowing a person to store up to 10% of their mana in it for later use. Effectively, it increased a person's mana by 20%. Its secondary ability was to grant the wearer a rare ability called *Tremor Vision*. The person would be able to to "see" using vibrations in the air, negating a form of invisibility.

"*Ring of the Serpent's Eye*?" he asked, looking at his party members. "Anyone other than Lucy."

"It's mine!" snapped the demoness. "That's the whole reason I joined this doomed mission."

Jace didn't know anything about the ring or what it did, but he didn't care. He was here for one thing - the sash. When no one else spoke up, he assigned it to Lucy, who quickly took it off the dead man's finger.

She then stepped back, dropped from the group.

"You all are a bunch of newbie morons!" she spat as she began casting a spell. For a moment, Jace thought she might attack them. Normally, she couldn't attack people in her own faction, like Jace, but since they were in the Outskirts, anyone could harm anyone they weren't grouped with.

Fearing an attack, Jace was about to activate one of his stealth abilities when he recognized the spell as a teleport spell. Before any of them could say anything, she vanished.

Jace relaxed for a moment since there wasn't going to be a fight, but then he remembered the demoness had been their "ride" home. She was supposed to teleport them all back to the city when they finished. Now it would take days to get back.

"That… that... hussy!" cried the normally timid Dharci. "She really just left us here?"

"Fraggin' demoness," cursed the dwarf. "I'm going to make sure my entire guild knows what she did."

Jace laughed as he realized something and both Dharci and Korgan turned towards him with angry expressions.

Holding up his hands, Jace explained. "She was in such a hurry to abandon us that she didn't get any of the money. And she didn't think about the loot on the lesser bosses - including a caster."

The dwarf and rabbit-kin's heads snapped to where the two lesser bosses lay dead. Then they looked back and smiled. That meant more loot for each of them.

In the end, Jace got his *Sash of the Kobadera*, which is what he really wanted. Grinning, he examined it.

Sash of the Kobadera
Type: Belt (Leather)

Armor: 512 + Masterwork (100) + Sturdy (100)
Level: 95
Wt: .3 lb
Special: +10 Defense,
Set Bonus: Kobadera
3 Piece Bonus: +10% to Critical Strikes, +10% to duration of Stealth or Invisibility Effects
4 Piece Bonus: +10% to Backstabs, +10% to Stealth skill
5 Piece Bonus: +10% Health, +10% Mana
6 Piece Bonus: Cooldown of Assassin abilities reduced by 25%, +25% damage to all Assassin abilities
Description: Given to Knights of the Griffon who had distinguished themselves in a tournament, this amulet gives the wearer extra protection.
Restriction: This item is soul bound. When picked up, it binds itself to the person and cannot be traded, sold or looted by others. They remain with the person through resurrection.

He slipped off his old *Belt of the Ninja* and put on the *Sash of Kobadera*. Finally! He had it! And with the complete set, all of his *Assassin* abilities were increased by 25%! Finally, he would be considered raid ready!

Realizing the rest of the group was looking at him expectantly, Jace continued the looting. He distributed the gold and got his share of the money from the two lesser bosses. The combined money from the mini-bosses ended up being nearly as much as the money on the boss himself.

In addition, he picked up two magic items from the two lieutenants. The first was a pair of boots from the healer called *Boots of Surefootedness*. The other was an amulet from the mage called the *Talisman of the Fire God*. Neither were useful to him but might fetch a decent price on the marketplace. The rest of the items had gone to his companions, giving them a nice haul.

While they were looting, Krogan had Dharci cast a *Divine Messenger* spell to send a message to one of his guild wizards, a gnome named Krockety Ratchet who had teleported to them. Since Krogan was a guildmate and Dharci was his girlfriend, Krockety had offered to teleport them for free, but he charged Jace the going rate, which was 100 gold per level, plus tip. The total came to 10,000 gold but considering it saved Jace days of hiking alone through neutral territory, it was worth it.

Krockety teleported Jace to the neutral port of Burrafirth and then quickly teleported away. Jace had never been to Burrafirth before but knew it was a home to many of the various furry races. He'd have to explore it later. He was tired and it was time to log off.

Bringing up his HUD, Jace selected the logout option and the game world faced into blackness.

Chapter 4

Jace groaned as he opened his eyes to the inside of the virtual reality pod. Jace sat up and climbed out of the FEVRE pod. FEVRE stood for Full Environment Virtual Reality Emulator and was pronounced fever. Right now, his muscles ached, and he almost felt like he had a fever. But that was normal after being in the pod for so long. The pod did something to stimulate muscles while you were in VR to keep them from atrophying. He had read something about exactly how it was done, but he couldn't recall. All he knew was that his muscles were sore. It didn't matter though, he'd sleep it off and be fine tomorrow morning.

Stifling a yawn, he walked over to his refrigerator and grabbed a water. Twisting the cap off, he drank it all down. While the pods somehow stimulated his muscles while he was in VR, they couldn't keep his hydration up. If he didn't drink before and after, he could very quickly get dehydrated.

His next stop was the bathroom. That's the other bodily function the pod couldn't take care of, at least not his FEVRE pod. He had read about long term pods and even medical pods that kept people in VR for months, sometimes even years using IV drips and some sort of waste processing. But he didn't have a million dollars to go out and buy one. For Jace, he still needed to come back to reality to eat, drink and use the bathroom.

He emerged from the bathroom and looked around his dimly lit apartment. It was a tiny studio apartment.

To his right was his "bedroom" area, which consisted of a closet, a small end table and his bed, which was still messed up from the night before.

In front of him was his "living room," which was completely taken up by the FEVRE pod. To his left was his tiny kitchen, as well as the door out to the hallway of his apartment building. There was a tiny table in the kitchen area that served as both his table and his desk.

Living the walls were posters of the last century's vidstreams, what they used to call movies. He was fascinated by the older culture and had spent some of his extra money on reprints of the original movie posters. He also had some retro gear he'd managed to buy as well as a library of pirated vidstreams from the 1980s, '90s and even some from earlier this century. Other than VEIL, it was his only hobby. The place wasn't much, and some people might call it claustrophobic, but it was all he could afford at the moment on a junior programmer salary.

Thinking of his job, he glanced at the clock. It was 1 a.m. in the morning. He'd been in VEIL for seven hours. He should have been in bed two hours ago, but he just couldn't pass up the opportunity to get the *Sash of Kobadera*. Finally, he'd be able to go on raids and start making real money in the game. That was worth being tired at work tomorrow.

Stifling a yawn, he walked over to the bed and picked up his alarm clock. Setting his alarm back on the end table, he accidentally knocked over the only picture in his apartment. Swearing, he bent over and retrieved it.

Luckily, the frame hadn't broken when it hit the floor and he took a moment to look at the picture. It was a picture of him on the day of his high school graduation. He was there in his graduation robes, along with his mother, his father and his sister. They were all smiling.

A pang of sadness hit him in the chest as he looked at the picture. It was the last time he'd seen them alive. They'd come to his graduation and were going to take him out to eat afterward to celebrate but he had begged to go with his friend, Michael. They'd relented and promised to take him out the next day but that had never happened. A truck in the opposite lane had blown a tire and swerved into their lane, hitting them head on. They were all killed instantly.

Jace hadn't even known until Michael's parents had dropped him off at his house to find the police waiting for him. They'd kept him to the station for hours until finally giving him to someone in child services. Since he had no living relatives, he'd been placed in foster care for four months until he turned eighteen. He'd never even been able to go to the funeral.

On his eighteenth birthday, he'd met with the lawyers who ran his parents' estate, or rather, what was left of their estate. His parents had been relatively young and the only insurance policy they had was the one through his dad's work. It had barely been enough to finish paying off the house and pay for funeral expenses. Then he found out that they also had no will, so the house was subject to some sort of inheritance tax and he'd have to pay 5% of the value of the house if he had wanted to keep it. Once you added lawyer's fees, court fees and all sort of other fees that seemed to ooze out of the woodwork, he would have needed to pay $30,000 to keep the house.

As an 18-year-old orphan with no job, who had been in foster care for the last four months, he had no money to his name at all. He'd been forced to sell the house just to pay everything, leaving him with $170,000 dollars. He used the money to send himself to the college to study programming.

Even with money from the house, he still had been forced to work a part time job to make sure he'd had enough to graduate. Now, this picture was all he had left of his previous life. That and the FEVRE pod. Everything else was gone.

Jace felt his eyes getting watery and he placed the picture back in its place on the end table. He blinked the tears away and collapsed on his bed. His guilt was clawing its way back out from where he kept it buried. He, Jace, had killed his family. It was all his fault. If he had just gone out to eat with them, they'd still be alive. His dad, his mom and his little sister. They'd all be alive if it weren't for him. And he wouldn't be alone.

With dark thoughts swirling around his mind, Jace finally fell asleep.

Chapter 5

Jace stared at his computer screen, not really seeing what was there.

"Earth to Jace," came a voice to his right, snapping out of his daze.

"What?" he stuttered and tried to look like he had been concentrating.

"Another late night?" asked Damian, a senior programmer on his team. He was a few years older than the rest of the team and loved to claim seniority to get his way. "I think I heard you snoring."

Jace cringed. He hoped he hadn't really fallen asleep at his keyboard. He started to reply and then yawned involuntarily.

"I'll take that as a yes," snickered Damian.

He took another sip of his energy drink before replying. "Yeah. I put together a pick-up group and raided Blackcoat Fortress. I finally got the *Sash of Kobadera.*"

"So, does that mean you're going to try the raid scene?"

"Yeah," Jace covered his mouth as he yawned again.

"You two and this game," came a disapproving woman's voice from the other side of the cube. "If you're not careful, that game will become your life!"

The voice had a pronounced Indian accent, marking it as belonging to Minu. She was one of the other programmers on Jace's team. Unlike he and Damian, she didn't play VEIL, despite the fact that all three of them worked for WorldCog, the creator of the game.

"Playing the game makes us better able to troubleshoot it," Damian countered.

"Hah," she snorted. "A good programmer should be able to troubleshoot code regardless of whether or not they have used the application."

"Yes mom," Damian replied in a mocking voice.

Jace was too tired to join in their back and forth ribbing. Normally, he'd try to throw in his two cents, but today, it was taking all he had just to keep his eyes open. Forcing himself to focus on the code he was supposed to be troubleshooting, Jace once again read through it.

His team was one of many who worked on troubleshooting the millions and millions of lines of code that made up the most popular VR game in the world, VEIL Online. It was actually Jace's dream job. Maybe being on the troubleshooting team wasn't exactly his dream job but working for WorldCog had been his since he was sixteen years old and he had seen the previews for the game.

Jace smiled at memory of the first time he'd entered the game. His parents had gotten the family a FEVRE pod for Christmas and Jace had used what little allowance money he had to purchase his subscription to VEIL. It was the same FEVRE pod that now sat in his living room. A bittersweet reminder of better days and a different life.

He still remembered his first character, a *Dwarven Paladin* named Rodrick Hammerhand. He'd played the Rodrick character with his friends in high school, all the way up to graduation. It was those many gaming sessions that had inspired him to become a programmer. Jace had been so enamored with the game that he had wanted to do more than just play. He had wanted to create. He had wanted to build. That desire had caused him to take as many programming electives as he could his senior year.

But then the accident happened, his world was thrown upside down. Once he was in foster care, he'd lost contact with his friends. Once he got into college, he had thought about reaching out to them many times, but something always stopped him. He wasn't sure what it was. Perhaps it was that they would bring back memories of the time before the accident. Memories of a family he had lost and could never have again.

Jace physically shook his head, as if doing so would shake out the dark thoughts that threatened to consume him. He pushed his attention back on the code. He scrolled through the code again, trying to force it to register in his tired brain. Then he saw it. Double checking, he verified that it was the issue. He made some corrections and put a comment in the code listing the change and the ticket number. Then he pushed the new code up into the repository and closed the ticket.

VEIL might be the most popular game in the world, but it was far from perfect. Yet, despite the small, and occasionally large, bugs, it earned more in a month than some small countries did in a year. All because it offered something that none of the other games on the market could. It could offer life after death. At least, a form of life after death. Jace still remembered when they had announced the technology that allowed specially designed machines to "backup" a person's brain and insert their consciousness into the game. They had stopped all of his college classes that day as people everywhere were stunned at the announcement.

In essence, a person could live on after death by having their consciousness moved into the world of VEIL. And because of proprietary technologies WorldCog had patented, they were the only company able to offer it. They had basically patented immortality. Jace smirked as he thought of their slogan "Play Forever". Of course, as religious and spiritual leaders were quick to point out, it wasn't really life after death. They claimed you became a soulless digital being, condemned to purgatory for all time.

Jace had attended a Christian church with his parents before they died. But since the accident, he hadn't stepped foot in any church. He couldn't. Not when their blood was on his hands. He could barely face himself. How could he face God?

His screen blinked, pulling him back to his job. The code was finished updating and the task was complete.

"Bug 734203!" he called out to his coworkers. It was a bit of a game that the members of his team played. Whenever one of them fixed some code, they yelled it out and the others would try to guess what had caused the issue.

"Logic error," guessed Minu.

"Forgot to declare a variable," Damion said from his cube.

Jace waited a moment for the other two members of his team to answer but remembered they worked from home on Fridays. They'd be online but obviously couldn't take place in the office banter. Lucky them.

"Both wrong," he told them tiredly. "They used the same variable name inside and outside their for… next loop. It was basically creating an infinite loop and caused the routine to return the wrong result."

He heard snickers and chuckles from his two team members.

"Amateurs," snickered Damion. The senior programmer had no tolerance for fools or bad coders. The guy was a great programmer and continually hinted that he had done some computer hacking back when he was younger. For all Jace knew, he still did hacking. Jace had often thought about trying his own hand at hacking. The idea was certainly thrilling but he just couldn't risk the legal penalties if he were caught. He'd worked too hard to get where he was, and he wasn't about to throw it away for a cheap thrill.

"Speaking of amateurs," Damian's head poked around the walls of his cubicle. "Any girls this weekend?"

Damian delighted in tormenting him about his dating life, or lack thereof. Jace had dated a few girls in high school but college had been so busy, he hadn't had time to do much outside classes and work. Most of the other kids had partied all the time. They weren't worried about failing out or making bad grades, since mommy or daddy would bail them out if they screwed up.

If he had screwed up, he would have had nowhere to go and no one to turn to. Consequently, his dating life in college had been nonexistent. After college, he'd worked two jobs to make ends meet. That hadn't lent itself to dating much either.

He'd actually had two girl friends in his first two years of college. They'd both been really nice girls and they'd shared some interests. But neither relationship had lasted beyond a few weeks. In the end, both had left him. After the second one, he'd just given up and focused on his studies.

Of course, now he had no excuse. And Damian knew it. Jace still wasn't sure whether the older programmer was actually trying to encourage him to date more or whether Damian liked to simply embarrass him. The man did seem to delight in the failures of his teammates for some reason.

"Your silence is its own answer. No girls again," Damian scoffed. "You need to put yourself out there."

Jace rolled his eyes but then Minu chimed in as well.

"Jace, Damian is right for once," came Minu's voice. "You need to put yourself out there. You are a nice guy. There are plenty of girls looking for nice guys."

Laughter came from Damian's cube. "Hah! Girls don't want nice guys. They want danger and excitement. That's why I'm hooking up with 3 girls this weekend."

"Oh yes, Mr. Danger and excitement," retorted Minu. "You 'hook up' with girls. But how many have you actually been in a relationship with?"

"Zero," the older programmer responded wistfully. "Why would I want a relationship. We use each other and then move on."

"Ugh," said Minu. "That's like rutting animals."

Damian only chuckled at her.

Jace knew better than to inject himself into their arguments about relationships. They were polar opposites. Minu believed in traditional relationships and marriage. Damian was the opposite. He seemed to like to "hook up" with women for brief periods of time, have sex and then move on.

The two were never going to see eye to eye and if he said anything, he'd get a lecture from one or both of them about how their way was the right way.

"Oh," Minu said suddenly. "I need to go. I have this afternoon off. I have to take Dinesh to the doctor this afternoon."

Sounds came from her cubicle as she cleaned her desk and gathered her stuff. A few minutes later, she appeared on his side of the cube.

"You two have a good weekend," she told them.

"You too," he replied, glancing over at her.

"See ya," Damian's voice said from inside his cubicle.

Jace watched her walk to the door. She stopped at the brain backup booth and stepped inside. Technically, it was called a Cranial Digitizer, but everyone just called them brain backup booths. Minu swiped her badge and entered a pin number on the keypad. When she did, the door slid shut behind her and a percentage countdown appeared on the screen in front of her. As it counted down, he knew there were invisible low-light lasers that were reading her neurons and storing the information in a memory crystal.

It took about a minute, but the counter reached zero and the door slid open. Minu stepped out, waved back at them and then turned the corner towards the elevators.

Tiredly, he raised his hand to wave back, but she was already gone.

"I'm going to grab some lunch," Jace told Damian and locked his computer. He heard some incomprehensible mutter from Damian's cube and assumed that was the older programmer's acknowledgment.

He walked around the office floor until he found an empty conference room. He looked up the conference room in the calendar to make sure it wasn't in use for the next hour and then ducked inside. Closing the door behind him, Jace sat back in one of the uncomfortable chairs. Before he knew it, he was dreaming of VEIL.

It wasn't uncommon for him to dream of the game since he spent so much time inside. But this time was a little different. He dreamed he was in the game, but as himself. And he was being chased. And whatever was chasing him was getting closer. It was right behind him. Then the alarm on his phone went off and he was back in the real world.

Chapter 6

Jace didn't really feel any better after his short nap in the conference room. He couldn't help but remember that feeling of being chased. Whatever it was that had been after him, it had almost got him. He grabbed a caffeinated soda and a candy bar from the vending machine on his way back to his desk. Candy and soda, the lunch of champions.

Dragging himself back to his desk, he went back to work and resolved several more code issues. Still tired, his mind still wandered back to the earlier conversation about dating.

Part of him did want to date. In fact, a tiny part of him even thought about marriage one day. But a larger part of him resisted. It told don't him not to get involved. Don't get too close. He couldn't open himself up to that pain again. That pain of losing everyone you love.

It was safer not to get involved at all. The closer you got to people, the more you had to lose. And Jace couldn't afford to lose any more.

He focused his attention on the issue he was troubleshooting. He had to read through the code several times before he spotted the error. It took him a few more minutes to program around it. Once Jace tested it, he documented the code and re-submitted it. One more issue resolved.

He glanced up at the clock. It was 4:30 p.m. Another thirty minutes and the work week would be over, and he could go home and rest before logging into the game. He wanted to be more excited about being ready for raids, but he was just so tired.

Jace rubbed his eyes and clicked on the next issue. He read the description and looked at the routine involved. Wow. It was an issue in the insertion routine. The insertion routine was the code which handled the process of inserting a new memory crystal into the game. The code looked like it scrolled for pages and pages. He began paging through it to see how many lines of code there were when something caught his eye.

He stopped and scrolled back. A few pages up, he found what had caught his eye. It was a large block of corrupted code. He looked at it closely. Maybe it wasn't corrupted at all. Maybe it was encrypted or obfuscated, making it completely unreadable to the human eye. He brought up the code history to see who had looked at the code last. It was currently checked out by Damian Teivel. He involuntarily looked over towards the older programmer's cube.

Should he ask Damian about it? Maybe there was a reason for it. Was it some sort of trade secret code? Yes, that must be it. The whole process of inserting a person's memory crystal into the game was very secret. It was one of the main factors that made VEIL Online the dominant game in the market. He definitely wouldn't put it past WorldCog to encrypt sensitive parts of it to prevent it from leaking.

"Hey Damian," he called out to his coworker. "What's up with this encrypted code in the insertion routine?"

He heard the other man's keyboard go silent. Damian's head peaked out of his cube. His face paled. "Encrypted code?"

That was interesting. Had Damian not found it? He couldn't see the other programmer missing something as obvious as a huge block of nonsensical code.

Maybe it really was corrupted. "Well, encrypted or corrupted. There's a huge block of it in the insertion routine."

The other programmer narrowed his eyes at Jace. His voice began icy. "What are you doing in the insertion routine?"

Jace was confused. The older programmer could be a jerk sometimes, but this seemed more extreme. "I was just clicking a random issue, and this came up."

Damian stared hard at Jace for a long moment. "And you didn't see that I was already working on it?"

Now he thought he understood. Damian must have already been working on the issue and must have thought Jace was checking up on him. He knew the other programmer hated that. He even hated it when their boss, Phil, did it.

Jace brought up his hands. "Sorry, I didn't even notice you were in it. I was so tired I didn't even check to see that it was checked out."

The older programmer's expression didn't soften. "You didn't notice that it was signed out to me?"

Trying to lighten the mood, Jace forced a smile. "Sorry man, I've been dragging all day."

Damian's eyebrow rose but his voice was still icy, almost dangerous. "What? You're so tired you couldn't read the checked out by but not tired enough to find some obfuscated code?"

"Obfuscated?" Jace asked, confused. Obfuscating code made it almost impossible to read. It took days, sometimes weeks or even years to make it readable. Why would WorldCog obfuscate their code? Especially from troubleshooters like his team.

He noticed the muscles of Damian's jaw tensing. The older programmer narrowed his eyes. "I meant encrypted, like you said."

Damian was acting weird, even for Damian. Was the code really encrypted or was it obfuscated? Whichever it was, it must be important.

"Does Phil know about the code?" he asked.

Damian's face went white, then red. He opened his mouth to say something then closed it. After almost a full minute, he did speak. "Of course, he knows. I'm looking into how the obfuscated code got in there. It's all hush-hush until I find who did it. Okay?"

Jace considered that. It would make sense. If someone had found some code that didn't belong, the company would want to find out where it came from and what it was doing. But why wasn't the Internal Audit department looking at it instead of one of the troubleshooting teams?

"Are you working with Internal Audit?" he asked Damian.

Once again Damian looked like he was about to say something, then paused and finally responded. "Yes, if you must know, I'm working with Internal Audit on this."

Jace opened his mouth to ask if he could help but Damian cut him off. "Listen, you're not even supposed to know about this. This is all very top secret stuff. Okay? Don't go telling anyone."

"I'll have to tell Phil," Jace told him. Phil would know anyway. The moment Jace had opened the issue, his id had been recorded as looking at it. If he didn't tell Phil before his boss noticed it in an audit report, he'd get in more trouble.

Damian's eyes went wide. "What?!"

"I opened the ticket," he explained. "My ID is already logged as reading it. If I don't tell him and he finds out, I'll be in big trouble."

Damian opened his mouth, then closed it. Then opened it again and closed it, as if he couldn't think of the right thing to say. That in itself was weird since Damian always had something to say about everything. But there was also a weird look to the man's eyes that Jace found unnerving.

Finally, Damian spoke. "Listen, I can erase your name from the audit log. Then Phil won't find out."

"What?!" Jace gasped. No one was supposed to be able to alter the logs. That was the whole point of an audit log, you knew it was a foolproof way to see who had done what to a file and when they'd done it. It was even possible to go back and see exactly what had been changed. If the audit log could be modified, then it was worthless. Someone could change the code, then remove any record that they'd made the change.

"How can you do that? It's supposed to be impossible," Jace asked curiously.

The older programmer gave Jace one of his cocky grins. "I could tell you, but I'd have to kill you."

Jace snickered. "No seriously, how can you modify the logs?"

Damian gave him a conspiratorial look. "I have heightened access at the moment, since I'm working on this. Don't say anything to Phil. I'll delete your log and he'll never know."

Jace considered that. What Damian was suggesting went against all sorts of policies. If they were caught doing it, they'd get fired.

If Jace just admitted to accidentally clicking on the ticket, he'd probably get a verbal reprimand - possibly a written one - but he'd still have a job. He just couldn't risk it.

"No thanks," Jace told him. "I'll just tell Phil and accept the consequences."

Damian eyed Jace for a long time before seeming to come to some mental decision. He shrugged. "Yeah, I kind of figured you'd say that. You're too much of a straight shooter. But listen, don't tell him by email. Tell him face to face. This is sensitive and no one's supposed to know."

Jace nodded. That mostly made sense. He looked over at Phil's office and then sighed. That's right, Phil was off today. He'd have to wait until tomorrow. "Fine, I'll tell him tomorrow."

"Good boy," Damian said and moved his chair back to his own cube. "You tell Phil tomorrow."

Jace logged out of the ticket and looked at the time. It was 5 p.m., time to go. He shut down his system and stood to go. Damian was still at his desk. "You leaving?"

"I need to get some more done on this project," Damian told him, not bothering to look at him.

"Okay," Jace said. "I'll see you tomorrow."

When Damian didn't reply, Jace walked over to the brain backup booth. Jace went inside the booth, swiped his badge and entered his PIN. A moment later, the door shut behind him and the screen in front of him began showing a percent remaining countdown. He closed his eyes to await the beep that would signal the end of the backup.

When the beep didn't happen after what seemed like a minute, Jace opened his eyes to find he was outside, and everything had changed.

Chapter 7

Jace blinked against the bright light of the sun and it took his eyes a moment to adjust. Even though things were blurry, it was clear he was now outside. How had he gotten outside? His vision cleared and he looked around.

He immediately scrambled back across the ground as he recognized the faces of goblins sitting around a bonfire. He fell as he backpedaled but kept moving backwards on his hands. The goblins around the fire stopped what they were doing and turned their heads to stare at him dumbly.

"You okay?" one of the goblins asked in a high-pitched voice. The other goblins shrugged and went back to talking.

Jace was continuing to back away when he caught sight of his feet. They were large and gray and had claws where the toenails should be. A costume. He must be wearing some sort of costume. Yes, he must be wearing those novelty slippers that look like monster feet.

Reaching down to pull the slippers off, Jace froze as he caught sight of his hands. They were gray and knobby with claws at the end of each finger. They were goblin hands. He wiggled his fingers and the goblin hands wiggled their fingers. He waved them around.

"You get hit in the head or something?" asked the goblin who was still looking at him.

"What?" Jace said reflexively. His voice game out high pitched like the other goblin. What was going on? Was he dreaming?

That must be it. He must have gone home and then fell asleep and for some reason was dreaming he was a goblin.

Relaxing, Jace sat up and looked around. He was in a small village of a half dozen mud and straw huts. There were a dozen more goblins in the village, most of them around the bonfire he'd just crawled away from.

Everything seemed so surreal, so vivid. It was just like being in the game - well, other than being a goblin. He wondered why his subconscious had chosen a goblin. Maybe it was something he ate.

He thought back to the last thing he remembered. He got the brain backup and then what? He didn't remember anything after the backup. He must have been really tired. It was strange that he didn't even remember the ride home on the train. Or, had he fallen asleep on the train?

Jace wasn't sure but he decided to check out things before he woke up. He had just picked himself off of the ground and started to brush himself off when the world went topsy turvy. There was a flash of blinding light and something hot lifted him off his feet and threw him into the wall of the hut behind him.

He wanted to cry out in pain, but nothing in his body responded. There were shooting pains in his back and his front felt like his skin was on fire. He slid down the wall into a heap on the ground, unable to move. But he could see now.

The place where the bonfire had been just seconds ago was now a large scorched circle. He heard several twangs and some goblin shouts and then everything went quiet. Was that the sound of a bow he'd heard? Was someone attacking them?

Jace fought through the excruciating pain and tried to stand up but his body didn't respond. Was he dead? Weren't you supposed to wake up if you died in a dream? Why hadn't he woken up? And why the heck did it hurt so much?

Then he heard voices and they were speaking English. He tried to move his head to find the source of the voices, but nothing worked. He was either dead or paralyzed. Except being dead shouldn't hurt so much.

The sound of talking caught his attention. It came from his left, but he couldn't see anything and still couldn't move his head to look in that direction. At first the talking was muffled by distance, but then he definitely heard people speaking English.

"I bet there's not even anything here," said a male voice.

"Me thinks there something," said a deeper male voice that sounded like it belonged to a simpleton.

"Geez, knock off the roleplaying… yes, we get it… you're Frankenstein," hissed another male voice. This one sounded much more guttural and somewhat serpentine.

"Frankenstein's monster," responded the deeper voice, this time sounding much more intelligent. "Frankenstein was the scientist."

"Whatever," hissed the guttural voice.

Four figures strode into his view, looking at the carnage in the village. The most striking was a seven-foot man who appeared to be stitched together. It was *golem*, a stitched together humanoid, very similar to Frankenstein's monster. They were one of the player races in the evil faction. They made excellent front line fighters.

To the right of the hulking golem was a small, slim midnight skinned elf with silvery hair. Jace recognized it instantly as a *dark elf*, another evil player race that did well at brigand work. This one held two hand crossbows at the ready.

To the golem's left was a tall, slim figure that moved with the grace of a snake. Not only that, but it looked like a snake, or more specifically, like a dragon. It was a *half-dragon*, another of the evil player races. Their dragon heritage made them talented mages. As Jace watched, a forked tongue slithered out of the half-dragon's mouth.

"Ugh," hissed the half-dragon. "It smells like burnt meat!"

"What? You don't like the smell of napalm in the morning?" said a new voice that stepped into view. Jace knew instantly that this was a *morlock*. It's pale shriveled body was a dead giveaway. Not quite dead, not quite alive, the morlocks were the natural necromancers for the evil player races. "Stop complaining and look for a chest or bag of gold or something."

They sounded like players. One was even trying to roleplay his character. Is that what they were supposed to be in his dream? Players? But who were they? Why had they attacked the village? Was he supposed to do something with them? Do something to them?

As Jace's mind swirled with ideas, he stared at them with his unmoving body. Right now, he couldn't do anything. Then he felt a tingling sensation in his fingers and toes that travelled up his body. He tried to move his fingers and found that they worked. Feeling the rest of his muscles come under his control, he slowly stood up.

The morlock noticed him first. "Hey, we got a live one."

"Seriously?" asked the golem in his deep bass voice. "One of them survived that blast?"

Jace wanted to scream in pain. He could see that his entire front side was burned. Not only that, but from the pain he was having breathing, he was pretty sure he broke a rib or two. He gritted his teeth from the pain but needed to find out what was going on.

"Who are you?" Jace asked in the same high-pitched voice he heard himself use before.

The four players, if that is what they were, looked at each other in confusion.

"Is it trying to speak to us?" asked the morlock. "Can they do that?"

"Wow," said the dark elf. "I've never seen one do that. Normally they just attack or run."

"Perhaps it's a quest starter," said the half-dragon thoughtfully. "Maybe even a raid quest."

The morlock scratched his chin. "You could be right. But then why can't we understand it."

Frankie, at least that's what Jace decided to call the golem in his mind, stepped forward and raised his voice. "WHAT… ARE… YOU… TRYING… TO… TELL… US?"

The other players rolled their eyes and the half-dragon smacked his forehead. Mordy, the morlock looked at the golem. "Do you really think saying it loudly is going to make him understand?"

"Maybe we have to kill him to start the quest," said the dark elf, which Jace decided to call Inky. Inky raised one of his crossbows.

"Just wait," said Draco the half-dragon. Now Jace had names for them all, which made it easier to keep track of them. "Why wouldn't it have just died if that's all we needed to start the quest."

Inky let his crossbow drop to his side. "Good point. Maybe there's something we have to do."

"Like what?" asked Frankie.

Jace was really confused. He knew dreams didn't make sense most of the time, but this was really confusing. What was he supposed to do? Did these players represent aspects of himself? Was he supposed to do something? It was hard to think with all the pain.

He wished he had a painkiller - or more like an entire bottle of painkillers.

As he wracked his brain for what to do, the players were having their own conversation.

"Let's offer him something," suggested Mordy.

"Like what?" asked Inky.

"What about a healing potion?" hissed Draco questioningly. "I mean… he's hurt right? Maybe if we offer him some healing, it will trigger a dialogue."

Mordy nodded and looked at the others who just shrugged. "Sure, why not. Anyone have a cheap healing potion?"

The four players searched their pouches for a long moment and then then Frankie held up a small red vial. "I have a cloudy potion."

Looking at the small vial in Frankie's fingers, the players nodded. "That'll do. Give it to him and see if anything happens."

Frankie started forward. "Okay, but if he attacks me, it's clobberin time."

"Don't kill him," Draco hissed. "Not until we find out what he does."

Jace watched the approaching golem. Goblins were only about three feet tall, and the closer Frankie got to him, the more the size difference became evident. He was basically a giant to Jace's little body.

Gently, Frankie bent down and held out the healing potion in his beefy hand. "Here little fella, try this." The big golem looked back at his friends. "Do you think it understands me?"

"I doubt it," Draco responded.

Jace took the vial and nodded his head.

"Hey," grinned the golem. "I think he understood me."

Jace took the vial, uncorked it and poured the content down his throat. Then he coughed and collapsed to the ground as his flesh mended itself. It didn't heal all the damage, but it certainly took the edge off the pain.

"You killed him!" cried Mordy.

Raising a gnarled hand to forestall any argument, Jace slowly climbed back to his feet. "Thank you," he rasped.

"What did he say?" asked the three players who had hung back. "What did he say?"

"I don't know," shrugged Frankie. "More goblin speak."

Jace let out an exasperated sigh. He could clearly hear himself speaking English, but apparently in his dream, he spoke goblin. That was frustrating. Was that part of what he was supposed to do? Was he supposed to communicate with the players? He really wished he'd paid attention in Psychology 101 back in college.

"I don't think he does anything," Inky said. "I think he just survived somehow."

"But what about the way he's acting?" asked Mordy. "That's not normal."

"Maybe he's the goblin village idiot," suggested Draco who laughed. "And we just wasted a potion on an idiot."

Jace didn't like where this conversation was going. In fact, he had a really bad feeling about this.

"Listen guys," Inky said. "I have to logout soon for supper, so I need to get back to a safe spot. Let's just kill him and go."

Mordy's eyes went glassy, much like real players did when they were looking at their HUD. "Yes, I have to go soon too. I guess just kill him."

Frankie pulled his sword from its scabbard on his hip. "Sorry about this little guy. I kind of liked you."

Jace waved his hands frantically trying to dissuade the giant golem. The last thing he saw was a huge sword descending towards his head. Then sharp pain. Then blackness.

In the blackness, glowing words appeared.

System message 4307895E - Entity killed.
Experience rewarded.
Loot generated.

Return code: __

Jace stared uncomprehendingly at the words. They looked like system messages but nothing like anything he'd ever seen before. Plus, wasn't he supposed to wake up if he died in a dream? Something was wrong. Something was very wrong.

A cursor blinked at the end of the words "Return code:" for several seconds before everything went black again.

AI module retrieved.
Selecting new host.
Inserting AI module.
Spawning…

And then more blackness… and light.

Chapter 8

Jace blinked against the bright light of the sun and it took his eyes a moment to adjust. Even though things were blurry, it was clear he was now outside. He got a sinking feeling in the pit of his stomach as a strange sense of deja vu overcame him. Didn't he just have this dream?

Things became clearer around him and he found himself in a small forest clearing but something was off. He looked down and was surprised to see how far it was to the ground. He held up his hands and this time, instead of short gnarly gray arms, he had huge, beefy arms covered in a tough greenish leathery skin. He recognized himself instantly from playing VEIL. He was an ogre.

Shaking his head as if that would make things go back to normal, he wondered what was going on? Why was he dreaming of being monsters? Was it a dream? What about those strange messages he'd seen when he had died as a goblin? They did seem remarkably like game messages.

Before he really had a chance to think about it, he felt a stinging in his knee. He looked down in time to see a stone bounce off it.

"Again?" Jace bellowed in frustration. Was someone attacking him again? Couldn't they just leave him alone and let him figure out what was happening?

"Get it! Get it!" came voices. Figures emerged from the wood and Jace recognized them as some of the "good" player races.

There was a halfling, a dwarf, a gnome and a nephilim, or half-angel, and they seemed intent on killing him. He frowned. Of course, they wanted to kill him, he was an ogre.

Two more rocks thudded into his arm, but he barely noticed as the dwarf ran up to him and bellowed a war cry. "Fight me!"

Jace did a double take. Had the dwarf just *Taunted* him? Would he be compelled to keep attacking the dwarf and only the dwarf? Was he going to lose control of himself? Icy panic flowed through him as he looked down at the dwarf.

Jace cocked an eyebrow. He didn't feel any different. He took a step away from the dwarf just to see if he could. The dwarf looked confused and then stepped towards him.

"Fight me!" demanded the dwarf again, this time a little louder.

Experimentally, Jace took two large steps towards the little gnome dressed in robes. The gnome appeared to be casting a spell and Jace didn't want to get burned, electrocuted, frozen or well… anything else that would hurt.

The gnome stopped casting with a frightened look as he moved closer. "Uh," she stammered. "Why is the ogre moving towards me?"

Emboldened by his success in ignoring the *Taunt*, Jace took another step. "Don't cast at me!"

The gnome took another step back and started moving in hands in the beginning of a spell. Angry for being ignored, Jace took another step and raised his club over his head, aiming it down at the gnome. "Stop it!"

When the gnome didn't stop, he smashed the club down on her, intending to knock her out. Unfortunately, he hadn't counted on the ogre's massive strength and flattened her instantly. Ouch.

"Sorry," he said, but she was already dead.

The other three players stood gaping in shock at the smear that used to be their caster.

"It killed Kenlee!" screamed the elf. "Why didn't you *Taunt* it?!"

The dwarf looked defensive. "I did! I *Taunted* it!" The armor clad dwarf faced him and banged on his shield. "FIGHT ME!"

Horrified at what he'd just done to the little gnome, Jace turned and ran off through the forest, quickly leaving the players far behind.

The ogre must have had a ton of *Stamina* because Jace felt like he ran for miles before collapsing. One minute he was running, the next minute he was flat on his face, unable to move. It was eerily like VEIL. In the game, when you ran out of *Stamina*, you just collapsed and were unable to do anything until your *Stamina* regenerated to 25%.

Stamina was one of those stats that wasn't really meaningful until you were either in a marathon fight, like a raid, or when you were trying to run. It was put into the game as an afterthought when players did nothing but run. The developers stated that it hadn't been their intention that everyone constantly ran, so they added in a *Stamina* stat. Now, it basically stopped you from running constantly and was really annoying in long fights.

The run had given Jace time to think. None of this really seemed very dream-like. It actually felt like being in the game.

Well, other than being a monster, it felt like being in the game. WAS he in the game? How was that possible?

Jace was a programmer. A troubleshooter. He had to think about this logically. First, how could he be in the game?

There were only two answers. One, he was logged in normally through his VR pod. If that were the case, he should be in his Mordred character and he should have a HUD. Experimentally, he tried activating his HUD. Nothing happened. He thought of the special keywords for major failures.

EXIT GAME.

He thought the command, but nothing happened. That was supposed to be hard coded into the pod itself to exit out of a virtual environment. It should have initiated a normal shut down, but nothing was happening.

There was another one, but it was only supposed to be used in emergencies as it had the possibility of messing up your brain. It did an emergency shutdown and could cause serious feedback to your mind. But what choice did he have? Not only was he stuck in the game, he was stuck in a monster. Closing his eyes and bracing himself, he thought the command words.

EMERGENCY EXIT.

Nothing happened. He waited longer. Still nothing happened. He felt his heart pounding as panic began to set in. Why couldn't he exit? Was it his pod? Was it malfunctioning? The pod was older. Maybe that was it!

He dismissed it. No, even if his pod was malfunctioning, it couldn't put him into a monster body. It only displayed the information that was sent to it. And all of that information came from the game computer itself.

Jace took a deep breath and realized he was still on the ground. It didn't really matter right now so he just stayed on the ground as he thought things through.

Okay Jace, think logically. How else could he be in the game? His blood went to ice in his veins as he realized the only other way he could be in the game. H must had died and been inserted into the game. He suddenly felt nauseous as he considered that grim alternative. If he had died, his Last Will & Testament currently told them to insert his last brain backup into the game. After all, that was why he played the game so hard. He had played so hard so that when he died, he'd become Mordred and live the rest of eternity in the game as a vampyre assassin. And the more money and loot he accumulated in the game, the easier his eternity would be. Now it looked as if that eternity had already started.

A deep sense of sadness and loss overwhelmed him. He thoughts of all the things he'd never do. The places he'd never go. Heck, he'd never even really had a serious relationship. Now he never would. There were so many things he wouldn't get to do.

It felt overwhelming but he also felt a sense of detachment. Like he was watching this happen to someone else. Was he experiencing denial? Wasn't that one of the stages of dealing with a death? He remembered one of the counselors he'd been forced to go to after his parents died had told him something about the five stages of grief. But that seemed a lifetime ago. He smirked as he realized that was literally true for him. It was a lifetime ago.

But how had he died? He thought back to his last memory before waking up the game. The last thing he remembered was the brain backup. He tried hard to think of anything after that, anything at all. There was nothing. Not even a hint or hazy memory after that point. He had no idea how he died. There were no memories after than brain backup.

He shook his enormous ogre head to clear away all the questions that were suddenly assaulting it. So now what? He was dead. That sucked. It really sucked. But if he were in the game, then he had a second chance. It wasn't the life he'd wanted but it was a second chance. The question was: why the heck was he in an ogre body?

He'd been goblin first, that was obvious. He'd been killed and, there was that weird system message and then he had jumped to a different monster body. Why

was he in a monster body? That made no sense at all.
Players couldn't be monsters. Period. The game rules
didn't allow it.

When he died, he should have been inserted into his
Mordred character. Inserted. That rang a bell. Players
who died had their brain backups uploaded into the
game permanent, a process called insertion. Insertion!
Jace's brain did a double take. Inserted. He should have
been inserted. *THE INSERTION ROUTINE*!

Why hadn't he thought of that sooner! Jace
remembered the encrypted or obfuscated code he'd
found in the insertion routine he'd seen at work! Was
there a bug in the insertion routine? Is that why he'd
been put into a monster body? If so, that would be
devastating to the company. That routine handled not
only the insertion of a person's brain backup into his
game character, it also handled the conversion of earthly
assets into game currency.

Despite everything, Jace chuckled. Who said you
couldn't take it with you?

You could specify in your will how much of your
assets you wanted inserted into VEIL with you to ensure
you had a comfortable eternity in the game. Only Jace's
assets hadn't made it over and even if they had, who
really wanted to be the richest ogre in the game?

But if there was a bug in the program and people
were being inserted into monster bodies instead of into
their characters, people would panic. WorldCog's stock
would drop. It would cost them millions. Is that what
had happened? Had they tried to hide it? Is that why
Damian was so upset when he learned about it? Was no
one supposed to know? Did Phil even know?

Jace swallowed. Had he blundered into some company conspiracy? Had WorldCog killed him to keep him quiet? Was that why Damian had been acting like more of a jerk than normal? Was he afraid for his life too? Had Damian tried to save him? That seemed uncharacteristic but maybe that had been why he was so upset.

And now, Jace had been inserted and subjected to the very bug he'd blundered into. How was that for irony? Or was it irony at all? Had WorldCog killed him knowing that he would become a monster? Was this a way to ensure his silence? But why insert him at all then? It didn't make sense.

He snickered unconsciously. They HAD to insert him. The government audited the company for insertions. If he hadn't been inserted, they'd have to answer to the government during the next audit. This way, everything looked on the up and up. He was inserted, but he was a monster and couldn't tell anyone about it.

But he wasn't just your average Joe. He was a programmer. And not just any programmer, he was a WorldCog programmer.

He had worked on nearly every routine in the game at some point. He knew how the code worked and he knew of the backdoors.

He laughed. In the ogre body, it came out as a wickedly loud, ominous sound. WorldCog thought they could silence him. Jace would show them. He'd use his knowledge of the game to get the word out. If he couldn't save himself, he might at least be able to save others by getting the word out and forcing WorldCog to fix their code.

In the process, hopefully they'd fix him too and he could live out his days as Mordred. It wouldn't be so bad. He had been about to become a raider and have access to the top content in the game. It would be fun.

He was still thinking that when he felt a heavy foot on his shoulder. He opened his eyes and looked up to see a huge bipedal bear. It was a *werebear*, one of the "good" races, which meant it was probably a player.

The werebear looked down at him with a huge, two-handed axe poised over his head. "Ello poppet."

The last thing Jace saw was the axe descending towards his neck and then a sharp pain and blackness.

After a few moments, just like before, glowing words appeared.

System message 4307895E - Entity killed.
Experience rewarded.
Loot generated.

Return code: __

Then, like before a cursor blinked at the end of the words "Return code:" Out of curiosity, he mentally clicked on the cursor and was rewarded with a virtual keyboard. He pressed the "1" key and then the Enter key. The words disappeared to be replaced by new messages.

Return code 1.
AI module retrieved.

Selecting new host.
Inserting AI module.
Spawning…

There was a darkness and then once again he was a physical body. He looked around. He was in an orc village. Looking at his arms, he was the same color as the orcs and guessed he was an orc this time. Just great.

Chapter 9

Jace looked around to see if there were any players nearby to kill him. When he didn't spot any, he found a nearby tree stump and sat down on it. None of the other orcs gave him more than a passing glance so he thought it would be safe to think for a while.

He tried to remember his train of thought before he'd been rudely interrupted by an axe to his neck. Jace involuntarily rubbed his hand across his neck and shivered. That had been a little too realistic. He made a mental note to avoid beheadings in the future.

Jace thought about his predicament until the sun went down without interruption. In the three or four hours, he'd come up with a few theories on what had happened to him. All had flaws except the last one.

In the game, everything was classified as an entity and each entity had a type. Unless he was mistaken, somehow, he'd been inserted with the wrong type. Instead of a player type, he was a monster AI type. That would explain why he was jumping from monster to monster. Each AI module, or AI entity, went to a pool until a monster was spawned. At that time, the monster "body" was given an AI to run it based on certain parameters. When the monster died, the AI module went back to the pool to get reassigned, which helped cut down on resource use.

That appeared to be exactly what was happening to Jace. He was put into a monster body until he died and then he was sent to a newly spawned body. But, since Jace wasn't really an AI, he wasn't bound by any parameters like real AI.

He didn't have to respond to *Taunt*s, didn't have to act "in character" for the monster. He could do whatever he liked - until he died.

If he could somehow change his entity type, he could change himself into whatever he wanted. He could even change himself into a player type and get back into his Mordred character. The problem was, without access to his data, he couldn't make any changes. And the only way to access his data was from the real world with a terminal connected to the game world.

Jace stretched. He'd been sitting for hours and he was getting sore - and hungry he noticed. He stood up and looked around the village. The orcs were going about their business, seeming oblivious to him. Apparently, he wasn't a very important orc in the tribe.

He did some quick stretching and then sat back down. Surprisingly, his stomach growled, and he looked down at it. Did monsters really feel hungry like this? It felt very real. But Jace couldn't think about stuffing his face right now.

He stopped in mid-thought. Stuffing his face. The thought had triggered something in the back of his mind. Stuffing his face. Stuffing his face. It was right on the tip of his brain. Something about stuffing.

Suddenly it hit him. Not stuffing. Injection. He could do an injection attack on the return code. By loading actual programming code into the return code, the system should run the code. In theory. And assuming the original developers didn't build in checks for an injection attack. But Jace felt certain they wouldn't have. After all, players would never be monsters, so why build security around a return code only AI's would have access to. But he couldn't be certain.

Jace needed to test it. He needed to be sure before he got his hopes up. Of course, there was only one way to test it. He had to die.

***

System message 4307895E - Entity killed.
Experience rewarded.
Loot generated.

Return code: __

It had taken Jace nearly an hour to get killed. This time, there were no players, and, in the end, he ended up punching the chief in the face. The chief was a boss and had killed him with one blow.

Once more he brought up the virtual keyboard. It was the moment of truth. Please let this work. Jace typed in his code:

System.out.printf("Hello World");

It was the most basic of code, but it would definitely let him know if he could use the injection exploit. He held his breath and hit the Return key.

Return code Hello World.
AI module retrieved.

Selecting new host.
Inserting AI module.
Spawning...

The messages flashed by quickly, but he had seen what he needed to. It had worked! And then he was in another body.

After a quick examination, Jace found he was in the body of a *kobold.* Kobolds were small reptilian creatures about the size of a goblin but looked more like a half-dragon. They were crafty little things that loved to set traps and lay ambushes for unwary players.

Jace didn't care right now. He was so overjoyed that he did a little dance, and then tripped over his own tail. Oops! He'd forgotten that kobolds had tails. It didn't matter, he just rolled around on the ground laughing. He was ecstatic that he'd found a solution. If he could do a code injection, he should be able to change his entity type to player.

He stopped rolling around as a thought struck him. He didn't actually know what the entity types were. He'd seen them before, sure, but he didn't have them memorized. Why should he when he could always just look them up in the documentation.

That sobered him up. He'd have to guess on the entity type. If he guessed wrong, he could end up permanently as a monster or worse, he could be a plant or even a sword. Spending eternity as a piece of ivy didn't appeal to him at all.

Jace turned over onto his belly and propped his head in his hands. He had thought this would be a solution - and maybe it still was - but there was a lot of risk involved. If he guessed wrong, he would be completely screwed - for eternity.

But what choice did he have really? Eternity as a monster, hopping from body to body? Is that what he wanted? Plus, if he stayed as a monster, he'd never be able to get justice against WorldCog for doing this to him.

And how many other people had been inserted with the same bug. They'd be doomed to live their eternities as monsters too. And unlike him, they had no choice. The people who had been affected by the bug would be doomed for all eternity if he didn't do something. Of course, if he screwed up and ended up a rock or an eggplant, they'd still be doomed.

Darn it! He was getting nowhere. He had to try. If he didn't, all the people who had been inserted with this bug were doomed. He was doomed. And WorldCog would get away with it. Jace couldn't let that happen. He would try.

Jace took a deep breath as he made his decision. He had to try. But what number should he use for the new entity type. He knew it was an integer, a whole number. And it would be a positive number. But which number?

He tried to think back to the last time he'd done any work with entity types. Something clicked in his mind and he thought maybe it was a number in the teens. Maybe 12 or 17. But which one? He didn't know. He decided to go with 17. It was as good as any. Now he had to die.

Looking around, Jace immediately saw a way to kill himself. Down the hall to his right, an area on the floor glowed red. It was the same ability he had as Mordred - the ability to detect traps. He picked himself up and ran towards the trap. As soon as his foot touched the red glowing area, a large spike shot up through the floor and impaled him.

He felt unbelievable pain and his body spasmed and then things went black. In a moment, the familiar text appeared:

System message 4307895E - Entity killed.
Experience rewarded.
Loot generated.

Return code: __

Jace mentally took a deep breath and summoned the virtual keyboard. He quickly typed in the code he would need.

this.entityType = 17;

His finger hovered over the Return key, but he hesitated. Was it 17 or could it be 12? He erased the 17 and put in 12 and hit Return before he could change his mind again.

Return code ERROR.
ERROR: WRONG ENTITY TYPE.
ERROR - INVALID FACTION. FACTION = 0.
ERROR - INVALID RACE. RACE = 0.
DNA DETECTED.
BODY GENERATION COMPLETE.
CLASS 0 DETECTED.

UNKNOWN ERROR.

UNKNOWN ERROR.
UNKNOWN ERROR.
UNKNOWN ERROR.
SPAWN ERROR.
SPAWN ERROR.

Suddenly, the darkness was gone, and he was back in the kobold body. Then pain like he had never experienced erupted across his entire body. He could feel muscles tearing, bones breaking and reforming and then breaking again. He tried to scream but the spike was still sticking through him, impaling him. All that came out was a gurgle and some blood.

The pain continued until he passed out. At least, he thought he passed out. Then the next thing he knew, the world was gray, and he was staring down at his body impaled on a stake. Only, it wasn't a kobold body, it was a human body. Looking closer, he saw that it was HIS human body. It looked almost identical to his real body except in much better shape.

Then familiar words popped up and he thought they were the most beautiful words he'd ever seen.

You have died.
Do you wish to respawn at your last spawn point? (Yes or No)

Without a moment's hesitation or even caring where he ended up, he mentally chose Yes. And everything faded away.

Chapter 10

Jace felt a sensation that felt like falling and tingling at the same time. Then his vision was obscured by a golden light that was almost blinding. It was an all too familiar feeling, though more intense than he was used to. It was the respawning process.

Respawn complete.
New spawn point: Sinking Springs
Do you wish to set Sinking Springs as your bind point? (Yes or No)

After mentally choosing yes, the prompt disappeared. He was still blinded from the golden light, but he could feel the grass beneath his feet, his bare feet. He blinked his eyes until he could see.

The first thing he noticed was that he was in a graveyard, on a grave with a tombstone marked "Unknown Adventurer". But that wasn't his primary concern. He held up his hands in front of his face. They were human. He felt elated. But then he realized that they were, in fact, human, not vampyre.

He looked down at the rest of himself. He was naked except for a loincloth and his body was definitely human and not vampyre. In fact, he actually looked like a version of his real-world body, but in peak condition and maybe a few inches taller. But he definitely wasn't Mordred. So, maybe he was a player now, but not in his normal character.

Bile rose in his throat. Had it deleted his Mordred character?

Please God no! He had so much time and money invested in Mordred! And he had been right on the cusp of becoming a raider! He could have made millions of gold!

Defeated, Jace dropped to his knees. He thought of the hours of work he'd put into his character, carefully crafting it and building up the skills. Then there were all the adventures he'd gone on to accumulate the equipment. The equipment! He'd finally gotten the full Kobadera set! And now it was gone?! This couldn't be happening!

"Noooooo!!!!!" he screamed to everyone and no one in particular.

For long minutes, he just sat there kneeling on the ground, thinking of what he had lost. Finally, he took a deep breath and stood up and looked down at his body. It was him, or at least his ideal body based on his DNA. In VEIL, players were always in their ideal body locked at age 25. Jace didn't know why the developers chose that age, but that was the way it had been designed. But that was BEFORE the race template was applied. And Jace should be a vampyre, not a human!

Was it the same bug? The bug had made him jump from monster to monster as some sort of AI. The bug was obviously WorldCog's fault. Once he brought it to their attention and they'd fixed the bug, they'd HAVE to restore his character. Wouldn't they? He hoped so.

For a moment, he remembered the stark reality that he was dead. That he would never be in the real world again. He shook his head to clear his mind. No, he couldn't think about that right now. He needed to contact support somehow. But how?

There was no in-game support. Everyone knew that. It broke immersion and the original developers didn't want things that broke immersion.

The main way to get support was on their website but Jace knew there were other ways most people didn't know about. He only knew about them because other developers complained when a player had stumbled onto them and they had to manually log a ticket for the players.

There was a hidden room inside the palace of every country sovereign. Inside the room, there was a desk - a *"Help Desk"*. On the desk was a book entitled "Entreating the Gods". If a player opened it in that room, it would summon the developer on call, and they would appear in game.

The method was in the original game code as a way to immersively ask for help. Unfortunately, they didn't anticipate how many users would use it and how much their staff's time it would take up. They quickly learned the error of their ways and moved all support to the website where it could be better managed. They left the code in the game but hid the activators where they thought players wouldn't find them. But it did happen occasionally.

When a player did find the *Help Desk*, its location was moved but it always stayed in the royal palace since that was one of the most difficult places for a player to get. In addition, the player was given a special buff called "Entreated the Gods" which gave them a permanent +1 to all their stats, which they lost if they told anyone about the room. It kept most players from telling and those that did could never lead the players back since the room had moved.

All Jace had to do was get to the capital, get into the palace, find the room and entreat the gods. He took a deep breath and let it out. It seemed overwhelming when he thought about it. He had no idea how he was going to do any of those things. He might have managed it with Mordred, but now. He paused. Actually, come to think of it, he knew nothing about his new character.

Curious now, he tried to activate his HUD. There was a weird flash and some strange characters he'd never seen and then the HUD flickered on and off, then back on. In the lower left of his vision was the system message icon and it was blinking. He had system messages waiting.

He mentally selected the icon and his screen filled with red error messages. He scrolled through them, trying to get a sense of what was going on. After several minutes of reading, he realized that he hadn't really respawned as a player, he had TRANSFORMED into a player. Because of the way in which he'd become a player, there were some issues. He appeared to have some sort of residual characteristics of the kobold he'd been before he became a player.

He brought up the General section of his status page.

Name: Dedrurrurth
Race: Human
Class: Rogue
Level: 1

Experience: 0

Jace frowned. It appeared that it either gave him some random name, or he'd kept the name of the kobold he'd been previously. Still, it wasn't the end of the world. What's in a name, after all. He'd been right that his race was human. It certainly wouldn't have been his first choice, but it was better than being a kobold.

Next, he looked at class. He had been given the Rogue class. He frowned again. Rogue was one of the base classes. No one took a base class anymore because the newer classes were so much better. It irked him that he hadn't gotten to choose which class he'd be.

Then, he looked at level and experience. Considering the way he become a player, he wasn't surprised that he was back to level 1 with no experience. That probably meant his Mordred character was gone completely. They'd have to restore it from a backup - assuming they would.

He decided to check out his *Attributes* and brought up that section.

Brawn: 10
Agility: 10
Hardiness: 10
Intellect: 10
Piety: 10
Personality: 10

Jace gritted his teeth. Could this get any worse?! His *Brawn, Agility, Hardiness, Intellect, Piety* and *Personality* attributes were all 10s. Those were the baseline attributes for all races. Each race started at 10 and were given certain bonuses based on race choice.

Elves got two points in *Agility* and *Intellect*. Halflings received more two points to *Agility* and *Piety*. Dwarves received two points to *Brawn* and *Hardiness*. Each of the premium races received a total of 4 points between their two attributes.

Even a single extra point would have been helpful. A *Brawn* score over 10 would have given an extra point of damage with his melee attacks for each point over 10, while *Agility* would have done the same for his ranged attacks. He would have received an extra point of health each level for every point of *Hardiness* over 10 and bonus points to man for each point of *Intellect* or *Piety*. *Personality* didn't affect any combat options, but it certainly did help to influence the type of reaction he received from NPCs, as well as allowing him to buy items cheaper and sell items for more.

Instead, he was a human. Humans were the original race. They normally received only two bonus points they could distribute wherever they want but would always be two points behind one of the premium races. And Jace didn't even have that. All of his scores were set at 10 with no bonuses whatsoever.

Jace was becoming more and more agitated. Although he wasn't a monster anymore, he was completely screwed as a player. Not only did he have a subpar class, but he was also a subpar race. No one played human anymore for a good reason. Those 2 extra attribute points didn't seem like much, but the higher level you were, the more they counted.

Not to mention, humans received no special abilities or skills like the premium races. The only boon they received was a lack of penalty for multiclassing, which was next to useless since no one multiclassed. You were much better putting your experience into leveling one class than trying to level several classes at once. You know the old saying, "Jack of All Trades but Master of None". And in VEIL, you needed to be a master.

Shaking his head at his misfortune, he looked at the *Skills* section. That gave him pause. He'd expect to have the base rogue skills and that's it. Instead, he had some extra skills.

Combat
Leather armor: 1
Piercing weapons: 1

Class
Acrobatics: 1
Bluff: 1
Dodge: 1
Lockpicking: 1
Pickpocket: 1
Stealth: 1

#$%#&
Monsterspeak: 1
Trapsetting: 1

Most of the skills were exactly what he would have expected. He had his *Rogue* class and combat skills. What grabbed his attention was the last category. The name of the category was corrupted, and he'd never seen the skills underneath it. *Trapsetting* seemed self-explanatory but no player class had access to it. And what was *Monsterspeak*? Could he speak with kobold-ish? Or was it kobold-ese? It was interesting but not particularly useful.

Considering his possibilities, Jace switched over to his Inventory section. He was not surprised that it was completely empty. He didn't have any items or money. Just great! How was he supposed to do anything without equipment?

He threw his hands up in exasperation as he dismissed his HUD. This was ridiculous. He was a subpar version of a subpar race with no equipment. Oh, but wait, he could talk to kobolds! Kobolds, who would attack him on sight! That would come in so handy!

He began pacing back and forth across the grave, trying to think of what to do. How could he get equipment without having equipment? He couldn't kill anything barehanded. Not with a *Brawn* score of 10.

He was still pacing when suddenly someone appeared in front of him in a golden glow. Unable to stop his momentum, he crashed into the person and they fell to the ground in a heap.

"Ow," said a feminine voice from beneath him. "Do you mind getting off me?"

"Sorry," Jace muttered as he pushed himself up. He rolled to his side, getting a good look at who had just respawned right in front of him.

The girl next to him had fiery red hair and long tapering ears, marking her as an elf. She had the lean, athletic frame of a dancer and was only clad in a loin cloth and something equally scant covered her small breasts. She had a pretty face that was lightly freckled, and she had dazzling bright blue eyes. Her proximity and lack of clothing made Jace both excited and embarrassed. He felt heat in his face and knew he must be blushing.

The girl blushed too and tried to get up, only to fall over on top of him. Jace looked down to see their legs were still intertwined.

"Sorry," she said, as she landed on him. She blushed an even deeper crimson and this time, the blush made it all the way to the tips of her pointed ears. She rolled off and stood up just as he did the same.

"Sorry about that," he said.

"It's okay," she told him. She had her arms crossed over her chest, obviously embarrassed at the small amount of clothing covering her. "It was an accident."

Jace quickly examined her in his HUD.

You have gained a new skill: Inspect

Almedha Pressalor
Race: Elf
Class: Scout
Level: 1

The *Inspect* skill was useful for evaluating other players, especially enemy players of other factions. It was the player equivalent of the *Monster Lore* skill for seeing the class, race and level of monsters. And he'd just gained it by using it.

Dismissing his HUD, he looked at her but couldn't think of anything witty to say. They both stood there for a long moment before she took a step towards the entrance of the small graveyard. "I have to go retrieve my body."

She started edging towards the entrance when Jace thought of something. "What day is it?"

The elf stopped and blinked. "What?"

"The date," Jace said. "What's the date?"

"Uh… May 8th," she replied, giving him the type of look only reserved for crazy people.

Inwardly Jace was stunned, but he recovered quickly. He gave her a grin as he said the first plausible thing that came to his head. "Sorry, I was pulling an all-nighter and fell asleep in my pod."

Her expression softened and she nodded. "Well, bye."

"Bye," Jace replied numbly as she hurried away. Even the sight of her half-naked bottom couldn't pull him from his thoughts. The girl had said it was May 8th. The last memory he had was April 5th. He was missing an entire month.

Chapter 11

He'd lost an entire month. How was that possible?
Normally, when someone died, their last brain backup
was inserted into the game within 24-48 hours.
Occasionally, it took longer if the backup had to be
shipped to WorldCog but Jace's last backup was done in
WorldCog headquarters.

Jace had never heard of it taking an entire month to
insert someone except when a will was contested. But
in his case, he had no surviving family to contest the
will. He should have been inserted minutes after he was
declared brain dead. It didn't make any sense.

Taking a deep breath, Jace pushed thoughts of the
missing month out of his head. He'd think about it later.
Right now, he had more immediate concerns.

The sun was sinking in the sky and that meant night
was coming soon. Since he couldn't logout, it meant
he'd be spending the night in the game. Right now, he
had no clothes to protect him against the cold and no
weapons to protect him from any monsters. He also had
no money to buy food. He didn't need food to live
anymore, but after a certain period of time, he'd get a
debuff called *Hungry* if he didn't eat. It was a penalty to
his abilities and skills and couldn't be cured until he ate
in-game food.

That meant, he needed to find food, clothing and
weapons. He looked to the right of the cemetery where
he saw an outcropping of crude, Tudor style buildings.

There was a village. And where there was a village, there were quests. It was time to do some quests.

Jace took a step towards the cemetery exit just as a golden form materialized in front of him. He couldn't stop in time and for the second time, he went down in a tangle of limbs with another player.

"Ahhh!" screamed a familiar voice underneath him. "Get off me!"

He rolled off and the elf he'd met earlier rolled on her side towards him. "You again?"

"Me again," Jace smiled. "I take it you died again?"

The elf made a sour face. "Yes! The goblins were still there, hiding. I went to get my body and they ambushed me." She looked him over. "You die again too?"

Jace chuckled. "No, I never left. I'm trying to figure out what to do."

"What do you mean? How far is your body?"

Knowing he couldn't really explain the truth, Jace came up with a believable lie. "I had to cover a co-worker's shift and my body aged out. Now I have nothing."

It worked. Her expression softened and she looked genuinely sympathetic. "Sorry to hear that. Maybe you could just delete your character and create a new one. You'd get new starter equipment, right?"

Jace raised an eyebrow. She was right. He was only level 1, so he could technically delete the character and create a new one. Of course, that required access to a pod, something he didn't have. He was stuck with this character until WorldCog fixed him.

"Good idea, but I'm kind of attached to this character," he said honestly.

She shrugged and stood up. "Well, I need to go get my body before it expires. Good luck."

Jace waved. "Nice bumping into you again."

The elf gave him a small chuckled and then turned to leave again. As she started to walk away, Jace realized he could help the girl get her body and called out. "I can help you get your body."

She stopped and spun around, eyes narrowing. "Why would you do that?"

Jace was taken back. He'd just offered to help her. Did she think he had some ulterior motive? He shrugged. "Because it's the right thing to do?"

She gave him a furious look. "Listen, I'm not going to have virtual sex with you or anything like that just because you help me get my body!"

Jace took a step backwards. This girl was crazy. All he'd done was offer to help and now they were talking about in-game sex. "Woah! Woah! Woah! Nevermind then! I just wanted to help. I didn't want you to be naked and penniless like me."

She looked at him for a long moment, her face slowly losing it's anger. "No catches? You'll just help me get my body and that's it?"

Jace held his hands up in a placating gesture. "No catch. I help you get your body back. That's it."

He could see the conflict on her face but finally she made her decision. "Okay. You can help. But I'm not doing anything for you in return."

Jace nodded. "Fair enough."

"Fine. We'd better hurry," she said, turning back around. "I have to log off soon."

Jace followed her out the cemetery and to the right through the village. They jogged through the village and then down a road through some hills. He noticed that the gravel on his feet felt remarkably painful. It felt real.

A terrible thought came to him then. Normally, a player could control the feedback level of the game using a sensory level. Most players kept theirs around 10-15% of normal, meaning they'd experience 10-15% of the pain (and pleasure) of the game. So when they were stabbed by an enemy, they'd only feel a fraction of the pain. Few people wanted to feel what a real fireball would feel like or a real spear thrust.

The sensory level was tied to the person's FEVRE pod and Jace had no pod. He quickly brought up his HUD and looked for the sensory level. As he feared, it wasn't there. He had no way to change how much pain he would be experiencing. Judging by the agony in his feet right now, he guessed he was permanently at 100%. He'd be experiencing everything as if it were really happening.

Mercifully, the elf finally called them to a halt between two large hills. She bent over to catch her breath and then pointed up the right hill.

"Okay," she said as she caught her breath. "My body is just on the other side of this hill. There were two goblins hiding nearby and they killed me each time I got close to my body." She looked him up and down, as if just realizing he was as naked as she was. "How exactly are you going to help me?"

Jace grinned. "By being bait." He savored the shocked expression on her face before continuing. "I'll run up and lure them away and you loot your body and run back into town."

She blinked but nodded. "That'll work."

Without another word, Jace ran up the hill waving his hands and screaming at the top of his lungs. Behind him, he heard the elf laughing. She had a nice laugh.

Then he topped the hill and saw her body about 20 feet from where he was. He didn't see any goblins but that didn't mean they weren't there. There were plenty of boulders and large rocks they could be hiding behind. Jace ran straight for the body as fast as he could.

As if by magic, two goblins stepped out from behind rocks and ran at him on an intercept course. If Jace had intended to stop at the girl's body, they would have caught him. Instead, he kept running right past her body as fast as he could. He could hear them puffing behind him.

He thought he might outdistance them until he slipped on some loose rocks and went rolling across the rocks. He felt the brush burns across his mostly naked body as he slid across the rocks and nearly screamed. Then the goblins were upon him.

"Stupid hoo-mon," said one and sliced him across the back with a rusty axe.

Forest goblin slashes YOU with rusty tin axe for 5 damage.

Jace arched his back as pain exploded from the gash across his spine. He tried to roll away but the other goblin was there with a large knife.

"Die hoo-mon," it said and then stabbed down at his chest. He felt excruciating pain as the dagger plunged into him. He tried to scream but it came out a gurgle.

Forest goblin pierces YOU with rusty dagger for 3 damage.
You have died.
Do you wish to respawn at your last spawn point? (Yes or No)

The pain ended and everything went black for a moment. Then the world went gray and he jumped out of his body in spirit form so he was looking down at his corpse.

This was good. When he had died as a monster, he'd jumped right into another monster body. What he was experiencing now was what happened when a player died. Thankful, he chose yes to respawn, and the world dissolved around him.

The next thing he knew, he was back in the graveyard, gasping and holding his chest. Looking down, he realized he was whole again, and the wound was gone. He sighed in relief. That might have been the most painful thing he'd ever experienced.

He stumbled away from the gravestone where he'd respawned and looked around. Had the elf gotten her body? He hoped so. Jace began to walk towards town, occasionally wincing when he stepped on a particularly sharp rock.

He had just gotten to the first building when he saw her coming from the opposite direction. Now she was dressed in a pair of tight fitting leather leggings the color of spring grass with intricate leaf patterns. She had a cropped leather top of the same leather that exposed her midriff and arms. On her feet she wore high leather boots that came just above her knees and she wore long leather gloves that came up past her elbow. These were the brown of tree bark. On her back was a quiver of arrows and in her hand she carried a recurve bow. She looked every bit the elf warrior maiden.

Jace flashed her a grin. "I didn't recognize you with clothes on."

She blushed but smiled. "Thanks for helping me get my body."

"No problem," Jace replied. He put on a mischievous grin. "Now about that virtual sex…"

The elf's face went red and she opened her mouth to say something, but he stopped her with a raised hand as he burst out laughing. "Just kidding! Just kidding! I couldn't resist."

"You…" She struggled for a moment to say something but then she broke into a smile too. "Fine, you had me going." She looked at him a moment and her eyes went glassy. She scrunched up her nose. "Your name is Dedrurrurth? That seems a bit hard to pronounce."

"Call me Jace," he told her and extended his hand.

She hesitated only briefly and then took his hand and shook it. "I'm Charlena."

"Nice to meet you," he told her. "What's a nice elf like you doing in a place like this?"

A cloud passed over her face. "I was tricked."

Jace gave her a curious look and motioned her to continue.

Charlena let out an exasperated breath. "Fine. Some wizard was in the elf newbie area and offered to take me to a special leveling place. He said it was a secret. I agreed and we grouped and then he teleported me here. Then he ungrouped and told me if I didn't give him sex, he'd leave me here - in the farthest village in Karlandia. When I refused, he teleported away and left me here. I've been stuck here ever since. What a jerk!"

Jace had heard of players doing similar things and then blackmailing the girls to have virtual sex with them. WorldCog was trying to crack down on it but it still happened.

"I'm sorry you had a bad experience like that," he told her. "Did you contact support?"

She grew more agitated. "Yes. But because I came here of my own free will, there's nothing they can do."

"Ouch," Jace sympathized. Given what he'd recently learned about WorldCog, he didn't put anything past them.

"Tell me about it!" she said angrily. "What a bunch of idiots!"

"On that we agree," he told her.

She looked at him curiously. "Did you get trapped here too? Is that why you're here?"

Jace thought about it. He didn't want to go into his whole story with someone he just met. He needed time to process it and think of what to do next. For now, he had to keep it to himself. "Something like that."

She suddenly brightened. "Well, since we're both stuck here, maybe we can work together to get to another village."

Jace thought about that. He needed to make it to the capital and that was going to be difficult by himself. Having another player help him would make things easier. At the same time, he would be helping her to leave this village. It did seem like a good idea.

A thought hit him. This almost seemed almost too convenient. He was in a small village with no other players except one. And that one was a cute girl who needed his help. It seemed almost like a setup.

Was it a setup? Could he trust her? Was she working for WorldCog? Were they watching him?

Did he have a choice? If she were the only other player around, what choice did he have? None. Not if he wanted to make it to the capital. But he wouldn't trust her. Not until she had proven herself. Maybe not even then.

Smiling, Jace nodded. "Sounds like a plan! Let's work together and get out of this village!"

Chapter 12

Charlena and he had agreed to meet the next evening and then she had logged off, leaving Jace alone. He looked at the sun and saw there wasn't much time before it would be dark and he'd be weathering the cold night in nothing but his loincloth. He didn't even have anything to make a fire with. Too bad that half-demoness wasn't here. She could warm him up.

He chuckled. Sure, she'd warm him up. And he didn't mean in bed. He'd rather sleep with a viper. The little backstabber would probably roast him alive. But that gave him a flash of inspiration. He brought up his HUD and looked at the human's special ability.

Adaptable: Humans can change classes with experience penalty. Note: Normal multiclass restrictions still apply.

Smiling to himself, he realized there was one class that could do damage and mount a defense in nothing but a loincloth. *Mages.* And since he was human, he could switch classes and not incur any of the normal experience penalties.

But did he want to do that? He'd grouped and fought with casters but he'd never played a caster. In fact, he barely knew anything at all about them, other than the useful spells they had at the higher levels. He didn't remember anything about the lower level mages.

The nice thing about switching classes was, he retained abilities from his other classes. The limitation was the health and mana. Only the highest class received an increase in health and mana.

So, while a player might have tons of abilities as a multi-class character, they were limited by their mana in how many they could use. Plus, trying to level multiple classes took time away a player's your main class and you advanced more slowly. There were definitely pros and cons to multi-classing. In Jace's case, the biggest drawback, the experience point penalty, wasn't an issue since he was human.

He debated for nearly half an hour before the sinking sun finally convinced him to just do it. After all, he could always switch back after he reached 2nd level. He went into his HUD, chose his class and hit the change class button.

Available classes:
Fighter
Rogue (current class)
Priest
Mage

All of his choices were the generic classes. He didn't have access to any of the more powerful premium classes like wizard, warlock or sorcerer. Jace gritted his teeth. He had no choice. If he wanted to switch to a spellcaster, he'd have to go with *Mage*. So be it. He would do the best he could. After all, this was just until he could get back into the Mordred body - assuming he ever could.

He chose *Mage* and received some warnings about the experience penalty. Since he was human and had

Adaptable ability, he wouldn't be penalized. He hoped. If that was broken too, he'd really be in bad shape.

He confirmed his choice and was instantly assaulted by a screenful of system messages.

Class changed. New class Mage.
Adaptable: No experience penalty for second class.

You have gained a new skill: Air Magic
You have gained a new skill: Earth Magic
You have gained a new skill: Fire Magic
You have gained a new skill: Water Magic
You have gained a new skill: Staffs
You have gained a new skill: Wands
You have gained a new skill: Quilted Armor

Ability gained: Summon Familiar
You wish to choose a familiar now? (Yes or No)

Jace read through the messages, noting the new skills he'd gained from the *Mage* class. They seemed fairly straightforward. He hadn't received any Health or Mana from the class since it wasn't his highest class. That was the way they kept balance. Only your highest class received health or mana. Too bad, he could have used the extra mana that *Mage*s received. He looked at the pitiful 4 mana in his pool and hoped it would be enough to cast the 1st tier spells.

He read further and noticed the *Familiar* ability. He'd forgotten about that. He'd seen the little fairy dragons that the wizards had or the imps that the warlocks kept. Excited by the prospect of having a little fairy dragon, he chose Yes. In response, he received a list of the available familiars.

Choose familiar type:
Baby Griffon (Sorcerer Only)
Cat
Faerie Dragon (Wizard Only)
Ferret
Imp (Warlock Only)
Lizard
Toad

Seeing the list of familiars he could actually choose from, Jace's heart sank. The best ones were reserved for the premium classes.

He looked at his available options and smirked. What, no owl? None of the familiars he could choose had the ability to fly. He didn't want a toad or lizard. That left Cat or Ferret. He thought about choosing the ferret and naming it Kodo or Podo and calling himself Dar, but he doubted anyone would get the reference.

He'd always wanted a pet cat when he was a kid but his mom had been allergic. Maybe now he'd finally have one. He chose Cat.

You have chosen Cat.
Is this correct? (Yes or No)
Note: Once chosen, a familiar cannot be changed.

He glanced at the other choices once more before choosing yes.

You have gained a familiar: Cat.
Use the Summon Familiar to summon your (cat)
Familiar.

Jace had expected the cat to appear but apparently, he had to actually summon it. He brought up his HUD and found the *Abilities* section. He selected *Summon Familiar (Cat)*. Instead of making the cat appear, he was prompted with a system message:

Summon Familiar (Cat)
Amount of Mana to invest in Familiar: (1-4)

This perplexed Jace. What did it mean? Was he giving the familiar some of his mana? Was it permanent? Would he lose access to the mana? Since he only had 4 points of mana from his Rogue class, he really couldn't afford to lose any.

He debated cancelling the *Summons*. It might not be worth it. Having a familiar could definitely come in handy, but losing some of his mana might severely restrict what he could do. He thought for a few more minutes and finally decided to do it. But he only invested 1 point.

After choosing 1 point of mana, it prompted him for the amount of health.

Amount of Mana to invest in Familiar: (1-7)

He read the prompt again. He had 8 health from his *Rogue* class, and it would allow him to invest up to 7 points. Would that leave him with a single point of health until he leveled? That seemed like a terrible idea. Once again, he chose 1.

Summoning Familiar...

Jace had just confirmed his choice when his world exploded. Pain like he had never felt wracked his entire body as it felt like his insides were being sucked out. He collapsed to the ground as blue and red streams of glowing particles burst from his chest and circled around a spot a few feet away. Through the haze of pain, he saw the blue and red particles swirl around until they formed the general shape of a cat.

Finally, the pain subsided, and the swirling particles solidified into a small orange tabby cat and he received new system messages.

Familiar (Cat) Summoned.
Ability Gained: Cat-Vision
Note: Familiar abilities are only accessible when familiar is summoned.

Cat-Vision sounded like a good ability to have. He wondered if it would allow him to see in the dark. He tilted his head so he could see his new cat familiar. It looked at him and tilted its head.

"Food?" it meowed.

Still recovering from the intense pain he'd just experienced, Jace did a double take. "What the -?! Did you just speak?"

"Yes," it meowed back in what he could have sworn was a condescending tone. "Food."

Jace shook his head, thinking perhaps the pain was causing him to hallucinate. He'd never heard a familiar speak to its master or anyone else. Pushing himself up, he looked down at the orange cat. "You can speak?"

The cat glared at him. "Yes."

He'd forgotten he was just outside the village until a man came walking over hesitantly. "You okay? I heard you hollering a moment ago."

Jace hadn't realized he'd been "hollering". He looked at the man and viewed him in his HUD.

Ernald
Race: Human
Class: Peasant
Level: 1

"Sorry," Jace responded. The man was one of the normal non-player characters (NPCs) that populated the villages and cities of the land. He saw no reason to lie to the man. "I was summoning my familiar and it was a little more painful than I thought."

The man harrumphed and shook his head. "One of those wizards, eh?"

"Mage," Jace corrected.

The man glared at him for a moment. "Wizard! Mage! Bah! What's the difference? All that magic and what do you do with it? Nothing!" The man fixed him with a stare. "Now, if you could make some sort of magic to find my dog, that'd be something. Poor thing ran off this morning and I haven't seen him all day."

Ernald of Sinking Springs has offered you the quest, "Find my dog?"
Reward: 1 gold, +5 faction with Residents of Sinking Springs, +50 faction with Ernald.
Accept quest? (Yes or No)

Jace looked at the quest. He'd been high level for so long, he'd forgotten how tedious and unrewarding the lower level quests could be. But it was offering gold and right now he had none. Not having any other prospects at the moment, Jace accepted.

"I'll find your dog," he told the man.

Ernald eyed him and then smiled. "Well, I'd be much obliged if you could find my dog Rusty. He ran off to the south this morning and I haven't seen him since. I'm worried something happened to him. My name's Ernald and if you do manage to find him, I might have a spare coin I could give you."

"No problem. Just one question," Jace told him as he got to his feet. "Which way is south?"

The man nodded towards his left. "Good luck!"

Ernald turned and walked off towards one of the houses. Jace looked down down at his familiar. "Ready to do our first quest?"

The cat eyed him. "Food?"

Jace shook his head at the persistent cat. "No, quest first, then food - if 1 gold is enough to buy food."

The cat just looked up at him.

Rolling his eyes, Jace turned and headed the direction Ernald had pointed. It was a path that led out of town towards a forest. He looked back and saw his familiar padding along behind him. He wasn't sure exactly what she'd be able to do to help him, but for now, at least he had company.

He suddenly remembered the health and mana he had used to summon her. Bringing up his HUD, he looked at his stats. Both his health and mana had regenerated. Both stats were at maximum. That was good to know. The mana and health he used to summon the cat would regenerate. It wasn't permanently gone. He smiled. At least something had gone right.

Once they reached the forest, Jace found he had another problem. The twigs and pine needles were wreaking havoc on his bare feet. Geez! Why did everything have to be so painful! Their pace slowed as he had to carefully navigate through the forest to minimize the pain to his feet.

They made it a hundred or so yards into the woods when Jace began calling out the dog's name. "Rusty! Rusty!"

As Jace walked, he thought about what he needed to do. He needed to get to the capital. Barring some friendly wizard teleporting him- and given Charlena's story he may not be able to trust a wizard - the only other way for low level characters to travel was either overland or via caravan.

Overland was out of the question. Even with Charlena's help, the area between towns was completely unpredictable. They could just as easily encounter ogres as they could goblins. Or much worse. And if you got far enough, there would be no possible way to retrieve your body if you died. You'd lose everything.

The other way was to ride a caravan. Players could use an auto-follow feature and march with a caravan, even while they were not logged in. Their character would robotically follow the caravan and the guards would fight off anything that attacked the caravan. Usually. Extremely strong monsters had been known to wipe out caravans. But the risk was minor.

Yes, a caravan would be the way to go and if memory served him right, they came to most towns once a week. He just needed to earn enough money to hitch a ride. Since Mordred was high level, it had been a while since he'd taken a caravan, but he thought it was either 100 or 150 gold to hitch a ride. That was chump change to Mordred but at the moment, Jace didn't have a single gold. He'd need to work to get the money before the next caravan came in. At least he'd get 1 gold from this quest.

Bringing his mind back to completing his quest, they kept moving into the forest with Jace occasionally calling out for Rusty. There was no answer and no sign of the dog. After about twenty minutes, the forest was growing almost too dark to see. Remembering the *Cat-Vision*, he brought up his HUB and saw a small icon of a cat in the lower right corner. He toggled it on and the world was transformed into what seemed like full daylight.

"Wow," Jace said and looked down at the cat next to him. "Is this how you see in the dark?"

The cat gave him a smug look. "Yes."

Jace smirked. She was certainly a sassy cat. "You need a name."

His familiar just stared at him unblinkingly.

He started thinking of names but quickly realized he didn't even know what sex the cat was.

"Are you male or female?" he asked.

He thought the cat actually glared at him. "Female."

"Sorry," he apologized. He began thinking of names, dismissing them as quickly as he thought of them until one popped into his head that made his eyes moisten. "How about Luna." He swallowed a lump in his throat. "It was my sister's name."

His familiar seemed to consider the name and then nodded. "Luna."

Jace smiled sadly. It had been years since he'd said her name aloud. It felt good. Sad. But good.

"Come on Luna," he said to the cat. "Let's go find this dog."

It took them another 30 minutes before they found a small, bare clearing. With his *Cat-Vision*, he spotted some tracks and bent down to look at them.

You have gained a new skill: Tracking

Noticing the new ability, Jace smiled. The tracking ability came in much handier later in the game, but right now, it was also a godsend.

He focused on the tracks and they began to glow faintly. Standing up, he saw a glowing trail of footprints that lead further into the woods.

"Let's go," he told Luna and they hurried after the trail. A short time later, they heard howling. It was a sad, troubled howling and Jace guessed it was the dog. He continued following the tracks until he came to a large pit. Looking over the edge, he saw a dog at the bottom of a six-foot pit. It saw him and began wagging its tail and barking happily.

Jace didn't see a good way to free the dog. He could jump down into the pit and try to lift the dog up, but there was no guarantee that would work and he could get stuck down there himself. He had no rope to loop around it and pull it up.

He began to look around the clearing until he saw what he needed. At the edge of the clearing was a large branch that must have broken off one of the trees. It was eight or ten feet long and maybe a foot wide. If he could push it into the pit, the dog could climb up it. Hopefully.

The log ended up weighing more than he thought and it took him a while to drag it to the edge of the pit. Once it was there, he pushed one half of it down into the put so it made a makeshift ramp.

"Come on boy," Jace called to the dog. "Come on!"

Rusty looked at the log but obviously didn't know what to do with it. Jace was about to jump into the pit and help the dog up when Luna scurried down the log. She went all the way to the bottom of the branch and stopped. She looked right at the dog, then turned and climbed back up.

Rusty looked from the branch to the cat at the top of the pit. Slowly at first, Rusty began to climb up but quickly picked up momentum and made it to the top.

"Come on," he said to the dog. "Let's go home."

Rusty seemed to understand "home" and lead them back through the forest to the village. The dog ran right to the door of a specific house and started barking. It only took a moment for the door to open, revealing Ernald. His face broke into a huge grin and he bent down to pet and scratch his dog. "Rusty! You're home!"

"He'd fallen into a pit in the forest," Jace told the man.

"Bad dog," Ernald said but there was no venom in his tone. He was obviously happy to have Rusty home.

Ernald stood up and reached into his pocket and brought out a gold coin. "A deal's deal. Here's a gold for finding Rusty. Thank you stranger."

You have completed the quest, "Find my dog?"
You gain 25 experience. Experience to next level 975.
You gain +5 faction with Residents of Sinking Springs
You gain +50 faction with Ernald

"Jace," he told the man. "Call me Jace."

"Thank you Jace," he said with a smile and held out his hand. Jace shook it and then bid each other good night and then Ernald let Rusty into the house and shut the door.

Jace turned to see Luna looking up at him. He sighed. "I know. Food."

He could have sworn he saw the cat smile.

Chapter 13

Jace went to the tavern, fully expecting that he wouldn't be able to buy anything. He was pleasantly surprised to find out his 1 gold would get him a plate of fish and chips. Then he remembered, this must be a newbie area. The prices were probably set to allow new players to purchase food and items.

No sooner had the fish and chips been placed on the table when Luna jumped, grabbed one of the breaded fish fillets and dragged it onto the floor. She began devouring it with gusto.

Chuckling, Jace turned back and took a bite of the remaining fish. He froze. It tasted incredibly delicious and a low moan escaped him. This had to be the best fish he'd ever tasted. Then he remembered, his sensitivity was set at maximum. He was experiencing the tastes as if they were real. And he had to admit, the flavor and textures were wonderful. In no time at all, he'd finished up the entire plate.

"I guess you were hungry," said the buxom barmaid.

Still chewing his last mouthful, Jace nodded. "That was the best fish and chips I've ever had."

The barmaid smiled broadly. "I'll let old Wimarc know you liked it."

Jace desperately needed money and since he didn't have to logout, he should be able to work through the night. He just needed to find some quests. Taverns were usually a good place to find work in cities, but he wasn't sure if that was the case in a newbie area. "Excuse me, he said to the barmaid, but do you know anyone around here who could use some help?"

The barmaid looked thoughtful and then pointed to a table in the corner with three men playing cards. "You might ask Maurice, Ralf, or Odo. They always have some odd jobs they need done."

"Thanks," he told her. "I'm sorry I can't leave a tip. I gave you my last gold."

She flashed him a smile and darted her eyes down his mostly naked body. "It's no problem. The view was my tip."

Jace felt heat rushing to his face and knew he must be beet red. The barmaid just giggled and then walked away to help other patrons.

Now acutely aware of his lack of clothing, Jace was suddenly self-conscious. Running around in a loincloth wasn't an uncommon thing, but many NPCs would react to it. Apparently, that included barmaids in newbie areas.

As casually as he could, he walked over to the table with the three men the barmaid had pointed out. "Excuse me good sirs, but I was wondering if any of you needed any help?"

Generally, asking a NPC if they needed help or need anything would trigger any quests they might have. Occasionally, there was something special that needed to be done or a condition that had to be met. And sometimes the NPC would approach you.

The three men looked up from their card game at him. One of them gave him a glance up and down, obviously noticing his lack of clothing.

"I think you're missing something boy," said the man who had eyed him.

"Yeah," chimed in the one to his left. "Some clothes!"

The three men began laughing and Jace was once again aware of being in nothing but a loincloth. To take his mind off of his embarrassment. He viewed each man in his HUD.

Maurice
Race: Human
Class: Peasant
Level: 1

Ralf
Race: Human
Class: Peasant
Level: 1

Odo
Race: Human
Class: Peasant
Level: 1

Jace quickly came up with a story to both explain his lack of clothing and possibly garner some sympathy. "I was waylaid by bandits on the east road. They took everything I owned.

Your Bluff skill has increased by 1.

Then men fell silent perhaps even looking a little guilty and Jace smiled inwardly. His story had worked better than he thought. Plus, he'd gotten a rank up in the Bluff skill.

"Sorry stranger," apologized Odo. "I'm not normally one to laugh at another's misfortune."

"Me either," agreed Maurice.

"We're awful sorry," chimed in Ralf.

Jace gave them a smile. "I'd consider it forgiven if any of you have some honest work I could do to earn a little coin so I can buy myself some clothing."

Ralf spoke up first. "Actually, I do have a problem with some rats down in my cellar. If you could get rid of them, I'd pay you 2 gold."

"I need 10 flat rocks from the lake to the west so I can put some steppingstones in my garden," Odo added.

"I fixed Ascilia's pipe," Maurice told him. "If you deliver it to her, you can keep the other gold she owes me."

Jace nearly laughed out loud at the almost comical way they stumbled over each other to give him their quests. He quickly agreed to all of the quests and took the pipe from Maurice, as well as got directions to Ascilia's house. He also got a key to the cellar from Ralf.

"Thank you, kind sirs," Jace told them. "I will take care of your tasks as quickly as possible."

Jace and Luna left the tavern and stopped just outside to think about the quests he'd been given. Maurice's quest seemed like a standard delivery quest. Hopefully, there wouldn't be any combat involved so it should be fairly easy. He should be able to do that one quickly and get the gold.

The second was a collection quest. He had to get 10 rocks and bring them back to Odo. It didn't seem difficult, assuming there were no monsters at the lake. It would just be time consuming to haul stones.

The last quest, Ralf's rat problem, would be the more difficult quest. He'd have to kill monsters - howbeit tiny monsters - with only his spells and very little mana. He opened his HUD and then found his *Spellbook* section. Since he'd never played a magic-user before, this was all new to him.

In his spellbook, he found one spell for each of the skills he'd gained. He took a moment to read them over. There was a *Fire Bolt*, an *Ice Blast*, a *Earth Grasp* and *Air Armor* spells. Unfortunately, they all used 4 mana, which meant he could cast one spell before being completely out of mana. His mana would regenerate but it would take him four minutes to get back to full mana after casting one of the spells. He'd definitely need to save the rat killing until last and hope he could find a weapon before he tried it.

Jace quickly dropped off the pipe to Ascilia, a tiny frail old woman who was extremely grateful. She dropped a coin in his hand and then began stuffing some sort of pipeweed into the pipe. He asked her if he could help her with anything and she gave him a letter to take to the innkeeper.

Leaving Ascilia, he found the lake Odo had mentioned and found him 10 flat rocks to use as stepping stones. There were no monsters waiting for him at the lake. With no monsters, the job was easy but time consuming. During the first trip to Odo's house, he dropped off the letter to the innkeeper, gaining another gold. It took him another 30 minutes to finish carrying all the stones but, in the end, earning another gold, bringing his total to 3 gold.

Completing the first two quests, plus Ascilia's quest, had also netted him some faction with the individuals involved and some additional faction with the residents. Jace had also received an additional 25 experience from each, putting his total experience at 100. That was a long way from level 2.

He paused after the second job and thought about the rat killing job. It had been a long time since he'd had one of those sorts of quests, but generally there were a number of little rodents you had to kill.

They could only do a little bit of damage and you could kill them before you died of their little wounds. But that assumed you had a weapon and some armor. He had neither.

The more he thought about it, the less confident he felt. If only he could get some armor. Perhaps he should wait until Charlena logs in. As he thought about Charlena, he remembered the goblins he helped her loot her body from. If they were still there, he just might be able to kill one with a spell. If he did, he could loot it and maybe get a weapon or a piece of armor. The other one might kill him, but he could respawn, go back and kill the other one.

"What do you think?" he asked Luna, who was the only other creature around. "Should I try to kill the goblins?"

Luna seemed to consider the question before answering. "Yes."

Twenty minutes later, he was reappearing in the graveyard. The goblins had still been there. He'd fired off his *Flame Bolt* spell and hit one of the goblins, but it hadn't killed it. With no weapons and armor, they caught him and killed him in short order. If he could just get one more spell off, he could have at least killed one and then maybe he'd have a weapon! At least he'd earned a rank in *Fire Magic*, so it hadn't been a total loss.

He looked around for Luna but didn't see her. As he was looking around, Jace realized it was oppressively dark and that he no longer had *Cat-Vision*. Scrolling through his logs, he saw that she had been banished as soon as he had died and he'd lost the *Cat-Vision* ability. That meant he had to resummon her.

Cringing as he thought of the pain he'd experienced before, Jace debated whether he should go through that again but realized he had no choice. Without the *Cat-Vision*, he couldn't see well enough in the dark to do anything. He needed that ability. Plus, it was nice having her around.

Steeling himself, Jace sat down and summoned her. This time, he chose the maximums for mana and health and completed the summons. This time the pain was even worse but since he was ready for it, he managed to grit his teeth through it and stay upright. When it was over, Luna had appeared and he felt completely drained.

"Summoner die?" asked Luna as she reappeared. Not waiting for him to reply, she began grooming herself as she didn't have a care in the world.

Shaking his head, Jace activated *Cat-Vision* and considered what to do next. He needed to go back to the hills and retrieve his corpse, that was a given. Unlike his previous death, where he had nothing, he now had 3 hard won gold pieces that he wanted back. Plus, he had the key to the cellar for Ralf's quest he needed to get back.

But, would the goblins be waiting for him? If they were, how could he hope to kill even one of them with the tiny amount of mana he had. Then it hit him. He still had his *Rogue* skills. He could sneak in and get his corpse.

Thinking about his stealth skills made him pause. He wondered if spells worked like regular weapons when it came to attacking from stealth. Having played Mordred for so long, he was familiar with stealth attacks and backstabs doing far more damage than a normal attack. He brought up his HUD and looked at his *Rogue* abilities. At first level, he only had one ability: *Critical Eye I.* It had been a while since he'd read the description.

Critical Eye I
Rogue Ability
Description: You are trained to spot weakness in others. When you strike from stealth or opportunity, your strikes are always critical hits.
Note: This does not stack with Backstab.

Jace smiled. If his idea worked, he now knew how to take out the goblins. If it didn't, he would be back in the graveyard shortly. He started to jog towards the hill and called back to Luna, who was still grooming.

"Come on Luna," he told her. "We hunt goblin!"

Chapter 14

Jace stalked silently across the crest of the hill desperately trying to spot the goblins. His body was 100 feet in front of him, very close to where Charlena had died. He wished he'd paid more attention to where the goblins had come from that time.

He'd taken the time to smear dirt on his bare chest and as much as his back as he could to prevent his pale skin from reflecting the moonlight. He wasn't sure if it would work. Some things that might work in real life didn't work in the game. Of course, in the fantasy world of VEIL, there were many things that worked that didn't work in real life.

Next to him, Luna crept along with the practiced grace of a feline. She looked up at him as if to say 'What's so hard about sneaking?' So far, he'd received two ranks in his *Stealth* skill, which meant they were nearby since you could only advance the skill by hiding from an enemy. But where were they?

Luna suddenly tensed and went deathly still, except for her tail which slowly moved back and forth. She'd sensed something he hadn't. Good girl. He followed her gaze but didn't see anything even with his enhanced *Cat-Vision* active.

"Goblin," came a voice in his head. Jace almost jumped out of his skin but stopped himself just in time from breaking stealth. It almost sounded like Luna.

Wait! Did they have some sort of way of talking like the *Far Speak* spell?

Tentatively, he directed his thoughts to her like he would using the *Far Speak* spell. "Luna?"

The cat looked up at him with an expression that told him she was not impressed with his deduction. "Yes."

"We can communicate telepathically?" he asked in astonishment.

If cats could roll their eyes, that was the expression she shot him. She looked at him in an expression that said "obviously".

He got over his shock and focused back onto the task at hand. He followed where she had been looking and tried to make out the shape of a goblin. Try as he might, he just couldn't see the thing. "I don't see it."

"Not see," the cat shot back silently. "Smell."

As if to emphasize her point, she sniffed in the direction she was looking. Now it was Jace's turn to roll his eyes. How the heck was he supposed to smell it. He didn't have a supernatural sense of smell like some animal-kin. This complicated things. Luna could smell the goblin from behind the rock but Jace couldn't see it. And if Jace couldn't see it, he couldn't target it with a spell.

"Do you know where the other one is?" he asked her.

"No smell," she replied, still fixated on the same spot, her tail swishing back and forth.

He knew what they needed to do. They'd have to circle around behind it. But that was a long way to go. If his Stealth skill failed, the goblins would see him and that would be the end. He glanced down at Luna. "We need to circle around until I can see it. Then I can cast the spell at it."

"Yes."

The two of them made a slow, quiet arch around the large rock Luna had pointed out. He was especially careful because somewhere out here was the second goblin. If Luna didn't smell it, they could blunder right into it and then they'd die again.

Jace received 2 more rank ups in *Stealth* and was just congratulating himself when Luna froze. He stopped himself in mid-movement and followed her gaze to a spot ten feet from them on the left.

He saw it. There was another rock, this one not as large as the other one. Lying on this his side of the rock was a goblin who was currently engaged in picking its nose rather vigorously. He froze, afraid to even breath. The only movement was the slow swish of Luna's tail.

Now was the moment of truth. Could he cast a spell from *Stealth*? If not, it was going to be a short, painful trip back to the cemetery.

Luna glanced up at him as if to say, 'What are you waiting for stupid human?'

Jace began casting, his hands moving on their own accord with the gestures of the spell. At the end, he whispered the words to the spell as quietly as he could. *"Minima fulmen ignem!"*

The flaming dart streaked through the air and hit the goblin in the side of the head.

You critically burn Forest Goblin with Flame Bolt for 7 fire damage.
Forest Goblin dies.
You gain 10 experience.

It had worked! Jace was elated. But he was also out of mana and casting the spell had knocked him out of Stealth.

"I kill you!" cried the second goblin as it charged towards him.

Wasting no time, Jace rushed to the dead goblin's body and looted it.

You receive Torn Leather Jerkin.
You 1 gold.

Jace dropped to his knees. The goblin hadn't dropped a weapon and he wasn't going to defeat its partner with a torn leather jerkin. A few seconds later, the goblin reached him, and two dagger strikes later he was back in the graveyard.

He hadn't really expected to live through that encounter. It would have been great luck had he gotten a dagger drop from the goblin. If he had, he might have had a chance. As it was, he had killed one of the goblins. That meant there was only one left. Since he knew he could cast a spell from stealth, he just needed to get into position, and he could kill it.

After summoning Luna, the two of them raced to the hill. All of the sneaking around had cost him precious

time and he didn't have long until his corpse expired.
Once that happened, he'd lose the gold he earned. He
needed that gold!

They reached the hill and Jace dropped into *Stealth*.
Steadily, he worked himself in the opposite direction as
last time, hoping the goblin would be in the same place.
He earned himself another 2 ranks in the *Stealth* before
he made it to a position where he saw the goblin. It was
exactly where it had been before, and it still hadn't
spotted him. Without any hesitation, Jace cast his spell.

***You critically burn Forest Goblin with Flame Bolt for
8 fire damage.***
Forest Goblin dies.
You gain 10 experience.

The bolt hit the goblin in the chest and the thing
topped over. Wasting no time, he ran over to his body
and looted it.

You receive 4 gold.
You receive cellar key.

"Whew," he said aloud to Luna. "We got our gold
back!"

Luna gave him a disinterested look.

"4 gold is 4 servings of fish and chips," he told her.

The little cat perked up. "Fish?" she asked hopefully.

Jace shook his head. "Not yet. We need to get the
loot from the goblins and hope there's a weapon."

Jace went to the first goblin and found his second
corpse. He retrieved the torn leather jerkin and

equipped it. He looked completely ridiculous. Now, he was wearing a ragged leather vest and no pants or shoes. He shook his head at himself as he walked back to the second goblin. He stopped in front of it, crossed his fingers and looted the corpse.

You receive Rusty Tin Knife.
You receive 1 gold.

"Yes!" he cried out as he plucked the dagger from the goblin's body. Now he had a weapon! He might actually have a fighting chance after his mana ran out. Maybe. He still had no armor to speak of since the jerkin by itself offered no defense bonus. Still, it was progress and he felt much better now that he had a weapon.

Bending down, he scratched Luna on the head and on the neck, eliciting some soft purrs. "We did good!" he told the cat.

Luna gave him a smug look. "Yes."

Motioning her to follow, he headed back into town. He had one more quest to do and it was going to be the hardest. He was still thinking about strategies when they found Ralf's house on the east side of the village.

By the lack of lights, he guessed Ralf must be sleeping. He walked around the house and found a cellar door with a large padlock. Retrieving the cellar key from his inventory, Jace unlocked the padlock and set it on the ground.

"We're supposed to kill rats," Jace told Luna who immediately perked up.

"Rats?" she asked excitedly and Jace chuckled.

"These rats might be pretty big," he told her.

"Big rats?" she asked with even more excitement.

Laughing, he pulled out his knife and started down the steps with Luna hurrying after him. No sooner had he made it to the bottom when there was a squeal from somewhere in the cellar. Luna darted towards the sound and disappeared behind some old crates.

"Big rat! Big rat!" she meowed in excitement. He heard a scuffling and then a Luna hiss and finally a howl from Luna. She came darting back, this time her voice was panicked. "Big rat! Big rat!"

Chasing Luna was a rat that was as large as her! Jace side stepped as Luna rushed past him, followed closely by the rat. As soon as it was past, he stabbed it with his knife.

You critically hit Cellar Rat for 5 damage.
Cellar Rat dies.
You gain 5 experience.

As soon as the rat died, Luna stopped, spun and pounced on it, wrestling around with the rat on the floor. Jace was laughing at her when he saw another rat racing towards her. Luna saw it too and jumped straight up in the air, came down and scurried out the cellar.

The cellar rat changed course and charged Jace instead. As it got near, he stabbed out and killed it.

Jace glanced at the system message and saw he'd killed the rat with only 3 points of damage. Apparently, this was going to be easier than he thought. And that's when 4 rats charged him from all directions.

Lashing out with his knife, he managed to skewer one of them but the other three slipped inside his guard, attacking his bare legs and feet.

Cellar Rat bites YOU for 1 damage.
Cellar Rat bites YOU for 1 damage.
Cellar Rat bites YOU for 1 damage.

Crying out at the nasty bites, Jace stabbed down at the rat in front, killing it. The other two bit him again, taking away another 2 health, leaving him with only 3 health left.

He pivoted and drove his knife in the rat on his left, allowing the one on his right to bite him again, dropping him down to only 2 health.

Jace spun again, burying his knife into the side of the last rat, dropping it. He looked at his health and *stamina* bars. Both were drained but he'd survived and finished the quest. Or had he? He waited for a quest update but nothing came. That's when he saw another rat darting towards him. This one was twice as large as the others and its beady little eyes glistened with malice.

Jace turned and ran up the cellar steps. He was half way up when the giant rat caught up with him and ripped into his leg.

Cellar Rat Den Mother bites YOU for 3 damage.
You have died.

After choosing to respawn, Jace once again appeared in the graveyard in only his loincloth. Pushing down his frustration, he sat down and summoned Luna back. When she appeared, she sat on her haunches, wrapped her tail around her and looked at him completely deadpan. "Summoner die again?"

Rolling his eyes at her, jogged back to Ralf's house. When he arrived, Jace crept over to the cellar door and looked down. He saw his corpse but no sign of the den mother. Entering stealth, he crept to his body and looted it. He quickly equipped the jerkin and pulled out the knife.

Then he crept further down the steps until he saw the den mother on the other side of the cellar. He earned another rank of Stealth as he crept to the bottom of the stairs. He was about to try stealth casting the Flame Bolt spell when the den mother charged him.

He cast the spell anyway, knowing it wouldn't be a critical hit. The flaming missile flew the distance to the rat and smashed into its face.

You burn Cellar Rat Den Mother with Flame Bolt for 2 fire damage.

Despite the burns, the den mother kept coming and Jace got in one thrust with the dagger doing 3 damage. Then the thing was on him and was latching its teeth onto his leg.

Cellar Rat Den Mother bites YOU for 2 damage.

He desperately stabbed down again, doing more damage but the huge rat didn't die. It released it's hold and hit him again.

Cellar Rat Den Mother bites YOU for 3 damage.

With only 2 health remaining, he knew he couldn't take another hit. He slammed his knife down into it's back, hoping his strike would kill it. It didn't. The den mother released it's hold and reared back to take the final bite that would kill him.

That's when an orange blur of fur streaked out of the shadows and landed atop the rat's face, biting, clawing and hissing.

Luna critically claws Cellar Rat Den Mother for 2 damage.
Cellar Rat Den Mother has died.
You gain 20 experience.

Stunned, Jace just looked at Luna, sitting atop the giant rat's corpse. She back on her haunches, with her tail wrapped around her. She looked straight at him. "Mine!" Then the little cat began to eat the dead den mother.

Chapter 15

Jace had looted all of the smaller rat bodies while Luna feasted on the den mother. He received some rat pelts but no worthwhile loot. When Luna had eaten her fill, which truth be told wasn't much, he looted the den mother and was happy to get a giant rat fang.

Giant Rat Fang
Type: Dagger
Damage: 4 + 1 (Sharp)
Wt: 1 lb
Description: Pulled from the mouth of a giant rat, this fang is large enough to be used as a weapon.

He now had two daggers and the Giant Rat Fang was definitely the better of the two. Like his Mordred character, Jace's Rogue class allowed him to wield two weapons at once. This would make fighting any more goblins much easier.

Jace turned in the quest and the cellar key to Ralf, who hadn't been very happy about being awakened in the middle of the night but who was very happy that his rat problem had been solved. He gave Jace the coins he'd promised and then promptly shut the door in his face.

He'd searched the town after that looking for anyone who might be able to give him additional quests but found no one. Unlike the larger cities he was used to, these NPCs in these small villages kept more traditional routines. Since Jace no longer needed to sleep, it appeared he would have plenty of wasted time.

To make matters worse, the evenings were very cold. Without pants or boots, the cold would cause him to shiver if he stopped moving for long.

Trying to keep busy and warm, Jace roamed just outside the village, looking for more goblins but hadn't found any. Next, he explored down the roads for several miles in each direction but hadn't found anything noteworthy. He'd found a few scattered farms in each direction, but they were dark as well.

He had been considering exploring further when he noticed the eastern horizon finally beginning to brighten. Dawn was coming. Hopefully that meant the villagers would be waking up and he'd be able to get more quests. Then he remembered Charlena. She'd told him she'd be logging in some time this morning so he really should wait for her. If they hoped to leave this village, they'd both need to get as much experience as possible. That meant they should do the quests together.

Five hours later, Charlena finally logged in. Jace was glad to see her. Not only was he anxious to get started with some quests, she was also the only person he knew in the game right now. And if he had to admit it, he was a bit lonely for human company. He'd always been an introvert, but he'd at least had face to face contact with people at school or people at work. While NPCs were programmed to act like people, they weren't people. They were just constructs.

Charlena smiled and waved when she saw him but then stopped and tilted her head, her brow furrowed. "Am I going crazy or were you a rogue yesterday?"

Jace smiled. "I switched classes to *Mage* since I had no weapons or armor."

"Isn't switching classes bad?" she asked. "I thought I read it would give you a penalty or something."

"You're usually right," Jace explained. "There is a penalty that grows with each class. Except with humans. Humans can multiclass without the experience penalty."

Her face brightened. "Ooo, that sounds neat! So, you can have all the abilities of all the classes! Is that why you chose human?"

"Sort of. You only gain mana and health from your highest class so generally you'd end up more versatile than someone who sticks with one class, but also less powerful in the long run." He didn't mention that he hadn't actually chosen to be human, it was thrust on him.

"Oh. So, why are you doing it?"

Jace debated telling her the full story but still held off. He really didn't know her, and he wasn't sure how'd she react. Right now, he needed her. Instead, he gave her as much truth as he could. "I hadn't planned on changing classes, but if we're going to make a run at getting out of this village, I thought we might need some versatility."

She seemed to consider that for a moment, her expression seeming to morph from appreciation to suspicion and maybe even wary. "So you did it to help me?"

Jace flashed her a grin. "Well, I assume I will be going with you!"

She smiled back and he noticed what a truly nice smile she had. Idly, he wondered if it was as nice in the real world. Then he remembered, he was dead. He'd never see the real world again.

"You okay?" she asked, breaking him out of his thoughts. "You looked really down just now."

"I'm fine," he told her. "I just remembered something sad. Oh, and I forgot, I have a familiar now." As if on queue, Luna stepped between his legs and sat down in front of him, looking up at Charlena. "Charlena, this is Luna. Luna, this is Charlena."

"Yes," meowed Luna impassively.

"She's so fluffy!" Charlena cried out and bent down to rub and pet her. "I want one!"

Jace laughed as Charlena lavished affection on his familiar. Luna tried to ignore it at first, but eventually gave in and began to purr happily.

"You like it?" he asked the cat.

"Yes," she replied contentedly.

Charlena looked up at him. "Are you… meowing… to the cat?"

Jace looked at her, confused. "No, I just asked if she liked the petting and she said yes."

"No, you didn't," she told him, shaking her head. "You… meowed like a cat… then she meowed back."

"What?!" Jace muttered. "I'm not speaking English?" Suddenly he remembered the *Monsterspeak* skill. He remembered he had understood the goblins. Did that mean he could understand ANY monster? And speak their language?! He could speak languages he didn't even know?!

"Sorry Jace," she told him empathically. "You were meowing like a cat."

He snapped his attention back to her, unsure what to say. "She's my first familiar. That must be the way mages talk with them."

"So, wait," Charlena said. "You mean, you can talk to her and she can understand and talk back?"

Jace nodded.

Once again, she flashed him her dazzling smile. "That is so cool! Now I really want one!"

"What do you say we do some quests and see how much experience we can get so we can get out of this one-horse town," Jace suggested, eager to change the topic. He had to think about this *Monsterspeak* skill and how it worked. There was something unsettling about speaking and understanding languages he didn't know - without knowing he was doing it.

"That sounds good! I really didn't get to do any quests. Are they fun?" she said with a gleam in her eye.

Jace laughed, remembering how long it had taken him to carry all the stones for Odo. "Sometimes. But they do give experience and money - usually."

"Great. Let's go!"

The two of them grouped and spent the next several hours running around town, doing various quests. Many of them were the simpler delivery or collect quests. In one quest, they'd had to clear spiders out of a woman's attic, which was very reminiscent of the rat quest, right down to the extra large spider at the end. Unfortunately, it hadn't dropped a dagger like the rat. Instead, it had dropped spider silk, which they could sell at the local store for an extra gold.

When lunch finally rolled around and Charlena logged off to eat, they'd each earned 250 experience and 13 gold. Combined with the 7 gold he'd earned previously from the quests and goblins, he had enough to buy a pair of leather boots and leggings. Putting on the clothes, he felt like a real character now. Finally, he wasn't running barefoot in a loincloth!

When Charlena logged in after her lunch break, she gave him an approving nod. "Much better! At least now you won't be so distracting."

Jace raced an eyebrow. "Distracting?"

Charlena's face went red. "I meant, because you looked so ridiculous."

Jace chuckled. "I did, didn't I."

Charlena giggled. "It was actually really hard not to laugh at you."

"I'm offended," Jace said with mock outrage.

"Yeah," she replied. "I'm sure you are. But at least you can be offended with pants now."

The both chuckled and then went back to doing quests around town. It surprised Jace at how well they seemed to get along. They chatted back and forth while they were running errands or collecting flowers or any number of other newbie quests.

Jace discovered Charlena was 22 years old and in school to become an internet gaming artist. She'd always loved art and dreamed of creating virtual reality worlds.

Since WorldCog and VEIL were the cutting edge, she had begun playing to experience the top virtual world. He'd had to stop himself multiple times from telling her he was - or had been - a programmer at WorldCog. Instead, he'd told her he was a contract programmer.

Charlena had mentioned that she lived in Wilmington, Delaware and he'd let slip that he lived in Philadelphia. Well, he used to.

"That's where WorldCog HQ is. You should go work at WorldCog!" she told him and punched him playfully. "Then you could put in a kind word for me!"

Jace's face must have betrayed him because she cocked her head. "I'm just kidding. You barely know me, you don't have to recommend me."

Jace forced a smile. "It's not that. I'm just not a fan of... big corporations right now."

She nodded in understanding. "I know what you mean. One of my professors says the same thing. Basically, how corporations hold the real power now.

Governments just exist to help them in their inevitable takeover of our rights."

Jace thought of his own situation. "You don't think corporations will sacrifice people to make a buck."

She looked thoughtful but finally shrugged. "I don't know."

Jace let the subject drop as they turned in another quest. They'd done 10 more quests and now the NPCs around town were no longer offering work.

"Thanks again," said Hazel as she handed them each a gold. "I appreciate you finding those mushrooms for my soup." The woman looked between Jace and Charlena. "You know, Gerta was just telling me today that she's afraid to go look for mushrooms because they've been having issues with wolves near their farm. Maybe you two can help them."

Jace smiled despite himself. It sounded as if Hazel had just pointed him to another quest. Judging by Charlena's smile, she realized it too.

"I'm sure we can help," she told Hazel. "Where do they live?"

Hazel pointed south. "Gerta and Thom have the second farm down the south road."

They assured Hazel they would talk with Gerta and then bid her farewell.

"So, we get to kill some wolves now?" Charlena asked enthusiastically.

"It sounds that way," Jace replied.

Looking up at them with a concerned expression, Luna meowed "Wolfers?"

Chapter 16

They found Thom and Gerta working out in the field when they arrived at their farm. The couple looked at them with suspicion as they approached.

"Can I help you strangers?" asked the man they assumed was Thom.

Jace gave them a smile and held his empty hands up in a sign of peace. "Hazel in town said you might be having some trouble with wolves. We came to see if we could help."

"Wolfers," Luna meowed softly.

The tension drained from their faces and Thom actually smiled and put his hand out. "My name is Thom," he said, shaking Jace's hand. "And this is my wife Greta. We'd welcome your help."

Thom related their recent troubles. For the last week, they'd been getting night-time attacks by what they thought were wolves. Every other night wolves would kill one of their livestock and eat part of it but leave the rest of their herds untouched.

"Just one animal, every other day?" Jace asked, perplexed. "And they only eat part of it?"

Thom and Greta nodded.

That didn't seem like a pack of wolves. Maybe a lone wolf but he'd think a pack would kill more or at least finish the entire animal. And every other day seemed too consistent. Then again, game logic tried to mirror the real world, but sometimes they took artistic license. This could be one of those times.

"Do you think you can do something?" asked Greta.

Greta of Sinking Springs has offered your group the quest, "Wolves By Night"
Reward (per member): 5 gold, +5 faction with Residents of Sinking Springs, +50 faction with Thom, +50 faction with Greta.
Accept quest? (Yes or No)

Charlena accepted the quest a second before he had the chance. "We'll do it!"

Thom and Greta both looked relieved and thanked them profusely before going back to their chores.

"Do you think it's a wolf?" asked Charlena after they were out of earshot.

Jace shrugged. "I don't know. Does seem like the behavior of a wolf or even a pack of wolves. Knowing the twists the devs love to throw into quests, it would surprise me if it were a wolf."

"I don't think so either," she agreed. "Why only one animal a night?"

"I don't know," he said honestly. "But I doubt this quest will be what we expect."

She frowned. "And it only comes at night. How late will I have to stay up?"

"I don't know. But generally, the quests and other things are designed around the prime play hours so I doubt it will be later than 10 p.m."

She bit her lip. "That's late for me. Plus, I have some homework I have to finish up for class. I should log out now and log back in around 9:30. How does that sound?"

Jace nodded. "That sounds good. In the meantime, I'll see if any of the other farms have quests."

"Great!" she told him and backed away. "See you in a few hours."

With that, her character faded away as she logged out. Jace looked down at Luna, who was staring off at the lambs in the farmer's pin. "I guess it's just you and me for now."

"Yes," she said.

Jace had run back to town to eat a meal so he wouldn't get the *Hungry* debuff. Despite her earlier meal of rat, Luna once again stole one of his fish fillets. Afterwards, he went to every farm and received as many quests as they would give him. Interestingly, he received an almost identical quest from a farmer to the west who had a similar issue with someone attacking his life stock - but on alternate nights. He spent the rest of the time going back and forth between the two farms, asking more questions. By time Charlena logged in, he had a lot to tell her.

"You're right," she said as he finished explaining the other similar quest and his theory. "Something between the south farm and the west farm is attacking both and it's alternating farms."

"And I checked with the other farms," he told her. "Only those two are getting attacks."

"It couldn't be… like… a werewolf could it?" she asked. He heard both excitement and fear in her voice.

Jace shrugged. "If so, we're way out of our league. They can only be killed by silver or blessed weapons."

She raised an eyebrow. "Do you know everything about this game?"

Laughing nervously, he hoped he hadn't given away too much. He didn't know how he'd explain having a level 95 character only a month or so ago. "If only. I certainly don't know what this thing is."

Once again, he saw the gleam of excitement in her eye as she pulled her bow off her back. "Let's go hunt it down!"

Jace could only smile and then he and Luna followed her into the woods.

They began a criss cross pattern between the two farms, both of them using their stealth skills to navigate through the dark forest. Luckily, elves had similar eyesight to cats in the dark and so neither of them needed a torch. In fact, now that he thought about, all of the premium races had enhanced sight. Perhaps that had been a complaint of the early users who had played humans.

"I'm lucky I chose you as my familiar," he told Luna silently, thinking of the *Cat-Vision*.

"Yes," came her smug reply.

They searched for almost an hour before Luna froze next to him. He held up his fist, signally Charlena to come to a halt. It was one of several gestures he'd used with other groups. He gave her a crash course before they'd started into the forest.

He watched Luna as she sniffed the air, first one direction, then another. Finally, her gaze locked slightly to the left. In his mind he heard Luna's voice. "Wolfer."

Wolfer? He still didn't know what Luna meant by that. Was that her way of saying wolf? Or was something wolf-like? Was it a werewolf? He really hoped not or they were going to die horribly.

Moving back to Charlena, he leaned in close so he was almost rubbing his lips against her ear. "It's close," he whispered. In the dark, he almost thought he saw her shiver.

"Lead the way," Jace told Luna silently.

Luna began stalking forward without a word, her attention fixed ahead of her. Jace and Charlena followed after her as quietly as possible. Suddenly Jace received a rank in Stealth. He knew that meant he was close to an enemy.

The wolfer. It was close but he still didn't see it no matter how hard he strained his eyes. He looked down at Luna, whose tail was swishing back and forth. Her head was still pointed in the same direction, ears rotating left and right.

Luna moved a few steps forward and they followed. That's when he saw movement. It was just a quick movement from one of the trees. A head poking out for just a moment. Jace couldn't be sure, but the brief glimpse he'd gotten was that of a canine head, like a wolf. And whatever it was was on two legs.

Signaling Charlena to the tree next to her, he ducked behind a tree to his left. Not for the first time, Jace wished he had the *Far Speak* spell so he could talk silently to her. Instead, he pointed to the tree where he'd seen the movement and then pointed to her. Then he gestured to himself and made a semi-circular motion, indicating he'd circle around. She nodded that she understood. He gave her a smile and then moved off to the left to circle around with Luna padding silently next to him.

Jace kept his eyes peeled on the spot where he'd last seen the wolfer, watching to see if it moved. Nothing moved as he slowly circled around to the side of it. He gained several more ranks in *Stealth* and saw that he'd gained rank 10, the highest rank he could achieve until he hit character level 11. He'd also gained a *Stealth* ability, but he couldn't take the time to read it at the moment. He had to keep his attention on the wolfer.

Coming around a tree, Jace was finally able to see behind the tree where he'd seen the wolfer earlier. It was there, with it's back to the tree. It definitely had a wolf's head and seemed to have gray-white fur. It was either shorter than he'd originally though or it was crouching down.

That was the moment the thing decided to look in his direction. He locked eyes with the wolfer's black orbs, dark as midnight and his blood went cold.

"Ahhh!" screamed the wolfer and it ran off to the right. "Stupid players!"

Jace blinked. Had the wolfer just referred to him as a player? That wasn't possible. The monsters weren't aware of players in that sense. It was like breaking the 4th wall. It wasn't possible.

A bow twanged and then the wolfer fell over as Charlena's arrow hit it. "Owwww! Not again! Freakin' players!"

Shaking his head, he heard the elf moving towards the spot where the wolfer had fallen. She was probably looking to finish it off.

Jace broke cover and ran to the fallen wolfer who was whimpering. As he got closer, he spotted the elf with her bow drawn, about to fire another arrow.

"Hold on Charlena," he yelled and saw her relax her grip on the arrow she had at ready and lower her bow. She gave him a confused look.

"Give me a second," he told her as he came to halt a few feet from the "wolfer". Only it wasn't a wolfer at all, it was just a goblin. It was a goblin wearing a wolf head headdress and wolf pelts it had tied to its body. He chuckled. It was a goblin who had disguised itself like a wolf.

"What?" asked Charlena who still hadn't moved.

"Come and look."

"What's wrong stupid player," the goblin said sarcastically. "You can't kill me without your elf bi-"

"Shut up," he snapped at the goblin. "Or I will kill you."

The goblin's eyes went wide. "You… you understand me?"

Charlena moved over and looked down at the goblin. She scrunched up her nose. "Can they… do that? Disguise themselves?"

"This one can," he told her. He had a bad feeling that he knew why this goblin knew they were players and why it could disguise itself.

"Were you… talking to it?" asked Charlena. "I heard you speaking in… what… goblin?"

Jace sighed. It looked like it was time to come clean with her. He really hoped she'd forgive him for not telling her the whole truth. But if what he suspected was true, he had no choice.

"Wait," the goblin said to Charlena. "Can you understand me too?"

Charlena looked from the goblin to Jace. Her expression had become colder. "You understand it don't you?"

"Yes," he admitted. "But there's a really good explanation."

Her icy expression didn't soften. "There'd better be. I don't like being played."

"What the heck is going on here?" demanded the goblin. "You guys aren't going to kill me? Or are you?"

Jace looked down at the goblin and put away his daggers. "What's your name?"

"My… uh… er… name?" stuttered the goblin. "It's um… Naj-nok… or was it Nag-rok? Definitely an N-word…"

Jace held up his hand. "No, your human name."

The goblin's eyes went wide as saucers. It hesitated for a moment and then answered in a whispered, "Duglas Morgan."

Chapter 17

"Hi Duglas," Jace replied. "I'm Jace Burton."

Jace knew now that Duglas had somehow been affected by the same bug that had afflicted him. Had it affected him the same way? Was he still hoping from monster to monster?

"Are you… are you a developer? Can you fix me?" asked the goblin pleadingly.

Jace was about to answer when Charlena cut in, her tone dangerous. "Are you going to tell me what's going on? And how it is that you can speak to cats and now… to goblins?!"

"He's not a goblin," Jace told her. "Well... I mean, technically he is right now. But he's a player. His name is Duglas."

Jace watched her face go from angry to shocked and then to disbelief. "Yeah, right."

"I know this," Jace told her. "Because I was a kobold before I became human."

"What?!" both Duglas and Charlena said at the same time.

"I'm sorry I didn't tell you right off the bat, but it's a little hard to believe - even for me," he told her. "But I'll tell you now if you'll listen."

Charlena's eyes were hard but she nodded and Jace spent the next half hour recounting what had happened to him. To their credit, both Charlena and Duglas listened without interrupting as he related his story. But as soon as he stopped, they both began blurting out questions.

When they realized they'd spoken at the same time, they both glared at each other and then Duglas gestured to Charlena to go ahead.

"Okay," she started. "If I believe you, then what you're saying is… you're dead. And when you were inserted into the game, you became a monster. But then you did some sort of programming thing and turned yourself into a human...oh…" Her mouth twisted into a sour expression. "And you really are, or were, a programmer for WorldCog. That about right?"

Both she and Duglas looked at him.

"Yes," he said simply.

"HOW did you turn yourself human? And is it permanent? Do you stop jumping from body to body?" asked Duglas, who evidently thought it was his turn to speak.

"I can tell you exactly how a little later, but yes, so far I've died several times and have respawned as the same character," Jace answered him.

He looked at Charlena who still had a troubled expression on her face. He opened his mouth to speak but she held up a hand. "Listen, this is a lot to process and I'll be honest, I'm not sure if I believe it or if this is some elaborate scam… No, just listen… I'm going to logout and think about this. I may or may not be back tomorrow. Don't look for me. If I want to talk to you again, I'll look for you."

Then, before Jace could respond, Charlena faded away.

"I think your girlfriend is upset with you," Duglas said quietly. "I guess it's my fault. Sorry."

Jace shook his head, still staring at the place where Charlena had been. "She's not my girlfriend. And no Duglas, it's not your fault. It's mine." He turned towards the goblin. He wanted to change the subject. "I told you my story. What's your story?"

"I… ah… used to be a day trader," he told Jace. "I made some really good trades at the right time and made a lot of money. I made sure it was all supposed to come into the game with me when I died. It was supposed to be my "retirement" nest egg. I even had a little in-game inn I purchased. Instead, here I am in a monster body. No character and no money."

Jace whistled. He knew players could buy in-game homes of all sorts, but an inn was right up there with a small mansion. It'd probably cost 10,000,000 gold, or about $1,000,000 in real money. Duglas must have had a lot of money. "What kind of character did you have?"

"Level 51 Werebear paladin," he said. "You?"

"Level 95 vampyre assassin."

"Wow," Duglas said with some surprise. "You were hardcore."

Jace smiled and then changed to a slightly touchier subject. "Do you know how you died?"

"Surfing I assume," he replied nonchalantly. "I had a backup right before we hit the Banzai Pipeline on the North Shore. I don't remember anything after that, so I assume I took a bad wipeout and here I am. You?"

"I don't know," Jace told him honestly. "I had my normal backup after work and the next thing I know I'm a monster. I lost a month too."

"No, you didn't," the goblin told him.

"What?! No, I did, I…"

Duglas shook his head. "I'm pretty sure you're not conscious while we're between bodies."

That rocked Jace. He'd guessed he went back into the AI queue, but he'd never thought he would be unconscious. He wondered how Duglas had figured it out. "How do you know?"

"Little things," Duglas told him. "I'd die during the day and then respawn in a monster at night or it would be raining, and I'd respawn, and it wouldn't be raining. The real tell was the moon cycles. Once I guessed I was losing time, I started keeping track of them. Then I started realizing how much time I was missing."

Jace was impressed. He hadn't even guessed he'd been losing time until he'd talked to Charlena. But he had only jumped bodies a few times. Which begged the question. "How long have you been in here?"

A pained expression came over his face. "At least a year, maybe two. I really have no idea how much time I missed before I started keeping track of the lunar cycles."

"I'm sorry," Jace told him. "That's a long time to be jumping between bodies."

"You get used to it," he said stoically. "I eventually figured out that I could stay in the same body longer if I left the area, I'd spawned in. Eventually players would find me and kill me if I stayed close. But if I left and went out to the middle of nowhere, sometimes I could stay alive for a month or two before a player found me or a more powerful monster killed me."

"I can tell you how I changed into a human," he told Duglas. "But it's not perfect. There are issues."

Duglas laughed mirthlessly. "Worse issues than becoming a new monster every time you die and being killed by players over and over?"

"Point taken. I just want you to know it won't be easy starting off."

"Thank you, but I'll manage."

Jace explained the process and went over it twice. As he finished, Duglas began nodding. "I always wondered what that return code was for! I must have typed hundreds of combinations of letters and numbers. Nothing ever seemed to do anything."

"Just type it in exactly like I told you and it will work," he said. "Or at least, that's what worked for me. I can't guarantee it will do the same for you."

Duglas nodded. "Trust me, I won't blame you if it doesn't work. Even if I go back to jumping from monster to monster, it will be good knowing I'm not the only one."

"I guess all that's left is for you to kill me," Duglas said.

"Now?" Jace asked.

"I've been in this hell for at least a year," he told Jace. "If there's even a chance I can break this cycle, I want to do it."

Nodding slowly, Jace pulled out his daggers. "If need help or want to find us, we're on our way to the capital."

"The capital? Capital of what?" he asked, confused.

"Aldor, it's the human kingdom. The capital is Whitecliff. We can meet you there," Jace told him.

Duglas. "Okay, I'll try to remember that. Anywhere specific?"

Jace wanted to kick himself. Whitecliff was the capital. It was a large city by medieval fantasy standards and they might never cross paths. "Good point. Let's say, the first pub inside the main gate. When we make it to the capital, we'll go there every night for dinner. Look for us there."

"First pub," Duglas grinned. "I can get behind that." He sobered and looked down at the knives in Jace's hands. "I guess we might as well get this over with."

"Turn around so I can get a critical hit and it will be faster."

"I've been burned, shot with arrows, frozen, beheaded, ripped apart, clawed, bitten in half and just about anything else you can think of. Whatever you need to do, just do it," he told Jace but turned around.

Nodding, Jace stabbed Duglas with both daggers.

You critically hit Swampskull Goblin for 9 damage.
You critically hit Swampskull Goblin for 5 damage.
Swampskull Goblin dies.
You gain 20 experience.

Duglas's goblin body slumped to the ground and Jace received updates for the two wolf related quests. After a moment, the body began to change and elongate until it looked like a blond human with tan skin and a surfer's physique. He remembered what had happened to his own body when he'd used the code and how painful it had been.

Looking at the human body in front of him, Jace had to assume that it had worked and that Duglas would respawn as a human. Tentatively, Jace tried looting the body but received a system message.

You may not loot a player's body until it expires.

Jace smiled at the message. It said "player's body" which meant it had worked. Excitedly, Jace wondered if Duglas would respawn in town. Since he had nothing else to do in the forest, he decided to go check. "Come on Luna!"

He and his familiar jogged back to town and checked in the graveyard but there was no sign of him. Leaving the graveyard, they made a quick circuit of the town but there was no sign of him. He must have spawned elsewhere. Silently, Jace wished him well wherever he was. And Jace promised he'd remember his name when he finally got someone in support to fix him. Then they could fix Duglas too.

With Duglas gone, Jace's thoughts turned to Charlena. He'd barely known her. They'd only played together a day, but he already missed her. He wasn't sure why. Was it because she was the only real person he'd met so far - except for Duglas? Or was it because she was an attractive woman? Or was it the way they'd seemed to get along so well today.

Jace didn't know. He just hoped she'd be back.

He turned to look at Luna, who'd been quiet since they'd met Duglas. "You okay Luna?"

The cat stared at him before answering. "Yes."

He wasn't entirely convinced, but he'd take her word for it. If he had to guess, her programming might be having a difficult time processing what had happened since it had occurred outside the normal game parameters. After all, monsters didn't normally morph into players. Jace hoped she would be okay. If he lost Luna, he'd be completely alone. And he was surprised at just how much that frightened him.

To keep himself busy, he spent the rest of the night scouting out the area between the farms. Most of it was forest, but to the west, where he'd killed the goblins, it was hilly. He hadn't found any monsters of any sort. Not even wolves or coyotes. That seemed strange. If this was a newbie town, there should be monsters to kill. After all, that's how new players mostly leveled up - killing monsters. Well, killing monsters and doing quests. He'd found plenty of quests, but almost no monsters.

Then he remembered the wolf furs and wolf head that Duglas had been wearing. Had he been killing the aggressive wildlife around the area? That would make sense. He'd need to eat and would have wanted to clear the area of anything that would be a danger to him. That made sense.

But while it made sense, it also made Jace's life a little more difficult. There was nothing for him to kill and gain experience. He was limited to only quests unless he wanted to venture further into the forests. But the further he went, the more likely he was to run into things far higher level than he was. Still, that might end up being an option.

As day broke, he made his way back to the town. When the tavern opened, he went inside and bought some breakfast. What he ordered was called a Full Halfling Breakfast and consisted of bacon, eggs, and sausages, as well as a grilled tomato, mushrooms, fried onions, and some toast.

While Luna didn't care for the sausages or bacon directly, she did enjoy licking up the bacon grease and the egg yolks.

After finishing breakfast, he wandered around town for several hours, waiting to see if Charlena was going to show up. The hours seemed to pass especially slowly and when noon came, Jace realized she wasn't coming back.

Chapter 18

When Charlena didn't appear, Jace and Luna ate a lunch of fish and chips at the tavern. This time, Jace had enough gold to afford an ale and washed down his meal with a pint of the tavern's finest. He briefly considered drinking himself into a drunken stupor. After all, it was possible to get drunk on in-game alcohol through some miracle in the way the FEVRE pods interacted with the person's brain. But in the end, he had so little money, he couldn't afford to waste any on getting drunk.

Instead, he went to the general store and bought a set of lockpicks and a fishing pole. The lockpicks would help him practice his *Lockpicking* skill. The fishing pole would allow him to catch fish in nearly any water source. That would allow him to save some money while in town and be crucial for catching food once he left town. Assuming he could find a lake or stream to fish from out in the wild.

Next, he went back to some of the farms and finished up the other quests they'd received. These weren't nearly as interesting as they were delivery quests, go fetch this for me and bring it back and I'll pay you. But despite the tedium, they each paid 2 gold and gave 50 experience.

Several hours later, as he turned in his 8th quest, a glowing aura surrounded him, and he saw the system message he'd been waiting for.

You have gained a level.

You are now level 2 in Mage.
You gain 6 health.
You gain 6 mana.

Finally, he had reached his second level in *Mage*. Because it was his highest class, he received additional health and mana. He now had 14 health and 10 mana, nearly double what he'd had before. He'd now have a fighting chance against monsters his level.

He now had a choice. Since *Mage* was now his highest level, he could switch classes again. That meant he could switch back to *Rogue*. Or he could switch to *Fighter* or *Priest*. *Fighter* would give him the ability to use any armor or weapon, whereas *Priest* would give him access to healing magic and buffs.

He considered what his next step was. He still needed to reach the capital in order to find the *Help Desk*. That was the only way he could contact support and get this situation resolved. And now he wasn't just doing this for himself, he knew from Duglas that others had been affected and he just might be the only one who could help them.

He needed to make it to the capital. And he needed to do it as quickly as possible. That meant he needed to leave Sinking Springs and brave the wilderness between towns. That was no easy task for a group of low level characters. There was no set level limit on the monsters in the wilderness. He could run into a level 1 coyote or a level 50 ogre. At his level, Jace couldn't hope to defeat high level monsters. He would need to rely on stealth and avoidance. And that meant *Rogue*.

Going back into his HUD, he switched classes to Rogue. He was now a level 1 Rogue again. He'd now have to hit level 3 in Rogue if he wanted to switch classes again and it would take some time for that to happen. He hoped he'd made the right choice.

He looked at the last two quests in his journal. They were the wolf quests he'd done with Charlena. He'd been putting off turning them in case she returned but it didn't look like that was going to happen. Still, he could wait one more day. The farms were still giving him quests, so he could keep himself busy for now. But if she hadn't logged in by tomorrow, he would turn them in.

With that decided, Jace looked at the sky. The sun was still several hours away from setting so he had time to do some more quests before the NPCs started their evening schedules. He should be able to get in at least ten more quests before sunset.

Resuming his circuit from farm to farm, Jace went to Coy and Haylei's farm to get another quest from them. They waved when they saw him approach.

"Hello Dedrurrurth," said Coy as he approached them. Jace cringed inwardly but forced a smile. After reaching a certain level of faction, people in town had begun automatically calling him by name, which was still Dedrurrurth.

"Hello Coy," Jace responded. The nice thing about having a HUD is that you never forgot a NPCs name. You could look it up instantly. Too bad he hadn't had one of those back in the real world. He was constantly forgetting names. "Can I help you with anything?"

Coy looked over at his wife who shook her head. "I'm afraid we don't need any help at the moment. Unless you're good with a plow."

Jace waited a moment to see if a quest would appear. When it didn't he politely smiled at the couple. "Maybe another time. I should see if any of the other farms are having any issues with … um… monsters or… things."

"Alrighty," said Coy. "Always a pleasure to see you Dedrurrurth."

"Make sure you're in before dark," Haylei called after him.

Leaving Coy and Haylei behind, Jace went to the next farm down the road but received the same thing. And he received the same thing from the next one as well. The odd thing was the way they ended the conversation. Both times they'd told him to make sure to be in before dark. That was new. To test his theory, he walked to the last farm down the south road, Jebediah's farm.

Jebediah was an older man whose wife had been killed by goblins a few years ago. Now he lived alone and had asked Jace to fetch various things from the village for him so he didn't have to leave his farm.

As Jace approached, Jebediah waved to him. "Good day Dedrurrurth. Not that I don't mind you visiting, but you should be heading back to town."

"Why is that?" Jace asked him.

"Ain't safe around here after dark," the old man told him.

"What do you mean? I've been out at night before."

Jebediah made a warding gesture. "On account of the Reaping."

The name gave Jace the shivers. "What is the Reaping?"

The old man looked around as if expecting to see someone. "We don't really talk about on account that it might scare people away. Especially the caravans." Jebediah motioned him closer conspiratorially. "But, since people around here know you, I reckon it's okay to tell you."

Jace nodded for him to continue.

"You know Aldor wasn't always a united kingdom. Five hundred years ago, it was two rivalling kingdoms, Stroania and Jothuela. As it happens, Sinking Springs was originally a border outpost of Stroania. This was all Stroania, but twenty miles west was Jothuela and their necromancers," Jebediah spit and made a warding sign again before continuing.

"Well, as you know, Stroania and Jothuela eventually went to war. What most people don't realize is that one of the first battles was right on this spot. Right here in Sinking Springs!" The old man waved his arms around indicating the entire area. "The black army marched up and attacked the outpost and almost took it before reinforcements arrived."

"King Ackert himself showed up through some magic portal with a whole mess of his Knights of the Griffon and they pushed back the Black Company and killed the leader, a necromancer general named Mimira Sanguis."

"Of course," the man spat again. "Them darn Jothuelans blamed Stroania and claimed they'd actually been the invaders. That's what's what started the Twenty Year War. And it would have gone on even longer if King Ackert's son hadn't killed Stauzor The Demon - only he won't a real demon, just a necromancer but people called him that."

Jace waited for Jebediah to continue but the man stayed silent. "So… what does that have to do with the reaping?"

The man gave him a disbelieving look. "What do you mean what does it have to do with it? Mimira Sanguis was buried not 5 miles from here." Jebediah emphasized his point by pointing west. "For two nights a month, when the black moon is full, the dead soldiers of the Jothuelan army arise to take their vengeance on the living! Been happening for the last five years."

The world of VEIL had three moons. The white moon, Geal, which was home of the good gods. Then there was Dearg, the red moon, where the neutral gods lived. And finally, there was Dubh, where the evil gods made their abode. Jace frowned. It was said that only evil beings could see Dubh. He'd been able to see it as a vampyre, but as he looked into the night's sky, he couldn't see it with his human eyes.

He eyed Jebediah suspiciously. "How do you know Dubh is full?"

The man's eyes went wide, and he made his warding gesture. "Don't say the name of the dark moon! Tis an ill omen! And no, I don't be calling on the dark gods. All farmers can tell. The day before and the two days of it being full, the milk curdles, and the hens lay nothing but rotten eggs. The dead will be out tonight. Mark my words. You best be inside before they do."

Jace looked around at the farmer's cattle and sheep. "What about your herd?"

Shaking his head, Jebediah gestured to the livestock. "The dead don't want them. Ain't them what killed the necromancer. They only go after humans… well and elves and dwarves and such. All them that served in Stroania's army." The man made a shooing gesture. "Get on back to the village. They'll let you board there tonight."

Nodding, Jace turned and ran towards the village. Behind him, he heard the Jebediah's parting words. "Don't come out at night! No matter what you hear!"

Jace ran until his *stamina* was nearly completely gone then slowed to a walk. Jebediah's farm was the furthest from town and he knew from experience it was a good half hour walk. Looking to the west, the sun had just touched the horizon. He had twenty or thirty minutes before it would dip below.

He should have time to reach the village, but he had no idea exactly when the undead would rise or from where.

From a game standpoint, he wasn't sure if this was some sort of quest, an event or if it were a dungeon. Perhaps all of the above. This could be a good opportunity to earn experience by killing the undead, but until he knew more, he wasn't inclined to risk it. One or two at a time he might be able to handle, but a swarm of undead who could easily overwhelm him. Best to play it safe or he could spend all night dying and respawning.

Jace kept alternating between walking and running until he reached the village. The sun had just dipped beneath the horizon, so he ran straight to the tavern. The door was locked and all the windows were shuttered. Desperately, he banged on the door but there was no answer. He ran around to the side and banged on that door. No one answered. He turned and ran to the store, banging on the door hard enough to make his fists hurt. There was no answer.

He turned to run to another building when he heard Luna hiss and he heard the first unearthly moan.

Chapter 19

Jace spun around, looking for the source of the moans but even with his *Cat-Vision*, he saw nothing. His heart was racing, and the blood was pounding in his ears but he tried to focus. Where were they?

Luna had moved behind him and was still hissing. He spared a quick glance down at her. "It'll be okay."

"No," she sent back, and her voice was frightened.

He needed to find shelter. He needed to get in one of these buildings, but how? He'd briefly thought about picking the lock but he guessed that if the windows were shuttered, the doors were locked and barred. He needed another way.

Scanning the buildings in the area, Jace got an idea. If he couldn't go in, maybe he could go up. Most low level undead couldn't climb, they mostly shambled. If he could get somewhere, they couldn't reach, he might be safe. He might be.

As Jace looked closer at the nearby buildings, he realized Tudor style buildings didn't make good climbing structures. In fact, nearly all of them had an overhang where the second floor met the first. He remembered reading somewhere that it was called a jetty. No matter what it was called, it would make climbing them much more difficult.

"Tree!" Luna meowed in something that was half meow and half whine. Following her gaze, he saw what she was referring to. One of the houses had a tree close enough that one of the branches overhung the top of the house.

The only problem was, there were no lower branches that he could use to get up.

The moaning was growing louder and now Jace could just start to see shapes moving at the edges of his vision to the west, making their way towards town. There were dozens of them, and they were moving fast! He didn't have time to figure out how to climb the tree. He needed to find a place to hold out. And he needed to find it fast.

His hands hurt and he looked down at his knuckles, which had gone white from his death grips on his daggers. He tilted his head as he looked at his dagger. He stared at the rat fang dagger he'd gotten from Den Mother. Then it hit him. Ralf's cellar! It might be strong enough to withstand the undead. And right now, it seemed to be the only place he might be able to get to. Without another thought, he took off towards Ralf's place with Luna at his heels.

It only took him a couple of minutes to reach Ralf's home and just like the others, the windows were shuttered, and he guessed the door was barred. He ran around the house to the cellar to find it had been relocked. He started to look in his inventory for the key but remembered he'd given it back to Ralf when he'd completed the quest.

Looking west, he could now discern the vague forms of skeletons running into town. Tall, thin forms with tattered pieces of armor or clothes. Some were stopping and pounding on doors with their bony fists. Others were continuing on to find other houses. He'd guessed it would only be a matter of minutes before they reached him.

He looked down at the padlock on the cellar and remembered his lockpicks! He didn't hesitate. Grabbing his picks from his inventory, he went to work on the lock.

Critical failure!
Your pick has broken.
Your Lockpicking skill has increased by 1.

Jace had been trying too hard and had broken one of his picks. He only had 2 left. Glancing towards the center of town, he could see the skeletal creatures were much closer. Their long, thin limbs moving unnaturally in the dark. He needed to get inside now!

Pulling out another pick, he got back to work. He thought he almost had it when there was another clink.

Critical failure!
Your pick has broken.
Your Lockpicking skill has increased by 1.

No! He'd broken another pick. He glanced up and saw the skeletons were close now. Too close. If he didn't pick the lock right now, he wouldn't be able to outrun them. He pulled out his last pick, took a deep breath and focused on the lock.

This time he focused, ignoring the moans which were getting closer. He had to focus. Suddenly, he felt the tumblers click into place and the lock opened with a snap.

Your Lockpicking skill has increased by 1.

He pulled the lock off the chain and yanked open the door. There was a flash of orange and he realized Luna had already bolted down the steps. He jumped in the cellar and pulled the chain inside. The doors didn't quite close all the way but he didn't care. He slipped the large padlock through the chains and slammed it closed just as the first skeleton reached the door.

Stumbling back, he retrieved his daggers and watched as more and more skeletons pulled at the cellar doors. When they didn't immediately give way, he relaxed slightly and started looking for things to pile in front of the steps. Luckily, there were plenty of things. There were shelves, crates and boxes of all sorts. And luckily, no giant rats.

He spent the next hour moving two large shelves in front of the entrance to the cellar and then stacking crates and boxes in front of it. The entire time, he could hear the skeletons pulling on the doors while others banged on the doors.

Once he had made his makeshift barricade, he slumped down in front of it to catch his breath and let his *stamina* recharge. The sounds of the skeletons trying to break in never ceased and he prayed the doors would hold.

Jace was glad he no longer needed to sleep since he would have gotten none that night. The sounds of the skeletons never ceased. They continued their pounding and pulling, but the doors to the cellar held.

Luna had gone to the furthest corner from the cellar doors and climbed to the top of a shelf there. At some point, she had curled up in a circle and fallen asleep, apparently confident in Jace's ability to protect her. Or more like, she's simply been too tired to stay awake. Occasionally she would pick her head up and look around and then curl back up and go to sleep. Jace smiled at the little feline. At least one of them could sleep.

Jace lost track of the hours but at some point, the noise from the door just stopped. It was sudden and after listening to it all night, the silence was profound. There were no windows in the cellar, so Jace couldn't tell if it were morning. If it were, then the undead may have retreated back to wherever they had come from. Unfortunately, there was only one way to find out.

It took him almost an hour to move all the crates and shelves in front of the door, but he could finally see the light seeping through the cracks in the cellar door. Creeping up to one of the cracks, he looked out. There were no skeletons that he could see. He took a look through each crack with the same result. He saw no sign of the undead.

Luna had jumped down from her perch and was now near him. She wasn't hissing and didn't seem to look stressed, so he guessed she wasn't sensing any skeletons either. He took a deep breath and retrieved his last lockpick and went to open the door.

This time he opened it on his first try, earning another rank in *Lockpicking*. After removing the padlock, he opened the door and peaked out. And almost got a pitchfork to the face.

"Watch it!" he snapped, and the pitchfork was withdrawn.

"I knew I heard something down in my cellar! Thought it was either more rats or… the dead," came a familiar voice.

Cautiously raising his head out, he spied Ralf a few feet away with his pitchfork poised.

Ralf looked at him, obviously trying to make up his mind about something. "You alive or dead?"

"Alive," Jace responded. "As long as I don't get a pitchfork through the head!"

Ralf didn't lower his pitchfork, but he did back up a few steps and motioned. Even still down in the stairwell, Jace could see the bags under his eyes and his haggard appearance. Probably most of the villagers hadn't slept last night. "Well, come on out of there, let me see you. I've never heard those dead fellas speak, just moan, but there's a first time for everything."

Jace climbed up the steps with his hands raised and paused at the top.

Ralf did a semi-circle around him before finally lowering his pitchfork. "Well, you don't look dead. But I warn you," he brandished his pitchfork again. "You try and eat my brain and you'll get a mouthful of pitchfork!"

"Fair enough," Jace said. "And sorry I broke into your cellar. I couldn't find any other place to hold up."

The man looked at the cellar and shook his head. "It's alright. No one ought to be caught by those things!

I'm just glad the doors held. Why didn't you take shelter in the tavern?"

"No one told me about the undead until it was too late," Jace snapped. "I was all the way out at Jebediah's farm when he told me about it just before sunset."

"Well then," whistled Ralf. "You're lucky you made it all the way back here in time."

Jace nodded and thought about what Jebediah had said. "And they'll be back again tonight?"

"Two nights, every month."

He handed the lock to Ralf. "Then I'd better make sure I have a place to stay tonight. Thanks again."

"Sure," Ralf called from behind him. "Good thing you had already cleared out them rats!"

Jace went straight to the tavern and ordered breakfast. The same crowd was there this morning, but they looked as haggard as Ralf had. There was also a much more sober mood. When people did speak, it was in hushed tones.

He ate his breakfast in silence and then left. He'd come back later and talk to the tavern owner. Jace had barely gotten a dozen steps when a portly man he hadn't seen before stepped in front of him.

"Dedrurrurth!" he called out and Jace sighed. He'd asked a few of the villagers to call him Jace, but they always reverted to his character name. "I'm mayor Absalom. Sorry I didn't get a chance to introduce myself before this but I also run the apothecary and it's always busy before... Well... You know that time of the month shall we say. I must gather extra herbs beforehand."

Jace smiled half-heartedly. He'd actually tried to go into the apothecary to see if he could get quests, but the door had been locked each time he'd tried. "What can I do for you?"

"Well," started the man and Jace couldn't help but feel like he was talking to a used car salesman. "I'm sure you are aware of our current, shall we say, predicament. You seem to be the adventurous sort and I thought perhaps you could look into exactly why these things occur and if possible, put an end to them."

Mayor Absalom of Sinking Springs has offered you the quest, "Plague of Undead"
Reward: 100 gold, +100 faction with Residents of Sinking Springs, +100 faction with Absalom, item.
Accept quest? (Yes or No)

Jace looked at the reward. It was substantial. That meant the quest was most likely difficult, and without Charlena, he'd be going into a potentially bad situation with no backup.

He hesitated in accepting the quest so long, he saw a line of sweat drip down the mayor's neck, though his smile never wavered. Finally, Jace decided to go for it. He accepted the quest.

"I'll check it out," he told the mayor and the man visibly relaxed.

Absalom grabbed his hand and shook it. "Thank you! Thank you very much Dedrurrurth!"

Jace released the man's sweaty hand and wondered what he'd gotten himself into.

Chapter 20

Jace had tried to find out from the mayor where the necromancer had been buried but he had been evasive and finally claimed ignorance. Jace wasn't sure if Absalom was lying or not but he didn't press it.

Thinking about the quest, he guessed he'd need to explore the burial site of Mimira Sanguis. He couldn't think of any other leads and according to Jebediah's story, that seemed to be where they came from. Or at least, that's what the old man believed.

"What do you think," he asked Luna. "Should we go to the dungeon?"

His familiar just looked at him as if to say, 'How should I know?'

Jace tried talking to a few of the other townsfolk about the skeletons but every person he talked to quickly changed the subject or had nothing to say. The most he got from the villagers who would say anything was that they came two nights every month and that it had started five years ago.

He found it curious that the undead started coming to the village five years ago. If he remembered correctly, the battle between King Ackert and Mimira Sanguis had happened over 500 years ago. Why then had the undead only started appearing five years ago? He needed to investigate the burial site.

Before heading back to Jebediah's, Jace stopped by the general store again.

He bought another set of picks and a 50 foot coil of rope. There were some other items he could have used but he was running low on gold. With his purchases stored in his inventory, he headed west, out of the village with Luna trailing along.

Jace cut through the woods to get to Jebediah's forest, taking his time. He remembered the crazy run walk he'd done last night to get from the man's home back to town and wasn't up for a reverse repeat.

"Let's not repeat that crazy run we did last night," he said aloud.

"No," Luna agreed quietly as she started stalking a butterfly. Jace paused to let her have some fun. She stalked it for several minutes as it flitted from flower to flower.

As Luna played, he thought about Charlena and wished he would have handled things better with her. She'd seemed like a nice girl and he'd appreciated her enthusiasm. He knew there was no way they could have a real relationship, but it had still been nice to have her around.

Jace turned his attention back to Luna just to see the butterfly fly high into the air and away from them. Luna stopped stalking and sat back on her haunches.

"You have fun?" he asked the cat as she watched the butterfly fly away.

"Yes."

When he reached Jebediah's farm, he found the old man tending his herds. Jace was surprised to see that the man had been right. The undead hadn't touched any of the animals. Apparently, they really did just want humanoids. Specifically, they wanted the good player races, he assumed.

"Oh, you didn't go into the burial mound," were the first words out of Jebediah's mouth.

"No," Jace interrupted. "But I will."

The old man shook his head. "Not surprising. To be honest, I'm surprised you survived the night. I have to admit, I didn't think you would. It's a long run back to the village and those undead are mighty fast. I was cursing myself all night for not inviting you in."

"I almost didn't make it back," Jace admitted, remembering the mad scramble last night. "But this morning, the mayor asked me to investigate the undead and if possible, put an end to their raids."

The old man raised an eyebrow. "Did he now?"

"He did," Jace nodded. "Funny thing is no one in town was really willing to talk about it."

"Weren't they now." Jebediah didn't act surprised.

"What weren't they telling me?"

The old smiled. "Oh, I'm sure there was lots they weren't telling you."

"Why wouldn't they tell me what I need to know if I'm trying to help them?"

"Why indeed?"

Jace could see he was getting nowhere with this line of questions, so he changed his tactic. "Do you know where the burial spot is for Mimira Sanguis?"

"I do," the man said.

Jace waited patiently for the man to continue, when he didn't Jace prompted him. "And will you tell me?"

The man seemed to consider that question. "I reckon I will. But it'll most likely mean I send you to your death."

A chill went down Jace's spine, even though he knew he could respawn. "That's why the others don't want to tell you nothing."

"Because they think I'll die?" he asked.

"You don't think you're the first adventurer to come into Sinking Springs do you? They come, they seem all heroic and then we tell them about the undead or they find out themselves. Next thing you know, they go marching off to the dungeon and we never see them again. You can only have so many adventurers on your conscience before you stop asking for help and just accept your fate."

"Wait," Jace said, his mind reeling. Was he saying they'd sent other players to this place and the players hadn't returned? There were NPC adventurers, but usually they were in the form of mercenaries you could hire to accompany you on your adventures. They weren't as powerful as players, but they could lend you some extra power if you needed it for certain dungeons or quests. But there was a cost. A steep cost. And not just in money. The mercenaries took part of the experience as well. Experience was more valuable than gold at higher levels.

Jace didn't think Jebediah was talking about NPC adventurers and that scared him. If players weren't returning, it most likely meant their characters had been perma-killed. Permadeath was very rare, but certain monsters could eat the "soul" of the character, permanently killing it and forcing the player to create a new character. Jace wasn't sure what would happen if he suffered a permadeath. Could he create another character? He wasn't sure and that scared him.

"If you're thinking about walking away," the old man seemed to be reading his thoughts. "No one would think the less of you."

That was exactly what Jace was thinking. He wouldn't have even risked Mordred on a quest that could involve permadeath. There was no way he was going to risk his actual life - digital or not - on a stupid quest. Not a chance. "I'm going to go back to town and wait out tonight in the tavern."

Jace turned to go. "Good fella. It's a shame that elf lass didn't listen to me."

His blood going cold, Jace froze in his tracks. He was sure he must have misheard. "Elf… lass?"

"Yah," the old man chuckled. "About ten minutes before you, she shows up asking where the burial chamber was. Need to find some fella named Jason… Jaxon… Something like that. I told her and off she ran.

I tried to yell after her, but she ran off so fast, she didn't hear me."

Jace around and caught Jebediah by the arms, his voice insistent. "The elf! What was her name!"

The old man was taken back by the sudden movement and Jace's tight grip on his arms. "Uh… It was… Um… Almedha… Almedha Pressalor."

Jace let go of the man and stumbled back. That was Charlena's character. Charlena had come back? She was looking for him? And now she was off to a place of possible permadeath.

"No!" he yelled, causing Luna to jump. Charlena was rushing to a certain doom because she had been looking for him. Worse, she didn't even know. He needed to warn her or, just like his parents, it would be his fault she died. He didn't want that on his conscious, even if it was just character death. Not if he could stop it.

Whirling on Jebediah, he took a step towards him. The older man cowered beneath his glare. "Tell me where the burial crypt is. Now."

The old man blurted out the directions and Jace took off west down the road. Even if he ran until his *stamina* was almost gone, he didn't think he could catch up with her. Jebediah had said she'd been running too. Still, he had to try. He had to get there and stop her or, if it came to it, go in after her and get her out before it was too late.

"We save elf?" Luna meowed.

"Yes," he replied, hoping it wasn't just bravado. "We save elf."

The two of them ran until their *stamina* was low and then walked until it had regenerated and then ran again. They kept it up the entire five miles to the dead oak Jebediah mentioned and then turned left into the forest. They followed an old game trail another mile before it led into a ravine. He and Luna followed the increasingly rocky trail through the ravine.

The entire time he thought about Charlena. She's logged off abruptly last night and he had feared maybe the fact that he was dead had freaked her out. But she was back and she was looking for him. And she'd gone into some place where potentially that character could be permanently killed and she'd have to create a new one. If that happened, his chance of ever seeing her again were slim to none. After all, it was only bad luck that wizard had stranded her here. He needed to find her before anything happened to her.

A small stream ran along the bottom of the ravine parallel to the trail but Jace couldn't stop and admire the scenery. He kept walking alongside the stream. As he walked, he noticed small bits of armor, pieces of dried leather or other things that he guessed had fallen off the undead as they passed this way. That meant he was on the right track.

The guesswork came to halt as the ravine turned a sharp right, into a wall of stone. In the wall of stone, a large doorway had been carved into the rock itself. A door that had once sealed the tomb shut was lying askew, leaving enough room for a fully grown man to pass into the darkness beyond.

Jace noticed that carved into the frame of the doorway were ancient runes - runes too old to be from 500 years ago when the necromancer was defeated. The runes were from an ancient race called the Veteribus, referred to as the Ancient Ones. They had been the first inhabitants of the world who had passed away before the gods came and created the current races. In truth, it was a made-up language that was unique to VEIL, invented especially for the game. There was no in-game skill for the language. Instead, WorldCog left it up to the players to learn on their own.

And while not all players could read Veteribium, it was extremely difficult to get by as a high level player without some knowledge of it. The most powerful raids and artifacts were related to the Veteribus and knowing their language gave you hints, clues or warnings about what to expect.

Like a real geek, Jace was one of the people who had taken the time to learn it. He couldn't quite speak it, but he could read it. He poured over the letters, reading from right to left.

Welcome to the City of Crystalburrow. Let those with evil in their heart be warned: The immortal guardians stand ever vigilant.

Jace frowned. This was not the tomb of the necromancer. This was something much older. Had Jebediah misled him? Or had he really believed this was Mimira Sanguis' tomb? Was this even the same place the old man had sent Charlena? Or was there really an actual tomb for the necromancer?

Thinking back to the bits of armor he'd seen on the way here, he had to assume that the undead were coming from here. If that were the case, then perhaps Jebediah and the other villagers did believe this was the tomb of Mimira Sanguis. After all, a common villager wouldn't understand Veteribium or even recognize it as the language of the Ancients.

Still, something didn't feel right. But one thing was clear to Jace now. If this really was a Veteribus rune, it could hold untold dangers and possibly the ability to permadeath characters. He needed to go after Charlena, but he needed to be careful. Very careful.

Jace looked down at Luna. "Ready to explore an ancient city that could kill us?"

His familiar gave him a cat look that he guessed translated into 'Are you crazy?' and meowed, "No."

"Yeah, me either," Jace said. He took a deep breath and stepped through the doorway.

Chapter 21

Jace was able to enter the doorway with no issues. In VEIL, there was nothing that prevented a low level player from entering a high level zone - one that would surely mean death and losing your body. However, after many complaints the first year, WorldCog had created a system that helped to warn players they were walking to their own death. If a dungeon or area was more than 10 levels higher than the player, they would feel a strong sense of foreboding. The greater the level difference between the player and the monsters, the greater the sense of foreboding.

Since he hadn't felt anything as he walked through the threshold, it meant either everything was within 10 levels of him or his character was corrupted, he hadn't sensed the foreboding. He was tempted to ask Luna, but guessed her reactions were based off of his. In the end, it didn't matter, he still needed to find Charlena, so he looked around the room he'd just entered.

There was a lot of rubble in the initial entry way that Jace had to climb over and he wondered if there had been some sort of earthquake or rockslide that might have opened up the city's entrance. As soon as he moved away from the doorway, there was very little ambient light so Jace activated his *Cat-Vision*.

With his enhanced vision, he could see that he was in a large chamber, perhaps sixty feet long by thirty feet deep. The domed ceiling was a good forty feet above him but parts of it looked to have collapsed.

It appeared that there had once been a statue in the middle of the room, but it lay scattered across the floor along with sections of the ceiling.

Focusing on the floor, he could clearly make out sets of footprints that marred the dust covered floor. Most of them appeared to have been made by skeletal feet. It appeared that would confirm that this was the source of the undead that had been plaguing the village.

Jace also found a set of small booted footprints. He bent down and examined them in his HUD, activating his *Tracking* skill.

Your Tracking skill has increased by 1.
Tracks:
Elf

The trail of tracks was slightly illuminated and according to his *Tracking* skill, the tracks definitely belonged to an elf. Unfortunately, his skill was too low to identify the specific owner. But since this was a human area and Charlena had been the only elf he'd seen so far, he could assume they were hers.

"Charlena," he said aloud.

Luna walked over the tracks and sniffed several times before she looked up at Jace. "Yes."

"You can smell her?"

"Yes."

"Good girl."

Luna sat back on her haunches and looked smug and Jace reached over to pet her head.

"Let's go find her before she gets into trouble," Jace said.

"Yes."

There were three exits from the main chamber he was now on. The tracks lead down the center passage. Worriedly, Jace noticed this was the same passage that the skeletons had emerged from. "That's not good."

Luna seemed to realize the same thing. "No."

Jace wanted to call out to her but doing so could alert the skeletons. He was sure if they were only active on nights of the full moon, or if they only came out on those nights. Trying to call out could put her into more danger than not doing so.

Motioning to Luna, he activated his Stealth skill and entered the center passage. The passage immediately began sloping down. Jace remembered that originally the Veteribus had cities on the surface but some catastrophe happened, and their latter cities were built underground. In fact, he knew of at least one dwarven city that was actually built by the Veteribus.

The passage looked to be about 10 feet wide and 8 feet tall, enough for several people to move side by side. Or one really big monster. He pushed his fears down and continued moving through the gloomy passage.

He'd traveled about 100 yards when the passage widened into a small circular chamber. There were three other exits from the chamber. There was one to the right, one to the left and one that continued in the same direction. Using his *Tracking* skill again, he was able to see her tracks going off the left. Once again, it was the same direction as the skeleton tracks. Was she trying to die?!

Jace shook his head. No, she was following the only tracks she could see, trying to find him. And she might be walking straight into a room full of undead. He needed to move faster.

"Come on," he whispered and quickened his pace. Beside him, Luna silently kept pace. As she ran, she was constantly sniffing the air. He hoped she would be able to warn him before they ran into anything terrible.

The passage split several more times and Jace continued to follow her tracks. From using the *Tracking* skill earlier and then her in the dungeon, he finally got his 10th rank and received a new ability Identify Tracks.

When he saw the system message, he bent down and examined the tracks again. With the new ability, he'd now at least see who they belonged to.

Tracks:
Almedha Pressalor (Elf)

He let out a sigh of relief. It wasn't that he didn't trust Luna's nose, he just appreciated the confirmation. At least now he knew for certain he was on the right trail and he picked up his pace.

At the very edge of his vision, he saw a flash of light. It was bright at first, then went dull.

"Ahhh!" A scream echoed down the passageway.

The voice came from up ahead and it was definitely a woman's voice. The echo and reverberation distorted it, but it had to be her. Unless there were other women hanging around in an underground dungeon built by an ancient race.

Jace ran towards the light as fast as he could and nearly. As he got nearer, he could see the light was coming from the floor. No, not the floor. It was coming from a partially closed pit on the floor. It was partially open with a bow sticking out. He rushed over to it and saw there was a slim hand still grabbing the bow, which was the only thing keeping the pit from closing.

"Charlena?" he called, no longer caring if the undead heard him.

"Jace?" Came a muffled voice.

"Yeah," he said as he grabbed her hand and started to pull.

"Pull me up! Pull me up!" she cried frantically.

Now that he was closer, he could see down into the pit. About 20 feet below Charlena was a swirling vortex. The vortex shimmered and rotated but in the middle was the scene of the outdoors with large, snow-capped mountains in the background. It was a portal. And if Charlena fell into it, she would be transported to wherever it led.

Grabbing her wrist, Jace leaned back and began to pull her up. He only had a 10 Strength, but she was light and soon she began to move upward.

"Don't let go!" she begged as her legs worked to find purchase.

"I won't," Jace promised. Inch by inch, he pulled her up. As he did, the scene in the middle of the vortex changed and it was a barren wasteland surrounded by volcanic mountains. Jace pulled harder. Finally, her other arm cleared the put and she was able to help pull herself out.

With one final heave, he pulled her free of the pit and she landed on top of him.

"Thank you! Thank you!" she panted. "I thought I'd be sent to who knows where."

"It's okay," he told her. A strange thought occurred to him as she lay on top of him. "Isn't this the way we met?"

She stopped and looked down at him underneath him and then began to laugh. "Actually, I think you were on top."

Jace grinned. "And we weren't wearing clothes."

They both laughed and Charlena rolled off of him onto the floor. "Where the heck were you? I came in here to find you."

Jace grimaced. "You actually beat me in here. Jebediah told me an elf had asked for some 'Jason' guy and demanded to know where the tomb was. I figured out where you went and came here as soon as possible."

Her voice turned angry. "Yeah! I was looking for you! I went into town looking for you and the mayor said you went to investigate some undead tomb or something and that the old guy on the last farm knew where it was. He said you left fifteen minutes before me. He said you probably wouldn't be back."

Lying on his back, he couldn't see her expression, but she was obviously frustrated and a little angry. "Sorry. I cut through the forest and…"

"And what?" she demanded.

"And we stopped so Luna could chase butterflies," he said, wincing.

"Butterflies?" she asked with a deadpan voice.

"Butterflies."

There was a long silence and then he thought he heard her crying, until it got louder, and he realized she was laughing.

"You are something else," she said. "By the way, I checked out your story."

Jace sat up and faced her. "My story?"

"Jace Burton, junior programmer for WorldCog," she repeated as if reading a newspaper clip. "Hit by a truck that ran a red light on his way home from work on April 5th. Pronounced dead at the scene."

Jace sat up and looked at her. His heart suddenly felt very heavy. Up until now, part of him hadn't believed it. Or maybe, part of it hadn't accepted it. Hearing her say it aloud suddenly made it all too real. He really was dead. This was his life now. "So, I am dead."

Charlena sat up and put a hand on his arm. "I'm sorry. I checked the newsfeeds in Philadelphia. I did a search on your name and got a hit in a news article.

Sorry I didn't believe you and freaked out. I mean, you have to admit your story sounds unbelievable."

Jace smirked. "Thanks, I think."

She punched him playfully. "Hey, a girl's got to be careful!"

"That's right," he said and gave her a wink. "That virtual sex stuff!"

She made a face and punched him harder this time. "Is that all you guys think of?"

Jace shrugged. "We also think about real sex."

She rolled her eyes and started to pick herself up. She looked over at the pit. "What was that?"

"I think it was a trap. My guess is, it was meant to send trespassers to some random part of the world. And if I had to guess, it resets your spawn point when it does it," he said.

"Resets your spawn point? Why do you think that?" she asked.

"Because Jebediah let slip that they've had other adventurers check this place out and that no one has ever come back," he told her.

"Great! So, what do we do?"

Smiling, Jace stood up. "We explore of course."

Charlena gave him an incredulous look. "We're going to explore the place no one comes back from? Are you crazy?"

Jace held his fingers up about an inch apart.

"A little crazy," she said. "Why do I not find that hard to believe." Charlena gestured back to the pit. "And what about the pit? And any others we run across?"

Jace had seen that there was about a foot of floor on each side of the pit. He guessed that's how the undead were getting around them. But how did mindless undead know to go around the pits?

He searched the floor around the pit and found the answer. There were magical runes on the inside of the pit. He wasn't sure, but he suspected that they were to repel undead.

"What is it?" asked Charlena as she moved up next to him. "Is that… writing?"

"Magical runes," he told her. "Some type of repulsion spell. We can guess what they're designed to repulse."

"Why would they…" she started to ask but worked it out for herself. "To stop the undead from going into the trap."

Jace nodded.

"This isn't a tomb and those undead aren't trying to get revenge on the village for King Ackert killing the necromancer," Jace told her. "Something else is going on."

Chapter 22

Both Jace and Charlena had decided they wanted to explore further. They grouped up and Jace shared the quest from the mayor. Just to make sure one of them didn't accidentally fall into a pit, Jace tied them together with the rope he had bought and was having Charlena test the passageway for pits with her bow. If one of them fell, the other one could brace against the floor until the other climbed up. At least, in theory.

He had originally thought to use it to climb someplace safe if the undead caught him in the forest. The plan had been to knot up the rope, climb a tree and tie it onto a branch. Then, if he needed to make a quick escape, he could run to the tree and shimmy up the rope to safety. He'd been in so much of a hurry to reach Charlena, he hadn't remembered the rope until he'd seen the pit.

"So, you must really know a lot about this game," Charlena commented as they continued down the passage. "I mean, you were a level 90-something character, plus you worked for the company who makes the game. You must know all kinds of inside information!"

Jace smiled. "I know some, but it's mostly about how the game works. I'm a," Jace stopped and corrected himself with a pang of sadness. "I WAS a troubleshooter, fixing bugs in the code. I didn't really do anything with the content. Plus, all the content is under heavy security. They monitor those guys like hawks. If they leak anything, they are not only fired, but sued into poverty."

Charlena scrunched up her nose. "That seems a bit draconian. I mean, it's still just a game."

Jace shrugged. "Yes and no. You can transfer real money into the game and you can convert game money into real money. Wherever there's money, eventually there'll be someone who wants to exploit it."

Jace trailed off as he thought of his own situation. WorldCog had wanted to cover up the bug so badly that they must have killed him and made it look like an accident. He knew how much power they had, it would have been child's play. That made him very nervous. What if he got to the capital and found the *Help Desk* and they just covered it up. And worse, what if they found his brain backup and simply deleted it. That was a terrifying and sobering thought.

"You okay?" Charlena asked beside him.

"What?"

"You looked scared or worried just now."

He didn't know how much of his concerns to tell her. She'd come back to tell him about his death and had been willing to go into a "supposed" tomb to do it. He wasn't sure if she knew about players disappearing or not, or even if she understood the ramifications. She could always just delete her character and create a new one. Jace wasn't sure that applied to him and he didn't want to find out the hard way.

"I'm fine," he lied. "Just remembering that I'm dead."

A pained look crossed her features. "Yeah, sorry about that. I guess I just blurted it out without thinking. In my defense, I had been dangling over a portal to who knows where right before that."

"Sometimes you just have to rip the band aid off." Jace gave her a smile. He understood. That was a devious trap and he had respect for whatever designer came up with the idea. It would be a great way to separate a party or raid. He was actually surprised he hadn't seen a trap like that before.

There was an awkward pause and then Charlena asked another question. "What do you think this place is?"

Happy for the change of topic, Jace related his thoughts about the city and an abbreviated explanation of the Ancient Ones. He also recited the inscription on the door. "Welcome to the City of Crystalburrow. Let those with violence in their hearts be warned: The immortal guardians stand ever vigilant."

Frowning, Charlena paused. "So this is like some ancient city that no one's ever explored?"

Jace thought about it. "It's possible. Remember how I said that adventurers had disappeared from here. None returned so maybe they fell victim to the traps. So they may not have made it into the city proper."

"That's exciting then!" She perked up. "We might be the first!"

Her enthusiasm was infectious and he found himself smiling. "We might be! As long as we're careful. Remember, we're following the same path as the skeletons. At some point, we may run into them."

That seemed to steal some wind from her sails. "What do we do if that happens?"

"Probably die," Jace said honestly.

Charlena smiled and motioned with her hands. "Come on, think positive!"

It was Jace's turn to smile. "Okay, I'm positive we'll die."

Making a dismissive gesture, she playfully punched him on the arm. "That's not what I meant."

"I know," he chuckled. "Hopefully, we'll think of something. There's usually more than one way out of situations in this game. You just have to use your head."

She flashed him a dazzling smile. "See, much better!"

Grinning, he motioned her to continue checking the corridor for pit traps as they moved deeper into Crystalburrow. They'd found two others so far and like the previous one, the skeletons moved around them to walk on the sides. That meant the first pit hadn't been a fluke. The skeletons were part of the city and the builders, or game designers, had made accommodations for them.

But something didn't seem right. He didn't remember the Veteribus using necromancy. In the other ruins and underground towns he'd explored or quested in, he'd never seen any undead. In fact, they'd used almost exclusively golems.

Jace stopped in his tracks causing Charlena to halt with a start. "What?!"

"I don't think those were skeletons," he told her, mulling the idea in his mind. It would make sense. They come at night. No one ever got a really good look at them. It was possible they weren't skeletons at all, but golems. Golems made to resemble the thin limbed Veteribus. "I think they might be golems."

She looked at him perplexed. "Golems?"

"Uh," he tried to think of how to explain them. "They're like robots, only animated and programmed with magic instead of technology."

"Robots," she said dubiously.

"Like robots," he corrected. "But animated creatures made of wood, stone, metal or even bone. The Ancient Ones were masters of creating golems."

Charlena still looked doubtful. "Everyone in the village said they were skeletons."

"Yes, but they always come at night and people are locked away in their houses," he told her. "They could be a band of babbling baboons for all they know. Plus, the Ancient Ones are tall, slender humanoids who look like aliens, with those large heads and bulbous eyes."

Charlena looked around. "What does this mean for us?"

"Not much difference," he told her. "When it comes down to it, golems and undead are fairly similar except in how they are animated. Golems are animated with magic and runes while undead are animated with necromancy."

Charlena pursed her lips. "I'll take your word for it. But basically, our situation hasn't really changed."

Jace thought about it. "Not really."

"We keep going?"

"We keep going."

They kept going for what felt like a mile before they saw light at the end of the tunnel - literally and figuratively.

"What is that light?" asked Charlena, coming to a halt.

"I have a suspicion," Jace told her and motioned her to continue. "Let's see if I'm right."

Another hundred yards and Jace's theory was proven right. The passage opened into an enormous cavern which went on for what could have been a mile or more. Inside the cavern was a city sculpted from some sort of ivory or pure white stone with unerring perfection. The alien look to the buildings with their sharp curves and nearly no straight lines, marked it as a Veteribium city.

"Oh wow," he heard Charlena gasp next to him.

He knew the feeling. Even though he'd seen the Ancient Ones' cities before, this one was different. What made it different was the illumination. Previous cities had used some sort of animated lamps on the buildings that gave the cities a perpetual night feeling. This city looked like it was nearly in full daylight. Glancing around the cavern roof, he realized why.

Embedded in the ceiling was some sort of enormous crystals that seemed to have a natural illuminance. There were hundreds, or even thousands, of them embedded in the roof. Had the Veteribus found this deposit of glowing crystals and built the city around them? Or had they discovered how to create the crystals and then embed them in their city?

"What's that?" Charlena said, pointing to something near the center of the city. It looked like some sort of giant observatory that was at two hundred feet taller than the rest of the buildings. At the top were three huge circular objects that resembled tinted mirrors. One was white, one was red and the last was black - the same color as the moons. As he strained his eyes, he could see that the red and white mirrors were cracked but the black one seemed to be intact.

"I have no idea," Jace told her. "But I think we should have a look."

"Won't we run into those undead… golem creatures?" she asked.

Jace frowned. If they were golems, then they had been programmed with a task. In other Ancient Ones cities, he'd seen where golems continued to clear the streets or clean houses, thousands of years after their masters had died off. He'd also battled guard golems programmed to protect a room or items in a room.

"We may," Jace told her as he started to untie the rope from them. Hopefully, there would be no pit traps in the city itself.

Undoing the knots, he looked down the stairs that lead from the passage to the floor of the city, nearly two hundred feet down. There were no signs of golems, but they could be anywhere in the city.

Bending down, he looked at the steps. Unlike the passageway, there was no dust on the steps at all. Something must be cleaning the steps. That presented two problems. First, something was regularly and consistently coming up to where they were now. And second, without dust, he had no idea where the skeletons or golems went. "The steps are clean."

"What does that mean?"

Jace considered the options. "Something or someone is keeping them clean."

"Golems?" she asked quietly, casting worried glances around the city. "Ancient Ones?"

"The Ancient Ones are all dead. But maybe some sort of cleaning golem," Jace said. "Keep your eyes open."

Charlena looked out into the sprawling alien city. "Are we sure this is a good idea? When will those undead or golems or whatever wake up?"

"At nightfall," Jace told her.

"When's that?"

"I have no idea," he told her.

"Oh geez," she said, looking at him incredulously. "You're crazy aren't you?"

Once again, Jace held his fingers up about an inch apart.

Charlena let out an exasperated breath. "That's right, you are a little crazy. Well, if I die, you'd better help me get my body!"

"Likewise," he shot back.

"Are you ready?" he asked her.

"As ready as I'll ever be," she retorted.

With that, the two of them began descending the long steps down into a dead city, made by a dead race. What could possibly go wrong?

As if to answer his question, a low moaning began in the center of the city.

Chapter 23

Luna hissed and Charlena stopped in her tracks, turning to Jace wide eyed. "What is that?"

His cat darted between his legs as Jace took a deep breath. "That would be the undead, or whatever they are."

"Are you sure you want to go down there?" she asked, her voice concerned and perhaps a little frightened.

"Not really," Jace confessed. "But I do want to understand what's going on here. Plus, we could be the first players to see this place. That would be kind of cool."

Her face brightened. "You think so?"

"There's so much of VEIL, I don't think everyone's seen everything. There's floating cloud cities, underground empires and that's not even talking about the oceans and what's under them."

"Wow, I didn't know there was so much. It's a lot to explore."

"And I'll have a long time to explore it all," Jace nodded sadly.

Her face softening, Charlena put a hand on his shoulder. "I'm sorry."

Jace shrugged. "Nothing I can do about it now but make the best of it. But it's off to a good start, I met this cute girl who plays the game." He gave her a wink.

Blushing, she punched him lightly and turned away. She wasn't quite quick enough to hide her smile.

"We'd better start down these steps," he said, bringing their attention to the reason they were here. "I don't know when they will start heading to the village but we should be someplace safe before they do."

Charlena nodded and the two of them began to descend the steps. Jace turned to see Luna reluctantly following them. "You okay?"

Luna didn't bother to look up at him. "Scary sound."

"I know," he told her. "But we'll be safe."

Luna gave him what he thought was a doubtful look but didn't reply. Turning back around they continued descending into the city.

Sooner that he would have thought, they were at the bottom, looking into a wide city street with the alien-looking buildings towering over them. As they had descended, the moaning sound had gradually gotten louder. It was definitely coming from somewhere in the city.

Jace looked down the street of strange buildings. Most of them were two stories tall with a few one and three story buildings scattered throughout.

"Let's look in one," he said, pointing to a nearby doorway. While the entire structure was smooth ivory stone, there was an outline for a door on the side of the building. It was made for a being at least two feet taller than humans, another tell-tale sign this city was built by the Ancient Ones.

The two of them walked to the door and stood in front of it. After a moment, Charlena turned to him. "And you know how to open this?"

Jace looked at the smooth surface of the door and the area around the door. Nothing stood out as a doorknob or anything else that might open the door. He looked back at her. "Theoretically," he said and then paused as he looked up and down the door again. "No."

Charlena let out a breath. "Well, our exploration is off to a good start."

Jace chuckled. "We're quite the great explorers. Can't even get in the first building."

That elicited a giggle and they moved on to a couple other doorways. In each case, they saw what appeared to be a large, smooth door by the outline but there was no visible way to open it. Jace even tried walking up to the door and waving his hands to see if it was motion activated. Nothing worked and the doors remained sealed.

As they got closer to the center of the city, Jace did notice that the moaning sound seemed to get louder. He checked with Charlena and she agreed.

"Maybe locked the doors when they left," Charlena said as they tried another door.

"I guess so," Jace shrugged. "Maybe we'll have more luck with the big building."

Charlena glanced up at the large observatory building and gave him a doubtful look. "Are you sure you want to go there? I mean, that does seem to be where the moaning sound is coming from."

She had a point. For all he knew that large building was where the skeleton things were. Still, he felt like he needed to know what was there. It was almost as if something was drawing him in. Maybe his sense of curiosity?

"We'll be careful," he told her. "When we get close, we'll switch to stealth and at least see if we can determine what that building is."

Carefully they move towards the center of the city, checking the alleys they ran across for any signs of the skeletons. The moaning definitely got louder as they moved closer to the center. Not only that, but Jace had an odd itching feeling on his skin the closer they got. He didn't think anything of it until he saw that Luna also became more agitated the further into the city they went.

"Are you okay Luna?" Jace finally asked her.

The cat looked up at him, ears flattened against her head. "Sound... bad."

He looked back at the large building. "The moaning?"

"Sound hurt," the cat whined.

Jace was taken back. Did the moaning actually hurt her? How could that be? He bent down and scooped her up and held her, petting her head. "I'm sorry Luna. I didn't know it was hurting you."

He looked back the way they came. "Was it hurting you at the top of the steps?"

"No," she retorted.

Putting Luna back down on the ground, he pointed back towards the steps. "Go back to the steps and wait for us there. Go as far as you need to so that it doesn't hurt."

"Yes," she said, and the little orange tabby took off for the steps.

Charlena, who had witnessed the exchange but obviously hadn't understood his "cat speak," gave him a questioning look.

"The sound is hurting her ears," he told her, "so I sent her back to the steps."

"The sound was hurting her?" Charlena asked, concerned. "Do you think it's some sort of high frequency sound like a dog whistle or something?"

Jace cocked his head. A dog whistle? Human's couldn't hear a sound at high pitches but animals could. Was that what they were dealing with? Some sort of sound that was out of normal human range? What would be causing that? "You could be right. But what would be causing it?"

Charlena looked around. "I don't know." She shivered. "But something about this place does make my skin crawl."

Jace snapped his head to her. "You feel it too? Like an itch all over your body?"

"Not really like that, just a weird feeling," she said.

Jace thought about it for a moment. "What's your sensitivity level set at?"

Charlena's eyes went glassy while she looked at her HUD and then they cleared. "15%"

"Can you do me a favor, turn it up to say 90% and see if you feel anything," he told her.

Charlena's eyes went wide. "90%?! Are you crazy? Wait… I know... "She held her fingers about an inch apart. "A little bit. I don't know if that's a good idea…"

Jace held up his hands in a placating gesture. "I know. Just turn it up and see if you feel anything and then turn it back down."

Grudgingly she nodded. "It's a good thing you're cute." And then her eyes went glassy.

Jace just stared at her. Had she just called him cute?

"Your mouth is open," she said smiling, her eyes clear again. Then suddenly she shivered and started scratching. "Okay… okay… it's seriously itchy! Geez! How do you put up with it?"

"You can turn it back down," Jace told her. "I learned what I needed."

"So, it's affecting both of us," she said, "and the cat."

"Yes," Jace said. "But I'm not sure what IT is. I think we need to get to the observatory - or whatever it is."

Charlena looked up at the ominous structure and swallowed. "I was afraid you were going to say that." She looked back at him. "Are you going to be able to deal with that - whatever that itching sensation is?"

"I'll have to," Jace told her. At this point, the only other alternative seemed to be turning around and going back to the village. They could also go back and explore the other tunnels. Yet something kept drawing him to the observatory. The strange and, if he admitted it, scary thing about it was, he wasn't sure why he felt so compelled to go there. It was almost as if he were thirsty and he knew there was water there.

"You okay?" Charlena asked, breaking him out of his thoughts.

"Yeah," he said. "Let's go. But keep in stealth. Something doesn't feel right and I'm not sure what it is."

Charlena rolled her eyes. "We're in an ancient, forgotten city that probably has murderous undead or golems or something and there's some unseen force making us itch and causing the cat to go nuts. Plus there's an insane moaning coming from where we're headed. And you're not sure what doesn't feel right?"

"Well, when you put it like that," Jace chuckled and they both shared a quick laugh.

The mirth was quickly over and they *stealthed* up and continued into the center of the city. It took another 15 minutes of creeping before they were within 100 feet of the building and they stopped.

"Do you see what I see?" Charlena whispered.

Jace nodded. Unlike the other structures they had passed, this building had a door that was twice as wide as the others. Also, unlike the other structures, this door was open. "Isn't this usually the part of the vid where the heroes go into the obvious trap and all die."

Charlena slowly turned to him and gave him an incredulous look. Then she brightened. "I'll give you a Scooby snack if you go in."

Jace stared open mouthed at her. Had she just made an obscure reference to the old vids? He loved the old vids from the turn of the century, but it was rare to find someone else who shared his love of, as people called it "antique vids".

"It's an ancient vid," she started.

"An old animation," he broke in.

"Cartoon," she corrected, smiling. "You know what it is?"

"Vaguely. Something about some kids who are detectives and they have a dog, right?"

Charlena smiled broadly. "You do know! It's on the retro streams. Good stuff!"

"We'll have to talk about it when we get out of here," he told her. "Let's sneak up to the door and see what's inside."

She nodded and followed him around one of the buildings nearby so they could come in from the side. This prevented them from being seen from anything inside, but also prevented them from seeing what was inside until they were right next to the door.

The itching sensation was almost unbearable at this point and the moaning was as loud as it had been when he was locked in the cellar with them pounding outside. Only now, in the absolute quiet of the dead city, it seemed much louder.

Staying in *Stealth*, they crept quietly along the side of the observatory. He'd checked with Charlena and her *Stealth* skill wasn't maxed so he told her to let him know if she got any skill ups. If she did, that would mean a creature was nearby that the skill was actively working to hide her from. It was sort of like a cheat, but it only worked until your skill was maxed out for your level like Jace's was. Once that happened, you were on your own.

Feeling Charlena's hand on his shoulder, he looked over to her. She gave him a meaningful look and nodded towards the door. She'd received a skill up. Something was inside. Jace nodded his understanding. He motioned her to stay and gestured that he was going to take a look.

Jace crept the last few feet to the door and stopped. Taking a deep breath, he slowly peered around the corner of the door and looked into the large circular chamber inside. What he saw was nothing like he expected.

Chapter 24

Jace wasn't sure what he had been expecting inside the observatory, but this wasn't it. The building was one large chamber. Lining the walls of the chamber were box-like alcoves that looked like upright coffins without lids. There were circles of coffins in the center of the room as well. Inside the coffins were skeletons, hundreds of them.

"We found the skeletons," Jace muttered quietly. Charlena gave him a worried expression. Stepping back, he motioned for her to take a look. She squeezed around him and peeked into the building.

"We are totally screwed," she whispered as she moved back behind him.

It was hard to disagree with her. Yet he still felt compelled to check it out. He might die. He might even lose his equipment, but he needed to check out the chamber. It was that strange compulsion that both prodded him on and frightened him.

"I'm going to go check it out," he told her quietly.

Her eyes went wide but she kept her voice low. "Are you crazy?!"

"I want you to stay here," he told her. "I'll give you my stuff. If I die and they come after you, run away from this building. Since the rest of the city is deserted, we can come back and get our stuff as long as it's not near the building.

"Are you serious?" she asked him, her face portraying her doubt.

"Yes," he told her. "I need to go into that room. I can't explain why. It's like something is drawing me in."

"Oh geez," she muttered. "Go down into the basement to check the breaker while there's a murderer in the house."

Jace chuckled quietly. "I know, it's almost a horror vid clique, but I need to do it."

Charlena rolled her eyes and let out an exasperated breath. "Fine. But you'd better be right about us getting our stuff back."

Jace gave her a boyish grin and a wink. "It's all right, trust me."

Charlena raised an eyebrow. "Channeling your inner Solo?"

Jace grinned broadly that she got the reference. He hadn't met any other women who enjoyed the old vids like he did. He definitely needed to talk with her more when they got out of this. He glanced back at the doorway. IF they got out of this.

Stripping off his gear, he initiated a trade and passed it to her. She accepted the trade and he was once again, completely naked except for his loincloth. He glanced back at her to see that she was eyeing his body and he immediately felt his face get warm.

Charlena noticed his blush and smiled wickedly. "Looks like there's a bright side to this after all."

Feeling both embarrassed and pleased by the praise, he turned to go. She caught his hand, leaned in and kissed him on the cheek. "For luck."

Her kiss was warm and wet on his cheek and sent shivers up his spin. He was thankful this one time that his sensory level was set to maximum. He smiled and then turned away so she wouldn't see him grinning like an idiot.

Taking a deep breath, Jace crept into the room and stopped. Nothing happened. The skeletons remained in their chambers unmoving. Now that he was inside the room, he could make out more details.

The first was that he noticed some sort of pipes lining the inside walls of the chamber. They were thin and ran the height of the enormous room, all the way up to the ceiling. Looking up, Jace could see that the ceiling was open and he could just make out the mirrors he'd seen earlier.

Second, this was absolutely the source of the moaning. The sound echoed around the chamber, making it impossible to pinpoint exactly where it was coming from but one thing was clear from the sheer volume - this was the source.

Looking around the chamber, he also noticed that the coffins weren't a uniform color. About a third of them were red, another third were white, and the remaining third were black. Jace remembered the mirrors at the top of the observatory. They were the same colors. Was there a connection?

The closest alcove was red and Jace crept around to the side of it. He peeked his head around quickly and then back around. It had been too quick to get a good look but he had seen enough to know there was a skeleton inside. He waited for the skeleton to come out of the alcove and attack him.

Nothing happened. Jace peeked around again, intending to take a longer look and then duck back around but he froze once he'd gotten a good look. These weren't skeletons. They were golems. They were made out of the same ivory stone that the city was made out of. The golems had long, slender arms and legs, as well as thin bodies that made them resemble skeletons. Up close, Jace could see their joints and crystal eyes. But the tell-tale sign was the large red gyroscopic device in the middle of the chest. It was most definitely a golem, no doubt created by the Ancient Ones.

The one he was looking at appeared to have the remnants of an ancient set of leather armor on it but the moment Jace touched it with his finger, it disintegrated into a pile of dust and small pieces at the bottom of the alcove.

Jace watched it carefully for any signs that it would animate but after several minutes of it not moving, he relaxed. It was deactivated. Or, it's power cell had run out. Like all constructs, a magical "battery," or power cell, animated them. How long the golem stayed animated depending on how much magic was put into the "battery." Unlike the rest of the city, Jace noticed that a thick layer of dust covered this skeletal golem.

Slowly, he moved to the next alcove, keeping an eye on the first golem. When it still didn't move, he relaxed and checked out the next one. The second golem was identical to the first and it also had a layer of dust on it.

Going from alcove to alcove, Jace examined several more of the golems. They were identical in every way. And none of them seemed to be active. Not only that, but they appeared not to have been activated for some time.

All the alcoves he'd looked at had been red, so Jace moved to the opposite side of the chamber to examine the white alcoves. These also had skeletal golems that were identical in every way to the others except for one thing. The golems in the white alcoves had white gyroscopic devices instead of red. Did that mean these golems had some other purpose? Or was it related to the mirrors?

He turned to the circle of alcoves in the center of the room. They were all black. He started to move towards them and suddenly noticed the floor had thick black metal lines on it that ran from the walls to the alcoves. He cocked his head and looked at them. They were almost like the lines on the old fashioned circuit boards that took current from one part to another part.

Going back to the white alcoves against the wall, he looked all around them until he spotted what he was looking for. The white alcoves had a white metal line running from the wall to the back of the alcove. He guessed if he looked behind the red alcoves he'd find red metal bands connecting them to the wall.

Jace looked up at the mirrors again and then followed the "pipes" down the walls with his eyes to where they intersected the floor. Was this what he thought it was? Was this some sort of recharging station for the golems? But what powered it? This was underground so the mirrors couldn't be powered by the sun. What else could…

It hit him then. The moons. The moons were said to be the source of all magical energy and the home of the gods. Had the Ancient Ones figured out a way to tap into that energy to power their constructs? He looked back up. There was a mirror for each of the moons, capturing their energy and then relaying it down the pipes. No, not pipes, they were cables of some sort. The magical energy was sent down the cables into the alcoves and must have recharged the power cells of the golems. He grinned, no, they weren't alcoves or coffins, they were recharging stations.

His smile faded as he remembered the black mirror was still intact. Was it possible it was still recharging the golems in the black recharging stations? There was only one way to find out. Taking a deep breath, he crept closer to the black alcoves.

Jace crept to the back of the nearest black station and paused with some trepidation. If the black pods were being recharged, then the golems inside were most likely active. That meant, if he peaked around, it might see him. But he had to know.

Slowly, Jace peeked around the recharging station. Inside was a skeletal golem, just like the others with two main differences. The first difference was the color of it's gyroscope. It was black. The second was that the gyroscope was spinning at an incredible velocity. The spinning was creating a whirring sound that closely resembled a moan.

He was congratulating himself for his discovery when the head of the golem turned and the glowing eye crystals stared right into his eyes. For a brief moment Jace froze, transfixed by those crystal eyes. Then he backpedaled away from the station only to bump into the station next to it. His bare feet lost their footing and he fell, tumbling into the middle of the black stations. Almost as one, the golems in the black stations which now encircled him turned their heads to regard him.

Jace froze for long seconds as the golems regarded him. Then, as suddenly as they had moved their heads to look at him, they all moved their heads back into their original positions. Still holding his breath, Jace waited to see if the golems would do anything else.

After nearly a minute, Jace finally let out his breath. Slowly, he got to his feet. None of the golems acknowledged his presence. He took a step back towards the entrance. Again, there was no reaction from the golems.

He took another and then another until he finally turned and started back towards the door.

That's when he heard a loud clicking sound from high up in the ceiling. He stopped and looked upward. The black mirror had started to move. Suddenly the entire room began to thrum and he saw the black cables coming from the ceiling start to glow. The black metal lines that went from the floor to pods began to glow as well and Jace felt the itching feeling starting to grow unbearable. He clenched his jaw to stop from scratching.

The pods themselves began to glow and the whirring sound of the golem's gyroscopes increased in pitch until it was beginning to hurt his ears. Then there was another clicking sound and the floor in the center of the room began to open.

Fascinated, Jace watched the center section of the flood split into two, revealing a large opening 20 or 30 foot in diameter. He noticed then that there were red, white and black metal lines running directly into the opening. Were there more pods under the floor?

He started to take a step towards the opening to look in when a new sound emerged from the hole. It was like the whirring from the golems, only higher pitched - almost a whine. That's when he saw a long, slender insect-like leg appear out of the opening and set down on the floor.

"Time to wake already?" said a whispery female voice as the rest of a spider-like body emerged from the opening. Eight crystal eyes stared down at Jace from a giant spider golem body. "Oh, and what delicious morsel has come to entertain me?"

Chapter 25

Behind him, Jace heard Charlena scream and that broke him out of his paralyzing stupor. He spun to run but with unnatural speed, then spider golem moved between him and the door. "Going somewhere, my little naked pet?"

Jace froze, once again staring at the spider's eight crystal eyes. He noticed that this golem too had a gyroscope in it's thorax that whirled with that high pitched whine.

"Run," he whispered to Charlena. "Run!"

"No, no," said the spider in its almost seductive female voice. "No one leaves the party until I say so."

There was no indication that the spider golem had done anything, but suddenly a dozen skeletal golems sprang from their alcoves and ran towards Charlena.

"Run Charlena! Run!" he yelled out.

The spider laughed. "Is that your girlfriend? Or maybe she's a virtual flame that you hide away from your real life wife."

"She's not my…" Jace had started to retort until the spider's words sank in. The spider had said "real life!" It knew about the outside world. Could this be another player? He realized the spider had stopped moving, as had the skeletons.

"Did… did you… understand me?" asked the spider golem with a hint of desperation in her voice.

"Yes," Jace said. He remembered back to Duglas and had an eerie deja vu. "You're a player who was inserted into the game when you died, right?"

"Yes," gasped the spider. "How did you know? And how do you understand me when no one else was able to?"

"Jace?" came Charlena's voice from behind him.

Turning, he saw that she had stopped running when the skeletons had stopped and had crept back to the door. "I think it's okay. I'm pretty sure she's another player like Duglas."

"Pretty sure?" she asked.

"She can't understand me?" the spider golem asked.

"No, just me," he told the golem.

"You want to stay there?" Jace asked Charlena.

She seemed to consider for a moment and finally gave a little shake of her head. She came towards Jace and the skeletons all parted for her as she did. Then, the skeletons ran back to their alcoves and went inert.

"Why is it only you can understand me?" asked the spider again, more insistent this time.

"Because I'm dead too," Jace told her, once again feeling that pang of regret and sadness. "I was inserted into the game as a monster."

"You were a monster too?" she asked incredulously.

"Yes, I… wait, do you have a name that I can call you?" Jace asked.

"Name," the spider thing muttered. "My name? Oh my god, I haven't said or heard my name since I died. My name is Anika Holden, but you might know me as Diana Stewart."

"Diana Stewart?" Jace repeated.

"Diana Stewart?!" Charlena exclaimed from beside him. "THE Diana Stewart?!"

Jace turned to her and asked, "Do you know her?"

At the same time the spider golem said happily, "You know me?"

Charlena looked between the spider and Jace, her face alight with excitement. "Geez! I wish I could understand her! Diana Stewart. She's a romance novelist. She wrote the *Scandalous Queen* series and the *Midnight Earl*. Wow! It's great to meet you. Well… you know… meet you in this life or game… or whatever."

"Yes," Diana told him sadly. "That used to be me. Once upon a time. And now, I am the Spider Queen, feared monster of the underground city."

"I'm sorry," Jace told her and then translated for Charlena. "The same thing happened to me. I believe there is a bug in the insertion routine. But I know a way you can turn yourself into a woman."

"Really?" Diana asked, her voice excited. "You mean, I don't have to be this… thing for all eternity?"

Jace smiled at her. "It worked for me and it worked for Duglas, another player who had the same bug."

"So, I'm in this body instead of a beautiful elf body, living a life of luxury because of a bug?" Diana demanded.

"I'm afraid so," Jace replied. He remembered that he was still standing in nothing but his loincloth. "Charlena, do you think I could get my clothes back now?"

"Oh cutie," purred the spider. "Don't get dressed on my account. I can't even remember the last time I saw some young stud mostly naked."

Jace blushed furiously and Charlena demanded that he translate what she said. When he told her, she burst out laughing. "Well, you are pretty cute."

"Oh dearie," said the spider as Jace equipped his gear again. "If I was 30 years younger and not in the body of a spider, I'd be all over that."

Blushing again as he translated, Jace tried to change the subject. "So yes, it is a bug."

"And here I thought it was a plot by my publicist to keep all my royalties," Diana said. "Either that, or I really did go to hell."

Jace gave her a questioning look. "You had your royalties transferred into the game?"

"Yes, every month my royalties were supposed to be transferred into the game. I was supposed to be living like a queen right now," she said wistfully.

"It's terrible," Charlena said, after Jace had translated. "You're such a good novelist! You deserved better."

"I like this girl. She's a keeper." Diana chuckled, a strange sound from the golem. "Let's get back to the part where you make me human."

Jace explained how he'd become human and then how he'd helped Duglas do the same. He found out that she'd actually never played the game before, she had just been coached by her publicist. He also found out that she was worth about 10 million dollars. But since she had no family to leave it to, she had donated most of it to charity and had the rest inserted into the game for her - along with the monthly royalties. She literally should be living like a queen with all that gold.

She'd also been responsible for the player disappearances. She'd fought off a few players before realizing they just respawned and came back. Then she'd figured out that if they fell into the traps, they didn't come back. She'd been having the skeletal golems grapple the players and throw them into the pits. Clever.

Unfortunately, she'd made the mistake of sending the golems to the city, thinking to scare them into not sending any more adventurers. But the game had compensated by creating a quest to end the "skeleton" scourge.

Finally, he learned that she had been inserted into this spider golem and she had never died. Which meant she had never monster hopped. This seemed to make her a bit skeptical when Jace mentioned she had to die for the process to work.

"So, you've actually only done this twice," she asked skeptically. "And I have to die for it to work?"

"Yes," Jace told her. "But there's no reason to believe it wouldn't work for you."

"But if it doesn't, I could end up as some other monster? What if I don't come back?"

Jace nodded. "There is no reason you wouldn't respawn. And if for some reason it wouldn't work, then yes, you would end up in some other monster's body."

Diana was quiet for a long while. "I don't know. It seems like quite a risk."

Jace shrugged. "I won't lie to you. It is a risk. And even if you do become human, you'll have to make your way in the game, starting from scratch. You will literally have nothing. But you can go out and adventure, earn things and make a life for yourself until they fix the bug."

"I... I don't know how," she admitted.

"It's not that hard," Charlena told her once Jace translated. "I'm a new player and it's not that hard. You just have to watch out for creeps. But that's no different than real life."

"That's the truth," Diana agreed. "Romance novels were my way of living vicariously. I had more than my share of creeps." The spider golem many eyes rotated. "You two make a cute couple though."

Jace blushed as he translated it and was surprised to see that Charlena did too.

"Oh," laughed Diana. "You two must be young. So adorable."

Diana was silent again for a long moment that stretched into an awkward silence. Just when Jace was about to say something she spoke up. "Okay, I'll do it. But how am I supposed to die. Do I… kill myself?"

"You could do that," Jace said. "Or we can kill you."

"If you kill me, you get the...uh… experience?" asked Diana. "And that makes you more powerful?"

Jace nodded, as did Charlena when Jace had translated. "Yes."

"If this does actually work, then I think you should get the experience as the only reward I can give you," she said merrily. Then her tone became more sober. "It will… hurt… won't it?"

"Just until you die," Jace offered. "Then you'll be in your new human body."

"Alone and naked," she retorted sardonically.

Charlena listened to the translation and walked up to the spider golem. She put her hand on it's head. "You won't be alone. We're going to the capital," she turned to Jace expectantly.

"The capital is called Whitecliff, it's the capital of Aldor, the human kingdom," he supplied.

"Right, we're going to Whitecliff. If you can make your way there, you can meet up with us," Charlena offered. "Then you won't be alone. If you get there, we'll try to meet you at the first pub inside the main gate. We'll go there every evening for dinner once we arrive."

"You're kind to an old lady," the spider golem said. "Whitecliff. Aldor. First pub. Got it. If it is possible, I will meet you there."

Diana paused again, her spider face an unreadable mask. "Okay, I'm ready." The spider golem turned it's back to them. In a sad voice, Jace heard her say. "Come, sir, your *passado*."

Jace wasn't sure what she meant, but Charlena both did sneak attacks on her back side. Unfortunately, their first attacks weren't powerful enough to kill her outright and he cringed as Diana cried out. "Death, death; oh, amiable, lovely death! Come, grin on me, and I will think thou smilest."

They struck a second time and finally a third time before the spider golem collapsed onto the ground, a broken ruin.

Crystalburrow Control Drone dies.
You gain 80 experience.

Seeing the experience, Jace guessed Diana must have been some sort of mini-boss. As they looked down at Diana's body, the whirring from the other golems slowly came to a stop and they were plunged into silence. Not only that, the itching sensation immediately disappeared.

Jace heard a sob and turned to see tears streaming down Charlena's face. He stepped closer and put an arm around her shoulder and she buried her face in his arm.

"That was so terrible!" she cried into his arm.

"I know," he said softly. "I know. But hopefully she'll… Charlena look!"

Jace had seen the body of the spider starting to change, much like Duglas' body. Charlena raised her head and watched with rapt fascination. Before their eyes, the spider golem twisted and twitched as it transformed into the body of an attractive raven haired woman.

"Does that mean it worked?" Charlena asked, wiping the tears from her face with the back of her hand.

"I think so!" Jace told her. "That's what happened to me. My body morphed from kobold into human and then I was able to respawn."

Charlena jumped into his arms and gave him a huge hug. "Thank you for helping her."

Jace smiled and patted her on the back. "Of course. I certainly don't wish that sort of hell on anyone."

She broke the embrace and stepped back. "You're a good man, Jace Burton."

Jace looked around conspiratorially. "Shh.. Don't let it out. I don't want to ruin my reputation."

"Oh, I'm sure," she said, jabbing him playfully with an elbow. "You have quite the reputation as a hell-raising, vagabond junior programmer!"

They shared a laugh. Curious, Jace walked over to the opening where Diana had emerged from. Looking down, he saw some sort of special recharging station that had obviously been made for the spider golem. He also saw a large chest next to it.

"Yes!" he cried out and Charlena came over to look down as well. "Loot!"

"You men," he heard Charlena say next to him, "and your fascination with big chests!"

Chapter 26

They had climbed down into Diana's chamber and looted the chest. It contained a compound long bow, called *Earthshadow*, as well as a rapier, called *Netherlight*. The bow went to Charlena, while the foil went to Jace.

"Wow," Charlena said as she tried out the bow. "This is really nice!"

Jace agreed but was looking at his own weapon with a degree of respect. It was nowhere near the daggers he'd had as Mordred, but it was nice for a low level character like him. He viewed the statistics in his HUD.

Netherlight
Type: Rapier
Damage: 8 + 1 (Dark)
Wt: 3 lb
Description: Found in the ancient underground city of Crystalburrow, this rapier is imbued with the dark energy of Dubh.

Charlena's long bow was almost identical to his rapier and she was itching to use it.

Earthshadow
Type: Longbow
Damage: 8 + 1 (Dark)
Wt: 5 lb

Description: Found in the ancient underground city of Crystalburrow, this compound longbow is imbued with the dark energy of Dubh.

After checking around the room for any other loot, they climbed back up and headed back to the entrance.

"So, all this," Charlena gestured to the city. "Just for that one little room full of golems? Was that all there was to it?"

Jace shrugged. "It's possible. But who we'll never know. The moment Diana was inserted into the Control Drone, things changed. She was bound by the monster's parameters and started doing her own things. The overall game AI adapts and generates quests accordingly. If she hadn't been put here, who knows what this area would be like."

"That's wild! So, players who've died with this bug could be wreaking havoc with the game?" she asked.

"Possibly," Jace smiled. "You hear about strange things happening in the game from time to time but usually they're chalked up to exaggeration or a player who just wants to get attention. Who knows, maybe they've been bugged players."

"Ghosts in the machine?" Charlena raised an eyebrow.

"Ghosts in the machine." Jace smiled. "Literally."

"But they'll be able to fix you, right?" she asked, her tone grown serious.

Jace pretended to be offended. "What? You don't like this version of me?"

"It's not that." She rolled her eyes at him. "It's just that you had a character you built up over years and all your money. You should have that!"

"Thanks." Jace smiled.

They walked the rest of the way back to the steps in silence. Waiting at the bottom of the steps, was Luna.

His cat was lying on the first step with her paws tucked under her body and her tail wrapped around her. She appeared to be sleeping but opened a single eye as they drew closer.

"Food?" she meowed hopefully.

"Yes," Jace assured the orange tabby. "We'll go back to the village and get some food."

"What is she saying?" Charlena asked.

"She wants food," he replied. "She always wants food."

Charlena giggled. "Just like a real cat."

They made their way back out of Crystalburrow and back to the Sinking Springs. Along the way, they stopped at two of the outlying farms where they had quests to turn in. It had been the quest that involved Duglas and turning it in was bittersweet. He hoped Duglas was human and doing well.

Once they reached the village itself, they went to the apothecary until Absalom answered. The squat mayor looked at them in surprise when he opened the door.

"You're… you're back," stuttered the mayor and then looked crestfallen. "Did you decide not to help us after all?"

"Quite the opposite," Charlena retorted. Jace saw that she had taken up a very heroic pose and worked to suppress a grin. Who was he to knock someone who wanted to roleplay a bit. "We took care of that pesky problem you were having."

"Wha-?! You… you took care of the skeletons?" the mayor stammered in surprise.

"We did, good sir, mayor," she replied, her chin held high. She was really hamming it up.

The mayor seemed pleased but skeptical. "It's.. uh… not that I don't trust you. I mean, you both seem very heroic." Jace noticed the mayor's eyes darted over his mismatched armor when he said it. "But uh… I need to, well you know… verify that you did, indeed… ah… well… solve our undead problem."

Charlena's heroic facade faltered slightly and she looked to Jace questioningly.

Jace checked the time of day. It was midafternoon judging by the sun. That meant they still had several hours before sunset. "I assume you want to make sure no undead show up tonight before paying us?"

The mayor's chubby head bobbed up and down vigorously. "It's not that I don't trust two fine adventurers such as yourselves. But I have … a… uh… responsibility, yes… a responsibility to the village to verify that the job was done. I'm sure you understand."

"Can we collect the reward tomorrow morning, assuming no undead show up tonight?" Jace asked him.

"I have classes tomorrow," Charlena leaned in and whispered quietly. "I can log in after classes."

"Oh yes," said the mayor. "If the undead do not come tonight, you may collect your reward tomorrow."

"That is acceptable, good mayor," Charlena said, once again resuming her heroic stance.

The mayor nodded and then bolted back into his shop and shut the door. Once the door was shut, Jace let loose the laugh he'd been holding in.

"What?" asked Charlena, giving him an indignant look. "I was in the role. I'm a heroic elf warrior." She gave him her heroic stance, but he could see the smile creeping on her face.

Jace stopped laughing and nodded. "So you are."

The smile finally broke through and she relaxed her posture. "Well, I figured… when in Rome."

"Indeed," he said. "No reason not to play the part."

"Exactly," she smiled for a moment. Then her expression went serious. "Sorry Jace, but I need to log out and do some homework for school."

Jace was disappointed, but he knew she had a real life, back in the real world. This was still just a game for her. He forced a smile. "No problem. I'll see you back here tomorrow?"

"Yes. I have classes and then homework. But after that, I'll log back in and we can collect our quest reward!"

"Sounds good," he told her. "See you tomorrow."

"Before I go," she started hesitantly. "Do you… do you want me to try to tell WorldCog about your predicament? Try to get help?"

"No!" Jace snapped, louder than he had intended and was her hurt expression. He took a breath. "No, please. I don't want you to contact WorldCog at all. They don't know about you and I want to keep it that way."

She looked at him questioningly and he raised his hand to forestall any argument. "I want to get to the capital and contact support directly. If they do nothing or, worse, if they try to take me offline. You're my ace in the hole. I might need you to go directly to the government gaming commission."

"I'm your ace in the hole, am I?" she smiled but it became wicked. "Is that some sort of sexual innuendo?"

"I...ah…" he stammered. He certainly hadn't intended it that way. "I mean…I..."

"It's okay," she elbowed him playfully. "I'm just kidding. I'll be your ace in the hole then. But if you change your mind and need me to contact WorldCog, I will."

"Thanks," he let out a relieved breath. She was his only friend now. He didn't want to screw things up. "I really appreciate it."

"Of course! See you Jace," she smiled and then he watched as she faded away.

Once again Jace was alone in the game world. He didn't remember it bothering him before he died. He used to relish the solo missions and quests he would go on. But playing with Charlena, he found he enjoyed questing with her.

"Food?" meowed Luna, and he looked down to see she was staring hopefully up at him.

"Okay," he told her. "I did promise you food. Let's go to the tavern."

Jace went back to the tavern and ordered their usual, fish and chips. He also used the last of his gold to buy himself an ale. After the ordeal with Diana, he felt like he needed it. As always, Luna attacked her fish with gusto and had it finished before he was done with his ale.

They finished their food and then Jace talked to several of the patrons about where Sinking Springs was in relation to the rest of the kingdom.

Unfortunately, the news was not good. The village was in the far west. It would be months of travel to reach the capital by foot. Frustrated, Jace thanked the patrons and left the tavern.

Jace checked with everyone he could find about quests but everyone was preoccupied with the undead attack tonight. It seemed like he would not be getting any new quests tomorrow. Thinking of other things he could do, Jace remembered the fishing pole he'd bought. Maybe it was time to work on a new skill.

Hiking back to the lake where he had collected the stones for Odo, Jace brought out his fishing pole. He dug up some worms and began to hone his *Fishing* skill. Luna, who had been watching intently as he found worms - and even ate one whole - became bored with fishing and found a sunny spot and curled up to take a nap. Smiling at his sleeping cat, Jace leaned back against a tree and began to fish.

When dark finally fell, Jace had only raised his Fishing skill to rank 5. He found it was much slower going that some of the other skills he'd worked on. And in all that time, he'd only managed to catch four fish. And he had to admit, they were pitiful. It would take two of the fish to make a meal. Still, since he had no more gold, he really had no choice. Beggars couldn't be choosers since he'd have to provide for himself until he could make more money.

Jace looked over at the three fish hanging from the tree and realized he'd need to cook them. He cast a glance down at Luna, who lay near the tree with a half-eaten fish in front of her. The sneaky little cat had climbed up the tree and managed to pull one of the fish down. At least, she could eat raw fish. It wasn't even an option for players. They had to cook it or prepare it - both of which took the *Cooking* skill.

Since he was a mage now, he hadn't bothered buying flint and steel to start a fire and he hadn't had enough money for the gnomish fire sticks - the expensive VEIL equivalent of matches. He just stacked up firewood and cast *Flame Bolt* at it. As Jace hoped, the spell immediately ignited the firewood and he smiled. In the past, as Mordred, he'd always had to carry around gnomish fire sticks to start a fire. It was nice to not have to rely on them. Especially since he couldn't afford them at the moment.

Once the fire was going, the next problem that presented itself was how to cook the fish without any pots or pans. He thought about it for some time before finally coming up with an idea. First, he gutted all three of the fish. Using a long, straight stick that he used as a skewer, he impaled one of the fish. He used two forked sticks on either side of the campfire and placed the skewer across the fire. He rotated the fish every few minutes, receiving several rank ups in the *Cooking* skill. After a half hour of turning the fish, he finally received a message.

You have lost an item: raw fish. Cooking failure.
You have lost an item: raw fish. Cooking success.
You have lost an item: raw fish. Cooking failure.
You have gained an item: Cooked fish fillet.
Your Cooking skill has increased by 1.

Jace looked down as two of the fillets turned to burnt husks. He sighed. It looked like he would go hungry tonight. On the bright side, he'd gained some valuable skill ranks in *Fishing* and *Cooking*. The more ranks he got, the easier it would be. He hoped.

He took his cooked fish fillet and bit into it. It wasn't bad. It wasn't nearly as good as the fish and chips he had eaten at the tavern, but it wasn't half bad. Since there wasn't much to it, Jace finished the fish fairly quickly. Surprisingly, it seemed to satisfy him.

Luna had come to lie near the fire and was curled up and he leaned back against his tree and enjoyed the warmth. It brought back memories of going camping with his dad when he was younger. His father had liked the outdoors and had taken Jace and his sister hiking and camping several times a year. They'd been fun times.

A howl broke Jace from the pleasant memories and he sat up quickly. He'd definitely heard a howl in the night over to his right. Another howl sounded in the darkness, this one to his left. He cursed himself as he realized the light and the smell of cooking fish probably attracted some wolves or coyotes.

Luna was up as well, moving behind his legs. She looked up at him and meowed a single word: "Wolfers!"

Chapter 27

As howls grew closer, Jace armed himself with his newly acquired rapier in his right hand and his rat dagger in the left. Luna scrambled up a tree and Jace briefly considered doing the same. Wolves couldn't climb. Maybe they'd go away.

No, he thought bitterly, they could wait him out and keep him pinned up in the tree for days. If that happened, he would be weakened by the hunger or starvation debuffs. He had to fight them now, while he was at 100%.

Putting his back against the tree Luna had climbed, Jace waited for the wolves to get closer. He didn't need to wait long. With his *Cat-Vision*, Jace saw three wolves bolt from the woods, running straight at him. Viewing them in his HUD, he saw one was the alpha male and targeted it with a *Flame Bolt*. "*Minima fulmen ignem!*"

The missile streaked from his hand and hit the lead wolf in the face eliciting a yelp from the beast.

You burn Alpha Forest Wolf with Flame Bolt for 2 fire damage.
Your Fire Magic skill has increased by 1.

The wolf stopped and rubbed it snout on the damp evening grass. When it's head came up, its eyes were filled with hatred. He'd hoped the fire spell would scare it off but no such luck. This fight was going to get up close and personal.

Jace had 6 mana left. Enough for one spell or ability. He briefly considered trying another *Flame Bolt* but he didn't think a second one would scare it off and he could use the mana for something better. Since he'd ranked his Stealth skill up to 10, he'd received the *Vanish* ability and he was counting on that to help him even the odds.

As the lead wolf came within range, Jace activated *Vanish* and, true to its namesake, vanished from sight. The wolves skidded to a stop and began growling and sniffing the air. Jace tumbled between two of the wolves, came up behind the alpha and stabbed both his weapons into the thing's back.

You critically stab Alpha Forest Wolf for 17 damage.
You critically stab Alpha Forest Wolf for 9 damage.
Alpha Forest Wolf dies.
You gain 30 experience.

The wolf yelped once and then fell over. Jace was very impressed with the new rapier as it did nearly twice the damage as his dagger. The other two wolves sniffed at the leader and then growled at him. Darn it. Couldn't they just run?

The one to his right lunged forward suddenly and clamped its teeth on his arm.

Forest Wolf bites YOU for 2 damage.

With his sensory level at maximum, he felt the teeth dig into his flesh and muscle and barely stifled a scream. The second one came in from behind and bit at his leg.

Forest Wolf bites YOU for 3 damage.

The second wolf's teeth dug into his calf and he almost collapsed with the pain. But if he did, they'd kill him and he'd be walking back here to loot his body. Gritting his teeth and blinking the tears of pain out of his eyes, he lashed out at the first wolf.

You stab Forest Wolf for 7 damage.
You critically stab Forest Wolf for 4 damage.

The wolf didn't go down and Jace realized he could be in trouble. By the number of experiences, the alpha wolf had been level 3. Since these wolves weren't going down with 14 damage, they had to be level 2. He was down to only 8 health and didn't have enough mana to cast a spell. He wasn't sure he'd make it through this fight.

Punctuating his thought, both animals bit at him again.

Forest Wolf bites YOU for 1 damage.
Forest Wolf bites YOU for but you Dodge.
Your Dodge skill has increased by 1.

His *Dodge* skill had kicked in and saved him from one of the bites, but he was still down to only 5 health. Two more bites and he'd be done. With experience born of playing an assassin to level 95, Jace drove his rapier into the wounded wolf, while stabbing his dagger in the other wolf.

You stab Forest Wolf for 9 damage.
Forest Wolf dies.
You gain 20 experience.
You stab Forest Wolf for 5 damage.

The second wolf went down but the last one sank its teeth into his thigh and this time his leg buckled. Jace didn't give up, but stabbed his blades into the final wolf, hoping he would do enough damage.

You stab Forest Wolf for 8 damage.
You stab Forest Wolf for 2 damage.
Forest Wolf dies.
You gain 20 experience.

The wolf fell atop of him and Jace just lay there for a long moment before pushing the creature off him and struggling to his feet. He could feel his wounds mending as he regenerated health and mana, but they still hurt - a lot.

Luna scrambled down the tree and sniffed the dead wolves. "Bad wolfers!"

Wincing from his healing wounds, Jace looked over at the little cat and laughed. "Yes, bad wolfers."

Jace looted the three wolf corpses and received wolf pelts for his trouble and pain. Then again, animals never dropped gold, so he hadn't really expected it.

Slumping down in front of the fire, he waited until he was fully healed and his mana was at maximum. The entire time, he was scanning the area around him and listening for any signs of other predators. Nothing appeared, so he put some more wood on the fire, dug up some worms and went back to fishing.

The rest of the night was uneventful. He managed to catch another six fish and rank up his Fishing skill. In the morning, he cooked the fish in two batches, getting his Cooking skill to increase several times despite burning two of the fish. Luna ate two of the small fish for breakfast and that seemed to satisfy her, though she did sniff at his cooked fish briefly before going back to her raw ones.

He and Luna returned to the village to see groups of happy villagers talking to each other. As soon as one of them noticed Jace, they came running over to him.

"You did it," said one of the villagers, grabbing his hand and shaking it.

"Are they really gone?"

"Was it a curse?"

"Did you vanquish the necromancer?"

"Will they be back next month?"

Jace backed away as the villagers hit him with rapid fire questions. Finally, he held his hands up for quiet and a hush fell over the crowd. Suddenly looking at a crowd of people waiting for him to speak, he swallowed nervously. Even in the game world, he didn't like public speaking.

"Good people," he began. "The elf and I went into the ancient underground city of Crystalburrow. There we found a...ah... controller... that was controlling some..."

Looking at the blank looks at the villagers, Jace sighed. He wasn't sure how to explain Diana and the drones. Even if he did, he doubted the simple villagers would understand the explanation. It was time for a plausible lie. "And we killed the necromancer controlling the skeletons!"

Your Bluff skill has increased by 1.
Your Bluff skill has increased by 1.
Your Bluff skill has increased by 1.

A cheer went up from the assembled villagers as his *Bluff* skill hit the maximum rank for his level, granting him the *Feint* ability. Jace smiled. *Feint* allowed him to burn some mana to set an enemy off balance and allow his next strike to be a critical strike. It was a very powerful ability. As Mordred, he'd used *Feint* for many levels before finally he upgraded to a better ability.

More villagers swarmed him then, shaking his hand or clapping him on the back. This went on for several minutes before people started to disperse and get back to their routine. Even so, Jace couldn't happen to notice that everyone seemed much happier.

"Well done, good master," said the mayor, as the squat man waddled up to him. "I have to admit I had my reservations but as you said, no undead plagued us last night and after the first few hours, I actually went to bed and got some sleep! Ha!"

He shook the mayor's beefy hand and then the man reached into his jacket and brought out a small jingling pouch. "This is yours. A reward well earned."

You received 100 gold.
You have completed the quest, "Plague of Undead"
You gain 200 experience. Experience to next level 440.
You gain +100 faction with Residents of Sinking Springs

You gain +100 faction with Absalom

"I may have something else that might interest you," the fat man told him.

Absalom motioned Jace to follow and then lead him to the apothecary shop. Stepping inside, the man walked to the back of the shop and disappeared behind a black curtain. Looking about the shop, Jace saw all sorts of beakers, vials, burners and other things that made the shop look like a mad chemist's lair.

The odor of the place nearly overwhelmed Jace's sense of smell with his sensory level so high and he nearly gagged. He forced himself to breath in his mouth, but even then he felt he was still smelling it. It was an odd combination of chemicals, herbs and possibly putrefaction.

Luna, whose nose had started sniffing the moment they walked in, hopped up on one of the tables and started to walk around the various equipment, nearly knocking it over. Luckily, Jace was quick enough to scoop her up before she did any damage.

"Smells!" she protested as her nose continued to take in the pungent aroma of the lab.

"No," he scolded her. "If you knock anything over, I'll have to pay for it!"

He was about to retort when there was a crash and a muffled cry from the other side of the curtain. Concerned, Jace started to walk towards the curtain just as the mayor burst from the backroom holding a large object. The mayor walked over to him and thrust it at him.

"Believe it or not, there was a time when I used to be an adventurer like you. But, sadly, I took an arrow to the knee and that ended my career," the large man told him wistfully. "But, this leather jerkin protected me through my many adventures! It's still in good condition and it's much better looking than that thing you wear now on your chest."

Taking the offered jerkin, Jace viewed it in his HUD.

Second Hand Leather Jerkin
Type: Leather armor
Armor: 2 + 1 (Masterwork)
Wt: 3 lbs
Description: Once worn by the self-proclaimed adventurer, Absalom the Magnificent, this leather jerkin is in excellent condition and appears to have never seen combat.

Stifling a laugh at the description, Jace equipped the jerkin and looked at himself in a small mirror attached to one of the pieces of equipment. He had to admit, it looked good.

"Quite fetching," Absalom said. "You cut nearly as dashing a figure as I did back in my day."

"Thank you," he told the big man and shook his hand again.

"Yes, yes," said the mayor. "Now, off with you! I must get back to my potions! Oh, and if you see your elven companion, you can tell her to see me for her reward too."

With that, the mayor waved dismissively and turned to one of the many pieces of alchemy equipment and began fiddling with one of it's knobs.

Jace continued to hold Luna until they got out of the shop and then set her down on the ground. He'd been serious about probably having to pay for anything she broke and from his days of brewing potions as Mordred, he knew alchemical equipment was expensive.

"We have money now," he told Luna. "Let's go shopping!"

Chapter 28

Luna followed Jace to the general store. Since Sinking Springs was only a starter town in a newbie area, its selection was limited. Regardless, Jace looked for items that would be useful for him while he was here in town and once he joined the caravan.

He bought two more sets of picks since there would be no place between towns to buy more. Despite his earlier success with cooking the fish with a homemade spit, Jace bought a metal frying pan and a spatula. He also bought some twine, some spikes and a shovel so that he could make some traps. Finally, he bought 10 days worth of rations, in case there were some days he couldn't find food. One could never be too careful.

Together, the items came to 23 gold, leaving him only 77 gold. Jace looked at the pitiful amount. He would still need 80 more gold for the caravan fare. While it was a good amount of coin for a new character, Jace remembered how much money he'd accumulated as Mordred. The difference was staggering. He really needed the company to fix this issue and put him back inside Mordred!

After shopping, Jace spent the rest of the afternoon running around from villager to villager to see if he could pick up any quests. It appeared that completing the "undead" quest had opened up some additional quests. Unfortunately, the new quests involved hunting, gathering or even fishing and took a while to complete. But fortunately, the new quests also rewarded twice the experience. By the time Charlena logged in, Jace had reached level 2 in *Rogue*.

"You're level 2 now?!" was the first thing Charlena said when she saw him.

Jace shrugged apologetically. "I don't sleep. Unfortunately, since it wasn't my highest class, I didn't actually gain anything from it."

Charlena made a frustrated sound, though her tone was playful. "You're not allowed to get too far ahead of me!"

"I'll try to hold myself back," he told her.

"You'd better!" she told him sternly, though he saw the edge of her mouth creep into a smile. "Okay! Let me go turn in my quest!"

They went to the apothecary and banged on the door until the mayor answered. The man's scowl turned upside down when he saw Charlena and he invited her in to get her reward, closing the door before Jace could follow. It opened a few minutes later and Charlena emerged before the door slammed and Jace heard the locks click into place.

"Charming guy," Jace muttered.

"He's not so bad. Besides, And I have something for you," Charlena said, smiling. She held out a pair of leather bracers and initiated a trade with him.

"Don't you want them?" he asked before accepting the trade.

Charlena shook her head and held up her arm. "They have the same stats as the ones I'm wearing. I thought you could use them."

Accepting the trade, Jace equipped the bracers. "Thanks! That's 2 more points of armor."

"Great!" she said. "Let's go kill some things!"

Jace laughed. "Too bad you weren't here last night. I could have used your help with some wolves that attacked me."

Luna's ears went back against her head and she crouched low. "Wolfers!"

"Aw," Charlena cooed as she bent down and scratched the cat on it's head and chin. "Did you deal with the mean ole wolves?"

"Yes." Luna purred, rubbing her head against the elf's scratching fingers.

"I seem to remember being there too," Jace muttered.

"Want me to scratch you behind the ears too?" Charlena teased.

"Would you?" Jace shrugged, bent over and tilted his head toward her.

She smacked him playfully on the head. They both laughed and then Charlena stood up and looked around. "So now what?"

"We need to get you to level 2," he told her. "Time to do some quests."

The two of them spent the rest of the time running picking flowers, gathering mushrooms and even gathering firewood for one of the older villagers.

The quests would have been boring, but having someone to talk to while running around gathering items definitely made the experience more enjoyable. Within an hour, Charlena gained level 2 in her *Scout* class.

"Level 2 now!" she said happily and did a little bow.

"Great job!" he told her and gave her a high five.

As if on queue, the mayor came puffing around the corner. "Dedrurrurth! Almedha!"

The rotund mayor skidded to a halt in front of them and tried to speak but was too out of breath. Absalom bent over, breathing heavily and trying to catch his breath. He stood up and tried speaking again but then just bent over. "Goblins… goblins… attacking… farms… south."

Mayor Absalom of Sinking Springs has offered you the quest, "When Goblins Attack"
Reward: 100 gold, +100 faction with Residents of Sinking Springs, +100 faction with Absalom.
Accept quest? (Yes or No)

"We'll take care of it!" Charlena grinned, accepting the quest. "Come on Jace! Let's get some goblins!" Not waiting for a response from the mayor, Charlena dashed off to the south. As she ran, she pulled out her bow. "Come one!"

Shaking his head and smiling at the gung-ho elf, Jace hurried to catch up with her.

The two adventurers ran quickly out of town and down the southern road until they came to the first farm. They slowed to a walk and looked around. There did not appear to be any goblins, so they ran to the next farm. There were no signs of goblins there either but they did spot some smoke coming from just south of them.

Running down the road, Jace and Charlena stopped as they cleared a small hill and looked down on the scene below them.

From the hilltop, they could clearly see the thatch roof of the farmhouse was on fire. Surrounding the farmhouse were at least six goblins who were intently watching the house. Jace thought maybe they enjoyed watching things burned until he heard a woman's plea for help from inside the house.

Charlena heard it too and started to rush towards the house but Jace caught her by the arm. She turned to him angrily. "We have to help those people!"

Jace nodded. "I know. But we're outnumbered. We have to do this smart. Dying won't help anyone."

She was still tense under his grip and he let go over her.

"What do we do then?" she said through gritted teeth.

As he'd looked over the situation with a practiced eye, Jace had already formulated a plan. They didn't have a full group nor did they have many abilities they could draw on. That meant they'd need to play it smart.

"You need to sneak over to that big oak. Stay in stealth and climb up," he told her, pointing to a nearby tree with a lower branch she could reach but the goblins couldn't. "As soon as you're in position, fire your first arrow from stealth. Then, keep firing at them until they come at you."

Looking at the tree, Charlena nodded. She wanted to help, but she was smart too. "What about you?"

"I'm going to go hide and wait until they come after you," he smiled and paused for dramatic effect.

She gave him a hard look.

"And then stab them in the back," he finished.

"So, I'm bait." She looked at the area around the tree and nodded. "That works!"

They both activated their stealth skills and got into position. Jace had just managed to hide behind some particularly dense bushes when he heard Charlena's bow ring out.

Unsurprisingly, her first arrow, fired from stealth, was a critical hit and the goblin she hit dropped face first in the dirt. The other goblins looked down at their fallen companion and the arrow sticking out of its head and began chattering and pointing around, looking for the bowman - or bow woman in this case.

Her bow rang out again and an arrow appeared in the chest of another goblin. It staggered but didn't drop. The other goblins looked over to the tree that Charlena was hiding in. This time, the sound had pinpointed her location.

"Elf!" he heard the one goblin scream. "Kill the elf!"

The wounded goblin and two others ran towards the tree while two others stayed behind and poked their spears at the windows, probably trying to keep whoever was inside from leaving.

Another scream came from inside and Jace had to re-evaluate his plan. The roof was blazing by now and two of the goblins were still preventing anyone from escaping. He looked over to the tree to signal Charlena but the elf was already lining up her next shot.

Hoping his companion would hold out on her own, Jace stealthily made his way around the charging goblins with Luna on his heels.

So intent were the enraged goblins, they didn't notice him at all. He heard two more bow shots as he moved in behind the goblins guarding the house.

When he was right behind the first one, he struck quickly with both his weapons.

You critically stab Firebelly Goblin for 17 damage.
You critically stab Firebelly Goblin for 10 damage.
Firebelly Goblin dies.
You gain 20 experience.

The goblin stiffened and dropped to the dirt. The kill had been silent, but the other goblin saw the motion and turned towards him!

"Me kills you human!" it screamed and charged him with its spear.

Jace was ready for him and used his *Vanish* ability, side stepping in case the goblin kept running. It didn't. The thing skidded to a halt and desperately looked around for its quarry.

Obliging him, Jace appeared just as his rapier and dagger stabbed the goblin through the heart and the throat.

You critically stab Firebelly Goblin for 18 damage.
You critically stab Firebelly Goblin for 7 damage.
Firebelly Goblin dies.
You gain 20 experience.

Looking into the window, Jace saw two farmers inside, huddling for protection. "It's okay. You can come out now."

The two villagers obviously heard him but they shook their heads. "What about the big one?"

Big one? Jace spun just as he felt pain explode from his side. The villagers were right. The goblin who had stabbed him was almost a head taller than the other goblins had been and broader. He didn't need to view it in his HUD to realize this was a mini-boss.

Firebelly Raid Leader stabs YOU for 5 damage.
You are Bleeding.

Jace gasped as he felt the barbed spear penetrate his side and something inside him and then gasped again as the goblin yanked it free. He activated his *Vanish* and stabbed back at the larger goblin.

You critically stab Firebelly Raid Leader for 17 damage.

You critically stab Firebelly Raid Leader for 9 damage.

The goblin raid leader let out a howl of pain but it didn't die. Jace knew he was in trouble. He didn't have enough mana for another *Vanish*. His health was down to 8 so he could take one more strike. The second one would kill him.

The goblin leader seemed to sense that Jace was outmatched and laughed. "You are puny, human."

"And you are ugly!" Jace spat back at him.

That surprised the goblin and bought Jace a few extra seconds. "You speak goblin tongue? Not as ignorant as other humans."

YOU Bleed for 1 damage.

Jace had forgotten about the bleeding message. It was a condition that caused you to continue to lose health for a specific time period from a few seconds to a minute. It wouldn't matter in this case, because he didn't think he had a minute.

Punctuating his thought, the raid leader struck out, quick as a snake.

Firebelly Raid Leader stabs YOU for but you Dodge.
Your Dodge skill has increased by 1.
YOU Bleed for 1 damage.

His dodge skill had saved him, but it had only just postponed the inevitable. The goblin's next strike would kill him.

Intent on going down fighting, Jace stabbed out with his thin sword and dagger. Both blades connected.

You stab Firebelly Goblin for 7 damage.
You stab Firebelly Goblin for 5 damage.

But it wasn't enough to kill the thing. Jace braced for the inevitable and hoped Charlena could finish it off once he died.

"Out of tricks human," the thing observed. "Now you die!"

"Use mine," came a voice in his head he recognized as Luna.

"What?" he sent back as he saw the goblin raid leader brace for another thrust.

"Use mine!" came Luna's voice again.

"Use your what?!" he sent back. Time seemed to slow as the goblin thrust his spear forward, aimed at Jace's chest. Suddenly, an orange blur darted into the path of the spear, taking the hit meant for him.

Luna uses Protect Master.
Firebelly Raid Leader stabs Luna for 5 damage.
Luna is Bleeding.

Luna howled as the little cat was impaled by the spear. She fell to the side, wounded but still alive. She'd used some special familiar ability to save him. And now she was wounded.

Jace felt rage fill him, but he knew it wouldn't be enough. He prepared to stab at the creature when he heard the cat's voice again.

"Use mana," Luna told him in a pained voice.

"I don't have any more," he shot back, getting ready to strike.

"Mine!" she nearly screamed at him.

Hers? What did she mean hers? Then he sensed it. She had mana too. The mana he'd used when summoning her. Experimentally, he reached for it and found he could touch it. She had 6 mana left of the ten he'd used to summon her. That ability she used must have drained some of it already. But 6 was enough.

Drawing on Luna's mana, he used *Vanish*, sidestepped the goblin leader and stabbed both of his weapons into the thing's back.

You critically stab Firebelly Raid Leader for 15 damage.
You critically stab Firebelly Raid Leader for 9 damage.

And he looked disbelieving as the thing didn't go down. "You've got to be kidding me!"

YOU Bleed for 1 damage.
Luna is Bleeding.

The raider leader spun around, about to stab Jace when there was a twang and an arrow appeared in its head.

Almedha Pressalor shoots Firebelly Raid Leader for 16 damage.
Firebelly Raid Leader dies.
You gain 120 experience.

Jace looked over to see Charlena partially behind a tree and smiled. He walked over to Luna, who was lying on her side.

"Are you okay?" he asked her.

She gave him that "are you crazy" look. "No. Hurt."

"You saved me," he said, stroking the cat's fur. He felt his eyes moisten and had to blink several times.

"Yes," Luna responded, her voice still pained.

"What happened? Will she be okay?" Charlena bent down and scratched the cat's chin.

"She used some special ability to save me," Jace said, his voice rough. "She took the hit instead."

"I don't think she regenerates like we do," Jace replied. His pain was already fading as his health and mana regenerated now that combat was over.

"What? So, she'll die?"

Jace shook his head. Her wound wouldn't heal and she would be in pain. He had to help her. He knew what he needed to do. Luna seemed to sense it as well.

"Yes," she said.

Bringing up his HUD, he found the cat icon mentally clicked it.

"Goodbye, Luna," he said. Choosing *Dismiss Familiar*, Jace watched Luna fade away.

Chapter 29

"Where'd Luna go?" Charlena asked as the cat faded away.

"I dismissed her," Jace grunted and fell back, gritting his teeth against the pain as his virtual flesh knitted itself back together.

Charlena winced and gave him a sympathetic look. "That looks like it really hurts."

"'Tis but a flesh wound," Jace smiled in his best British accent, but the effect was ruined as a spasm of pain wracked him from the regeneration process.

"At least your arm's not missing," she said and winked.

An older man and woman came running out of the house. They were coughing but otherwise seemed to be unhurt. "They… the…" the man started but fell into a coughing fit. "Goblins… gone?"

"We killed them," Charlena told them gently.

"Thank you," the woman told them. The two villagers held each other as they continued to cough and watch the flame devour their burning house. He thought he heard the woman softly sobbing.

Jace knew they were just NPCs in a virtual world but he found it difficult not to sympathize with them. What would happen to them without a house? Jace looked around the farm. Most of their livestock had been killed by the goblins or had run off. Would they even have food to eat?

As if reading his mind, Charlena moved closer and bent down and lowered her voice to a whisper. "Are these people going to be okay? Should we… give them money or something?"

Jace thought about it for a moment. Perhaps there was something they could do. The game created quests based on changing events. They might be able to help the villagers and help themselves at the same time.

Groaning as he got to his feet, Jace turned to the couple. His HUD identified them as Aiden and Chastity.

"Aiden, Chastity, I'm sorry this happened to you," he told them sincerely. They may be artificial people, but they were still people. "Is there anything we can do to help you?"

Both of the farmers spoke up at the same time, stopped, looked at each other and then continued speaking.

"Dem goblins need to pay for what they did!" Aiden demanded. "We's peaceful folk! They had no right attacking us like that and slaughtering our cows! Especially old Bessy"

Aiden of Sinking Springs has offered you the quest, "Payback for Bessy"
Reward: +100 faction with Residents of Sinking Springs, +100 faction with Aiden.

Accept quest? (Yes or No)

"All of hens done ran off! We'll need them for their eggs, and maybe for eatin' if they don't lay no eggs!" Chastity told them.

Chastity of Sinking Springs has offered you the quest, "A Bird in Hand"
Reward: +100 faction with Residents of Sinking Springs, +100 faction with Chastity.
Accept quest? (Yes or No)

"We'll be glad to help," Jace accepted both quests and ignored a pointed look from Charlena.

"Once you finish those," Chastity said. "I'm sure we can find you more work. If'n your up for it."

"Thank you, we'll get right on those," he told them and then motioning for Charlena to follow him, walked over to the road.

"That's not what I meant," Charlena said as soon as they were out of earshot. "I meant, help them rebuild their house or buy them food or give them money."

"I know," Jace nodded. "And we can still do that. But this is how the game works. When NPCs need something, they give out quests. Completing the quest helps them and also helps us."

Charlena opened her mouth to protest but Jace held up his hand. "If we do all their quests and they still need help, we can decide the best way to help them then. But in the meantime, we can help them AND gain some experience. Deal?"

She considered for a minute and then nodded. "I guess that makes sense. But let's get the hens first so they'll have some food…"

"Okay," Jace agreed. "But let me summon Luna first."

Jace checked his health and mana and seeing they were both full, he moved off the road and sat behind a tree.

He then summoned Luna, pushing as much health and mana as he could into the summoning. The process was just as painful as the last time and he was left on gasping on his side when she finally appeared.

Charlena bent down and put a gentle hand on his shoulder. "It really hurts when you summon her?"

"Every time," Jace said as Luna walked over and rubbed herself against him. "Feeling better?"

Luna purred. "Yes."

"Thanks for saving me. You're a brave little cat," he told her and scratched her chin affectionately.

"Yes."

It took Jace and Charlena over an hour to find the eight hens that were missing. By the time they returned, almost a dozen other villagers had come to help the couple. Jace and Charlena turned the hens over to Chastity and completed the quest.

"Now we go after the goblins," Jace said.

"How do we do that?" Charlena asked. "Do you know where the goblins came from?"

"No, but I know where the trail is," he told her. He'd been using his tracking skill while they were hunting down the hens and had found the goblins trail. They'd come from the south, which Jace found odd. He'd scouted further south after his encounter with Duglas, wondering if there was a tribe nearby. Even after searching for miles around, he hadn't found any trace of any other goblin. So where had these come from?

"Something wrong?" Charlena asked, breaking him out of his thoughts.

"I found their trail when we were looking for the hens," he told her.

She looked him in the eyes. "I hear a BUT…"

"But," he continued as he felt a smile creep across his face. "I searched this area after Duglas, looking for more goblins. I was hoping I could get more armor pieces from them."

She frowned. "But you didn't find any did you?"

"No," he replied. "Which begs the question…"

"Where did these come from," she finished, looking around. She looked thoughtful for a moment. "Did the game just spawn them?"

"It's possible," Jace responded, but he wasn't convinced. It seemed too convenient. Plus, he felt somehow drawn to the south without quite knowing why. Something just didn't feel right but he couldn't put his finger on it.

"Do you not want to go?" Charlena asked him. "I mean, it's not like we have to do every quest."

"No, we should go," Jace told her. He didn't know what the strange feeling that was drawing him south was, but he wanted to find out. Perhaps he'd find the answer south. "Yes, let's go."

They set off south, following the trail Jace had found earlier. While the footprints were a little older, there were so many of them that it was easy to follow. The trail continued south for what Jace guessed was five or six miles before they came to a river.

Charlena had maxed out her *Tracking* skill following the trail and she bent down to examine the tracks to get a new heading. Jace felt that odd feeling pulling again but this time to the east.

"East," she said as she stood up. "The trail turns east along the river."

Jace felt uneasy. Whatever the feeling was that was pulling him along seemed to be in the same direction the goblins had come from. He looked down at Luna, who had been dutifully following them. "Do you feel like something is drawing you to the east?"

The little cat looked up at him curiously. "Drawing?"

"Do you feel like something is pulling you in a specific direction?" he tried.

The cat moved it's head from side to side and then looked back at him. "No."

"Is that a private conversation or can anyone join?" Charlena chimed in and Jace looked up to see her smirking at him. "You were talking cat language again."

"Sorry," he apologized. "Do you feel drawn to any particular direction?"

"What do you mean?" she asked, cocking an eyebrow.

"I have this feeling," he told her. "That seemed to be drawing me in the same direction as the trail of goblins. Do you have anything like that?"

Charlena seemed to go introspective for a long moment and then shrugged. "Not that I can tell." Her face suddenly brightened and then her eyes went glassy for a moment.

When her eyes came back into focus, she bit her tongue as she went introspective again.

"Darn. I thought turning my sensory level up might let me feel something, but I don't feel anything pulling me in a certain direction."

"Bummer," Jace said and gave her a head nod. "But that was a good idea. I didn't even think about that."

She looked pleased. "Thank you! What do you think it means?"

"I don't know," Jace told her. "But I think we should be careful."

"That sounds like good advice."

They followed the river east for a few miles until they entered a hilly area. The river weaved in between the hills. The trail followed the river and so did they. All the while, the odd feeling kept growing, and Jace was feeling more and more nervous. He almost felt like he'd had too much caffeine and his nerves were on edge.

Finally, they rounded a bend in the river and realized they'd found their destination. They'd found the goblin village. At least, Jace thought it might be the goblin village. Huts dotted the hillside in front of them. They looked like typical crude huts. All except the large one in the center.

The center hut wasn't a hut. It looked more like a very crude log cabin. But that wasn't the strangest thing about the village. The goblins had constructed a fence around their village of sharpened sticks and logs driven into the ground. Jace had never seen goblins do that. They weren't builders. Was there another creature in charge of the goblins?

It wasn't uncommon for a lone bugbear or orc to take command of a goblin tribe. It wasn't difficult. They just challenged the leader and killed him. Then they promised the tribe riches, food or loot and generally they were made chief. Was that what had happened here? Something more intelligent had taken over? Or had they simply found the cabin abandoned and built up the goblin village around it?

"That seems like a lot of goblins," Charlena whispered to him.

Jace nodded. "Too many for us to take in a frontal assault. Plus, I think someone else might be leading them."

"Something else," she gave him a worried look. "Like what?"

"I don't know," he replied. "An orc, a bugbear, heck, it could even be an ogre."

Charlena went pale. "An ogre? Aren't they like… really big and mean?"

"Ogres aren't all big and mean." He smiled. "They have layers."

"Layers?" Charlena asked dubiously.

Jace shook his head. "Never mind. The point is, we need to do some recon before we attack."

"Darn it!" Charlena said. "I'm going to need to go soon."

Jace looked around and realized it had gotten dark at some point. With his *Cat-Vision*, he hadn't even noticed.

"Can we wait until tomorrow to attack them?" she asked hopefully.

"Of course," he told her.

"Great!" she said and leaned in and kissed him on the cheek. Then realizing what she had done, she blushed. "I'll meet you here tomorrow after school."

And with that, she faced away leaving Jace alone. Well, almost alone. He looked down at Luna. "You're still with me, right girl?"

"Yes."

Jace started walking back towards where the trail had first met the river. He was nearly there when the ground gave way beneath him and he was falling.

Chapter 30

After falling for what seemed like a minute but was in reality probably only a few seconds, Jace hit the ground with bone jarring force. He felt Luna land gingerly on top of him before hopping off and coming around to sniff his face.

You take 10 falling damage.
You are Stunned for 30 seconds.

"Summoner okay?" the cat asked him.

Since he was stunned, Jace couldn't speak. In fact, he couldn't do anything physical. Remembering their telepathic link, he replied. "I'll be okay. Just stunned for a bit."

Luna sat down near his head. Effectively paralyzed, Jace could only lay there at the bottom of what he guessed was a pit. He had ended up face down so for the moment, his view consisted of the dirt floor.

Jace cursed his luck. Of all the things, he had fallen into a pit trap. A pit dug by goblins no less? He'd gotten so used to Mordred's detect traps ability, he hardly gave traps a thought any longer. He needed to hit rogue level 5 before he'd get that ability. It couldn't come quick enough in his mind.

A thought occurred to him then. The goblins in this area should be low level. They shouldn't even be digging pits! Then again, they also shouldn't be building log cabins either. Was there some other higher level monster running the tribe? That possibility was looking more and more likely.

You are no longer Stunned.

After what seemed like an eternity, Jace could move again. His health was already starting to regenerate and he felt the all too familiar pain that accompanied it. Jace felt like every bone in his body had been broken and were now putting themselves back together. Along with the pain, Jace still felt that nagging sensation that seemed to be drawing him towards the village.

Standing up, Jace looked around the pit, because it was definitely a pit. It was too square shaped to be some random random sinkhole. That meant, the goblins really had dug it and there was most likely a more intelligent and probably higher level monster leading them.

Jace didn't like that idea at all. A tribe of goblins would be hard enough for the two of them to handle. If there was some other boss, one that was showing how to make traps and fortify their village, then this quest just got much more complicated - and dangerous.

Luna suddenly hissed and Jace looked up to see two goblin heads poking over the side of the pit.

"Hey," said one of them. "Dat not deer or pig, dat human!"

"Hoo-mon?" said the other as it squinted down. "Dey good eatin?"

"Me not know," the first shot back.

"We kill it?" the second one asked.

"Um," the first one looked doubtful. "We need ask Big Cheese!"

"Yah," agreed the other. "Not kill without Big Cheese."

Big Cheese? Was that the name of the leader? What kind of monster had a name of Big Cheese? Or was that just how the goblins pronounced it.

"I want to speak to Big Cheese!" Jace called up to him.

"Ah!" screamed the first one. "It speaks! It speaks!"

"Hoo-mons speak?" asked the second one, wide-eyed. "Maybe it not hoo-mon. Maybe it baby ogre?"

The first squinted down at him. "Nah. Too ugly to be ogre."

"You shuddup!" yelled the first. "You not talk Big Cheese."

"Not less Big Cheese want talk you!" nodded the second.

The two goblins looked at each other. Almost in unison they said. "We tell Big Cheese."

As quickly as they had appeared, the goblins disappeared from view and Jace was left alone. "Hey! Let me out! I want to speak with Big Cheese!"

There was no reply. Jace wasn't sure what to do. Not that there was much he could do. If the creatures came back and killed him, his body would most likely be irretrievable. If they took him into the village to see this "Big Cheese" monster and he died in the village, his body would definitely be irretrievable. Either prospect didn't sound appealing.

He looked around for anything he could try and throw his rope around but found nothing. He started to panic. He couldn't afford to lose all of his money and items - especially the rapier he'd gotten from Crystalburrow. Jace knew he wouldn't be finding anything like that any time soon.

Suddenly he thought of a desperate plan, but he needed to be fast. He used his hands to dig a small hole in the button of the pit.

Next, he removed his rapier, the rat fang dagger and his coins and placed them in the hole. Then, he placed the jerkin he'd gotten from the mayor and the bracers from Charlena into his shallow hole. Those were the most important items he had, and he quickly piled dirt on them and patted them down. After covering them up, he smoothed out the dirt the best he could to make it look as natural as possible.

If one of the goblins came down and searched, they'd probably find it and they'd be able to take it since it wasn't on his body. He would just have to take that chance since the alternative involved him losing it as well. At least this way, he had a chance.

He equipped his old tattered jerkin, so it didn't look obvious that he had taken off some of his equipment. He also equipped his original dagger. It was battered but was better than not having any weapon.

There was a commotion above him, and several goblin heads appeared over the lip of the pit.

"Yah," said a goblin he hadn't seen before. It had some sort of pattern painted on its face and wore a feather headdress. "Dat a hoo-mon. Big Cheese say bring him."

Jace heard muttering between the goblins and then they retreated, and a thin pine trunk was lowered down into the pit. The branches had been hacked away after a few inches but there were enough of them that they could be used to climb up. Seeing no real alternative and wanting to keep the goblins from climbing down and finding his loot, he grabbed Luna and climbed up.

"Oh," said one. "Cat! Good eatin!"

"No!" said the goblin in the headdress. "Take to Big Cheese. Him decide."

Jace relaxed. He had been about to blast the cat-eating goblin in the face with a *Flame Bolt*. He wasn't about to let them hurt Luna. And they certainly couldn't eat her. Even if they killed her, she'd fade away.

Reaching the top, he was immediately seized by several goblins and his hands were bound by roughly made rope. They tried to grab Luna but she darted away with feline grace and ran into the woods.

"Let it go," the painted goblin barked. "We have hoo-mon. We take to Big Cheese."

The goblin with the headdress, which Jace's HUD identified as Forest Goblin Shaman, led them back towards the village. Four other goblins surrounded him as they walked, occasionally prodding him with a spear.

While he walked, Jace could once again feel the pulling sensation getting stronger, the closer he got to the goblin settlement.

Before he knew it, they had reached the village and he was ceremoniously marched through the makeshift gate. Goblins gathered around to watch him as they paraded Jace up the hill. When they reached the log cabin, they stopped and did a special knock on the door. Jace raised an eyebrow. Was that 'Shave and a Haircut'?

Before Jace had time to think about it, the door opened. The goblins behind him prodded him forward with their spear tips and he had no choice but to step into the log cabin. He would have entered anyway since whatever the pulling sensation was, it was coming from inside.

Stepping inside was like leaving the goblin village behind and stepping into a completely different area. The inside of the smoke filled room was draped with silks and other expensive cloth, giving it an exotic look. On the floor were carpets and pillows that no goblin had made and in the center was what looked like a home-made hookah.

Lounging around the room in various states of undress were what Jace guessed were goblin women. Jace could only tell they were female because of their, in some cases very large, breasts. Most of them had long hair, but not necessarily and longer than the bushy manes some of the males sported.

His attention was drawn to a large, human sized chair on the far end of the cabin. Like the rest of the items in this room, it was most likely stolen from a caravan. But it wasn't the chair that grabbed his attention. It was the creature that sat on it.

Seated on the chair was what appeared to be a normal goblin. And while it looked like any other goblin, it was wearing what Jace guessed was a child's navy silk bathrobe. On the goblin's fingers were gold rings, many of them jeweled, and around its neck were a dozen thin golden chains. On the goblin's head was what appeared to be a crudely hammered crown. In all his years of playing the game, he had never seen anything so ridiculous.

"Oh Great Big Cheese!" said the shaman, bowing low to the goblin in the chair. "I bring the talking hoo-mon as you ordered!"

The "Big Cheese" sat in his chair holding a long tube from the hookah. He looked Jace over, mumbling something quietly to himself. Then he took a long draw from the hookah before dropping the tube and hopping to his feet.

As the goblin leader approached him, Jace continued to hear the thing mutter softy to itself. He also noticed something else. The goblin leader was the source of the pulling sensation. The thing he felt drawn to.

Big Cheese walked over to him, stopping in front of him to look Jace up and down. "Hmmm." The goblin leader then slowly walked around him, continuing to look him up and down. "Mmm..hmm."

The leader made a complete circuit around Jace before coming to a halt in front of him. The little goblin turned to regard him.

"So," the Big Cheese said. "You're the human who can speak goblin, huh?" The goblin leader looked at him expectantly. Just under his breath, he heard the goblin mutter. "Tell us."

He wasn't sure what the muttering was about. Was the goblin leader saying it under his breath so only Jace would hear? Was that some message to him, telling him this goblin was a player too?

Jace had already put two and two together. Given everything he was seeing in this room, the log cabin and spiked walls goblins shouldn't be able to build, Jace knew this goblin had to be a player. He couldn't think of any other rational explanation for the strange things he was seeing.

"Yes, I'm a player like you," he told the goblin.

"A player," repeated the goblin. "It wants us to believe it's a player." The goblin's right eye twitched as it spoke. "It thinks it can fool us? Kill us? Force us into a new body?"

Jace shook his head. "No, I can help you."

"Help us," the goblin cackled. "Help us? Help the Big Cheese? The Big Enchilada? The Head Honcho? It thinks it can help us?" The goblin looked at him suspiciously then began to shake its head violently. "No! No! No! It wants to kill us! Send us somewhere else! That's what the players do! They kill us! Over and over and over again!"

Jace tried to back away, but the goblins behind him prodded him with their spears, forcing him to stay in place.

The goblin leader was holding its head in its hands now, rocking back and forth. "They kill us! Force us to jump! One body! Two bodies! A thousand bodies! No more! No, now we stay! No more!"

"I know how to make you human again," Jace told him. "It worked for me…"

"Lies!" the Big Cheese spat. "Lies from players! Death from players! That's what players do! Kill us! Kill us over and over!"

"Not anymore!" the creature screamed, it's eyes wide now, spittle flying from its mouth. "Never again! It won't kill us!"

Suddenly it straightened, its face a mask of calm once more. "No. No more killing us. Now we kill players and take their loot when their bodies expire."

Calmly, as if signaling a waiter to stop over at his table, he gestured to the guards. Immediately Jace felt the spears thrust into him. Somewhere not too far away, he heard a cat howl. The goblins stabbed him over and over until his body collapsed and he was in spirit form looking down at his corpse.

You have died.

He looked at the Big Cheese as the goblin climbed back into his makeshift throne and realized the truth. This player was insane.

Shaking his head, he chose the option to respawn.

Chapter 31

Jace gasped as he reappeared in the Sinking Springs graveyard. It was dark out and without the *Cat-Vision* he received from Luna, the darkness was oppressive. In addition, he was naked except for his loincloth and the cool night air chilled him to the bone.

He quickly resummoned Luna, giving her as much health and mana as he could despite the pain it caused him. As usual, the energy flowed out of him and formed into the familiar shape of an orange tabby cat.

"Summoner die?" the cat asked him when she reappeared.

"Yes. The goblin leader killed me."

"Bad goblin," she said angrily.

"Yes, bad goblin," he smiled and scratched Luna's head. He remembered back to the goblin's rantings. He had no idea how long the person had been in the game, leaping from body to body as he was killed, but it must have driven the person insane. "Crazy goblin."

Thinking about the crazy goblin, Jace remembered his equipment he'd hidden. He needed to get his stuff before one of the goblins found it. "I need to get back to that pit. Do you remember where it was? Can you lead me back to it?"

That cat sat back on its haunches and wrapped its tail around itself. In a very smug tone it replied, "Yes."

Jace didn't wait for his mana and health to replenish, they could regenerate on the way. He and Luna ran off towards the goblin village with his familiar in the lead. Without boots, every step hurt as the stones, twigs and sticks dug into his feet. Unfortunately, he had no choice but to endure the pain and kept pace with Luna.

Before long, they had passed the farms and were running down the rocky trail Jace and Charlena had followed earlier. It didn't take long before Luna slowed and began sniffing. She stopped and looked back at him. "Hole."

Jace looked closely in front of the cat until he was able to see the dimensions of the pit. He had to admit, it was cleverly hidden. It was no wonder he'd missed it before. He looked over the entire area and found a piece of twine tied to several metal cups. The twine ran across the pit and he guessed the metal cups would make noise when someone fell into the pit. It had probably done the same earlier but he'd been too busy falling to remember it.

Very carefully, he untied the cups from the twine that connected them to the pit and put them in his inventory. Next, he searched the area for a log the goblins had used to get him out of the pit. He didn't find it and guessed they must have carried it from the village.

Without the goblin's makeshift ladder, Jace had to search for nearly half an hour before he found a large branch that was adequate. After dragging it to the edge of the pit, he pushed it in and tested it before climbing down.

At the bottom of the pit, Jace dug into the ground and started to panic when he didn't immediately find them. He expanded digging and finally found them. He spent several minutes digging everything up and placing it in his inventory. Once he had everything, he climbed back up the branch.

Jace walked over to the river and washed off his gear before equipping his breastplate and bracers. They were cold on his skin but he didn't care. He just felt better having some of his equipment back. He was just glad Charlena wasn't here because he looked absolutely ridiculous with nothing but a breastplate, bracers and a loincloth.

He shivered and realized he needed to get some more equipment. Of course, the only way to get more equipment was to buy it tomorrow in the village or get it off a monster. Jace glanced back at the hill with the goblin camp and smiled. He had an entire village of monsters. He just needed to figure out how to get a few of them alone.

Looking at the pit below him, he got an idea. He pulled the branch out of the pit and dragged it a few dozen yards away. Next, he used a leafy branch to wipe his tracks away. He found a good hiding spot between the pit and the goblin camp. When he was ready, he took the cups from his inventory and shook them around to make a clanging noise. Now, he just needed to wait.

He didn't have to wait long before two goblins came down the path from the goblin village. They didn't seem very alert and they walked right past Jace without noticing him. Jace moved silently up behind them and struck down out with his rapier and rat dagger, aiming one weapon at each goblin.

You critically stab Firebelly Goblin for 17 damage.
Firebelly Goblin dies.
You gain 20 experience.

You critically stab Firebelly Goblin for 9 damage.

The goblin he had struck with his rapier dropped with a sound. The other goblin screeched and spun around, its eyes going to Jace's bare legs and loincloth. The moment of gawking at Jace cost the goblin.

Jace used his *Vanish* ability to disappear. He then stabbed both his weapons into the goblin, dropping it next to its companion.

You critically stab Firebelly Goblin for 16 damage.
You critically stab Firebelly Goblin for 7 damage.
Firebelly Goblin dies.
You gain 20 experience.

"Watch for more goblins," he told Luna, who dutifully began to look towards the village and sniff the air.

Bending over the bodies, Jace quickly looted them. He received four gold, a short sword and helmet. He held up the helmet and looked down at his bare legs and feet. Of course, it would be a helmet. Trying not to think how ridiculous he must look he equipped the crude goblin helmet.

"Any sign of other goblins?" Jace asked Luna silently.

"No," she told him, her nose still sniffing the air.

Jace dragged the bodies to the pit and threw them in. Using the leafy branch, he obscured any signs of a struggle and wiped away his tracks.

He took his position in some thick brushes and sent Luna closer to the goblin village to see whether more goblins came to investigate and if so, how many. His mana had completely regenerated by then so he clanged the cups together again and waited.

"More goblins," he heard Luna say in his mind. "Two."

Jace used the tactic as before, killing both goblins with barely any noise. This time he was slightly luckier and received a pair of boots from one of them.

He also received a sling but since he didn't have the *Missile Weapons* skill, it was useless to him.

After cleaning up the area, Jace was able to do the same routine again but the third time, there were three goblins and they had their weapons out. One of the goblins was larger than the other and his HUD identified it as a warrior. That one would be the toughest.

Jace carefully watched them pass him, ready to bolt if he was discovered. Yet despite being alert, they didn't detect Jace in his hiding spot and as they passed. Jace stepped in behind the large one and stabbed it with both of his weapons.

You critically stab Firebelly Goblin Warrior for 17 damage.
You critically stab Firebelly Goblin Warrior for 9 damage.

The goblin cried out in pain but didn't die. That was not good. He had been counting on taking out the lead goblin with his first strike and then dealing with the other two with his *Vanish* skill. He grimaced. The best laid plans of mice and men.

The moment of surprise ended as the goblins turned to confront their attacker. Before they attacked, Jace did some quick calculations in his head. Long hours of playing the game helped him as he quickly formulated a plan.

Popping his *Vanish* and savoring the look of surprise on the goblin's faces, he drove his dagger into the warrior, while simultaneously running through the goblin on his right with his rapier.

You critically stab Firebelly Goblin Warrior for 9 damage.
Firebelly Goblin Warrior dies.
You gain 30 experience.

You critically stab Firebelly Goblin for 18 damage.
Firebelly Goblin dies.
You gain 20 experience.

The warrior and the goblin he'd struck both collapsed onto the group but Jace couldn't avoid the spear of the remaining goblin as it caught him in the chest.

Firebelly Goblin stabs YOU for 4 damage.

As if the explosion of pain wasn't bad enough, the remaining goblin began to scream at the top of his lungs. "Hoo-mons! Hoo-mons! Help! Help!"

Jace used his remaining mana to activate *Vanish* again and stabbed the goblin through its black heart. The thing dropped bonelessly to the ground.

Luna's frantic voice popped into his head. "More goblins! Many!"

"Come back to me," he told the cat and looted the bodies so quickly, he wasn't even sure what he received. He and Luna retreated to the river and then walked a hundred yards down river and hid in some bushes, watching the area with the pit.

Within minutes, a group of a dozen goblins appeared and began chattering as soon as they came across the bodies. Among them, one seemed to be giving orders and Jace pegged it as the shaman from its feathered headdress.

As the goblins spread out searching for him, Jace decided to circle around and head back to the village. Then he paused. He ran the numbers in his head. He'd killed seven goblins and there were about a dozen currently looking for him. How many were there back in the camp? A dozen? It was a big camp for a dozen goblins to guard.

Changing his mind, he circled back towards the camp. While so many of the goblins were out here searching for him, it was time to get some payback for Aiden and Chastity.

Jace made a wide arch around and came at the village from the opposite side. He moved as quickly as possible without giving away his position. Creeping up to the wood fencing, Jace made sure there were no goblins within eyeshot and cast a *Flame Bolt* at the thatch roof of the cabin and then cast another at the hut nearest it. He quickly re-stealthed and crept along the parameter, but towards the gate.

Behind him, he heard the commotion as goblins realized the buildings were on fire and went to try and extinguish the fire. By then, he'd move fifty yards along the fence and, drawing on Luna's mana, Jace cast *Flame Bolts* at two more huts, setting their roofs ablaze too.

"Poetic justice?" Jace asked Luna.

The cat considered the growing flames with her feline eyes. "Yes."

As more anarchy ensued, Jace crept back to the cover of the forest and then made a wide arc back to the river. He stayed in stealth until he was back on the trail. Once he was a few hundred yards up the trail, he figured it was safe enough to pick up the pace and then jogged the rest of the way to Aiden and Chastity's farm.

Looking at the destroyed farmhouse, Jace stopped in his tracks. He'd been so intent on getting some more equipment and getting revenge on the goblins, he hadn't really thought of the consequences. What if they formed a large war party and came to burn more farms? With a crazy player in charge of the goblins, who could guess what the guy would do?

He cursed himself for his short-sightedness. His actions may inadvertently cause an even larger attack on

the farms, and possibly the village. He looked around
and then crept over to the barn where he heard snoring.
The two farmers were cuddled up on some blankets in
the hay.

Should he wake them and warn them? He wasn't
even sure whether or not the goblins would come. He
should just let them sleep. But that meant he needed to
stay and watch over things and make sure he could warn
them if the goblins did come.

He looked up into the sky and checked the position
of the moons. He still had a few hours before daylight.
He made his way to the tree that Charlena had used
when they'd attacked the goblins and climbed up. From
his perch in the tree, he would maintain his vigil until
the farmers awakened.

Chapter 32

Jace waited until daybreak but there was no sign of the goblins. He had lots of time to think during the hours before dawn and he's considering many possibilities. At one point, a few hours ago, he'd sent Luna to check the other farms in the area. Considering how insane the player was leading the goblins, he thought they might attack farms at random. But no attack had come.

During the hours, he'd had a chance to go back and take a look at what he'd looted. He'd gotten 7 gold, a shortbow, an axe and another goblin jerkin. That was two items he couldn't use and one he didn't need. And he would have traded them all for a pair of pants.

Just after sunrise, Aiden and Chastity had awakened and started to do their farm chores. It hadn't taken them long to see Jace in the tree.

Aiden walked over to the tree and called to him. "Son," he yelled up. "Is there some particular reason you're half naked up in our tree?"

Sighing, Jace climbed down. "I was keeping an eye out for more goblins."

"You think they might come back?" asked the man, clearly alarmed.

"Remember when you told me you wanted revenge?" Jace asked.

The man nodded.

"Last night, I killed seven more of them and set several of their huts on fire," he told the man. "Including the goblin leader's."

"Did you now," the man grinned. "I reckon that's good revenge. That'll teach those goblins to kill my poor defenseless Bessy!"

You have gained a level.
You are now level 3 in Rogue.
You gain 8 health.
You gain 4 mana.

You have gained a new ability: Backstab I

"And tell your elf friend that I'd like to thank her too," he told Jace. "When you see her."

Jace hardly heard Aiden. The experience from the quest pushed him to *Rogue* level 3, giving him 8 more health and 4 more mana. More importantly, he'd also gained the Backstab ability, which would allow him to do triple damage when attacking from behind. At the moment, it wasn't much more damage than a critical strike, but the higher level he achieved, the more damage it would do.

"I'll tell her," Jace assured the old man. "I need to go into town and um… buy some pants."

"I reckon you do," Aiden agreed and left to help his wife with the chores.

Jace left their farm and went back into town. He ignored the stares of the villagers and went straight to the apothecary. Once again, he banged on the door until the rotund mayor answered it.

"Oh," said the mayor, breaking into a grin. "It's you! I heard you drove off those goblins but not before they burned down the couple's home. A pity but at least they're alive!"

You have completed the quest, "When Goblins Attack"
You gain 400 experience. Experience to next level 1510.
You gain +100 faction with Residents of Sinking Springs
You gain +100 faction with Absalom

Jace nodded and caught the mayor's eyes flit down to his bear legs.

"Ah well," the Absalom said. "Come in! Come in!"

Absalom didn't wait for Jace but turned and hurried to the back of his shop where he disappeared into another room. Jace and Luna were left in the main area, waiting for the mayor to return.

It took several minutes for him to emerge, but when Absalom finally did, Jace smiled broadly. In the mayor's arms was a pair of leather leggings. Finally, he'd have some pants again.

The mayor handed him the pants. "These go with the jerkin. It looks like you could use them." He then pulled out a pouch of gold and handed it to Jace. Jace received both items and immediately equipped the leather leggings. He felt so much better being fully clothed.

You receive 100 gold
You receive leather leggings

"Thank you again for helping poor Aiden and Chastity," the mayor told him. "Now, I must be getting back to my…"

"When is the next caravan," Jace asked the mayor before the man could usher him out of the apothecary.

He knew he now had the 150 gold it would cost to hitch a ride on the caravan that would hopefully take him to the capital.

The mayor stopped and blinked. "The caravan?"

"Yes," Jace confirmed. "When does it arrive? I'd like to get a ride to the capital."

"Whitecliff?" said the mayor. "That's a goodly distance. Yes, yes. Let's see, the caravan." The man tapped his head. "Oh yes, it was just through here a week ago. So, it will be back in… Uh… A month and three weeks!"

Jace just stared at the mayor. "A month and three weeks?"

"Yes. It was last in just before you and the elf arrived. "It takes a month to get back to the Whitecliff and a month to get back here, so that would be … about a month, three weeks and a few days."

He felt his shoulders slump. Almost two months? It would be almost two months before he could catch a caravan to the capital? Sinking Springs must be on the outer boundaries of Aldor, the human kingdom. He was more familiar with the Visimar, the vampire nation that

Mordred was from but he had been to Aldor for higher level quests. In fact, he'd found one of the pieces of the Kobadera set in the human kingdom.

He sighed. Travelling at higher levels was much easier. Players could pay a few thousand gold to a high level mage and they could teleport their entire group. There were also mage gates in every capital that allowed travel to any other capital in your faction. Add in ships, horses, flying mounts and special teleportation items and there were many ways mid to high level characters could get around the world easily.

Unfortunately, he was not a mid or high level character at the moment. He was a low level character with not even two hundred gold. Did he wait two months? Or brave the wild lands? Would Charlena come with him? It would be dangerous. Very dangerous. He'd need to talk to her.

The mayor cleared his throat. "Milord Dedrurrurth, are you okay?"

Jace snapped back to where he was and saw that the mayor was staring at him expectantly.

"I'm sorry," Jace apologized. "What did you ask?

"I asked if you were okay," the mayor said. "You looked quite crestfallen just now."

Jace nodded. "Sorry, I had been hoping to get to the capital sooner."

Absalom nodded. "Yes, well, it is a long journey and getting goods is sometimes a pain, but we do like our privacy out here on the border."

Jace perked up. "This is the border?"

The mayor nodded. "Oh yes, to the east are the Outlands. Monsters of all sorts call those lands home. But we are a rugged folk here in Sinking Springs."

The Outlands. That meant Jace was on the far eastern edge of Kushor, probably the furthest he could be from Whitecliff and still be in the human kingdom. No wonder it took two months for the caravan to get from Sinking Springs to Whitecliff and back.

"I'm okay," Jace told the mayor. "I just forgot how far away I was."

"Understandable," Absalom told him and glanced at the door.

Jace understood the hint. Absalom wanted him to leave so he could get back to, well whatever the man got up to get his apothecary. Looking around, he was suddenly curious exactly what the mayor did in here.

"Mayor," he looked at the squat man. "What exactly do you do with all this equipment?"

The mayor looked surprised but quickly recovered. "I am working on a new alchemical mixture. One that will make me both rich and famous!"

"What kind of alchemical mixture?" Jace asked, impressed.

"I am working on a formula which will, when taken, fortify the body, mind and spirit," the mayor said excitedly. "Permanently."

"Permanently?" Jace looked at him quizzically. There were already various potions that could temporarily increase attributes. If Absalom created an alchemical potion that did so permanently, he'd have every player knocking on his door. Of course, that was assuming he could create such a mixture. Could the Game AI create new potions? Or did the developers have to add those to the game? It was an interesting question. One he could have asked the developers if he were still alive.

He smiled at the mayor. "That sounds incredible. Have you made any progress?"

Now it was the mayor's turn to be crestfallen. "Some, but it's slow. As I just mentioned, the caravans take two months to return so getting rare ingredients has been trying. But I'll figure it out eventually."

"I really need some Opigon," the mayor told him. "But it's such a rare plant and the only known samples have been found in the Outlands."

Jace raised an eyebrow. "Is that why you came here?"

The mayor laughed mirthlessly. "Of course. I thought there would be adventurers coming out here, going into the Outlands all the time."

"But no one comes out this way.".

"Exactly. Adventurers don't come out here at all. Well, present company excluded of course. And on the few occasions they did come out, they appear out of thin air, mount their horses and ride off before I even get a chance to talk with them."

"What does this…"

"Opigon," the mayor supplied helpfully.

"What does this Opigon look like?" Jace asked. If he ended up sticking around, maybe he could go hunt for some.

The mayor described it as a seven pointed leaf that sounded to Jace like a cannabis leaf, only it was black with red around the edges and tips. He made a mental note of it and would keep an eye open for it.

"If you come across any," the mayor said. "Make sure you handle it with extreme care. They are very fragile. And bring it back to me as soon as possible."

Jace agreed and left the mayor's lab. He went back to the store, where he brought another fishing pole, a frying pan and spatula, as well as another coil of rope to replace the items he'd lost to the goblins.

Leaving the store, Jace checked the time. He still had a few hours before Charlena would log in and he wanted to do a little recon of the goblin camp before she did. Who knew what that crazy player leading the goblins would do.

Before he left, he decided to go to the tavern and eat. Jace was starting to feel hungry and he knew it wouldn't be too long before he'd get the debuff. He started to walk over when he heard his name being called. It was distant and he could barely make it out, but it was definitely someone calling his name. And not his character name, his real name. It sounded like Charlena.

"Jace!" came her faint voice and he looked around for her. His ears were just not sharp enough to pinpoint where the sound was coming from. But he did know someone with very sharp ears. He looked down at Luna. "Find her! Find Charlena!"

Luna's ears twitched for a moment and then she streaked off to the south, forcing Jace to run in order to keep up with her. They ran through the village, dodging between buildings before they finally broke into the open and onto the southern road.

He immediately saw Charlena lying on her stomach in the middle of the road. He couldn't tell if she was dead or not and poured on the speed.

Reaching her body, he turned her over. She was alive but she wasn't speaking. Jace realized what had happened. She must have ran all the way back and used up all of her *Stamina*. She'd be fine once she regenerated some.

"It's okay," he told her. "Sorry I was there. I'll explain it to you when you can move."

She shook her head slightly and he thought he heard her say something. He bent over her and lowered his ear to her mouth to try and make out what she was saying.

"You… you're alive," she rasped.

Jace sat up and smiled down at her. "Yes, I'm alive. The goblins killed me, but I respawned."

Charlena shook her head again, a little stronger this time. She reached up with her hand and pulled him back down. "No… I think… you're alive… "She gasped, straining to get the last words out. "... in the real world."

Chapter 33

Jace sat up quickly. He didn't think he had understood her correctly, but his heart still did a flip flop. She thought he was alive? That wasn't possible. He had to be dead. Didn't he?

His heart was racing but he tried to think of things logically. He'd be in the game for days without logging out. He would have had to eat and drink in that time, not to mention taking care of other bodily functions. Even if he wouldn't have dehydrated by now, he hadn't slept the entire time he'd been in the game. It didn't make any sense. There was no way he could be in a pod. He must have misunderstood her.

As he waited for her to recover from *Stamina* depletion, a thought occurred to him. She said he had been in an accident. A car accident. What if he was in a coma? He could be in a long term medical pod. That would explain how he could survive this long. Jace had only read a little about them but if he remembered correctly, a person could be in one for months.

But if he was in a coma, inside a medical pod, why wasn't he sleeping? Could that be it? Was he still alive in the real world, inside a medical pod that was keeping his brain stimulated? It was too much for him to process.

"I think you might be alive," Charlena said as she climbed to her knees. She'd recovered from the *Stamina* depletion and had regenerated enough that she could sit up.

Jace just stared at her. "How? Are you sure?"

Charlena shook her head and took Jace's hand. "I don't know for certain. But remember when I told you I did a little search for your name when you first told me your story?"

He nodded numbly. "Yeah, that's when you told me about the car accident."

"Right," she said. "I don't remember if I told you, but that was the only thing I could find on you."

"Did you find more?"

"No," Charlena said and must have seen Jace's puzzled look. "No. I didn't find anything else. That's the whole point. I kept an automated search on your name so I could see if there was a funeral or anything."

Jace still didn't know where she was going and it must have shown on his face.

"It's been over a month since the accident," she explained. "I went back and looked at the search results when I got home from class. There's still nothing."

Jace felt a little depressed at that. He'd died and there had been nothing about him, other than some brief mention on an accident report. It was as if he had never existed. He was an average Joe. He died and no one noticed. The world went on. "Well, it's not like I was a celebrity."

"No," she shook her head, tightening her grip on his hand. "You don't get it. I was searching everything. Public records, the internet, everything. There was no obituary. And there was no certificate of death."

That hit Jace like a ten ton hammer. Could it be? Was it really possible that he was alive?

If so, that meant he was probably in some sort of coma and his body must be in very bad shape. Why else would he still be in a coma? He could still die.

"That's good news," he said, though he was too numb to convey any real emotion.

Charlena gave him an incredulous look. "Good news?! That's great news! You're still alive!"

Jace held a hand up. He wanted to believe that. He wanted to believe that he was alive and that he'd recover. Thinking that he was dead for all this time really made him realize how precious his life really was. He would love a second chance at it. But he needed to be sure before he got his hopes up.

"I need to be sure," Jace told her. "I need to have some sort of proof before I can accept it."

Giving him a sympathetic look, Charlena nodded. "I understand. If you are alive, we need to find your body!"

"Yes," he told her. "If I am alive, I'm probably in a coma, in one of the long term medical pods."

"A coma?" she asked and seemed to take a minute to absorb that. "Why do you think that?"

"I haven't logged out, slept, eaten or drank anything for days by my reckoning. I think I would have either died of dehydration or something before now. A long term medical pod could take care of all of my bodily functions: feed me intravenously, etc."

"But why do you think you're in a coma?"

"Because I haven't slept. It wouldn't make any sense for them to keep me immersed if I was well enough to wake up. So, I must be in a coma."

Charlena looked saddened by his explanation but after a moment, she nodded. "I guess that makes sense."

"This may make finding me easier," he told her. "How many hospitals would have a coma patient in a long term pod?"

"That's right!" Charlena said excitedly. "I should be able to call up the hospitals and find out if they have long term pods and if so, do they have a car accident victim in a coma in one of them."

"That might work," Jace told her. He remembered WorldCog and how he had thought they had killed him. That was still a possibility. They could have tried and failed. If so, they may still be after him. "Charlena, be careful. If WorldCog did try to have me killed, I don't want you getting on their radar."

"You still think they tried to have you killed?" Charlena asked him. "I mean, it's possible you were just hit by a car and then ended up in a coma."

Jace shook his head. "Except for the fact that I ended up in a monster body."

"Oh," Charlena scrunched up her face. "I forgot about that. You're right. Just ending up in a medical pod wouldn't explain that. Except, what if it's a problem with the medical pod and not the game?"

Once again, Jace shook his head. "That doesn't explain the other players I found in monster bodies."

Charlena's face went sober. "That's right. Like Diana Stewart."

"Like Diana Stewart and Duglas," Jace agreed. "And that goblin chieftain."

Charlena's shot up. "Goblin chieftain?"

Jace smiled sadly. "I got captured by the goblins after you left last night. They took me to their leader, who called himself 'the Big Cheese'." He remembered the person's ravings. "He'd gone insane from being in here so long and being a monster."

"He was crazy?" Charlena asked. "Are you sure?"

Jace nodded empathetically. "Oh yeah. He was ranting about being killed over and over by players and kept talking about himself in plural form."

Charlena made a face. "Poor guy or girl. It's frightening to think that could be happening to others."

Jace agreed but remembered something else. "And I think there must be some sort of residual code from me being a monster."

"You mean the fact that you can talk to monsters?"

"Something more. I can sense other players inside monsters. I actually feel drawn to them," he told her.

She considered that for a moment. "I'm not sure if I understand. Aren't you a regular player now?"

"Not really completely normal," Jace told her. "I wonder if the way I turned myself into a player didn't completely change me. It could have made me a hybrid. I may have code from both entity types."

"I don't know if I understand," Charlena told him.

Jace shrugged. "I don't know if I understand either. What I did shouldn't be possible. It's a situation the original developers never anticipated: A player who is a monster and happens to know how to code and knows something about the game, doing an injection attack to change his entity type."

Charlena ran her hand over her head. "Most of what you said went right over my head."

Jace laughed. "Sorry. But let's just say, the developers never meant for a hybrid like me to exist, so there's no telling what side-effects may occur. Me sensing other players in monsters could be one of those side-effects."

A dark look crossed Charlena's beautiful elven features. "Wait. If you can sense them, do you think they can sense you?"

Jace considered that. "It's possible. I didn't ask Duglas or Diana and I don't think Big Cheese was lucent enough to understand and even if he did, I don't think I could have trusted his answer."

"So, what now?" Charlena asked. "Want me to log out and start calling hospitals?"

Jace considered for a moment. It would be nice to have confirmation that he was actually alive. But at the same time, if she started calling every hospital in Philadelphia, it might set off some red flags. "No, wait until tomorrow and then call one or two."

She gave him a confused expression.

"I don't want you to set off any red flags," he told her. "If WorldCog did try to kill me, we don't want to alert them to the fact that they didn't succeed. I think I'm better off if they think I'm dead."

Charlena nodded. "That makes sense. I'll try to be discrete. I'll start with the ones around where the accident occurred. I think the address is in the accident report."

"That sounds like a plan."

"So then," she looked around. "Do you just want to keep playing like nothing happened."

He smiled. "I guess so." He remembered the news about the caravan, and it must shown on his face.

"What?" asked Charlena.

"I found out from Absalom today that the caravan was here right before we arrived," he told her. "It won't be back for nearly 2 months."

"TWO MONTHS?!" Charlena exclaimed. "That little piece of --"

The colorful language she used to describe the mage who had brought her here could have made a sailor blush. Jace was pretty sure he was blushing.

"I can't believe that idiot would just dump me here to wait for 2 months!" Charlena fumed. "And I can't believe WorldCog wouldn't do anything about it! If we find out WorldCog was behind trying to kill you, I will personally help you burn their headquarters to the ground!"

Jace nodded but didn't interrupt her tirade. He was afraid that if he did, she might redirect some of that ire onto him. And he had enough things to keep his mind occupied right now.

When she'd gotten her ranting out of her system, she turned back to Jace. "So then what do we do? Wait here?"

"That's one possibility," he told her. "The other is, we try to make it to the next town on our own."

"On our own?" Charlena asked disbelievingly.

"It's possible," he told her. "If we could make it to a different town, closer to the capital, we might catch an earlier caravan."

"Isn't that dangerous, especially if we can only move when I'm logged in?" she asked.

"Actually," Jace began. "We could be moving 24 hours a day. If you auto-follow me."

"Auto-follow you?" she asked, wrinkling her nose.

"It's how you attach yourself to a caravan or ship. You auto-follow the captain or caravan leader and you will basically go where they go," Jace explained. "You can also auto-follow another player."

"How does that work? I stay logged in?" she asked.

"Basically, when you log out, your character will keep following me," he told her. "It's very robotic and unnatural looking but it does work. Players do it, but usually with people they really trust. So we could do it, if you trust me." He raised an eyebrow at her.

Charlena looked right into his eyes and took his hand. "I trust you with my life. Well, maybe my character's life."

He wanted to laugh but her eyes held him. So caught up in her eyes was he that he was surprised when her lips found his.

Chapter 34

Her lips were warm and sweet and Jace had just begun to kiss her back when she pulled away suddenly.

"Darn it!" she said, taking a step back.

Jace looked at her in confusion. He knew it had been a long time since he kissed a girl, but he didn't remember being that bad.

She seemed to notice his look and her expression turned apologetic. "I forgot to turn up the sensory level. No offense, but it was sort of like kissing you through a few layers of cellophane."

Jace gave her a mischievous smile. "You can dial your sensory feedback up to maximum and we can try that again."

"Oh really?" she asked, her eyes glinting with mischief too. "Maybe I'll do just that."

Her eyes went glassy for a moment and Jace stepped in and kissed her. This time she didn't pull away and a little moan escaped her. When they finally broke away, they were both breathless.

Jace had been attracted to her from the start, but his predicament had taken up most of his thoughts. And the news of him possibly being alive had really thrown him for an emotional loop. But he genuinely liked Charlena. He'd always been so focused on his career and building up his "retirement" with Mordred, he'd barely had time for relationships. Now it seemed he had inadvertently found one.

He really liked Charlena. She was intelligent, funny and best of all, she seemed to like the old vids that he did. If he was alive and he did recover, would their relationship spill over into the real world? Would they like each other once they met the real versions? Jace decided to think about it later. Right now, he'd just enjoy whatever it was they did have.

"Better that time?" he asked playfully.

Catching her breath, Charlena gave him a broad smile. "Much better!"

They both laughed for a moment but then Charlena turned serious. "I trust you Jace. I will definitely auto-follow you. But do you really think we can make it to the next town? Do you even know what the next town is?"

Jace shook his head. "I didn't ask. The two months until the next caravan thing kind of threw me for a loop."

"Me too," she nodded. "It's hard to believe this is a starter town when it's that far away from the capital."

"When the game first started, people ended up all over the place. It was completely random.," he told her. "There were tons of complaints because it took so long for friends or family to find each other in the game - if they ever did."

"God forbid any of them ended up out here," Charlena chimed in.

"They did," Jace assured her. "And other equally far away places. Remember, back then, you could only be human so they had lots of human villages scattered across the world so that the starter areas wouldn't be overcrowded. But they had so many complaints that they did that big update and introduced the other races as 'premium' races and introduced new starter cities - all near the capitals."

"Total money grab!" Charlena said bitterly.

"At the time," Jace agreed. "But now when you sign up, you get three free premium options."

Charlena nodded. "True, I got three. I tried a gnome but I didn't like it so I deleted it and created this elf."

Jace stared at her for a long moment, trying to picture her as a gnome. Gnomes and halflings had very youthful looks to them. Combined with their small stature, they almost resemble children. It almost seemed a bit creepy to have a relationship with someone who looked like a child, even though they could be 50 years old in real life.

"What?" asked Charlena, who must have noticed his odd stare.

"Just imagining you as a gnome," Jace said, blushing slightly.

"I'll have you know I was a really cute gnome," she told him with mock indignation. "But they make better wizards and I just didn't like the magic."

"Me either," Jace said. He remembered how he'd set the goblin huts aflame. "But it does have its uses."

"Oh shoot," he said as he remembered the goblin camp. He'd forgotten about it. What were they up to now? Were they planning an attack on Sinking Springs? Even if he was leaving, he didn't want Sinking Springs to get wiped out because of something he did.

"What?!" Charlena asked, suddenly alert.

"The goblin camp," he said. "I kind of set it on fire last night after they killed me. They might be planning an attack on the village to get revenge. We should go check on it."

Relaxing, Charlena shook her head. "They're gone. I logged in near them and thought you might be scouting them out, so I went to find you. The whole place is deserted."

"Deserted?" he asked in disbelief.

"They're all gone. Most of the huts have been burnt to the ground," she told him. "When I saw that, I figured you were back in the village and ran back here to tell you the news."

"And ran yourself completely out of stamina," he chided.

"Yes," she said, remembering. "That's never happened. I just collapsed. I couldn't do anything. It was scary."

"When you run out of stamina completely," he explained. "You collapse and can't do anything until you regenerate. If that happens in a fight, you'll die. So make sure you keep an eye on it."

"I will from now on," she told him. "I wasn't sure what was going on."

He thought back to what she said about the goblin village. He had only started fires on a few of the huts. Had that crazy player burned down the rest of the village and left? Had he been afraid of more retaliation? Did he think a group of players was coming for him? Jace remembered his talk of being killed over and over by players. Had he been afraid?

Jace shook his head. Who knows what the Big Cheese was thinking? He was obviously insane now and it was probably a mistake to assign rational decision making to him. The goblins were gone. That was all that mattered. At least they could leave Sinking Springs without worrying about it being wiped out.

"Speaking of the goblins," Jace said. "Did you turn in your quests?"

"No, I came right here."

"Let's go turn in your quests and see how far away from level 3 you are," he told her. "If we're both level 3 when we leave, it will be a bit easier."

Her eyes glazed over briefly and then she punched him playfully. "You're level 3 already?!"

Jace related the events of the previous night in more detail than his earlier description. He told her about the pit trap, being taken to the Big Cheese and being killed. He went on to relate the ambushing of the goblins and the torching of their huts before stopping.

"Wow," she said. "You did have a busy night."

"Wish you would have been there," he told her.

"Some of us have to sleep," she told him but then her smile faltered. "I'm sorry, I shouldn't joke about that."

He waved away her apology. "On the bright side, even caravans stop for the night. I can keep going all night."

She smiled wickedly at him. "Good to know you can go all night."

Blushing, Jace turned back towards the mayor's place. "Let's go turn in your quest."

She giggled behind him but followed him to the mayor's apothecary. They turned in her quest but asked the mayor about the next closest town before they left.

"Next closest town," repeated the mayor thoughtfully. He scratched his chin for a moment. "That would be Skystead, in the mountains to the west. It's a good week's journey from here. Why do you ask?"

"We were thinking about heading there," Jace answered truthfully.

"Oh my," the mayor looked startled. "Just the two of you?"

"Yes," Charlena said warily. "Why? Is that a problem?"

"Well...uh," stammered the mayor. "I mean… it's just that… you know… it's dangerous in the wild lands. Normally the adventurers that go between towns are...uh… much more… um… experienced."

"Are there specific monsters between here and Skystead that you know about?" Jace asked.

"Well, no… I meant… nothing specific," he said. "But the caravans always speak of beasts attacking, bandits and all sorts of other nasty things."

"Are their stories specifically about the area between here and there?" Jace asked again.

"Well, um, no. Not specifically," the mayor replied, now looking a bit embarrassed. "I mean, not that I remember."

"Thank you," Jace told him. "Char… Almedha will talk about it."

They left the mayor and walked a short ways away before Charlena stopped him. "What do you think?"

"About the monsters?" Jace asked.

Charlena nodded and he saw worry on her face.

"I don't think it will be as bad as he says," Jace tried to reassure her. "For one, we will attract much less attention than a caravan. And for two, he couldn't name any specific monsters between here and there. If there was really a problem, he would know."

She considered that and then nodded. Then her face went from worried to serious. "Jace, you never told me why you need to get to the capital so bad. Is there something there that can help you."

Jace hesitated. The *Help Desk* was supposed to be a secret. If he were alive and they found out he'd said something, would WorldCog try to enforce his NDA.

Jace stopped and mentally kicked himself. Why did he care? If he wasn't dead, his NDA was going to be the least of WorldCog's problems. Once he exposed the bug, they were going to have a lot of explaining to do - not just to him, but to the gaming commission.

"Technically, we're not supposed to talk about it," he told her, leaning in conspiratorially. "But in the castle of each capital city is a hidden room that can shift around. Inside the room is a thing called a *Help Desk*."

"A help desk? As in, customer service?" she broke in.

Jace smiled and nodded. "It's left over from the first revision of the game where they tried to handle support in-game. It's been discontinued but ripping out the actual *Help Desk* would have involved a ton of code change, so they just hid it where no one should be able to find it."

"But you can?" she asked.

Jace frowned. "Hopefully. But first, we need to get to the capital. Once we're there, I'll figure out a way to get into the castle and search it."

"Aren't only royalty allowed in the castle," asked Charlena dubiously.

"Yes," Jace confirmed. "One step at a time."

"Okay Jace," she said. "I'll trust you know what you're getting into. What next?"

"Let's go turn in your other quest and then go grab some rations at the store," he told her. "If we can get you to level 3, we might as well start off tonight."

Charlena stopped and looked at him, her eyes boring into his. "Are you sure about this Jace? I know your situation but we could wait."

"Yes," Jace said, holding her stare. "If I am in a medical pod, I may need to get this resolved as soon as possible. I have no log out option. No pod references at all. I could be stuck in here even if I come out of the coma."

"Couldn't they just turn the pod off?" Charlena asked, the concern showing on her face.

"No," Jace shook his head. "Well… yes, but there are serious risks just turning off a pod - like frying your brain. It's why they have battery backups. The sudden loss of input can lead to all sorts of problems. I'm sure they know that at the hospital, but I don't want to take that chance."

"I had no idea," Charlena told him.

"Most people don't. It's in the manual but no one reads that. And since they have battery backups, there is almost never a problem. I only know about it because I worked at WorldCog."

"So, we need to get to the capital and we need to find your body in real life," she said adamantly.

"The sooner the better," he told her.

Chapter 35

Even after turning in her goblin revenge quest to Aiden, Charlena was still a few hundred experience shy of level 3. They went around to the various farms and villagers until they had completed enough quests to get her to level 3.

After she hit third level, they bought some more rations and a few other supplies Jace thought they would need. After their shopping, they went into the tavern to plan their next step. Jace ordered fish and chips, as usual, and a cup of their mead. Although skeptical at first, Charlena tried the mead and the fish and chips and then ordered her own.

"This is so good," she said, savoring a mouthful of fish and chips. "And the best thing is, it's not fattening!"

"Zero calories," Jace agreed. Luna was purring on his lap. He stroked her fur and changed the conversation back to their plans. "So, you're okay with me leaving tonight once you log out?"

She smiled over at him. "I'm okay. I don't have to do anything. You're the one that gets to start walking."

"True," Jace admitted. "Hopefully, the next time you log in, we'll be a day closer to Skystead."

"Just be careful. I don't relish making a second attempt naked."

"I don't know, that could be interesting." Jace smiled evilly.

Charlena rolled his eyes at him and took another drink of her mead. Her mood turned serious. "Do you really think we can make it?"

"I don't know," he told her honestly. "I never tried something like this when I was low level. But if we don't try, we're going to be stuck here."

"What about me contacting support?" she asked. "Maybe if I told them about the situation, they could intervene."

"I don't know how much I trust them," Jace told her. "And I don't want you to get involved until we know."

"I don't mind..."

"No!" Jace said adamantly and saw her face go steely. He softened his face. "Listen, we don't know if WorldCog is involved or if they're just ignorant of the error. Until we do, we can't let them know about you."

"But..."

Jace reached across the table and put his hand over hers. "Look what happened to me. What if they are involved and they come after you? Right now, you're my only link to the outside and finding my body - assuming I really am alive. You need to stay off their radar. At least for now."

She stared into his eyes for a long moment and finally nodded. "Fine, for now."

"Thanks," he told her and she gave him a smile.

She looked around. "I think it's late. I need to log out and you need to start your journey."

Jace sighed. "You're right. I'll see you tomorrow evening?"

"Of course," she said and she stood up from the table. She walked over to him and kissed him. The kiss lingered for a long moment before she backed away. "So, I just auto-follow and log out."

"Yes," he told her. "And then your body stays online and follows me."

She shrugged. "Good luck!"

Jace watched as her eyes went glassy and this time they stayed glassy and Charlena's body took a step towards him. Setting Luna on the floor, he stood up and took a step back. Charlena's body took a step forward. The movement was stiff and looked a bit unnatural but she did follow him. It was actually a bit unnerving to see her body there but know that Charlena was not inside.

He walked outside and Charlena followed him a few steps behind. Once outside, he experimentally jogged and then ran to see how she would react. In each instance, she mirrored his movements and kept up with him.

"Well, at least we know it works," he said to Luna.

"Yes."

He looked down at the little cat. "It looks like you're going to be my only companion for a while."

Luna looked up at him and blinked. "Yes."

He realized he was stalling. Jace felt a certain sense of trepidation and maybe even a little foreboding about the journey. He had a lot to lose - well, relatively speaking. If he died out in the wild lands, he'd never make it back to his body. He'd lose everything he had. If he didn't go, he could lose even more if he were alive.

He needed to reach the capital and he needed to figure out how he could access the pod controls if he were actually alive. Only support could help him to that. He took a deep breath and held it. Letting it out, he took the first step towards Whitecliff.

Jace walked west out of Sinking Springs, past the farms and into the wild lands. In the distance, he could make out the mountains. That was his destination. Somewhere on the mountain was Skystead, his destination.

Once they entered the wild lands, Jace began to jog. He kept a watchful eye on his *Stamina*. Whenever it dropped to 50%, he would stop and walk again. It was important that he keep enough *Stamina* to fight if he ran into something hostile. If he ran himself too low and then met something that wanted to kill them, he would be at a severe disadvantage.

They kept walking through the night and into early morning. When they came upon a stone bridge with a small river, Jace took the time to fish for their breakfast. It only took him an hour to catch several fish and fry them up in his pan. He burned one but did manage to finally max out his *Cooking* skill.

After giving Luna one of the fish to eat, he ate his own fried fish. The fried ones were much tastier than the fish he had cooked over the improvised spit and he was glad he'd picked up the frying pan. It was somewhat disconcerting to have the glassy-eyed Charlena staring at him the entire time, but he was starting to get used to it.

After their breakfast, Luna and Jace continued on through the forest. Jace was just thinking to himself that this might not be as bad a trip as he thought when Luna stopped suddenly. Having learned to trust her instincts and sharper senses, Jace immediately skidded to a halt and heard Charlena do the same.

"What is it?" he whispered.

"Wolfers."

Luna had barely finished answering when three large wolves burst out of the bushes and Luna hissed. Each one was as large as the alpha wolf he'd fought before, maybe even a little larger. One of them went for him, one went for Luna and the final one went for Charlena.

Jace hesitated for a moment, torn between defending himself, Luna or Charlena. He made his decision and hoped it would be the right one.

"Luna," he told her. "Lead it away then lead it back."

"Yes," she snapped back, already bolting away.

Jace stepped next to Charlena. He only had 14 mana and there were three wolves. He thought about using *Vanish*, but opted to use his *Feint* ability instead. It used only 2 mana, instead of 4 so he could get more out of it.

At his level, the two abilities were nearly the same and he'd get twice as many *Feints* than he would *Vanishes*.

As his wolf lunged for him, Jace used *Feint*. The wolf was off balance for a moment and Jace stabbed his knife and rapier it, praying it would go down.

You critically stab Wild Wolf for 17 damage.
You critically stab Wild Wolf for 10 damage.

It didn't. The wolf was still up and snapped at his leg with its teeth.

Wild Wolf bites YOU for but you Dodge.
Your Dodge skill has increased by 1.

His Dodge skill saved him but he heard Charlena cry out as her wolf bit into her. He glanced at the logs.

Wild Wolf bites Almedha Pressalor for 5 damage.

That was a powerful bite. He needed to hurry and kill his wolf so he could help her out. Once again using *Feint*, he slammed both his weapons into the wolf.

You critically stab Wild Wolf for 15 damage.
You critically stab Wild Wolf for 9 damage.
Wild Wolf dies.
You gain 50 experience.

He didn't even wait until he saw the result but immediately used *Feint* again, stepped forward and drove his weapons into the other wolf.

You critically stab Wild Wolf for 18 damage.
You critically stab Wild Wolf for 10 damage.

The wolf yelped but bit Charlena again. His damage hadn't been enough to pull it off.

Wild Wolf bites Almedha Pressalor for 7 damage.

Jace heard Luna scream and saw that the wolf which had been chasing her had caught her. Anger searched through him and he *Feinted* and attacked the wolf in front of him just as it was about to bite Charlena and kill her.

You critically stab Wild Wolf for 16 damage.
You critically stab Wild Wolf for 6 damage.
Wild Wolf dies.
You gain 50 experience.

The wolf died and he immediately ran over to where Luna was, but as he did, the wolf bit down savagely on her and she disappeared.

Your familiar has been banished.

Rage surged through Jace and charged the wolf. The creature was still trying to figure out where it's prey had gone when Jace used his *Feint* and stabbed it.

You critically stab Wild Wolf for 17 damage.
You critically stab Wild Wolf for 8 damage.

It yelped and snapped back at him, it's teeth finding his leg. The teeth tore through muscle and he stifled a scream as the pain flooded his awareness.

Thinking of Luna, he once again used his *Feint* and drove his weapons down into the creatures exposed neck.

You critically stab Wild Wolf for 18 damage.
You critically stab Wild Wolf for 7 damage.
Wild Wolf dies.
You gain 50 experience.

The wolf dropped to the ground and Jace stumbled back, his leg barely able to support his weight without pain shooting up to his head. He looked around, making sure there were no others and then moved back over to Charlena.

Like him, she was starting to regenerate and he could see her wounds closing. Slumping down next to her standing form, he looked up at her glassy eyes. "Well, we survived the first encounter." He thought about how close she'd come to dying and of Luna. "Barely."

That had been close. Too close. He had barely been able to get the wolf off of Charlena in time.

One more bite and she might have died and then she would have lost her body and he'd have to go all the way back to the village to get her.

He needed a tank to *Taunt* the enemies but of course, he didn't have a tank. It was just the two of them and a cat familiar. Future fights could go even worse. What if two of the wolves had attacked Charlena or even all three? He needed to be able to pull them off her quickly.

There was only one way he could do that. He didn't want to do it, but he knew it was the only way. He needed to switch classes to *Fighter*. *Fighter*s were front line fighters. They could use nearly every weapon or armor. They could take blows that the other classes couldn't.

At first level, *Fighter* had the *Taunt* ability, which would force creatures to target him. It was the only reliable way he could ensure that he could get future enemies to attack him instead of Charlena or Luna.

He laughed mirthlessly. He was just starting to make progress in Rogue and now he had to switch. Cursing the game mechanics and WorldCog, he brought up his class menu.

Available classes:
Fighter
Rogue (current class)
Priest
Mage

He hesitated only briefly before choosing *Fighter*. He really didn't want to play a fighter, but he had no choice. It was the only way to keep Charlena safe. Reluctantly, he confirmed his selection and watched the system messages fly by.

Class changed. New class Fighter.
Adaptable: No experience penalty for third class.
You have gained a new skill: Crushing Weapons
You have gained a new skill: Missile Weapons
You have gained a new skill: Slashing Weapons
You have gained a new skill: Throwing Weapons
You have gained a new skill: Two-Handed Weapons
You have gained a new skill: Metal Armor
You have gained a new skill: Shields
You have gained a new skill: Block
Ability gained: Taunt

Jace sighed. It was done. He was now a *Fighter*. Shaking his head, he really couldn't wait to be Mordred again.

Chapter 36

Jace stood alert until his health and mana regenerated and then resummoned Luna, dumping as much mana and health into her as possible. The streams of energy formed into the familiar shape of the orange tabby and she appeared.

The cat spun around, looking around at the dead wolves before finally relaxing. "Bad wolfers!"

"Bad wolfers," Jace agreed. He scratched under the cat's chin. "Sorry I couldn't save you."

"Protect Charlena," the cat meowed.

He smiled at her. "Yes. I have to protect her. We can't let anything happen to her."

"Yes," agreed Luna.

Within a few minutes, Jace's health and mana had recovered from the summoning and they were able to continue on. He kept up his jog and walk routine until early evening. As the sun dipped into the trees to the west, he slowed to a halt.

He had expected Charlena to have logged into the game by that time but her character was still glassy eyed. The time of day in game corresponded to the time of day in the real world, more or less. She'd generally been logging in before nightfall each night.

Why was she tied up with schoolwork? Or was it something else? Had the kiss scared her away?

Wait, hadn't she initiated the first kiss? Was he a bad kisser? Jace hadn't had any complaints from the few girlfriends he'd had.

As the minutes ticked on, Jace began pacing back and forth across the road as Luna sat near Charlena and followed him with her head. Why wasn't she logging in? Had something happened? Had WorldCog found her somehow? But how would they? She shouldn't be on their radar at all.

Jace went from scenario to scenario, each as unlikely as the last, as the minute ticked by and the sun's glow had completely disappeared. He'd already goggle his *Cat-Vision* on, so the change wasn't as noticeable but now he could see stars in the sky. And still Charlena wasn't logged in.

Unable to take it any longer, he motioned to Luna. "Come, let's get going."

Luna looked at him. "Noms?"

Jace gave her an apologetic look. "Sorry Luna, there was no place to fish. If we find a river or lake, I can fish for one."

He checked himself to make sure that he didn't have the Hungry debuff. Jace didn't but he knew it wouldn't be long. He hadn't eaten since breakfast. Another few hours and he'd definitely have it. If he hadn't found a place to fish before then, he'd need to eat one of his rations.

Turning towards the west, Jace began his job again, keeping a watchful eye on his *Stamina*. He threw backward glances at Charlena running behind him, but she remained glassy-eyed. Trying not to worry about her, Jace continued on.

Hours later, when the moons hit their zenith, Jace knew it was midnight. Charlena hadn't logged in and he was really worried. His mind had conjured all sorts of scenarios about what might have befallen her, adding to his foul mood.

He kept up his pace throughout the night with no sign from Charlena. By morning, the trees began to change, as did the surrounding landscape. The trees became shorter and more twisted, while the landscape around him grew wetter. He realized the forest was giving way to swampland.

The mayor hadn't said anything about a swamp. In the game, swamps were a breeding ground for all sorts of monsters and creatures. Generally, it was not a place low level characters wanted to go. Not to mention, it was starting to stink.

As if on queue, Luna complained. "Smell bad!"

He reached down and petted her. "I know. But we need to go this way. Hopefully, it won't be long."

By noon, or what Jace thought was noon, Jace realized he had been wrong. The swamp had not only continued but as he got deeper into it, a mist or fog of some sort permeated the area, obscuring the sun and cutting his visibility. Not only that, but things had grown louder. If he'd thought the forest animals made noise, the swamp was alive with all sorts of life - though none of it visible.

The worse thing was the biting insects. They bit and stung him mercilessly. They were tiny and did no damage but Jace cursed the developers who decided to include them. He realized a normal player could just turn down their sensory feedback but not him. He had to endure their full biting fury.

The only positive thing was that the swamp seemed to hold fish and he had been able to catch a fish for Luna to eat. It looked a bit foul and Jace guessed it was a catfish but his familiar ate it raw nonetheless. He didn't eat any, choosing instead to use some of his rations. He wasn't about to risk getting poisoned or contract some sort of swamp disease. Without a healer, a disease could give him some major debuffs.

When Luna had finished her meal, they continued through the misty swamp but this time the going was slow. With the reduced visibility, he dared not jog. It would be too easy to run right into an ambush or even stumble blindly into some swamp creature. Instead, Jace and Luna continued at a brisk walking pace.

Throughout the day, Jace saw movements in the swamp on both sides of him. Once he glimpsed what looked like a log until two large eyes opened, revealing it to be an alligator of some sort. The second time, he'd seen what looked like a falling branch on a tree that ended up being an enormous snake nearly a foot thick.

Jace kept them moving, making them walk single file down the middle of the road. The movements and sounds kept his nerves on edge the entire day to a point where he could swear they were being followed just out of his sight range.

He wasn't sure when exactly it had begun. He'd caught little glimpses of movement out of the corner of his eye but as soon as he turned to get a better look, he hadn't seen anything. He even asked Luna if she could smell any enemies but she just responded with "smell bad."

When darkness came to the swamp, his visibility dropped almost nothing as the mist seemed to get thicker. He could barely see the road in front of him, even with his *Cat-Vision*. Jace was forced to reduce their pace to a slow walk.

Worse yet, there was no sign of Charlena logging in. Her character continued to follow them with its glassy eyed stare but she was not there. Jace really began to worry about her. She knew they were traveling between the towns. Why wouldn't she log in? Was she okay?

He kept walking, even as the dark swamp seemed to be closing in around him. He looked back to make sure everyone was still with him and once again caught a glimmer of movement to his right. Then there was movement to his left and he snapped his head around to see. There was nothing there. At least nothing that he could see.

Moving in the mist shrouded in darkness, he lost all track of time. It was night, that was all he knew. Had he been walking for one hour, two hours or six hours? He didn't know. The movement continued on either side of him, just out of his view and his nerves were raw from fear and concern. That's when the sounds started.

There were plenty of swamp sounds but these broke through the normal swamp animal sounds. It was like a hissing to his right but a strange hissing, almost like someone letting air out of a balloon or air coming in through a cracked car window. Now it was on his left. And behind him. They were surrounded.

Jace's weapons were already in his hands and he strained his eyes to see the sources of the noises. He glanced down to see that Luna's fur was standing up and her back was arched. She knew something was out there too, but she couldn't see it any better than he could.

The sounds were moving now, circling them. There were at least three, maybe four of them. But what were they?

He couldn't tell exactly where they were but he knew they were close. And they were slowly getting closer. Still he couldn't see anything but swirling mist.

The other swamp sounds went quiet and all he heard was the hissing, slowing circling them. He stepped back so that he was straddling Luna and right next to Charlena. He had no idea what was out there, but he would do his best to protect them. He checked out his new *Fighter* ability.

Taunt
Range: 15 ft
Cost: 4 mana
Description: Scream out a primal challenge to your foes that force them to attack you for 60 seconds.

It seemed straightforward. Unfortunately, unlike a real fighter, he didn't have the armor or extra health to take blows from multiple enemies. He also didn't have the benefit of a healer to keep his health topped off. He had only himself. And he didn't think that was going to be enough against what could be at least four opponents.

The hissing was growing louder and now he could make out shapes in the mist, moving slowly - almost hypnotically around him. It was still hard to make them out but they seemed to be bipedal but they weren't human. At least, not like any human he'd seen. Was that a tail swishing behind them? Darn this mist!

They couldn't be more than 10 or 12 feet from him now though still mostly obscured by the mist. They were slowing circling but Jace could see that they were definitely bipedal. He could tell that they were side stepping around on almost human legs and they definitely had tails. He could see them swishing back and forth in the mist. They held something in their hands. It could be a club but he wasn't sure.

Suddenly they stopped moving and Jace braced himself. He only had 14 mana. That was enough for one *Taunt* and five *Feints*. If these were anything like the wolves, they would each take at least two critical strikes each. That was eight critical strikes, which meant eight *Feints*. He wasn't going to have enough mana. And if each of them landed a blow, he'd wouldn't last past the second round.

Luna rubbed up against his leg, looking up at him. "Use mine."

Use mine? What did she - ? It hit him. He remembered he could pull from her mana. That changed things. That gave him another seven *Feints*, which was enough to take them. If they just lined up and let him kill them. Unfortunately, they weren't going to just stand there and let them hit him. They'd be fighting back.

He thought about their weapons. They definitely looked like clubs. If so, that meant they did the same damage as a dagger - 4 points of damage. He was wearing four pieces of armor, giving him 2 *Defense* - enough to reduce the damage by 2 points. That might do it. If only he had a shield or plate armor.

A shield… plate armor. That sparked a memory and he brought up his spellbook. He remembered seeing an armor spell. He looked through it and sure enough, he was right. The *Air Armor* spell provided 1 defense plus 1 point of armor per rank of *Air Magic*. Unfortunately, he only had one rank but that extra point of defense would reduce his damage by 1 more point.

With *Air Armor*, he might just have a chance. Of course, it only lasted a minute at his current rank. He'd have to wait until combat began to cast it. But did he use the *Taunt* ability first or the *Air Armor*?

Casting the armor spell would use up another 4 mana. That cut his *Feints* down by two. He prayed it would be enough.

The figures in the mist were still not moving, standing unnaturally still. Even their hissing had stopped. There was no sound at all in the swamp. He looked from figure to figure, trying to gauge when they would attack. He didn't have to wait long.

"Kill the soft skins!" hissed the figure to his right and then everything went to hell.

Chapter 37

The creatures sprang forward and Jace could see that they were some sort of bipedal lizard creatures. He didn't have time to analyze them in his HUD. As soon as he heard the cry, he immediately cast Air Armor. *"Aeris Armatura!"*

Wind swirled around him and coalesced into a sparky suit of armor made of hardened air. He couldn't feel it but hopefully it would do its job. "Come get some!"

The lizard men skidded to an abrupt halt, weapons still raised to attack but making no move. Now that they were closer, Jace could see that they were wearing leather loincloths not dissimilar to the one he had when he respawned. They also had leather bands tied around their arms and legs that had many colorful feathers attached to them. Their scaly green bodies were decorated in white and red war paint, giving them a very primitive look.

They looked back and forth at each other. Finally, the one that had called out tilted its head, a long forked tongue slipping in and out of its mouth.

"You speak the language of the scaled ones?" it asked, looking over him curiously.

Now that they were closer, Jace recognized them as lizard men, or *saurians*. They were intelligent reptilian humanoids. They weren't inherently good or evil but stayed away from civilized society. His *Monsterspeak* skill was allowing him to speak and understand even the lizard men. Jace answered the saurian, "I can speak your language."

Since they weren't attacking him, Jace scanned them in his HUD.

Swamp Saurian Hunter
Level: 4

The lead saurian flicked his tongue again and looked over Jace. He seemed to stare at the distortion caused by the *Air Armor*. After a moment, he lowered his weapon and signaled the others to do the same. He gestured at Jace. "You are… magic man?"

Jace nodded. "I know some magic."

The leader gestured to the others who came over and they whispered too low for Jace to hear them. Occasionally one or the other would pop his head out of the huddle and look over at Jace. After several minutes, they broke apart, and the leader stepped forward.

"I am Kagask," he said. "Hunt leader. Will you come back to our village?"

Jace tried to keep the frown off his face. He may or may not be able to handle these four, but there was no way he could handle an entire village. And just a minute ago, these things had been ready to kill him. Still, he needed to be diplomatic.

"I cannot," he told them. "I am on my way to the human village Skystead. I am in a hurry."

Kagask shook his head. "You will not make it."

"Why? Will you stop me?" Jace asked, tightening his grip on his weapons.

Did they intend to fight him? Or try to stop him? His Air Armor had expired, but his mana had regenerated, so he could cast it again. He'd been willing to fight them just a few minutes ago and he still could.

The saurian shook its head. "I will not stop you but ahead, maybe half a day, are the Dying Grounds. The Raagaax hunts there. You may have magic, but it will still devour you. Many of our braves have we lost to the Raagaax."

That bothered Jace. There was some creature ahead of them that killed the lizard men. "What is the Raagaax? What type of monster?"

"It is a swamp dragon," Kagask told him. "Even with your magic, you cannot win against him. It destroyed your human caravan almost 7 suns ago."

"Swamp dragon?!" Jace asked in shock. Dragons were powerful raid bosses. They took a full raid of 40 people to bring down. If it really was a dragon, he had no hope at all against it. Perhaps he could sneak by on his own, but not with Charlena walking next to him. The dragon would spot them and kill them.

Dragons didn't live long in VEIL. Once players learned about them from NPCs or quests, the raiding guilds quickly organized a raid to kill the monster. They would teleport in, kill the dragon, loot its hoard and then go back to their normal activities.

That meant they would teleport into either Sinking Springs or Skystead! He and Charlena might hitch a ride back to the capital. Jace got excited until he realized he would still need to make it one of the villages. Maybe he could just die. Then he'd reappear back in Sinking Springs and he could hitch a ride.

Except, he'd he naked with no money. He wouldn't have anything to offer them. Darn it! He needed to get to one of the two villages, and he needed to get to it now.

"If you come to our village," Kagask told him. "I will show you a way through the swamp."

Jace's head snapped around to the saurian hunter. "What?"

His HUD updated unexpectedly with a scrolling message. He did a double take as he read the message.

Kagask of the Willow Marsh Clan has offered you the quest, "Speak to the Elder"
Reward: +25 faction with Willow March Clan, +50 faction with Kagask, Safe Passage.
Accept quest? (Yes or No)

The lizard man had offered him a quest! Jace knew it wasn't unheard of for intelligent species to offer quests, but it was rare. And it was limited to creatures who spoke the common tongue? Was he getting the quest because he could speak and understand them? Had the game AI adapted its programming to allow for any intelligent creature to give quests?

This was a major development if it were true. Did that mean only he could get these quests from monsters -

assuming he could live long enough to talk with them? The notion was mind blowing, as it opened up a virtual world of possibilities.

"If you and your companion come to my village and speak with the elder," the lizard man repeated, snapping Jace back to the situation at hand. "I will lead you around the dragon, to the mountain."

The lizard looked at him suspiciously. "Why do you want me to speak with your elder?"

"You speak with the elder," he said. "Maybe save the village."

Jace considered that. It sounded like a quest. And if part of the reward was safe passage, he'd be a fool to say no. Still he hesitated a moment longer. Could he really trust these lizard men?

Realizing he didn't really have a choice unless he wanted to turn around and walk all the way back to Sinking Springs, Jace agreed and accepted the quest.

The lizard men lowered their weapons and guided him off the road and into the swamp. Jace hadn't thought it was possible, but the insects became even worse and he felt like he was going out of his mind with all the bites.

"Soft skin no protection against the insects," said one of the saurians. "You need scales like us."

"Right now," Jace told him, swatting another biting insect on his arm. "I agree with you."

The saurians hissed rhythmically in a way that reminded Jace of laughter.

"Ha," hissed another one of the lizard men. "Or maybe you just need pointy ears like that one. She no bothered by insects."

Jace looked at the glassy eyed elf next to him. She wasn't reacting to anything because there was no one home. In auto-follow mode, she wouldn't react to anything. The real Charlena was somewhere else.

Once again, Jace found himself worrying about Charlena. Where was she? Why hadn't she logged back in? He could understand one night. But this was the second night.

Jace wasn't sure exactly what time it was but it was definitely later than the times she had logged in before.

As Jace worried about Charlena, the lizard men continued to lead him deeper into the swamp. In the dark, with all of the mist, Jace quickly became lost. At this point, he knew he couldn't find his way back to the road on his own. He was now at their mercy. Not for the first time, he hoped he had made the right decision.

After what seemed like an hour, they came to solid ground. After walking in the fetid water for so long, it was a welcome change. They walked through tall reeds and other large vegetation for several minutes until it suddenly opened in a large clear area full of crude huts. They'd found the saurian village.

The village was very crude and the huts appeared more like wigwams were made of reeds and animal skins, giving them a very distinct Native American appearance. Jace wondered if the similarities had been programmed in by a developer or was it something the game AI had adapted them to do.

Saurians were coming out of their huts to watch the party as it made its way through the village. A few times, saurians reached out and touched his hand or touched Charlena out of curiosity. Very possibly, they were the first non-saurians they had ever seen and Jace found their actions eerily lifelike.

After only a minute or two in the village, the group stopped in front of a large wigwam. The structure was larger than the others and had poles in front of it. On the tops of those poles were what Jace guessed were alligator skulls.

"Elder," said Kagask, "we have brought someone for you to speak with."

There was a rustling from inside the hut and the hide that served as a door was thrown aside revealing a thin saurian. The saurian was not only thin, but his scales had faded to a light grey color in most places, though here and there were patches of green. The elder ducked through the door and then stood.

"May the sun shine on your scales, Kagask," the elder said.

"May the sun shine on your scales, Elder," Kagask repeated back.

"Why have you brought the soft skins to our village," the elder asked, looking over Jace and Charlena. "Would it not have been easier to skin them in the swamp? Certainly, less messy."

There was a hissing from the gathered saurians that Jace guessed was laughter and he began to feel nervous.

He'd put his weapons away but he let his hands fall near them, just in case.

"No Elder," the hunt leader said. "These soft skins are not for eating. They speak the language of the people."

The elder looked surprised and looked at Kagask for confirmation. "Truly?"

"Yes," Jace answered for him, willing himself to speak the saurian.

There was a communal gasp from the assembled saurians and then whispered hissing. The elder overcame his shock and walked to stand in front of Jace. The older saurian's forked tongue tested the air as he tilted his head to the left and right to get a good look at him. Jace couldn't help but notice the white scaled lizard man's eyes were cloudy with age.

"How is it you know the tongue of the people?" the elder asked him.

Jace thought about a suitable answer. He couldn't just say 'because I used to be a kobold.' He thought back to what Kagask had called him. "I am a magic man."

There was another gasp from the lizard men who had come to watch, and more whispered hissing.

This seemed to surprise the elder as well and he looked at Kagask. "You have seen the magic?"

Kagask nodded and motioned to his three hunters. "We all saw him use the magic."

The other hunters nodded and the elder looked back to Jace. "You speak the tongue of the people and you are a magic man when the need of the village is great. It is a sign." He then spoke louder so the rest of the village, who had gathered. "It is a sign. The Swamp Mother has sent us a soft skin who will help us."

A hissing murmur went up from the gathered lizard men.

"Come," the elder told him and then ducked into his wigwam. "We have much to discuss."

Chapter 38

Jace followed the elder into the wigwam. Luna padded in behind him and Charlena even ducked and came in, still auto-following him.

"Is your female all right?" the elder asked as he seated himself on some mats and gestured for Jace to do the same.

Sitting, Jace looked up at the glassy-eyed avatar of Charlena. That was the question, wasn't it? Was Charlena all right? Had something happened to her? Or she suddenly received a ton of schoolwork that kept her busy? Still, she seemed like a girl who would have logged on quickly and told him.

Had he been wrong about her? Was she just using him to get out of Sinking Springs? Was that possible? Was he just a sucker who would get her out of a nasty situation? He'd known girls like that - users. They used guys for money, gifts and other favors. Was that what was happening? He didn't want to believe that. He really felt like he and Charlena had shared a connection. Had he been fooling himself?

"Are you all right?" asked the elder and Jace realized he had never answered the saurian's question.

"We're both all right," he said. "My companion… hit her head a few days ago and hasn't been the same since. All she can do is follow me around until she feels better."

The old saurian nodded as he put a log on the fire, which burned inside a small pit in the middle of the wigwam.

"Head wounds can be serious. You must watch her closely." The lizard man paused and looked at Jace. "But you are a magic man, you must know these things."

Jace looked at Charlena. "Yes, I should."

The elder nodded, prodding the fire with a reed. "In all my days, I have never met a soft skin who spoke our tongue. Why have you come?"

Jace smirked. "You don't believe the Swamp Mother sent me?"

The old saurian hissed softly. "The Swamp Mother would not send one such as you. I know the soft skins. You come with steel, killing my people."

"But you told the village the Swamp Mother sent me," Jace retorted.

The elder made a dismissive gesture. "The village loses hope. The Raagaax killed the chief and our magic man. Now there is no chief now. And only a magic man can anoint the chief with the blessing of the Swamp Mother."

Jace was seeing where this was going. "And any old magic man will do?"

The elder shrugged. "I do not know. All I know is that without a chief, we will perish. Will you act as our magic man in this?"

Ejoklixl of the Willow Marsh Clan has offered you the quest, "Anoint the Chief"

Reward: +200 faction with Willow March Clan, +50 faction with Ejoklixl, tribal membership.
Accept quest? (Yes or No)

Jace hesitated before he accepted the quest. There were still a lot of unknowns, and what was the tribal membership part of the reward?

He looked over at the old saurian. "And what does anointing him entail?"

"You must kill an alligator and collect its blood. Then you must infuse the blood with your magic. Only then will you choose one of our braves to be the new chief. Smear the blood on him and it will grant him the strength of the Swamp Mother. Only then can he lead us," Ejoklixl said.

"Alligator?" Luna asked suddenly.

"Like really big, mean lizards," he told her. "With lots of sharp teeth."

"Bad lizard," she said.

"You speak with the animals too?" asked the elder, switching his gaze between Jace and Luna. The lizard man nodded. "You are magic man."

"So, I kill an alligator, get its blood, put magic into the blood somehow and then put the blood on one of the saurians… er… the people, and that's it? That's all I have to do?" Jace asked.

Ejoklixl nodded and threw another log on the fire.

Jace thought for a moment about the time. He was pressed for time but he needed to get past the dragon and get to Skystead. The fastest way seemed to be to do a quest for the saurians. "I'll do it."

The elder gave him an expression that might have been the saurian equivalent of a smile, or the lizard man might have been ready to bite his hand off. When the attack didn't come, Jace assumed it was the former.

The old saurian gave Jace directions and then he exited the wigwam. Kagask was outside the hut waiting for him.

"You agreed to help my people?" asked the hunter leader.

"Yes," Jace told him. "I will kill the alligator and choose the next chief."

The hunter nodded. "It is good then. But know that even if you hadn't agreed to help, I would still have shown you the way to your sky village."

Jace nodded and then looked around the village. He turned back to Kagask. "Which way is north?"

"This way," the saurian hunter pointed to his right. "May the blessing of the Swamp Mother go with you."

Jace turned and headed north. He was to follow the trail north out of the village until it split. Then he was supposed to take the left fork to a black pond. The alligator he was looking for would be in the pond.

It took Jace a half hour to reach the black pond with Luna and Charlena's body following him around. It had been as straightforward as the old lizard man had said.

Looking at the still, inky waters of the pond, he didn't see any alligator. Was it underwater? Had it left?

His first instinct was to sneak closer and try to glimpse the gator, but he realized that wouldn't work with Charlena following him. Jace would need to take the direct approach.

Equipping his weapons, Jace started towards the pool when an enormous alligator rushed out at him. Luna hissed and seemed to jump straight into the air before hitting the dirt and scrambling away. It would have been funny if a huge alligator wasn't trying to have him for dinner.

Jace *Feinted* and struck out, landing two solid hits on the creature.

You critically stab Swamp Gator Bull for 13 damage.
You critically stab Swamp Gator Bull for 5 damage.

He noticed his blows did less damage. That meant the alligator had natural armor. Why was nothing ever easy!

The alligator didn't seem phased by his attacks and snapped its jaws on his leg.

Swamp Gator Bull bites YOU for 9 damage.

Jace couldn't stop the scream of pain that involuntarily escaped as the rows of razor-sharp teeth dug into his lower leg. It had taken nearly half of his health in one bite. Two more bites like that would kill him!

Jace *Feinted* again and attacked.

You critically stab Swamp Gator Bull for 12 damage.
You critically stab Swamp Gator Bull for 6 damage.

The attacks seemed to have no more effect on the alligator as the last attacks and Jace prepared to die. It would be a long walk back to the village.

Swamp Gator Bull mauls YOU for 3 damage.

The alligator hadn't let go of his leg but ground its teeth together, causing more damage to him as well as excruciating pain. Jace once again *feinted* and attacked. Once again, he damaged the beast, but it didn't seem to show it.

Swamp Gator Bull mauls YOU for 4 damage.

Jace had one more hit left before he died. He was about to *Feint* again when he smelled a strangely familiar odor. It was almost like oil or petroleum. He looked down at the gator and realized the creature was covered in the black liquid from the pool. Could that be oil? If so, would it be flammable?

Instead of his *Feint*, he cast *Flame Bolt* at the alligator's head. Fire erupted from where the *Flame Bolt* had struck and quickly consumed the alligator. The thing released him and began rolling around on the ground, trying to extinguish the flames. Unfortunately for it, the ground was soaked in the same liquid and it caught fire too, speeding the creature's demise and forcing Jace to back away.

It took only a minute or two before the thing stopped moving and Jace received new system messages.

Swamp Gator Bull dies.

You gain 400 experience.

It amazed Jace just how much experience he had received from the creature. The alligator must have been a mini-boss or some sort. And he certainly wasn't going to complain about it.

Luna came out then and walked within a few feet of the dead alligator. She sniffed at it before turning her back on it. "Bad lizard!"

Walking over to the body, he sliced the thing's throat and collected its blood in his metal frying pan. He turned to leave but froze.

If this was a mini-boss, it had to have treasure. Setting the frying pan down, he began searching around the area until he found a pile of bones. It looked like it had piled up the remains of its victims. Jace sifted through the bones and came across a small leather buckler. It wouldn't offer much protection, but he could use shields now and every little piece of armor helped. He also found a pouch with some gold coins and tucked that into his inventory.

Jace strapped the buckler onto his left arm and viewed it in his HUD.

Alligator Skin Buckler
Type: Shield
Armor: 3 + 1 (Masterwork) + 1 (Sturdy)
Wt: 1 lb
Special: +1 Defense

Description: This buckler was worn by the famous Alligator Hunter, Zan To'al, who bit off more than he could chew when he came across a Swamp Gator Bull.

Jace whistled as he looked at the description. Not only did the buckler supply 4 points of armor, it also supplied a point of defense, which would absorb a point of damage. It was a very nice item for his level.

After spending a few more minutes picking through the remains, he found nothing else worth taking. He looked around the area to make sure he had missed no loot, but he found no other items.

He retrieved the frying pan full of alligator blood and hurried back to the village. Now Jace just needed to figure out how to put mana in the blood and anoint one of the lizard men as the chief.

Using his *Tracking* skill, Jace began following his own trail back to the village. As he did, he thought about how to get mana into the blood. Having never played a mage before, he had no idea how to put mana into an object.

He looked down at Luna. "Do you know how to put mana into things?"

Luna kept walking without looking up. "No."

He hadn't thought she would, but it was worth a shot. After all, she had known he could pull mana from her.

That made him pause. He had pulled mana from Luna. Once he realized he could do it, doing it was fairly straightforward. Could the same work with pushing mana? He examined the blood in the pan using his HUD.

Bull Alligator Blood
Wt: 1 lb

Description: Blood gathered from a swamp alligator bull.

The blood was an object. That was interesting. Could he just push mana into by doing the opposite of pulling? Tentatively, he focused on the object and then tried drawing his mana into it.

For a moment, nothing happened. Jace felt something leave him and the liquid began to glow.

You have gained a new skill: Enchanting
You have gained a new skill: Alchemy

Jace gawked at the new system messages. Players unlocked those skills by paying vast amounts of gold to trainers. He couldn't remember any players getting them on their own. Of course, players didn't always share everything - especially things that gave them an advantage.

Encouraged by his success, Jace tried to push more mana into the blood but it resisted. No matter how hard he tried, he could push no more mana into the blood. After several minutes, he gave up. There must be a limit to how much mana the blood would take.

Feeling better than he had in a long time, Jace made his way back to the saurian village.

Chapter 39

Jace arrived back at the village to a mass of saurians gathered for his return. A collective hiss went up from the crowd of lizard men when he entered the village. He hoped that was their equivalent of a cheer and not them calling for a soft skin four course dinner.

He looked down at Luna, who had moved behind him. She didn't seem to like the hissing sounds they made.

The crowd parted, giving him a path to the elder's hut. In front of the hut, Ejoklixl waited for him. As Jace approached, the elder spoke with a loud voice. "The magic man has returned, and he brings the blood of choosing!"

There was another collective hiss, and then everything fell silent. The crowd of reptilian faces looked at him expectantly.

"Now what do we do?" he asked Luna silently but Luna had no reply.

As if reading his mind, Ejoklixl hissed that was his equivalent of a whisper. "You must choose a brave to honor as chief."

Looking around the crowd, Jace wasn't even sure he could tell the males from the females. Was he even allowed to pick a female? A sea of reptilian faces stared at him expectantly. How was he supposed to choose?

Did he just pick one at random? He started to panic when he remembered he knew one of the saurians - the one who had offered to lead him to Skystead.

"Kagask! Come forward!" Jace announced in the deepest voice he could muster.

There was a hissing and saurians parted to allow Kagask to come forward. The lizard man stepped in front of Jace and knelt, which he assumed was part of the ceremony. Reaching his fingers into the blood, Jace smeared the blood on Kagask's face, mirroring the war paint that was already there.

The glowing blood lingered on the saurian's scales for a moment before being absorbed by Kagask's skin. Before his eyes, the already sizable lizard man seemed to grow several inches in height. The saurian's muscles also seemed to grow, making him look like a bodybuilder version of a lizard man.

Kagask stood and faced the crowd, now a good hand span above the others.

"We have a chief!" cried the elder, and the assembled saurians hissed loudly. Ejoklixl leaned close to Jace and hissed. "You must drink the rest of the blood so no others can be anointed chief."

Jace stared at the elder in disbelief. Did they really expect him to drink blood? He knew it wasn't real blood, just virtual blood, but the idea still appalled him. Noticing it had gotten quiet, Jace turned and saw that everyone was staring at him, expectantly.

Darn it. Given their somber mood, there was no way he was getting out of this. Well, didn't the British eat blood pudding? Maybe it wouldn't be so bad.

Before he did, he dipped his fingers in the blood and tucked them into his fist. Forcing a smile, Jace brought the pan to his lips.

Taking a deeper breath, he began to drink. The warm, thick liquid had a distinct, coppery taste and Jace wished he could cut it with some peppermint schnapps. He nearly retched it back up but forced himself to keep drinking until he had consumed it all.

The saurians hissed again as he finished the last of it. Jace forced a smile and concentrated on not losing the contents of his stomach while the crowd hissed. Then he felt a tingling in his stomach that quickly spread around his body. It was a very odd feeling, but not entirely unpleasant. His skin glowed for a moment and then disappeared.

You gain 2 mana.

Excitedly, Jace pulled up his HUD to read the system message. He checked his mana level and saw that his maximum mana was 2 points higher! Before he could even close down his HUD, new system messages appeared.

You have completed the quest, "Speak to the Elder"
You gain 400 experience. Experience to next level 200.
You gain +25 faction with Willow March Clan
You gain +50 faction with Kagask

You have completed the quest, "Anoint the Chief"

You gain 1000 experience. Experience to next level 200.
You gain +200 faction with Willow March Clan
You gain +50 faction with Ejoklixl

You have gained a level.
You are now level 2 in Fighter.

He had reached 2nd level in *Fighter* and was now only 200 experience away from 3rd level. Plus, Jace had permanently gained 2 points of mana, which was almost unheard of in the game. He felt his stomach lurch. Drinking the blood might have been worth it.

Kagask stepped toward him and put a large, clawed hand on his shoulder. "Thank you for doing the will of the Swamp Mother. We honor you as magic man. You will always be welcome in our tribe."

You are now a member of the Willow March Clan.

The new chief looked to Charlena standing next to him. "And this is your female?"

Jace wasn't sure exactly what to say, but he thought the safer answer was to tell them yes so they didn't cook her up in a celebration dinner. "Yes, she is my female."

"Then she will be a part of our tribe as well," Kagask pronounced. "Let there be feasting!"

The mood of the saurians had changed completely. They were no longer forlorn but seemed happy and festive as food and drink was brought forth and somewhere some of them began to hammer out a tune on drums.

With the saurians' attention elsewhere, Jace reached down and petted Luna, smearing her face with the blood. She shook her head and her fur glowed briefly but nothing else seemed to happen. Maybe it didn't work on familiars? He was about to ask Luna if anything felt different when someone got his attention.

"So, I'm you're female am I?" came Charlena's voice from behind him.

Spinning around, he crushed her in a hug. "You're back!"

She returned the hug and kissed him. "Sorry I couldn't log in, I kinda...got... arrested."

Jace stepped back. "You were arrested!? For what?"

"Trespassing," she said sheepishly. "I took the train up to Philadelphia to check out a few of the hospitals and tried to get into their coma ward."

"And you were caught?" he asked, even though he already knew the answer.

"I was caught," she confirmed. "I got arrested but the hospital decided not to press charges."

"You're lucky," Jace told her.

"Yes," she responded. "I had to spend a couple nights in jail. I think they let me sit in there to scare me. It worked."

"What were you thinking?" Jace demanded.

Charlena put her hands on her hips. "I was thinking that I was trying to find your body but since I'm not a relative, they weren't forthcoming with any information."

"I know you were helping," Jace said, making his voice more neutral. He realized he'd put her on the defensive and needed to back peddle. After all, she wasn't his girlfriend. She was a girl who was helping him out. At least, for now. "But you could have gotten into real trouble and I can't help you from in here. I didn't even know what happened to you."

"I know," Charlena said sympathetically. "I kept thinking about you and wishing there was some way I could contact you and let you know."

"At least you're okay," Jace said, and he hugged her again.

Charlena's eyes went glassy for a moment and then she gave him a wary look. "You're a *Fighter* now? And a 2nd level one to boot? What happened?" She lowered her voice to a whisper. "And why are we in a village of Sleestaks?"

Jace laughed and pulled her away from the festivities and explained what had happened since they had left. He related the wolf attacks and his decision to switch to *Fighter*. He told her about nearly being attacked by the lizard men and the quests he'd received from them.

"You actually got quests from monsters?" she asked.

"And they were good quests," he told her. "Theoretically, they will guide us to Skystead, around the dragon."

"Dragon?!" Charlena exclaimed. "Like, an actual dragon - I meant a real virtual… oh, you know what I mean!"

Chuckling, Jace nodded. "Apparently. Not only that, but according to our recent friends, it wiped out the caravan from Sinking Springs. We would have been waiting a VERY long time before another one showed up."

"Wow," she said, shaking her head. "That's crazy. Do dragons usually do that?"

"Sometimes, yes," he told her. "They've even wiped out villages and small towns before players bring them down with a raid.

"I guess we're lucky we missed it," she said.

"Definitely," he agreed.

Charlena yawned. "Sorry, it's like 3 a.m. here. I just got home and logged in to tell you what happened. I need to get some sleep. It's Friday so I don't have many classes, but I need to show up to explain what happened."

"Will you be on tomorrow?" he asked hopefully.

She gave him a dazzling smile. "Unless I get arrested again." She flirted forward and planted a quick kiss on his lips. Her avatar went glassy eyed and Jace knew she'd logged out.

He shook his head and turned towards the festivities. Things were in full swing and there was dancing and more drum music. Jace realized he would get no one to lead him to Skystead at the moment. Not until the festivities were over.

All the lizard men seemed to be having an enjoyable time, so Jace joined in where he could. He ate some sort of cooked meat. Jace tried not to think about what kind of meat it was as he bit into it but found it tasty. Searching until he found the cook, he managed to procure some of the meat for Luna. After a few sniffs, she ate it.

"Good chicken," she said and Jace didn't have the heart to tell her it wasn't chicken. At least he hadn't seen any chickens around. Best not to think about what it really was.

He tried some of their beverage and was pleasantly surprised to find that it was mead. The rest of the night was a blur at one point, he tried dancing with the lizard men but it didn't quite work out with Charlena following him.

As the sun came up, the saurians finally ended their celebration and began retreating to their huts, most of them drunk on mead.

Kagask found him near the elder's wigwam. "I will sleep now but I will keep my promise. When I awake, I will lead you to the soft skin village to the west. You will be ready?"

"I'll be ready," Jace told him.

"Follow me," the large saurian told him and Jace did as asked. The new chief led him to a larger hut and pointed at it. "This belonged to the old magic man. You and your female may use it. I will come for you when we are ready to leave."

Not wanting to offend his new friends, Jace thanked Kagask and ducked into the wigwam. Charlena's body followed him in awkwardly, as did Luna.

Despite being a larger hut, it was still a small area. Jace guessed no one had been in the magic man's hut in some time - probably since he died. It was rather sparse. Whatever meager possessions the magic man had possessed had probably been on him when he was killed by the dragon.

Despite that, Jace did a cursory look around to see if there was anything useful. When he found nothing more than some cups, bottles and plates made from carved gourds, he gave up.

Instead, he gathered up some stacked firewood and made a fire with his magic to keep them warm while they waited. He hoped he wouldn't have to wait long before Kagask and the other saurians got up.

Chapter 40

It was a boring wait for Jace in the wigwam. Unlike his reptilian friends, he didn't need sleep. Even Luna had curled up next to the fire and was quietly sleeping. He reached out and stroked her fur softly and she opened one eye briefly before shutting it again.

Jace still wasn't sure why he wasn't sleeping. He had originally assumed he didn't sleep because he was dead and just a brain backup inserted into the game. But if he were alive, why wouldn't he be sleeping?

Was it because he was in a coma? Was his constant awake state because of direct brain stimulation? Jace didn't know. He only knew he hadn't slept in the week he'd been in the game. He hadn't even been tired.

After what seemed like half a day, Kagask's voice came from outside the hut. "It is time magic man."

Jace left the wigwam to find Kagask and four other saurians. They inclined their heads at him, and he returned the gesture. From the diffused light in the mist, Jace guessed it was after midday.

"As I promised," the chief said. "We will take you to the path that leads to the human village. It will take one sun to reach the path. Come, we go."

With no further fanfare, the group left the village. Their odd group walked single file with Kagask leading the way, followed by two of the lizard men, then Jace,

Charlena and Luna. The remaining saurians followed behind them.

The saurians knew the terrain well, and they ran into no trouble. Unfortunately, for Jace, once they were outside the village, the insects seemed to return with a vengeance, biting and stinging him all over. He ignored it as best he could, but it wore on his nerves.

A few times, Kagask stopped the procession and then turned down a different path. This continued for two hours before suddenly Charlena stumbled into him.

"Sorry," she apologized and stepped up next to him. "That's weird to appear in your avatar while they're walking." She looked around. "Where are we?"

"We're on our way to the path that leads to Skystead," Jace told her, taking her hand.

"Great!" she said and then looked around in the misty swamp and lowered her voice. "Are we sure they know where they're going?"

Jace chuckled. "Let's hope so."

"Oh," Charlena changed the subject. "Sorry if I was out of it last night… or this morning or whatever it was. I didn't sleep at all on the train and not much in jail."

"Sorry about that," he told her. He'd never been in jail, and he was glad of it.

"It's my fault," she said. "I should have been sneakier. Unfortunately, I'm not this graceful in real life."

"None of us are," Jace observed. Unless a person was a top athlete, it was hard to compete with a virtual body that responded to your every thought.

"I found out you're not in Thomas Jefferson or Cristiania," she told him. "I'm not sure about the University of Pennsylvania hospital, that's where I got caught."

"You really shouldn't have…"

"I know, I know," she interrupted irritably. "I get it. It was stupid. But what else was I supposed to do? How else can we find out where your body is?"

Jace had no answer. "I don't know, but I don't want you putting yourself at risk for me."

Charlena stopped and grabbed his arm. "Listen, it's my choice. Okay?"

Seeing he would not win this argument, Jace just nodded and she released him.

She was quiet for a long time before she spoke again. "We have to find you. You said it yourself. Someone needs to tell the doctors you can't log yourself out."

Jace thought for a moment and suddenly an idea hit him. "Do you have access to a public phone at your college?"

"Sure."

Jace smiled. "Call the hospitals and tell them your Luna Burton and you're calling to speak to your brother.

Tell them someone from the hospital called you and said your brother is there because you're next of kin."

Charlena was quiet. She looked down at the cat padding along next to him. "Luna. Like your cat?"

Jace pushed down the painful memories. "My sister, Luna. she died in a car accident with my parents."

"I'm sorry."

"It was years ago."

Charlena put her hand on his shoulder. "I'm still sorry."

They walked in silence for a time. Finally, Charlena looked over at Jace. "When you come out of your coma. Do you think you'd want to meet in real life?"

Jace couldn't help the smile that crept on his face. "You're an optimist."

She nodded. "I try. So, is that a yes?"

"That's a yes," he chuckled. "But if I really was in a nasty accident, I have no idea what shape I'll be in."

That thought had tumbled around the back of his head since she had told him he may be alive. What sort of shape was he in? How much damage had been done to his body? Could he walk? What about his hands? Waking up inside a body he couldn't control was a possibility he'd been contemplating for some time. It wasn't a pleasant prospect.

"I still want to meet you," she told Jace. "I don't care what kind of shape you're in. You're still the person mentally."

Jace forced a smile. He hoped he was the same person. After all, he was in a coma. That meant he must have suffered a head trauma. It was a frightening thought and he pushed it out of his mind.

He stirred the conversation to more pleasant topics, like old vid streams, the things once called movies. Apparently, they both like the retro streams and had watched many of the same ones. They went back and forth for a long while. Finally, Charlena needed to log off but promised to log back in tomorrow morning. She kissed him goodbye.

When they finished their kiss and her body went back to the glassy-eyed state, he noticed the saurians were all staring at him. Jace blushed but raised an eyebrow at them. "Yes?"

"If you want to mate, you must clamp your mouth down on her neck and hold her until she stops struggling to show your dominance!" said one of the lizard men in the rear. The others bobbed their heads.

Jace blushed furiously, but thankfully, the leader signaled them to begin moving again. Jace quickly fell into step and tried to avoid the glances from the saurians.

Shortly after she had logged out, Kagask dropped back to walk alongside Jace. "The sun has fallen. Soft skins usually sleep during the time of the moon. Do you want us to make camp?"

"I can go as long as you can," Jace told him.

"This is good. We will walk through the night and get you to the path before the sun touches the sky."

"Thank you," Jace said sincerely.

The chief moved back to the head of the column and picked up the pace. Jace could keep up, even in swampy terrain, but it was a long night. By the time the swamp thinned out and they reached the road, he was glad to slow the pace.

"I have delivered you to the road," Kagask told him. "As I promised."

Jace held out his hand and the large saurian shook it. "Yes, you did. Thank you, Kagask."

"My tribe owes you a great debt," Kagask told him and the other saurians bobbed their heads. "Without you, we would be lost."

Smiling, he released the lizard man's scaly hand. "Glad I could help."

"Farewell, Dedrurrurth," he said.

Jace sighed. "Call me Jace."

"Jace," the saurian mouthed, his name sounding strange when hissed by the large lizard man. "Farewell... Jace."

With no further fanfare, Kagask hissed an order to his hunters and they turned and disappeared back into the swamp.

"No smell bad," said Luna suddenly, and he looked down at her.

"Was the swamp that bad?" he asked.

"Yes," she told him. "Smell bad!"

Chuckling, Jace turned to look at the mountains that stood between him. The snow-covered peaks were enormous and reminded him of pictures he had seen of the Rocky Mountains. He wondered how high Skystead was up on the mountain. He had no winter clothes of any sort so things could get very cold if it were near the top. Who knows, maybe he'd get lucky.

"It looks like you'll have lots of fresh air from now on," he said.

Luna sniffed the air. "Yes."

With Luna trailing behind him, he set off up the road. The saurians had said it was two suns from where they would leave him, but since he could walk all day, he was hoping he could make it in one. He tried to focus on that thought as the mountains loomed ever closer.

A few hours later, Charlena logged in, brightening his mood. His first hint were the arms that were suddenly thrown around his neck and the pressure of her body pressing against his back. "Good morning!"

Smiling, he twisted in her embrace until he was facing her. "Good morning to you too!"

She kissed him then and then broke away. "Ha! That's one nice thing about the game. No morning breath."

They laughed as he set her down and she looked around. "We're out of the swamp! Thank goodness! That place was dreary."

"It wasn't so bad," Jace offered. "Except for the insects!"

"I guess I missed them," she smiled innocently.

"I think I'm seeing a method to your madness," he teased.

She rubbed her hands together. "So, you've figured out my evil plan." She flashed him one of her dazzling smiles, and he couldn't help but smile himself.

"How long before we get to Skystead?" she asked, moving next to him and taking his hand.

"The saurians…" He started but Luna's hissed snapped him into combat mode and he yanked Charlena to the ground as arrows wheezed over their heads from both sides.

Charlena recovered quickly and her bow appeared in her hand. "What is it?"

"I don't know," Jace said, and he looked over the little cat. "Luna's like a little danger magnet."

"Do you know what they are?" he asked his familiar.

Luna looked at him blankly.

"You have *Vanish*?" he asked Charlena. They'd worked on her *Stealth* skill, but he'd forgotten to ask if she's reached rank 10.

"Yes," she told him.

"Good," he told her. "Use *Vanish*, standup and fire at anything you see on the left. As soon as you do, I'll use *Vanish* and rush to the right."

"Right," she nodded seriously. She was all business now. She waited a moment. "Go!"

She went shadowy for a moment as she activated *Vanish*. Because they were in the same group, he could see her shadowy outline, but she would be invisible to anyone else. She stood up, and after only a moment, fired her bow.

As she did, Jace activated his own ability and rushed right, his eyes searching for enemies. He saw them then, in the tall grass, looking for a target. They were orcs, and there were two of them right in front of him.

Orcs were taller and broader than goblins, with wide, flat noses, tusked mouths and large, pointed ears that were thicker and wider than an elf's. Their skin was an olive green and their hair coarse and charcoal black. They wore various pieces of armor that looked cobbled together from many sources.

Jace's *Vanish* wore off just as he reached the orcs, startling them. He took advantage of their hesitation and using *Feint*, jabbed both of his blades into the closest.

You critically stab Mountain Orc for 15 damage.
You critically stab Mountain Orc for 8 damage.

The orc squealed and dropped its short bow, reaching for a long knife at its hip. The other orc took aim at Jace and fired.

Mountain Orc shoots YOU for 3 damage.

Jace's armor absorbed most of the damage, but the arrow still penetrated his side, causing him to wince. He saw Charlena get hit.

Mountain Orc shoots Almedha Pressalor for 2 damage.
Mountain Orc shoots Almedha Pressalor for 4 damage.

She was taking more damage than he was and he knew his new buckler had something to do with that. He needed to finish these off so he could help her.

As the first orc cleared the long knife from its sheath, Jace stabbed again, hoping the orc was only 4th level.

You stab Mountain Orc for 7 damage.
You stab Mountain Orc for 4 damage.
Mountain Orc dies.
You gain 40 experience.

Even as that orc died, the other one shot him again, but this time his left hand moved on its own and deflected the arrow.

Mountain Orc shoots YOU but you BLOCK.
Your Block skill has increased by 1.

It thrilled him he had blocked the arrow since he'd completely forgotten about the *Block* skill. He closed with the other orc and, using *Feint*, stabbed both of his weapons into its torso, eliciting a squeal. With Jace too close for it to use its bow, it reached for an axe hanging from its belt.

He saw that Charlena took another arrow, but only one this time.

Mountain Orc shoots Almedha Pressalor for 3 damage.

"I got one!" Charlena cried.

Smiling at her enthusiasm, he focused on his orc. It had just cleared its axe when he struck again.

You stab Mountain Orc but it DODGES.
You stab Mountain Orc for 3 damage.

Darn it! It had dodged and was still alive. He flinched as the thing swung its axe at his arm.

Mountain Orc slashes YOU for 0 damage.

The blow hurt but didn't penetrate his *Defense*. The orc looked dumbly at its axe. It was still looking when Jace ran it through with his blades.

You stab Mountain Orc for 6 damage.
You stab Mountain Orc for 4 damage.
Mountain Orc dies.
You gain 40 experience.

Jace turned and started to run towards the remaining orc but stopped.

"Take that pig face!" Charlena shouted as another of her arrows found its mark.

There was only one orc left, and it was trading arrows with Charlena, whittling each other down. She must have been out of mana because she was no longer using *Vanish*, just firing regular arrows.

Rather than spoil it for her, he called out. "Need help?"

"I got this creep!" she shot back, keeping her eyes on the orc.

Trusting her to take care of the last one, he walked back to the orc bodies and looted them. He received 4 gold from each of the bodies, along with a leather cloak and a pair of leather boots. The boots were in slightly better shape than the ones he was wearing. He equipped both.

"Gotcha!" Charlena shouted, and Jace saw the orc's death in the system messages.

Grinning, she looked over at him. "That was fun!"

Walking over, he kissed her. "To the victor goes the spoils!"

"I want more spoils!" she smiled up at him and kissed him again.

Chapter 41

Charlena searched her orcs and received an axe and a short bow. After looting the orcs, they continued following the road towards the mountain. The terrain became hillier, and the walk became more of a hike. Around noon, they reached the base of the mountain and the path became more difficult as it sloped up the mountainside.

"It looks like this will be a good hike," Charlena said. "Do you think there will be any more monsters?"

Jace considered her question. Mountains tended to be the home to more powerful monsters who thrived in the harsh conditions. They were not the sort of creatures new adventurers wanted to run into. "Let's hope not."

Charlena threw him a glance. "Oh, come on, maybe more orcs or goblins or something!"

"It's the *or something* I'm worried about," Jace told her.

"You're no fun," she teased.

They continued their hike up the mountain road as it wound around the mountain, leading up and towards a pass between two snow-capped peaks. The view was amazing, but Jace kept a wary eye out.

The road was taking them higher and higher up the mountain and Jace noticed the change in temperature. It was gradually getting colder. He looked behind him to see Charlena had her cloak wrapped around her.

When she noticed him looking, she smiled. "It's getting a bit cool."

Jace raised an eyebrow. "What's your sensory level set at?"

Charlena's eye went glassy for a moment and then she came back and let the cloak go. "I had left it on maximum from when we were kissing. I just turned it down and this feels much better."

"Be careful with that," he told her. "You don't want your feedback level at maximum when we get in a fight."

She winced. "Sorry, I keep forgetting you can't adjust your level."

Jace shrugged. "I'm getting used to it."

"You shouldn't have to," she said and gave him a sympathetic look. "Once we get to the capital, you can get this sorted out with the help desk thingy."

Jace's face went grim. "Getting to the capital is just the first part. Once I get there, it's a whole other thing to get into the royal palace and then find the *Help Desk*. I haven't worked that part out yet."

"Is it really that difficult?"

"The royal palace is meant to be a reward for higher level players who gain enough money to buy a title. Access to it is restricted to those with titles."

"That doesn't seem very fair."

"Yes, but it is fairly period. Other than workers, peasants - that's us - weren't really allowed into the royal palace back in medieval times."

"So how are you doing to get in?"

"Obviously not by getting a title. Those cost hundreds of thousands of gold. I was thinking one of two ways: Sneaking in or trying to get a job inside."

Charlena stopped and Jace turned towards her. "Wait, you can get a job in the castle?"

"Oh yeah," Jace told her. "Quite a few players work in the castle….in all sorts of capacities." He gave her a meaningful look.

Charlena's eyes went wide. "You mean like… prostitutes? Players are prostituting themselves?"

Jace shrugged. "There's nothing in the rules that say they can't. After all, it's virtual sex so it's not subject to regular laws. It's considered 'entertainment' and since it has to be consensual, they allow it."

"That's disgusting."

"Believe it or not," he told her. "That's how some people make money in the real world. Remember, you can convert real money into gold or gold into real money. So, some men and women come in the game, trade virtual sex for gold and then convert the gold to real money."

Charlena's face had become red. "I can't believe they allow that!"

"The government has tried to step in, but it's hard to make a case about regulating a virtual action for a virtual good since technically none of it exists in the real world," he remembered. "Plus, when people have virtual sex, there's no chance of a disease or anything like that."

"It's still disgusting," she retorted. Charlena's eyes went wide as saucers and her mouth fell open as she looked at him. "Wait… Jace… you're not thinking about… I mean… you wouldn't…"

Jace suddenly understood what she was asking and started to deny it but stopped. He stood up straight and poked out his chest. "What? You don't think I could get top dollar for this body?" He flexed his biceps for her.

"Ha. ha," she replied. "But seriously, you're not, right?"

Jace shook his head. "I was thinking more of a server or something along those lines - not a boy toy."

Charlena's eyes narrowed seductively, and she moved closer to him, running her hands up his chest. When she spoke, her voice was husky. "But if you did, I'd hope you'd give me a discount."

Jace felt the heat in his cheeks and started to stammer a reply before Charlena burst out laughing. "You're too easy."

She skipped away up the trail and Jace was left staring after her as his cheeks returned to their normal color. He shifted uncomfortably. His cheeks hadn't been the only place the blood had been going. Shaking his head, he hurried after her.

The incline of the road became more noticeable, and they were both puffing as they continued to climb.

It was also getting colder and unlike Charlena, Jace couldn't just turn down his sensory level. It wasn't as bad when they were moving, but as soon as they stopped to rest, the cool air chilled him.

Suddenly a loud primal roar cut through the air and Charlena turned to him fearfully. "What the heck was that?"

Unfortunately, Jace knew exactly what it was. He fought tons of them in the mountains of Visimar when he had been Mordred. It was a mountain troll. "Troll!"

As if it had been waiting for an introduction, a huge mountain troll jumped out onto the trail twenty yards in front of him. The troll towered over them at eight foot tall and looked like a cross between a man and a gorilla with gray and white fur. It had the general proportions of a muscular man but the elongated arms of an ape. The creature roared as it pounded its chest with its muscular arms and charged them.

"Use everything you've got!" Jace yelled to Charlena as he cast *Air Armor*. "I'll try to keep it on me as long as possible."

He heard the twang of her bow as the thing thundered towards them.

Almedha Pressalor shoots Mountain Troll for 14 damage.

Jace retrieved his weapons as he stepped in front, steeling his nerves against the incoming juggernaut. As soon as it came into range, Jace shouted his *Taunt*, forcing it to focus on him. "Come get some!"

The troll missed a step as it switched from charging Charlena to now coming straight at Jace. It came in fast, raising its fists for a strike, and Jace ducked in and drove both his weapons into its exposed stomach.

You stab Mountain Troll for 6 damage.
You stab Mountain Troll for 3 damage.

The mountain troll didn't react to his blows and brought both his fists down at Jace.

Mountain Troll slams YOU but you Dodge.
Your Dodge skill has increased by 1.
Mountain Troll slams YOU for 4 damage.
Your Air Magic skill has increased by 1.

Jace had dodged its right fist, but the left fist had connected solidly with his shoulder, nearly tearing it out of its socket. Struggling to keep a grip on his weapon, Jace felt the pain shooting up and down his left arm.

With the *Air Armor* and his recently acquired leather cloak, he had 6 *Defense*. That meant each of the trolls fists normally did 10 damage. Even with his armor, he wouldn't last long.

Another twang from behind him and another arrow appeared in the troll's chest. Again, it didn't seem to notice the damage except to roar.

Almedha Pressalor shoots Mountain Troll for 13 damage.

Jace was already at half mana, but he needed to do as much damage as possible to help bring this thing down. He *Feinted* and then attacked the troll's groin.

You critically stab Mountain Troll for 12 damage.
You critically stab Mountain Troll for 5 damage.

This time the troll reared back in pain but then slammed both its fists forward into the ground, creating a concussion wave that threw Jace back.

Mountain Troll used Ground Smash.
You are Stunned for 3 seconds.
Luna is Stunned for 3 seconds.
Almedha Pressalor is Stunned for 3 seconds.

Jace lay on the ground, unable to move. He followed the creature with his eyes as it thundered over to him and slammed both of its massive fists into his chest.

Mountain Troll slams YOU for 3 damage.
Your Air Magic skill has increased by 1.
Mountain Troll slams YOU for 2 damage.
Your Air Magic skill has increased by 1.

The sledgehammer like blows knocked the wind out of Jace but he did see the system message he'd been waiting for.

You are no longer Stunned.

Scrambling to his feed, Jace was just in time to get two more of the trolls fists to his shoulders.

Mountain Troll slams YOU for 4 damage.
Your Air Magic skill has increased by 1.
Mountain Troll slams YOU for 4 damage.

Your Air Magic skill has increased by 1.

"I'm going to go down," he yelled to Charlena. "2 more health."

"No!" she screamed and fired another armor. "You can't!"

Almedha Pressalor shoots Mountain Troll for 14 damage.

Another arrow thudded into the troll, but it refused to go down. It reared back to deliver another blow and Jace had to make a quick decision. The next blow would kill him. He could either attack and hope he could take it down. The other option was to use an old trick he'd learned from playing Mordred. It didn't always work, but it might give him a chance. He decided on the latter.

As the creature's fists came down, Jace used *Vanish*. The moment he disappeared, he sidestepped, did a somersault and ended up behind the troll.

Your Acrobatics skill has increased by 1.

The mountain troll's fists crashed into the dirt and it looked in confusion at where its target should have been. That was when Jace stabbed both his weapons into its exposed back.

You backstab Mountain Troll for 21 damage.
You backstab Mountain Troll for 9 damage.

His backstab seemed to get the thing's attention, and it roared in pain. The troll spun to finish its attacker, raising its club-like fists in the air.

Before it could bring them down and kill Jace, a large orange blur slammed into the troll's head, knocking it off balance. The thing staggered, slipped and fell off the road. It tumbled down the steep mountainside until it came to rest far below.

Mountain Troll takes 37 falling damage.
Mountain Troll dies.
You gain 100 experience.

You have gained a level.
You are now level 3 in Fighter.

Ability gained: Shield Bash

Jace briefly saw the messages but turned to face the new threat. The thing had been large and he guessed it was a mountain lion. He was down to only 2 health and 2 mana. It was going to be a very short fight.

"Summoner okay?" Luna asked but her normal meow was much louder and deeper, coming out almost as a growl. Then Jace saw why.

Sitting on her haunches where the troll had been was Luna, except she was huge! She had grown to the size of a mountain lion or maybe even a tiger. Just past his familiar was Charlena, who was gawking at the small tabby turned giant.

"She can grow?!" gasped

Jace put away his weapons and walked over to Luna, using his fingers to scratch her shin. "Since when can you do this?"

Luna looked smug. "Since blood."

"Blood?" It took Jace a moment, but he remembered he had smeared her with the mana infused blood hoping it would strengthen her. When he had done it, it hadn't appeared to do anything. He had been wrong.

"And you can just grow big like this?" he asked her.

"Yes," she said smugly. "Use mana."

"It uses mana?"

"Yes."

Suddenly, she shrank down to a regular sized cat. She was her normal self for only a moment and then she faded away.

"That was amazing!" Charlena said excitedly and Jace couldn't help but agree.

Chapter 42

"Since when can she do that?" Charlena asked as they both recovered from the fight.

Jace flinched, rolled his shoulders as the wounds healed. Sometimes, he felt the healing hurt nearly as much as the actual damage. "Back when I anointed the chief. I MIGHT have taken a little blood and anointed Luna." He winked at her.

Charlena gave him a mischievous look. "You might have? I see. And now she can grow big?"

"I guess the blood gave her that ability. But it seems to use up a ton of mana. She was only in the shape for a minute and it burned through all of her mana."

"Poor thing. When can you re-summon her?"

He checked his HUD. He was at about half his mana and health at the moment. "A few more minutes."

Charlena glanced over the edge of the road to the fifty-foot drop below. "Think the troll had any loot?"

Laughing, Jace walked over to the edge. "If so, do you really want to walk all the way down there and get it?"

"I guess not," she said.

After a few more minutes, Jace summoned Luna, giving her all the mana and health he could.

As always, it felt like his insides were being yanked out, but he fought down the pain and finished the summoning.

Charlena rushed over to Luna and petted her. "You're such a good kitty!"

After lavishing Luna with affection for a few more minutes, they continued up the road. They walked on for several more hours. The higher they went, the more the temperature continued to drop. It forced Jace to keep his cloak wrapped around him at all times just to stave off the chill. They kept walking until the sun dipped below the mountains and night came.

"Jace," Charlena called out. "I need to log out. I have some homework I need to catch up on. Will you be alright until tomorrow?"

Teeth chattering, Jace looked back and nodded. "Yeah. Hopefully, we're not too far from Skystead."

Charlena walked up and hugged Jace, her body heat temporarily providing him some extra warmth. "See you tomorrow." She planted a quick kiss on his cold lips and then backed up and went glassy eyed.

Alone now, Jace turned back to the road and began walking. He looked down at Luna. "It's just you and me now."

The familiar turned to Charlena, sniffing. After a moment, she turned back. "Yes."

To keep warm, Jace broke into his familiar jog/walk sequence. It helped, but the temperature had dropped precipitously since the sun had gone down. If he didn't find the village soon, he'd need to find a cave or other shelter and make a fire.

Luckily, there was no frostbite in the game, but he was shivering so much it made focusing almost impossible. Jace found it interesting how the game had implemented certain aspects of the environment, like shivering and chattering teeth, but not other parts, like losing fingers and toes to frostbite. He guessed it wasn't very heroic to lose fingers because a player was caught outside.

Luna hissed next to him and his frozen fingers scrambled for his weapons. He looked around but saw no enemies.

"What is it?" Jace looked down at Luna, flattening herself against the ground. Her gaze was skyward. He suddenly had a sinking feeling in the pit of his stomach.

Looking up, he saw the amazing star-filled sky of the VEIL. That was all he saw until he caught a glimmer of movement. As he zeroed in on it, he realized something was blotting out the stars in the eastern sky. Whatever it was, it was moving. It was moving his direction. And it was big.

Jace scrambled off the road as quickly as he could, maneuvering himself and Charlena under a thick pine tree. There were only two possibilities. One, it was one of the gnomish flying ships. Jace had ridden in one once and some of them were the size of a galleon. But gnomish flying ships, while common in the gnomish lands, are not often to be found in human lands.

The other possibility seemed much more likely. It was a dragon. Considering it was coming from the direction of the swamp, it seemed likely that it was the Raagaax, as the saurians had called it, the swamp dragon. But what was it doing this far west? Was it hunting?

"Dragon," Jace sent Luna silently.

"Yes," said the little cat.

They stayed quiet while the dragon flew closer. As it did, Jace began getting a familiar feeling in the back of his mind. It was the same feeling he'd had back with Diana. The longer he waited, the strong it got. Could it be coming from the dragon?

Could a player really have been put inside a raid level monster, like a dragon. Should he reach out to the player, try to get the dragon's attention? Jace knew they had no chance against a raid level monster. If he got its attention and it just decided to investigate, it could just end up killing him from the sky before he ever got a chance to talk to it. Or, it could be insane like Big Cheese. Either way, he couldn't risk a long walk back from Sinking Springs. He'd lose his body and all of his belongings long before he could make it back here.

The black shadow across the sky flew closer and closer to their location, and Jace involuntarily backed into the shadows. The feeling was stronger, but he couldn't be sure it was the dragon. He stayed still since he knew dragons had the eyesight of an eagle. Even in the dark, it could spot them if they made any movement that attracted its attention. Player or not, he didn't want it's attention.

The seconds ticked by as it flew over them, blotting out the stars. Jace held his breath as the dragon continued west past them and he lost sight of it through the trees. As it did, the feeling subsided. "Looks like we lucked out."

Luna looked up at him, ears still back against her head. "Yes."

Jace started to leave the safety of the tree when Luna screeched in his head. "No!"

He stopped and looked at her. Her voice had sounded terrified. "What is it?"

"Dragon near," she said, freezing him in place.

"How near?"

Luna just looked up at the sky, her little eyes darting around to the west. Jace followed her gaze, but even with the *Cat-Vision* she granted, he saw nothing. She had been right too many times for him not to trust his familiar. So he stayed hidden.

The chill was getting worse now that they weren't moving. Since he couldn't build a fire, he needed to figure out another source of heat. He looked over at Charlena, remembering the warm hug she had given him. He moved in close to Charlena's body and draped his cloak around both of them to trap in their body warmth. Her proximity helped, but he wished the real Charlena was here so they could really huddle together for warmth.

Jace wasn't sure how much had passed, but Luna's voice in his head abruptly brought him to full alert. "Dragon coming."

He felt the feeling returning, that strange attraction came. It had to be either the dragon, or something riding the dragon. Scanning the sky, he spotted it coming from the northwest. The dragon was moving quickly. Within minutes, it had flown directly over them and then turned due east, back towards the swamp.

He waited until the shadow had completely disappeared from the sky. When Jace could no longer see it, he turned to Luna. "Is it okay to move?"

The cat's ears weren't as far back and it started to leave the shelter. "Yes."

Bundling himself in his cloak, he left the safety of the tree and walked back to the road. He scanned the sky in every direction, making sure the dragon had circled around. There was no sign of it anywhere.

Turning back west, Jace began alternating jogging and walking to keep himself warm. This time, he kept one eye on the road and the other eye to the sky.

He kept up the pace for another three hours before the road flattened out and Jace realized they were near the top of the mountain. If the village wasn't up here, maybe he could at least see its lights on the other side of the mountain.

"Keep your eyes open for lights," Jace told Luna.

"No lights," Luna responded.

"You don't see any?" he asked.

"No lights," she repeated. "All dead."

Jace stopped and looked down at her. "What do you mean: all dead? You mean the village? Skystead?"

His familiar looked up at him. "All dead. Dragon bad!"

Jace's head was spinning. Did she mean the dragon had killed the entire village? How could she possibly know that?

"How do you know the dragon killed them?" he demanded.

Luna's ears went back a little. "Hear."

"You heard the dragon attacking the village?"

"Yes."

Jace's head was spinning. Had the dragon really attacked Skystead? Had it killed the entire village? Why? Had it been looking for food? Wouldn't there be plenty of food in the swamp? Was it looking for treasure? Or was this a territorial thing?

Another, more frightening, possibility occurred to Jace then. Could it be a player inside the dragon? And the player was doing whatever they wanted? If it were a player, could even a full raid bring it down? What would happen when a player, unbound by rules of a monster, met a group expecting certain behavior?

Jace brought his attention back to the problem at hand. He needed to find Skystead and discover whether it truly had been destroyed.

They broke out into another jog. Jace stopped looking in the sky and focused his sight on the road and surrounding mountainside. He looked for any lights that might be a telltale sign of the village's location.   Within fifteen minutes, Jace had found the village - and his answer.

As he rounded a bend in the road, the area opened into a flat mesa. On the mesa were the ruins of homes and shops. Jace looked around at the total devastation the dragon had wreaked. Not a single building still stood intact.

"You were right," he said aloud to Luna.

"Yes," she responded quietly. "All dead."

He trusted Luna, but he needed to see it with his own eyes. He needed to search and make sure there were no survivors. If he were honest, he also needed to search and find anything useful he could use. He'd been planning to buy more provisions and cold weather gear in Skystead. That wouldn't be happening now unless he could scavenge some.

As Jace got closer to the structures, he realized the dragon hadn't razed the buildings with fire. They had been melted by some sort of extremely potent acid. It dissolved things into sticky puddles of goo that he was careful to avoid. Unfortunately, that meant most of the items in the houses had been completely or partially destroyed.

Each building he searched only confirmed Luna's assessment. Everyone was dead and there was nothing worth taking. The town was just... gone. Eventually, he found the graveyard - or what was left of it. Every tombstone had been dissolved away, leaving only puddles of gray goo.

Jace should have gotten a prompt to change his respawn spot. The graveyard was the normal respawn point for players. Whenever a player walked into a graveyard they hadn't bound themselves to, it always prompted to bind there. There was no prompt for him. It was as if Skystead had been wiped from the game map.

A regular monster wouldn't do that. It wouldn't wipe out an entire village, including the graveyard. Monsters wouldn't understand the significance of the graveyard - that it was a place where players spawned. But a player. They would know. They would understand exactly what it was. That meant one thing.

The dragon was a definitely a player.

Chapter 43

Jace saw the truth of it. The dragon was a player and he was destroying the towns around the swamp to prevent players from teleporting in for a raid. It wouldn't stop players indefinitely, but it would slow down the players from reaching him.

None of that mattered to him at the moment. He had come to Skystead hoping to get a caravan to Whitecliff. Once word spread that there was no Skystead, there would be no caravans. Not to mention, caravans would make a much more obvious target for the dragon player.

With the dragon having destroyed the bind point, they couldn't make Skystead their respawn location. If they died, they would respawn all the way back in Sinking Springs. That would mean they'd be right back where they started, only without gear or money.

Angry and frustrated at the events, Jace looked over the ruined husk of Skystead. He wouldn't even be getting a single night's respite. There was nothing for him here and every reason to put as much distance between him and dragon as possible. He had to push on to the next town.

"It looks like no fish and chips for us," he told Luna.

Luna looked at the village sadly. "No."

He turned away from what used to be Skystead and continued down the road. Jace struggled with the despair seeping into him. Or was that just the biting cold? Probably both, he decided as he trudged slowly down the western road. Nothing had gone according to his plans and now he wasn't sure if he could get them to the next town. Heck, he didn't even know what the next town was, how far it was or where it was! He still had the weird feeling he associated with a monster player but there was no sign of the dragon.

Luna seemed to sense his sullen mood and rubbed up against his leg. Looking down at her, he smiled, but there was no real joy in it. He wasn't sure how far he had walked, lost in his dark thoughts before something jarred into awareness. He'd been walking in a haze and it was several steps before his mind registered the hissing sound from Luna.

Freezing in place and drawing his weapons, he looked back at his familiar several paces behind him. The player feeling was stronger now and he feared the dragon was nearby. "What is it?"

"Something," Luna sent him. "Watches."

Jace looked around but saw nothing in the snow-covered foliage. Whatever it was, it was good at hiding. It couldn't be the dragon, could it? "Do you see it?"

"No. Smell."

"What does it smell like?"

"Like troll," she told him.

Jace blanched. Charlena was still in auto-follow. He couldn't take down another troll by himself, even if Luna could change into a big cat for several seconds.

Did he try to make a run for it? How fast could trolls run? Having seen how quickly it had changed him in the last fight, he didn't think he could outrun it over short distances. But was the troll the player or was the player nearby and the troll happened to be here too?

A flicker of movement caught his eye and his head snapped towards a large mound of snow near a tree. He looked up and down the tree, trying to identify the movement. Had it been a bird? Some snow falling?

He took a step closer to get a better look when the mound of snow suddenly stood up and began scrambling up the hill. Whatever it was, it was nearly as large as the troll. Like the troll, it was covered in long fur, but unlike the troll they'd killed, this thing's fur was pure white.

As it scrambled away, it was saying something. "No! No! No! No! Not again!"

Jace stared after it for a moment before realizing that it had been the player he sensed. "Wait!"

The thing stopped and ducked behind a tree, turning to stare down at him with two enormous brown eyes. It didn't say anything, but just blinked a few times as it considered him.

"Are you a player?" he asked. "Trapped in a monster body?"

The creature's gigantic eyes opened wide. "Can you... understand me? You... you know what I am?"

The voice was rough and deep, but he had the distinct impression it was female. There was also a desperate quality, which Jace could understand. He thought back to the Big Cheese and hoped this person hadn't gone insane.

"What's your name? You real name?" he asked the creature.

"Mika Mizuno," it replied, still staying behind the tree trunk that didn't really hide its large body.

"My name is Jace Burton," he told it. "I was like you. I hopped from monster body to monster body until I figured out a way to make myself human."

"You made yourself human?" she asked, its tone hopeful and desperate. At least, Jace thought Mika was a female name.

"I did. And I can tell you how to do it too," he told her. "Can you come down here so we can talk?"

Mika looked around fearfully. "No, no. We can't talk here. There are trolls and other people and a dragon. Follow me. I know a safe place."

With no other words, the large white creature turned and ambled up the slope. Jace watched her for a second and then started after. Moving gracefully for a creature of its size, Jace found it hard to keep up with her. As he followed, he took the time to examine her in his HUD.

Yeti
Level: 8

She was a Yeti. Jace had never run into a Yeti as Mordred, so he wasn't sure what abilities they may have. He saw she was several levels higher than he was, which meant she was probably as dangerous as the troll.

If she was insane like Big Cheese, he couldn't take her down without Charlena. He hoped it wouldn't come to that. He wanted to help these people, not condemn them to everlasting insanity.

It took several minutes before they came upon a small cave that looked too small for Mika to fit into, but she paused and motioned him to follow her, then squeezed inside. Jace hurried over to the cave entrance. Ducking, he looked inside. The cave opened into a large round chamber that was tall enough for the yeti to stand up. Hoping he was doing the right thing, Jace slipped inside with Luna and Charlena following him.

As soon as Jace and Charlena were inside, Mika slipped around him and pushed a large rock over the entrance. She turned around and must have noticed Jace tightening his grip on his weapons. She waved her hands. "To make sure trolls do not smell us. They cannot fit in, but if they come, it is a long wait until they grow bored and leave."

Jace relaxed some, but only some. There was no way he could have defeated her before and in the enclosed area of the cave, it became much more unlikely.

Mika looked at Charlena. "Can you understand me too?"

"She can't hear you," Jace told the yeti. "She is logged off in auto-follow mode. But to answer your question, no, she can't understand you. If she were here, I would translate."

"Oh," Mika replied, looking at Charlena. "She is not… there?"

"No," Jace shook his head. "She was sleeping while I got us to Skystead."

"There is no Skystead," the yeti blurted out. "It was wiped out last night."

"I know. We were nearby. The dragon destroyed it. It even destroyed the graveyard so we can't bind my respawn point."

Mika was silent for a long moment before speaking again. "You said you were a monster, like me. That you hopped from monster to monster."

"Yes."

"Tell me," she whispered. "Are we in hell?"

Jace shook his head. "No, there's a problem with the game. The game thinks we are monsters. But there is a way to make yourself human."

"I can be human again?" she asked quietly. The yeti had squatted down and wrapped its arms around its knees in a very human gesture.

"Yes," he told her. "If you do what I tell you, you will respawn as a human."

"I thought I was in hell," she told him quietly. "I thought… I had been a wicked person, and this was my punishment."

He heard her weeping then and his heart went out to her. He walked over to where Mika was, bent down, and put an arm around the yeti's broad shoulders. Someone watching would probably think it looked comical, but he didn't care. The yeti turned and buried its enormous head into his shoulder and sobbed.

Jace wasn't sure how long she cried into his arm, but finally she lifted her head. "Tell me, how do I become human?"

Taking his time, Jace explained the process and how to use the code. She listened intently and nodded as he spoke. When he was done, he asked her if she had any questions.

"So, I must die again," she said. "And at the prompt, I type in the code and I will become human?"

"Yes," he said. "Your body will morph and then you will respawn at some random starting town."

"Then what?" She asked.

"Then you play the game," he told her. "Until I can make WorldCog aware of the issue and we all get put back where we should be. Have you played the game before?"

The yeti bobbed its head. "I played for a while as a cat-kin."

"Good," he said. "You'll start with nothing, but it can be done. If you get to Whitecliff, you can group with us."

"Whitecliff?" she repeated.

"It's the capital of the human land of Aldor," he told her. "Just get there and we'll help you anyway we can.

Just get to the first pub inside the main entrance. When we reach Whitecliff, we will go there every night. Hopefully, we'll see you there."

She bowed her head. "You are very kind. I will try to meet you in Whitecliff." The yeti raised its head to look at him. ""You will… kill me?"

"I can," he told her. "Or you could jump off a cliff."

"You will get experience if you kill me," she said.

"I will," he told her.

"Then you should kill me," she said adamantly. "I can offer you nothing for your help. The least I can do is give you the experience for killing me."

Jace wasn't sure what to say, so he nodded. Then he remembered Charlena. "Do you mind if we wait until Charlena logs in so she can get the experience too?"

"I don't mind," the yeti replied. "I have been a monster this long, I can wait a few more hours or even a few more days."

"It should only be a few hours," he told her. "She said she would login this morning."

"That is fine," Mika replied. "While we wait, tell me more about you."

Jace didn't enjoy talking about himself, but he related his story. He told her about his job at WorldCog. He told her about the code and then waking up in the game as a monster. She listened intently to his story about how he'd met Charlena and how she thought he may not be dead.

"So, you may still be alive," the yeti said brightly.

"It's possible," Jace told her. "But I don't want to get my hopes up until there's proof."

The yeti smiled, which was a truly horrifying sight. "I hope you are alive. You are a kind person. You should be alive."

Jace blushed and smiled. "Thank you but you seem like a good person too." Then a thought occurred to him. "If it's not too painful, what happened to you? How did you die?"

Mika looked down at her feet. "I inherited my grandmother's estate since I am the only living member of our family. I flew down to Tokyo and signed the papers. The last thing I remember was getting a brain backup in the airport before the flight home. Something must have happened to the plane. When I woke up, I was in a monster. Soon after, I was killed by players and then went into another monster. That is how it has been. Go into monster, then get killed. Yeti is the first time I have not been killed in a long time."

"Wait," he interjected. "You're from Japan? Like, you actually live in Japan and not in America?"

"Yes, I live - lived - near Aomori in the north," she said. "But I had flown down to Tokyo."

He heard what she said, but it didn't make sense. She shouldn't even be on Aldor, the continent for American players. She should be in Meiguo, the in-game continent for Asian players. Whatever bug had caused them to be thrust into monster bodies was obviously also screwed up her default continent. One more thing to add to the list of items to report to the *Help Desk*.

"I see you made a new friend," came Charlena's voice.

Jace stood up quickly. He wasn't sure, but he felt a little weird being so close to Mika with Charlena around. He smiled. "Charlena, this is Mika. Mika, Charlena."

The two girls exchanged greetings and Charlena looked at him. "Did you tell her how to become human?"

"Yes," he replied. "We were just waiting for you so you would get the experience too."

Charlena brightened. "Thank you!"

"It is the least I can do," Mika said, standing up. "You two are very kind to help me."

"We're glad to help," Charlena told her.

There was a long awkward silence. They all stood there looking at each other until Mika finally spoke up. "It is time. I am ready."

Jace had her repeat back the code to him and then, after remembering just in time, asked her to move the rock blocking the door. She did and then walked outside. "You may kill me now. I will see you in Whitecliff, if I am able. First pub inside the main gate."

They killed her then, as quickly so she wouldn't feel as much pain. Mika did not cry out at all but stood there through all of their attacks until finally, she fell and he received a system message letting him know he'd received experience.

They watched her body, waiting for it to morph into a human. It seemed to take much longer than the others, and Jace was afraid she'd forgotten the code when the yeti's corpse began twitching and popping. The body shrank. As it did, the fur fell out, and the features morphed into those of an attractive Japanese girl clad in a loincloth and a tattered bra.

Jace smiled. It had worked. Mika was human again.

Chapter 44

Charlena looked over at Jace. "It worked, right?"

Jace nodded. "I really hope so. I assume if I see their body transform like mine did, that it worked. If not…" He trailed off, realizing he may have just sentenced her to more monster body jumping.

"We'll think positive," Charlena chimed in cheerfully. Then her eyes narrowed. "I can't leave you alone at all can I? I'm gone for a few hours and you're finding some other girl to snuggle up with in a dark cave."

Jace grinned. "It was the big, fur-covered body. Oh, and the maw of razor sharp teeth. Gets me every time."

They shared a quick laugh and then Charlena looked around. "I take it we didn't make it to Skystead."

Jace let out a breath. "We did. It's gone."

Charlena gave him a confused look. "Gone?"

"Remember the swamp dragon?" Jace continued. "It flew past us and destroyed the entire village. It even destroyed the graveyard!"

Charlena's blank look which told him she didn't understand the significance of the graveyard being destroyed.

"The graveyards are where players respawn," he explained. "If it's destroyed, the town's spawn point is destroyed. It's like the town doesn't exist anymore."

She gawked at him. "Are you serious? So, it's gone… forever?"

"I don't know about forever," Jace shrugged. "But for the immediate future it is. I don't remember this happening before. There are very few things capable of destroying a graveyard. A dragon is one of those things."

"So now what?"

Jace sighed. "There's really only one choice. We go to the next closest town." Charlena opened her mouth but Jace forestalled her next question. "And no, I don't know what that is or where it is."

Charlena shut her mouth, her brow creased.

"But I have an idea," Jace told her. "You have access to the internet. You will find some player made maps posted online. If you can look one up that has Skystead and the surrounding area…"

"I can find out where we need to go!" she exclaimed brightly. "I'll do that right now. I'll be right back!"

Jace stopped talking as her avatar went glassy eyed. "And now I'm by myself, talking to myself…"

Walking over to the cave entrance, he looked out. He didn't see any monsters around and the sky were thankfully clear of any dragons. He turned to Luna, who had come to brush up against his leg.

"Do you smell anything dangerous?" he asked.

Her little head bobbed up and down as she sniffed the air. Her ears were rotating left and right and he knew she was listening too for sounds he couldn't hear. "No."

Bending down to stroke her fur, he thought about their next move. They'd been lucky so far. They hadn't run into anything they hadn't been able to handle, even if just barely. He wasn't sure what was between here and the next city. If they ran into anything much higher level, they could easily be killed. Then they'd end up naked back in Sinking Springs.

He had been staring out at the snow-covered landscape for several minutes before he heard Charlena stir behind him.

"I got it," she said, but her tone was not as chipper as it had been. "Airedale. Airedale is the next closest city to the west." She hesitated, biting her lip and Jace knew what was coming next. "The FAQs say it's for characters level 10+, 20+ recommended."

Jace nodded glumly. He had expected this, but actually hearing it made his heart sink. They had little hope against a level 10+ monster and no hope against a level 20+ monster. In VEIL, every 10 levels, the monster strength jumped up significantly. Besides additional health, they did almost 50% more damage. They'd barely managed to kill the mountain troll. And that was just one troll.

"You don't think we can make it?" Charlena asked from behind him.

"I don't know," he told her. "The monsters will be much tougher than anything we've faced."

"Maybe we can avoid them," she suggested cheerfully. Jace couldn't help but smile at her optimism. He just wished he could share it.

"Maybe," he echoed.

She came up behind him and put a hand on his shoulder. "If we die, we end up back in Sinking Springs, right?"

"Yes," minus all of our gear.

"If that happens, we can do some quests and wait for the next caravan."

"No. There won't be any more caravans until the dragon is killed and I have a feeling that might be a long time. Players will not be ready for a dragon that doesn't adhere to the normal game rules. It's one of the most powerful monsters in the game and it will be completely unpredictable. And whoever it is, they're smart. Smart enough to destroy the graveyards in the surrounding towns."

"So, what do we do?" she asked, her normally cheerful voice muted.

Jace didn't have much hope, but he knew he needed to stay strong and not dull her enthusiasm. He turned around and put a smile on his face. "We make our way to Airedale, of course!" He made his voice low and gave her a wink. "Real sneaky like."

Charlena gave him one of her dazzling smiles. "This will be exciting. We'll be like Frodo and Sam sneaking into Mordor."

Jace did a double take. "Did you just make a Hobbit reference?"

She smirked. "Lord of the Rings… not The Hobbit!"

"It's like I designed you on a computer," he said and drew her in for a kiss. The kiss lasted for several minutes before they broke away, panting.

The kiss and the Lord of the Rings reference aside, Jace wished he shared her optimism. It would be very dangerous. One wrong encounter and they'd be dead. And if they died, it would be back to Sinking Springs for who knows how long. Who knew how long it would take raiders to kill the dragon?

"You okay?" Charlena asked him.

He forced a smile. "Oh yeah. Just remembering I need to find out where Airedale is."

"Right!" she said and went to the middle of the cave floor. "I can draw you a map."

She grabbed a stick, bent down and began sketching a crude map of the area. It took her several minutes, but when she had finished, Jace admitted he was impressed. The map had the location of the two cities with the roads, rivers and forests drawn out.

Jace whistled. "Nice map!"

"I AM an art major," she grinned.

He went back to studying the map. It looked straightforward. They just followed the road until the first intersection, then turned southwest until the road eventually met a river and followed it west to Airedale.

"I guess we just follow the road," she said.

"It looks like it," he told her, trying to commit as much of the map to memory as possible. After studying it for several minutes, he thought he had learned what he needed.

"Time to go?" Charlena said enthusiastically.

"Time to go," he agreed.

The two of them left the yeti cave and found their way back to the road. They made their way down as quickly as possible. They were still close to what used to be a 2nd tier village, so the creatures nearby should still be manageable.

They talked quietly about the journey and about the next week. Charlena still had homework to catch up on and she wanted to make some calls to the various hospitals in Philadelphia as Luna Burton to see if she could find out if Jace was at one of the hospitals so she wouldn't have much time to play in the evenings.

Jace understood but he didn't like it. The time passed more quickly and more enjoyably when she was with him. She was funny, witty and her enthusiasm was infectious. She just made his whole day better.

He thought about what would happen if he were alive. Would she like the real him? Would he like the real her? They'd be the same people, at least they would have the same personality. Physically, they'd be different. The real him was a thin, geeky version of his current avatar. He had no idea what the real Charlena looked like, but obviously she wouldn't have pointy ears. Would they be attracted to each other? Or would he end up in the friend zone in real life?

"A penny for your thoughts," Charlena said suddenly and Jace realized he'd been quiet for too long.

"Just thinking about the best route," he lied. He wasn't about to lay bare his fears about their relationship in the real world.

She gave him a confused look. "I thought we were following the road."

"Yes," he replied. "But I was also remembering the rivers. There aren't really many water monsters - at least, not in rivers. I was wondering if we could somehow build a raft and drift down the river."

"A raft?" she asked. "Can we do that?"

"I don't know," he replied honestly. "I've never really tried to build anything in the game. I didn't even bother with the crafting skills."

He checked his inventory. He still had rope and twine that he had bought to replace the stuff he'd lost when Big Cheese had killed him. If they could cut down some trees and lash them together, it should be theoretically possible to make a raft.

"And you're sure there are no water monsters," she asked.

"I'm not 100% sure," he told her. "But the only things I ever encountered in fresh water was in lakes or very deep rivers."

"What did you encounter?" she asked.

"Some river trolls who could breathe water and liked to pull us under, a giant hippo - which is much meaner than it sounds, and maybe some very large, predatory fish," he said, remembering his few river encounters. "I've never ran into anything in shallow rivers."

"So, it would be like white-water rafting?" she asked hopefully.

Jace chuckled. "Let's hope not. I'm not sure what kind of raft we can build, but I'm sure it wouldn't hold up to strong rapids. Not to mention the rocks and other obstacles that would smash us to bits."

"You're such a party pooper," she teased.

"Let's see what the river looks like once we get to it," he told her.

They had walked another few miles when Luna hissed. "Dragon comes!"

Charlena must have seen his expression. "What?!"

"Luna just said the dragon is coming," he told her. "Quick, into the trees."

The two of them dashed into the trees and tried to find a place to hide. Charlena found a rock outcropping surrounded on the sides by thick pine trees. The three of them rushed over and hid underneath. Then they waited.

It was several minutes before he caught sight of it. The dragon, black as night, was gliding through the air near the mountain maybe 500 or 600 feet above them. Even from such a height the thing looked gigantic and Jace wondered how big it really was.

And then, as quickly as it had appeared, it was gone. They watched as it turned west and flew off into the distance.

"It's enormous," Charlena whispered in a trembling voice. As it flew off to the west, she added. "Please tell me that thing isn't heading for Airedale."

Jace had the same thought. After flying west for what appeared to be several miles, the dragon turned around and headed back. It flew over their position without noticing them and then disappeared around the mountainside.

They waited for five minutes, then ten, and finally Luna looked at them. "Dragon gone."

Charlena looked over at him. "What was it doing?"

"It was scouting," he told her. "Looking for incoming players."

"Why?"

"So, it can kill them in small groups before they can form the raid."

She looked at him. "How do you know?"

Jace smiled. "It's what I would do."

Chapter 45

Once the dragon was gone, they quickly made their way back to the road and down the mountain. As they descended the mountain, the temperature became more moderate. Jace was very happy for the change. He'd had about enough of wintery temperatures for a while.

When they reached the bottom of the mountain, it was dark. Charlena had to log off for the evening. Tomorrow was Monday, and she had classes. She kissed him good night, set her auto-follow and logged off.

Alone once more, Jace set off down the road. He wasn't sure how soon the higher level monsters would start showing up. He was still fairly close to Skystead but given the troll he'd already encountered higher level creatures could be anywhere.

Jace set a normal walking pace with Luna beside him. Even with the *Cat-Vision*, he trusted Luna's instincts more than his sight. Her superior hearing and sense of smell would hopefully gain him the edge he needed to avoid any high level monsters.

They travelled west through the night until the sun rose behind them. The night had been chilly but not nearly as cold as the mountain. Just before dawn, the road had run parallel to one of the rivers he remembered from the map.

He took the time to catch some fish. They were larger than the ones he'd caught in Sinking Springs and he thought they might be trout. Jace risked a fire to cook them, but set Luna to watch for enemies once she ate her trout.

After his breakfast, Jace continued along the river road. Distances had been hard to judge on the map, but he guessed he had at least a day before reaching the crossroads and then another two days to Airedale. As long as he didn't run into any monsters, he should make good time.

As if the game had read his mind, Luna suddenly stopped and crouched low. "Monster."

Jace reacted instantly, ducking low and going into Stealth. "Which way?"

"Road," she sent back.

Jace scanned the area for hiding places. To his right the earth dropped away about 10 feet away to the shore of the river. They could try to hide there, but if the creature looked over the lip, they'd be in plain site. To his left was the ground sloped up and was littered with trees and other foliage. He saw a thicket twenty yards up the slope that looked like it would make a suitable hiding spot. "This way."

The three of them ran to the thicket and ducked down. At least, that's what Jace had planned. Charlena just stood there next to him. Darn that auto-follow. He tried laying down, but she continued to stand.

He tried to get Charlena to duck or lay down but nothing he did worked. Then he heard large footfalls. Whatever was coming closer was big. Very big. Was that a giant? He needed to work quickly.

Looking around, Jace ripped some branches from nearby trees and began stuffing them into the elf's outfit and various angles. He manipulated her until she stood behind a large oak next to the thicket.

Then he ducked down with Luna and waited, praying whatever was coming wouldn't take notice of the leaf-covered elf.

Over the next two minutes, the footsteps became louder. Finally, a shape came into sight. The thing was humanoid but was at least ten feet tall. It had thick leathery skin that was a blotchy olive green. The thing dressed in shabby furs and carried a huge club. Judging by the size of that club, Jace guessed it would take him out with one swing. Jace recognized it from his previous play experience. It was an ogre.

Ogres were stupid but powerful. They were constantly hungry and enjoyed smashing and eating anything they came across. Examining it in his HUD, Jace could see this ogre was level 15 - strong enough to squash him like a bug.

Forest Ogre
Level: 15

The ogre was seemingly out for a stroll and didn't seem to be particularly alert. At one point, it stopped and dug into his nose with a finger. It searched enthusiastically for almost a full minute before removing the finger and wiping it on its furs. Then the ogre resumed its walk as if it had never stopped.

When it reached the spot where his group had run off the road, the ogre paused. It moved its head around and Jace realized it was sniffing the air. Oh shoot!

Could it smell them? If so, they were totally screwed. With Charlena in auto-follow, they couldn't hide. The ogre's large stride would make it impossible to outrun.

Jace watched the ogre as it continued to sniff the air, walking around in circles. It did this for several minutes before finally turning towards them.

It sniffed the air in their direction, then took a step forward. It sniffed some more and took another step.

Feeling panic rising, Jace looked around for any way out, but there was nowhere to go at this point. He went through his abilities, but nothing he could do would help them against such a powerful foe. He couldn't even sacrifice himself for Charlena since she would auto-follow him to her doom.

As the ogre took another step towards them, he looked to Luna. "This might be it."

Luna was cowering but spared him a sad look.

Suddenly an idea struck him. "Luna, I want you to grow big and then run past the ogre as fast as you can. Run to the riverbank and then turn back the way we came as long as you can. Can you do that?"

Luna considered for a moment. When she answered, her voice was firm. "Yes."

She scrambled out from behind the thicket and the sound caught the ogre's attention. The thing squinted their way and suddenly there was a lion-sized cat in front of the thicket.

The ogre's face split into a wicked grin and slapped its club into its meaty palm. "Kitty!"

At that moment, Luna bolted down towards the trail. The ogre gave a grunt of surprise as the giant cat went past, just out of reach of its enormous club. "Kitty come back!"

The ogre turned and barreled after Luna who continued down the embankment to the river where Jace lost sight of her. He waited a moment longer until the ogre hopped down the embankment and then he ran as fast as he could up the slope, making sure Charlena was following.

Breathing heavily, they made it to the top of the embankment. He looked down but couldn't see the ogre which hopefully meant it couldn't see him either.

From far below, he heard the ogre calling out. "Kitty! Where are you kitty?"

Jace raced along the top of the slope the way the ogre had come. He looked back constantly to make sure Charlena was keeping up and not running into trees. Keeping a fast pace, he wanted to put as much distance as possible between them and the ogre.

His *Cat-Vision* had winked out a few seconds after Luna made it down to the river, meaning her mana had run out and disappeared. He didn't think the ogre had seen her disappear and there was no telling how long the ogre would look for her. Jace just knew they needed to be far, far away from the ogre when it stopped looking.

They continued as fast as they could without the benefit of the *Cat-Vision*. It was early morning, but the thick tree cover meant the light that filtered down wasn't giving him much to see by. Jace kept the pace as fast as he could for as long as he could.

Pausing when he had a quarter of his *Stamina* left, he waited for it to regenerate. He looked back and listened to make sure they weren't being followed. When he didn't see or hear anything, he sat down.

For the moment, it appeared they were out of danger. He used the opportunity to re-summon Luna. He took off his leather bracer and bit down on it while he summoned her so he wouldn't accidentally cry out when the pain began.

In a few minutes, Luna was back and walked over to rub against his leg. "Ogre gone?"

"Yes," he told her. "Ogre is gone. You did a great job!"

The little cat gave him a smug, satisfied look.

While he waited for his *stamina* to regenerate, he removed the branches from Charlena. As he did, he imagined what she would think if she logged in and saw herself like that. He chuckled to himself as he pictured the look on her face.

Soon his *stamina* was back to full and he began his jog/walk routine. He knew jogging would attract attention. On the other hand, he didn't want the ogre picking up their scent and following them. He didn't think the Luna trick would work twice.

He continued to jog and walk. The slope they'd been traveling on gradually leveled out. The further they moved from the mountains, the flatter the terrain became. That made traveling easier. It would also make spotting them easier and hiding more difficult.

They continued to move all morning and into the afternoon, eventually moving back to the road along the river. They hadn't run into anything else other than the normal wildlife one would expect in a forest.

It was late afternoon when he heard a voice behind him. "How are we doing?"

He stopped and turned only to have Charlena, who had kept walking, plow right into him. They went down, bodies tangled together with her on top. She smiled down at him. "Just like old times."

"Almost, except we're wearing clothes," he replied and leaned up and kissed her. She returned the kiss for a long time before finally the awkwardness of their positions forced her to sit up.

Charlena looked around and spotted the river. "How far did you make it?"

Jace looked around. "Honestly, I have no idea. We ran into a problem. A big problem."

"A big problem?" Charlena asked with concern.

"We ran into an ogre," he told her. "A level 15 ogre."

"I take it that's bad," she said blankly.

Jace remembered she was still new to the game and wasn't familiar with the creatures or the level differences like he was. "An ogre has a tough skin that basically acts as armor. It also carried a large club that could likely kill either of us in one hit. And it probably has at least 200 health."

"Oh," she said with a deadpan face. "In other words, a big problem. Why didn't you just say that?" She winked at him. Then her face became serious. "But you got away, right?"

"I think so," he grinned. "But it had a decent sense of smell. I don't know if it's enough for it to track us. I also don't know where its lair is. It may come this way just to get home."

"Is there some other way we can go to avoid it?"

"I don't think so. If I remember your map, we have to follow this until the crossroads."

"Could we try to cut across?"

Jace thought about it, trying to picture the map in his head. "No, we're on the fastest way right now. We could walk out a few miles and run a parallel course, but then we risk getting lost."

"So, we have to stay on the river road?"

"Yes, at least until we reach the other road."

"What does that mean for us?" she asked.

"It means we're going to need to be on guard all the time," he told her. "If that thing catches us, we're as good as dead."

Chapter 46

While there was still daylight, Jace asked Luna to retrace their trail and let him know if the ogre was following them. "Run until dark. If you find it, let me know. Either way, I will dismiss you and re-summon you back here with us. Can you do that?"

Luna was getting chin rubs from Charlena and didn't answer right away. Finally, Charlena stopped scratching his familiar, and the cat looked at him with a content expression. "Yes."

Rubbing her head up against Charlena's leg, Luna scurried off the way they had come.

"Where'd she go?" Charlena asked at the cat's abrupt disappearance.

"I sent her back along the trail to see if the ogre is following us," he told her.

Charlena brow furrowed. "Do you think it really will come after us?"

"I don't know," Jace shrugged. "But I would rather know if it is coming."

"That makes sense," she said. "Do we wait here until she returns?"

"No. We keep moving. When it gets dark in a few hours, I'll dismiss her and re-summon her."

"Oh," she said thoughtfully. "That's a pretty good idea."

"Always the tone of surprise," he grinned.

She elbowed him playfully, then leaned in and kissed him. After they broke apart, Jace took her hand, and they started down the road.

"Oh," she said suddenly. "I forgot to tell you! I started making some calls today to the hospitals, telling them I was Luna Burton."

Jace perked up. "Did you find out anything?"

Her face fell a little. "No. And I didn't get to make as many calls as I wanted because there were other students around."

"That's okay," he told her. "Just do a few a day."

"But we need to find your body."

"We will," he said soothingly. "But I don't want you getting in any more trouble. If you go to jail, then what."

"Yeah, yeah," she said grudgingly.

They walked until nearly dark, talking about their shared interests. He enjoyed having her to talk to and not for the first time, he wished he had met her in real life. Assuming they found his body, would she still like the real him? Would they get together veil real life?

Could he even get together with her in real life? Assuming he was in a coma in a medical pod, how badly was he hurt? He seemed to be cognitively okay. At least, he hadn't noticed any issues. Would he notice?

And how was he physically? Were things broken? Could he walk? Was he paralyzed? The last one was the most terrifying. The thought of being trapped in a non-working body was what he feared the most.

If he had been deformed, crippled or paralyzed, would Charlena want to be with him? Would he want to be within anyone under those circumstances? He didn't want to be a burden on anyone, least of all Charlena.

He was getting ahead of himself. He still needed to get to the capitol. Once he got there, he still had to figure out a way to get into the castle and find the *Help Desk*. He knew it wouldn't be easy, but he was confident he could figure something out.

In the middle of his thoughts, Jace heard an urgent voice in his head. "Ogre coming!"

Your familiar has been banished.

"Oh shoot," Jace said aloud.

"What?"

"The ogre is coming," he told her. "And I think it just killed Luna."

Charlena's eyes went wide. "It what?!"

Jace sat down on the ground.

"What are you…" Charlena started but then realized what he was doing. "You're summoning her back."

Jace didn't reply, but instead began the summoning process. He poured all of his mana and the health he could into her and it a moment she appeared again.

"Bad ogre!" she snipped as she appeared.

He scratched her head. "Brave little cat. Did the ogre kill you or did you use your big form?"

"Ogre kill," she said. "Throw rock."

"It threw a rock?"

"Big rock," Luna clarified.

Jace nodded grimly. He remembered that ogres could pick up large rocks and hurl them to devastating effect. Being hit by one was almost as bad as being hit by its club.

"What's going on?" Charlena demanded. "You know I can't understand her."

"She found the ogre and it must have seen her and it threw a large rock at her and killed her," he told her.

"You poor kitty," Charlena said, bending down to give Luna some chin scratches. "How far away is it?"

The ogre was moving fast, that much was obvious. Jace had been alternating between jogging and walking all day, and yet the creature had kept pace with them. It couldn't be more than a few hours behind them. Would it stop for the night? Or would it keep coming? How long could they stay ahead of it?

Jace looked to the river. The current was flowing fairly quickly, and he remembered back to Charlena's comment about rafting. He thought about it. If they built a raft, and rode it down the river, they wouldn't expend any *Stamina*. The river might also help mask their scent and confuse the ogre.

"Want to go whitewater rafting?" he asked her.

After explaining the idea to her, she logged off to search the internet on how to make a raft. Neither of them built one before and they wanted to make a raft that wouldn't sink or fall apart while they were in the middle of the river.

Jace sent Luna to scout down the trail to give them some advance warning in case the ogre caught up to them. Once she was in place, he took out the axe they'd looted from the orcs and began chopping trees. Almost immediately he received a system message.

You have gained a new skill: Woodcutting

The only crafting skill he'd used as Mordred had been *Poisonmaking*. At low levels, he'd also used gathering to collect his own herbs to make the poisons, but after a while, he just bought them from the auction house. He shook his head. Now he had all sorts of skills.

As he cut down a dozen trees, his skill went from rank 1 to rank 10. On reaching rank 10, he'd received the *Logger* ability that halved the time to cut down a tree. Once he reached character level 10, his skill cap would increase to 20 and he'd be able to cut down tougher trees. With his improved woodcutting skill, it took him less than an hour to cut down all twelve trees. By the time he had felled the trees, Charlena had returned. She explained the basics, which seemed fairly straightforward.

The design she'd found called for 10 logs. First, they use four logs to create a frame. Once the frame was complete, they would lash the remaining logs to the frame and to each other. It sounded easy. But it was not.

Using the axe, he was able to cut the logs to uniform size, more or less. The problem came when they tried to tie the logs together. The logs were heavy. Positioning and then holding them together was difficult and required both of them.

"You really think it will float?" Charlena asked as they put another log into place.

Jace considered her question and realized he had no idea. Jace knew nothing about rafts, let alone building a raft. He didn't even know if it would float if they built a similar raft in the real world.

"Let's hope so," he grunted as he tied another log onto the frame. "Only one way to find out."

Working together, it took them over an hour to get the crude raft assembled. It looked crude, but it floated when they tested it. The next test was to see if it floated with one of them on it. Jace got into the water to pull the raft out and learned that it was ice cold.

"What?" Charlena asked in concern when she saw the face he made.

"The water's cold," he said sheepishly.

"You and that 100% sensory thing!" she shook her head. He had to agree. This entire experience would be much more enjoyable if he could just turn down his sensory level like she could.

Wading out into the water, which was up to his hips, he held onto the raft. "Okay, hop on."

She gave it a dubious look and then hopped on. The raft sank slightly when her weight hit it, but then rebounded. He stood there for a moment, shivering, but the raft held. "Looks…. Good… to… me…"

Jace pushed the raft back to shore and then waded out. His pants and boots were soaked but he knew a little trick he'd learned as Mordred. He unequipped his pants and boots, letting items go back into his inventory. Then he re-equipped them. They were completely dry. He wasn't sure exactly why that worked, but he was glad someone had shown him back when he was Mordred.

"Giving a girl a show?" Charlena teased. She'd obviously seen his clothes disappear momentarily, leaving him briefly in his loincloth.

"It... uh... dries them off," he told her, feeling the heat in his cheeks.

"Neat trick," she smiled.

"Yeah," he said. "It dries them off instantly."

"Oh," she grinned wickedly. "I meant the disappearing trousers."

She giggled, walked over and kissed him. "You're so easy." She broke the kiss and stepped back.

"I'm sorry, Jace," she pouted. "I have to go. I have to do a little studying for an exam tomorrow. I already stayed longer than I should have, but I wanted to make sure we got this done."

"Thanks," he told her. "If you hadn't stayed, I don't think I could have gotten it done on my own."

"I know," she said playfully, then her mood turned serious. "Can we auto-follow on the raft?"

Jace looked down at the raft. "It should." Then it was his turn to give her a wicked grin. "But I think I need to tie you up!"

Before she logged out, Jace had her lay spread eagle on the raft and then he tied her to the corners of raft as she snickered.

"I must REALLY like you," she told him. "Because this is the first time I've let anyone tie me up."

Jace couldn't help the grin on his face. "If it's any consultation, I've only tied one or two other girls up like this."

She glared at him until he burst out laughing. "Just kidding. I can honestly say I have never even thought of tying a girl to a homemade raft before."

When he was done, he nodded to her. "Okay, set yourself to auto-follow and then logout."

Her eyes went glassy and Charlena's body struggled briefly against the restraints before giving up. That was good, he'd been afraid that the auto-follow would try to make her stand up. There was no way she'd stay on the raft standing up. He needed to tie her down to prevent her from standing, and it seemed to work.

Charlena's eye came back into focus and she tested the restraints. "Did it work?"

"Are you still in auto-follow mode?"

Her eyes went glassy for a brief instant as she looked at her HUD. "Yes! So, it worked!"

Jace smiled. "Looks like it." He bent over her and kissed her. "You know, I could get used to this."

"Don't even think about it," she warned teasingly. "See you tomorrow!"

And with that, she was gone. Her body struggled against the twine briefly and then stopped, staring glassy eyed into the night sky.

"Ogre coming," Luna's voice came in his head.

"Run back as fast as you can," he told her. He could have dismissed her, but he didn't want to lose his *Cat-Vision* now that it was dark. Especially not with an ogre coming after them.

Jace scrambled up to where he'd cut a long sapling about 10 feet long. Since he had no idea how to rig a rudder, he'd had to think of another idea. He'd finally thought of the stick when he'd remembered gondolas and how some of them used a long pole to help navigate. He wasn't sure it would work for him, but it was the best he could do.

He grabbed the pole and hopped back onto the raft. Luna came streaking down and stopped at the edge of the water. He cat-eyed the raft.

"Go water?" the cat asked him warily.

"Yes," he said urgently. "Come on."

"Get wet?"

"Maybe a little," he told her. "Come on! Or do you want to stay with the ogre?"

Luna seemed to consider that and then hopped onto the boat and settled onto Charlena's stomach.

Immediately, Jace pushed off from the shore and steered them to the middle of the river. The raft moved slowly at first but quickly picked up speed. He'd gone maybe two or three hundred yards down the river when he heard noise behind him.

There, where they had been only a few minutes ago, was the ogre. Even over the sound of the river, Jace heard it cry out. "Come back kitty!"

Chapter 47

Jace watched the ogre disappear behind him as the river made a turn. He had no idea if the creature would follow them. All the time he'd played as Mordred, he'd never known an ogre who tracked players. This one seemed intent on finding them. Or at least, it was intent on finding "kitty."

Sitting cross-legged in front, he could see the incoming rocks and then use the pole to steer them away. He could also push off left or right to keep them in the center of the river where it was deepest. It seemed like Charlena's white-water rafting idea might work out.

The river began moving more swiftly, carrying their raft along with it. Jace had to stop glancing behind them and focus on pushing them away from large rocks in the river. It was tense work. Not only did it keep him on his toes, it also tested his balance. The constantly shifting raft kept him struggling just to keep from being thrown off.

Your Acrobatics skill has increased by 1.
Your Acrobatics skill has increased by 1.
Your Acrobatics skill has increased by 1.

Jace barely had enough concentration to see the system messages and stay on the boat. Apparently, the act of trying to stay balanced on a moving raft was enough to increase his *Acrobatics* skill. At least he was getting something out of the experience.

Somehow, he managed to avoid the rocks and stay on the raft. Luna managed to stay on as well by digging her claws into Charlena's leather armor.

Unfortunately, that didn't prevent her from getting drenched. Her fur was soaked and slicked back against her tiny body.

"Sorry," he apologized. It seemed even virtual cats hated water.

Luna just glared at him.

"But it is better than being eaten by the ogre," he offered.

She continued to glare.

The water spared no one. Looking down at Charlena, she was still strapped down and was thoroughly drenched like him. Water splashed her and occasionally some would go into her mouth. When that happened, her character body involuntarily coughed it up. Jace was amused that the developers had added that level of complexity to their avatar's reactions.

Jace shivered. He was as soaked as Luna and Charlena, and the cold was starting to get to him. He was shivering and his teeth were chattering uncontrollably. That part, at least, he could have done without the developers adding. But then again, they probably didn't expect people to endure it on the highest sensory setting.

Luna's ears perked up and twitched, then her head came up. She looked back up the river. "Ogre come."

"Are you serious?" he said through clenched teeth.

How was this ogre following them? And why?
Why the single-minded determination to find them? Or
was this the way ogres were, and Jace had killed them
too quickly as Mordred to notice? That seemed as good
a reason as any. Not that it mattered at the moment. All
that mattered was keeping away from it.

Keeping his focus on the swirling water, Jace
continued to navigate a path down the middle of the
river. After what he thought was an hour, the river
widened, and the current slowed. Jace was able to relax
somewhat. He took the opportunity to equip and
unequip his gear to dry it off. That helped warm it up
slightly, but he wished he could build a fire.

Despite, or perhaps because of, the lull in the
current, Jace kept looking over his shoulder to look
back. He didn't see the ogre, but that didn't mean
anything. He looked down at Luna. "You still hear it
following us?"

"Stomp! Stomp!" the cat replied.

Jace ground his teeth in frustration. He didn't know
how to stop the ogre. Or even stop it from following
them. He was out of ideas. His character was just too
weak to take on the ogre, even with Charlena's help.

It was an unfamiliar sensation for him, feeling this
powerless in the game. He'd worked hard building up
Mordred to be a powerful character. With his vampyre,
he would have had so many options. But as a low level
human, he had none. He didn't like this feeling of
helplessness.

The worst part was knowing the consequences of
being killed by the ogre. They'd lose all their equipment

and money and end up naked all the way back in Sinking Springs. That would mean trying the journey again, only with even fewer resources.

It wasn't a pleasant prospect. He needed to get to the capital and find the *Help Desk*. And it wasn't just himself he was concerned for. There was Duglas, Diana, Mika who had lost all of their assets and who knew how many others who were still trapped in monster bodies. He needed to get WorldCog to fix them all. And fix him.

The raft shifted, bringing his attention back to his current predicament. The current was picking up in speed, and he focused all of his attention on steering the raft. He was trying his best, but the raft slammed into several rocks. Luckily, it held together.

Ability gained: Safefall

The rougher current maxed out his *Acrobatics* skill and he received the *Safefall* ability. It was a fun ability he'd enjoyed as Mordred. It allowed you to fall an additional foot per Acrobatics rank without taking any damage. He had loved to jump off buildings and land without a scratch. Unfortunately, it did not help him in his current situation.

They smashed into another rock and the raft groaned in protest. He was doing his best to avoid the larger rocks, but they were hitting the smaller ones more and more often. How long could the raft take this pounding?

The river suddenly dipped several feet. Jace suddenly found himself momentarily airborne and his stomach did a flip-flop. Then he dropped hard onto the raft and was nearly thrown overboard. At the last minute, he used the pole to push himself back onto the raft and ended up sprawled over Charlena's legs.

He resumed his position at the front of the raft just in time for the raft to smash into a rock. The force jarred him and caused the raft to spin around. Jace was now on the wrong end of the raft. He scrambled over Charlena to the opposite side, which was now the front.

The new position was awkward because Charlena's head was on this side. He barely had enough room to sit, making his perch even more precarious. One good jolt or another dip and he'd tossed off the raft.

Jamming the pole into a passing rock, he spun the raft around. He once again climbed over Charlena to get to the new front. Or was this the old front? Either way, he had much more room sitting between Charlena's legs than trying to fit next to her head.

The current slowed once more, giving Jace a respite. The waters calmed, allowing them to drift lazily down the river. Jace dried off his clothes once more but still couldn't get rid of the lingering chill. He wished the sun was out, but sunrise was still hours away.

He checked on Charlena and Luna and both were wet but were otherwise okay. While he could dry his own clothes by equipping and unequipping them, he couldn't do anything for Charlena. She would have to do that herself when she logged back in.

Jace looked back the way they had come. There was no sign of the ogre. "Is it still following us?"

The wet cat lifted its head up. Luna looked utterly miserable. He wished he could dismiss her, but right now he needed the *Cat-Vision*. If he couldn't see the rocks, they would be torn to pieces.

Luna's ears twitched and moved, and she sniffed the air. "No hear. No smell."

Had they finally lost the ogre? Or had it given up? Or had they just outpaced it? It was impossible to know. He would have to stay vigilant. "Keep an ear out." He looked back down to Luna. "And a nose."

"Yes."

The river continued its leisurely pace, allowing them to ride the current westward. If he remembered correctly from the map, they could take this all the way to the bridge at the crossroads. There the river turned to the south. Once they reached that point, they'd no longer be able to use the raft. It would be back to walking.

Jace shivered. Walking didn't seem so bad right now. At least it would be warmer. He had enough of freezing and being soaked to the bone. If this were real life, he was sure he would have died of hypothermia. As it was, he had to keep enduring the mind numbing cold.

Something changed just then and Jace wasn't sure exactly what it was, but Luna's head perked up. Whatever he'd picked up on subconsciously, she'd picked up on it too.

"Quiet," Luna said.

Jace listened then. He hadn't realized it at first, but she was right. Other than the sound of the river, he couldn't hear any other sounds. Even the crickets and

frogs had grown quiet. He gripped the pole tighter.
Was it the ogre?

"Is it the ogre?" he asked Luna.

Luna sniffed, her head moving back and forth, trying
to get a scent. Finally, she looked over at him. "No."

If it wasn't the ogre, what else was it? He scanned
both shorelines but saw nothing. Was there something
out there hiding? Was it some sort of ambush?

He looked down to Charlena strapped to the raft. If
there was an attack, he'd need to defend her and the raft.
And he'd need to keep the raft from capsizing.

And stay on the raft himself. He smirked. And he
was thinking it was going to be too easy.

The raft continued to drift down the river and Jace
could make out vines hanging across the river up ahead.
He could also see that it was darker ahead. There was
no reflection of the moons on the water.

Jace was getting a bad feeling about this situation.
Something wasn't right. He checked the shorelines
again, but there was nothing. Then something thin
brushed against him. He jerked back from it and looked,
but there was nothing there. Then it happened again.
This time it brushed against his hand and disappeared.
What was it?

Then something brushed against his face. It was like
a fine piece of thread and broke apart immediately.
Jace's breath caught as he realized what it was. It was
strands of spider web. He looked around with new
realization, and things fell into place.

His heart pounded in his chest as he looked over the section of the river they were headed into. Those weren't vines hanging down. They were huge spider webs. He looked up and realized with horror that those weren't stars he was seeing above him. They were eyes. Lots and lots of eyes - all staring down at him.

This was a spider's den. And they were floating right into the heart of it.

Chapter 48

Jace tried steering the raft to the shore, but now that he knew what to look for, he saw that the shore was webbed up as well. If they got too close, they would get caught in the webbing. At least in the water, it might be harder for them to come at him.

He looked up. He could see them now. There were dozens of them crawling around a web canopy that stretched above him. They were watching him with those alien looking eyes. He had flashbacks to the spiders he'd had to kill in Sinking Springs except each one of these spiders was larger than the final spider had been in the attic. Much larger.

One of the spider's descended towards them on a thin line of webbing. It came faster than Jace would have expected and he barely had time to equip his weapons. He stood up, rocking the raft, and stabbed at it with his rapier and fang dagger. He'd considered using *Feint* first, but with so many, he decided to conserve his mana for the moment.

You stab Spider Drone for 8 damage.
You stab Spider Drone for 4 damage.

His blows damaged it but also knocked it out of the path of the raft so it fell into the water. He looked at where it had fallen. Could spiders swim? A moment later, his question was answered as the spider's legs latched onto the raft from the water. Lunging down, he stabbed it through the eyes the moment it pulled its body onto the raft.

You stab Spider Drone for 9 damage.
You stab Spider Drone for 5 damage.
Spider Drone dies.
You gain 40 experience.

He didn't have time to congratulate himself as he saw another one floating down at him. He repeated his attack but this time it landed on the raft, causing Luna to leap straight into the air to get away. Afraid it would bite Charlena, Jace stabbed again, throwing himself slightly off balance.

You stab Spider Drone for 7 damage.
You stab Spider Drone for 5 damage.
Spider Drone dies.
You gain 40 experience.

As he picked himself up, he watched as two more spiders crawled along the canopy to get into position and then dropped at him. He really wished Charlena were here to help. This time, he did use *Feint* to attack the first one to come into range. Two mana down. Fourteen left.

You critically stab Spider Drone for 17 damage.
You critically stab Spider Drone for 9 damage.
Spider Drone dies.
You gain 40 experience.

The second one landed on Charlena's stomach with its back to him. He smiled. Bad luck for him. Never show your back to a *Rogue* with *Backstab*.

You backstab Spider Drone for 21 damage.

You backstab Spider Drone for 14 damage.
Spider Drone dies.
You gain 40 experience.

The second spider shuddered and died. Looking up, Jace could already see other spiders skittering above him to get into place.

Two more dropped and Jace took the first with a *Feint,* killing it. This time the second spider landed close to him. Before he could attack it it shot forward and bit him with its mandibles.

Spider Drone bites YOU for 0 damage.

He felt the pressure of the bite, but the spider couldn't penetrate his Defense. Jace knew he was lucky. If the bite had penetrated his Defense, and he'd taken any damage, he knew the spider would have injected him with venom. But no damage meant no venom. He smiled evilly. Time to kill some spiders.

He took out the second spider with two volleys of strikes but was immediately set upon by two more. One was unfortunate enough to land with its back to him and he *Backstabbed* it. The other he killed normally.

Jace continued to kill them as they came in one's and two's. He lost track of how many he killed and how many had bitten him but he was happy that his *Leather Armor* skill, *Dodge* and *Block* maxed out with all the attacks. This gave him three new abilities.

Ability gained: Deft Warrior
Ability gained: Evade
Ability gained: Bastion

Deft Warrior and *Evade* were both familiar to him since he'd had them on Mordred. *Deft Warrior* gave him an extra point of *Defense* when wearing at least three pieces of leather armor. *Evade* would allow him to expend 4 mana to avoid the next attack. Both were useful abilities. He wasn't sure what *Bastion* did and at the moment, he didn't have time to check.

He killed several more and saw a new system message that made him smile.

You have gained a level.
You are now level 4 in Fighter.
You gain 10 health.
You gain 2 mana.

He'd gained a new level in *Fighter* and since it was now his highest class, he'd gain more health and mana. Looking at the mana, he cringed. Two points wouldn't help much, but he liked the health boost.

More spiders kept coming, and he kept killing them when he noticed his *Stamina* level. He was down to a quarter. If this fight didn't end soon, he would find himself face down in the raft, unable to move. And while they may not be able to hurt him with his *Defense*, he guessed Charlena didn't have the same level of protection. They'd kill her, and she'd have to respawn without him.

Desperate, he started looking for some way out or someway to stop them but the web canopy stretched on above him. If there was only some way he could cut down the canopy or burn it. He blinked. Burn it. Rolling his eyes, he wanted to face palm himself. He was a *Mage*. He had a fire spell!

Aiming at the web canopy in front of him, he cast his *Flame Bolt. "Minima fulmen ignem!"*

The fiery bolt rocketed upward and slammed into the webs, igniting them instantly. What happened next was well beyond his expectations. Layers upon layers of webbing, probably spun over years, ignited, turning the canopy into a blazing inferno. He watched as spiders fled from the blaze, skittering to the safety of the trees that lined the river.

Except, the trees weren't safe either. Everything in the area was covered in webs and the fire ignited the web-covered trees. Unable to escape, many of the spiders burned alive. Jace couldn't see all of them dying, but he saw the experience gain in his system messages.

Realizing he might be wasting an opportunity, he quickly brought up his HUD and switched back to Rogue. Experience continued to come in as more spiders died, finally giving him the message he was waiting for.

You have gained a level.
You are now level 4 in Rogue.

He was feeling pretty good with himself until he heard a voice hissing out. "Who has done this to my children?!"

Up ahead, he saw a huge spider on part of the canopy in front of him that hadn't burned. She was perched on a huge branch that overlooked the river and he saw the thing look down at his raft, now illuminated by fires. "You! You will pay!"

Jace swallowed involuntarily as the eight eyes fixed on him. He tore himself away from its hateful gaze and examined the thing in his HUD.

River Spider Queen
Level: 10

It was level 10. The same as the Mountain Troll and that had taken both he and Charlena to bring it down. Could he solo this thing? Probably not, but he needed to try. Either that or die.

Just then, the flames reached the Spider Queen, and she skittered across the branch to avoid them. As fast as she was, the flames were faster. He heard her scream as they caught up with her but she didn't die. If anything, they made her angrier.

"You will pay human!" she hissed. "Oh, you will pay! I will suck your juices out slowly so that you take a very long time to die!"

Jace had zero desire to have his juices sucked out. He was pretty sure he'd just die and respawn, but the prospect of being slowly killed by a giant spider held absolutely no appeal.

Flames licking her, the queen seemed to realize there was only one escape, and she dove into the water. The spider hit the water and went under, extinguishing the fires on her body. Jace prayed that the thing was too large to swim or float or whatever spiders did on water.

A moment later his prayers were answered, but it wasn't the answer he wanted. The spider seemed to rise to the surface and stood there on top of the water. It snapped it's mandibles loudly. "You have burned my home and killed my children. I shall enjoy killing you and your mate…" The spider's eyes seem to rotate slightly and settled on Luna. "…and your cat."

Jace stood his ground. Keeping himself between the spider queen and Charlena. "Come get some!"

The spider queen let out a primal hiss and charged him. He could see the spider was burned in places, but he had no idea how much damage it had actually sustained. Jace hoped it was enough to give him a fighting chance.

"*Aeris Armatura!*" he cried out, casting his *Air Armor* spell. The spell would give him more *Armor* and improve his *Defense* and he had a feeling he'd need all he could get.

She reached him faster than he had expected and snapped at him with her mandibles.

River Spider Queen bites YOU for 0 damage.
Your Air Magic skill has increased by 1.

He almost laughed when her mandibles didn't penetrate. This fight would be easier than he thought. And then her two front legs jabbed at him like spears.

River Spider Queen stabs YOU for 3 damage.
Your Air Magic skill has increased by 1.
River Spider Queen stabs YOU for 1 damage.
Your Air Magic skill has increased by 1.

He grunted as the spider's forelegs stabbed into his arm and side, almost pushing him off the raft. Ignoring the pain, Jace regained his balance and struck out at the huge spider.

You stab River Spider Queen for 7 damage.
You stab River Spider Queen for 4 damage.

The queen hissed but otherwise ignored his blows, striking out again at him.

River Spider Queen bites YOU for 0 damage.
Your Air Magic skill has increased by 1.
River Spider Queen stabs YOU but you Dodge.
Your Air Magic skill has increased by 1.
Ability gained: Persistent Spell.
River Spider Queen stabs YOU but you Block.

Jace was a blur of motion as he blocked one leg and then dodged the other. Unfortunately, the one he dodged hit the raft and drew him off balance and he fell onto the raft. The Spider Queen didn't waste the opportunity and pressed her attack.

River Spider Queen bites YOU for 0 damage.
River Spider Queen stabs YOU for 1 damage.
River Spider Queen stabs YOU for 1 damage.

Jace received two more minor wounds from the spider queen as he got to his feet but clenched his teeth against the pain. He *Feinted* this time and stabbed the thing.

You critically stab River Spider Queen for 14 damage.
You critically stab River Spider Queen for 6 damage.

Other than hissing, the giant spider ignored his blows and continued to stab and bite him, hitting in the chest and stomach.

River Spider Queen bites YOU for 0 damage.
River Spider Queen stabs YOU for 4 damage.
River Spider Queen stabs YOU for 2 damage.

The stomach wound was the more painful one, but he recovered quickly and *Feint*ed. Then he drove his blade at the queen's eyes.

You critically stab River Spider Queen for 16 damage.
You critically stab River Spider Queen for 6 damage.

This time the effect was obvious. Two of her eyes were gone, but the remaining eyes glared at him with hatred and she reared back. Jace didn't recognize it as a special attack until it was too late.

River Spider Queen spits at you.
You are Blinded for 6 seconds.

Sticky burning liquid hit him in the eyes and the world went black. Jace tried to swing where he thought she would be but missed completely.

You stab River Spider Queen but miss.
You stab River Spider Queen but miss.

Desperately trying to stay balanced on the raft, he felt the queen's legs stab into his arm and leg.

River Spider Queen bites YOU for 0 damage.
River Spider Queen stabs YOU for 3 damage.
River Spider Queen stabs YOU for 1 damage.

Without seeing where the blows were coming from, he couldn't brace for them and he was once again knocked down. The queen didn't relent and continued attacking him.

River Spider Queen bites YOU for 0 damage.
River Spider Queen stabs YOU for 2 damage.
River Spider Queen stabs YOU for 2 damage.

Jace lashed out with his weapons, judging where the body should be, based off where the legs had hit him.

You stab River Spider Queen for 7 damage.
You stab River Spider Queen but miss.

His rapier stabbed something, but his dagger met only air. Still the queen just hissed and from the sound of the splashing, was circling.

"Maybe I should give your mate some attention," the queen hissed. "Or maybe your cat."

"I attack?" asked Luna in his mind.

He knew she meant using her mana to grow big. While she might damage it in her giant cat form, as soon as she did, she would disappear. Once she was gone, he'd lose *Cat-Vision*. The *Blindness* was almost over, and he needed to be able to see in the dark.

"No," he told her. "Wait."

But Jace couldn't just let the spider queen attack them either. Luckily, he knew what to do. Using his *Taunt*, he yelled. "Get over here! I'm the one who killed your little brats!"

Compelled by the *Taunt*, Jace heard the queen's footsteps splashing back toward him.

"You dare!" she hissed. "I will kill you first, then I will kill your mate!"

You are no longer Blinded.

Jace blinked and could see again. As the queen came back around, he *Feinted* and struck out at her eyes again.

You critically stab River Spider Queen for 14 damage.
You critically stab River Spider Queen for 8 damage.

She hissed and reared back, then struck out quickly.

River Spider Queen bites YOU for 0 damage.
River Spider Queen stabs YOU for 1 damage.
River Spider Queen stabs YOU for 1 damage.

He only had two more mana before he'd need to tap into Luna's mana. He *Feinted* once more and stabbed the queen in the eyes. This time, the blades slid in deeper.

You critically stab River Spider Queen for 15 damage.
You critically stab River Spider Queen for 7 damage.
River Spider Queen dies.
You gain 100 experience.
The spider queen's body twitched and spasmed and then collapsed into the water in front of them.

Breathing hard, Jace put away his weapons and looted the queen's corpse.

You receive Giant Spider Fang.

You receive Venom Sac.

The mandible was a lot like the Rat Fang, it was the same general shape as a dagger so Jace examined it.

Giant Spider Fang
Type: Dagger
Damage: 4 + 1 (Sharp) + Poison
Wt: 1 lb
Description: Extracted from the mandible of a giant spider, this fang is large enough to be used as a weapon and still retains some of its venomous qualities.

Jace put both items in his inventory and collapsed onto the raft. He'd killed a ton of spiders and their queen. And lived to tell the tale. He was feeling pretty good about himself.

That's when his world turned upside down.

Chapter 49

At first Jace wasn't sure what had happened. One minute he was sitting on the raft and the next minute he was in the river unable to move.

Forest Ogre hits you with Draining Rock 12 damage. You are Disabled.

Jace saw the system message but couldn't believe it. Was it the same ogre? Where had it come from? How had it tracked them? *Draining Rock* was obviously some special attack. It had taken the last of his *Stamina*. Even worse, it had put him into the negative. He was helpless until he regenerated his *Stamina* to 10%.

There was a cat's roar, and then an ogre's cry. "Aargh! Bad Kitty!"

Luna claws Forest Ogre for 5 damage.
Luna claws Forest Ogre for 3 damage.
Luna bites Forest Ogre for 7 damage.
Your familiar has been banished.

Even though he was face up, the world went dark for Jace as Luna was dismissed and he lost his *Cat-Vision*. Luna had tried to save Charlena and used her giant form to attack the ogre. Considering the level of the ogre, his familiar had done some fair damage. The transformation had used all of her mana and now she was gone. And Jace was literally in the dark.

"Oh… Pretty elf," he heard the ogre say and then splashing.

Desperately Jace tried to move or even turn his head, but it was impossible. He raged and cursed, but to no avail. He couldn't even move his toes. The game simply would not allow him to move until his *Stamina* regenerated.

Helpless, he waited for the system message that would let him know it had killed Charlena. Or waited to see the ogre looming over him with its giant club. It felt like an eternity, as he waited for the death he knew would come.

Yet nothing happened. The ogre didn't smash him and he didn't see Charlena's death message. Had it left them alone? That seemed unlikely, but maybe it was just after Luna? He was still entertaining that thought when a new message popped up.

Almedha Pressalor has moved out of range and is no longer following you.

Jace's blood went cold. Charlena wasn't following him anymore. Had she moved out of range? Had he drifted too far away? How far away were they? He could feel himself lodged on something. The raft must have kept drifting.

He checked his HUD to make sure her character was still logged on. It was. That was good. He was afraid her character might have automatically logged out when the auto-follow disengaged. Jace just needed to get back to the raft and keep her tied to it until Charlena logged back in.

Again, he struggled to move his body and again he failed. He looked at his *Stamina*. He was just over 5%. Just five more percent to go. He watched his HUD as it regenerated agonizingly slow. All he could think of was how far Charlena was getting from him.

Finally, he could move. Standing up, Jace looked around.

It was dark but he could see that he'd landed on the spider queen's body. Her body had prevented him from being carried down river. He looked around for the ogre but it was nowhere in sight. Hopefully, they'd seen the last of the thing.

Jace wanted to rush after Charlena, but first thing was first. Clenching his teeth against the pain he knew was coming, he summoned Luna. His health and mana had regenerated to full and he poured them all into her summoning.

"Ogre?" asked Luna as she materialized on the spider queen's body. He smiled. At least she was dry now. He immediately activated his *Cat-Vision*, and the world brightened.

"It's gone," he told her.

"Charlena?" she asked, looking around.

Jace looked down the river. "She floated away on the raft."

He reached over and picked up Luna and carried her to the shore. The spider webs around the area had burned away. There was no sign of any spiders either, so he set her down and dried his clothes before setting off at a brisk pace down the river. He wanted to jog or run but didn't dare risk it with his *Stamina* so low.

He and Luna hurried along the river for several minutes without seeing the raft. He wasn't out of commission that long. She couldn't go that far in only a few minutes. His *Stamina* was up to 15% so he broke into a jog, keeping his eyes peeling on the river for any sign of her or the raft.

He kept it up for ten minutes before he was forced to stop or run out of *Stamina*. This made no sense. The water wasn't even moving fast.

Where could she have gone? Had she gotten caught up on the other side of the river and he'd just missed her?

They crossed to the other side of the river and walked back towards the spider area. He kept a close eye out for her and tried to fight the rising panic he was feeling. He had to find her. He had to. If they got separated, he had no idea how he would find her again.

They reached the spider area with no sign of her or the raft. Jace was in full panic mode by this point. He had no idea what had happened to her. He looked again at his HUD and could see that they were still grouped and that her character was alive.

Had she died? Had the ogre killed her and he had just missed it? Was she back in Sinking Springs right now? Jace collapsed onto the ground. They'd gotten so far and now she might be back where they started. Or she might be further down the river. He had no idea where she was! What was he supposed to do?

Charlena was his only friend at the moment and his only link to the outside world. Plus, he had to admit he had feelings for her. He couldn't lose her! He had to do something. But what? He didn't know if she were down the river or back in Sinking Springs. What the heck was he supposed to do?

He could find a way to kill himself or get killed and respawn in the starter town. But what if she wasn't there? He'd be there alone with no equipment to make the trip back here. And then even if he did make it back here, how would he find her?

He could continue searching down river, but what if he missed her? There were small tributaries that snakes off the main river. What if she drifted down one of those?

He might never find her. And what if something killed her? She'd end up back at Sinking Springs.

And what if she were still alive when she logged back in and was all alone out in the forest? What would she think? Would she think he had abandoned her? Would she try to make it to Airedale? How long would it take her with only a few hours a day to travel? A week? Two weeks? Longer? Could she last that long on her own?

Jace put his head in his hands as he thought about the impossible situation he was in. He didn't know what to do. He'd lost Charlena, and he had no idea where she was or how to get her back.

Maybe he should just kill himself. Chances were, if Charlena hadn't already died and respawned in Sinking Springs, she would soon. Her body would be alone and unable to defend itself. The first monster that came along would kill her. Then she'd be in the starter town with him.

He knew that's what he should do, but part of him hated it. It was quitting. Giving up. He was used to living with the hand he was dealt. He'd come so far and was so close to getting to Airedale and the capital. But he knew that when he did get to the capital, he wanted it to be with Charlena.

"We're going to have to die," Jace said aloud.

"Die?" Luna asked.

"Yeah," he told her. "I need to die so we can go back to the town."

"Why?"

"So, we can meet up with Charlena."

"Meet Charlena?"

"Yes, meet Charlena in the town."

"No."

Jace looked at the cat. "What do you mean no?"

"No town," the cat responded, and looked up the river. "Ogre."

Jace stood suddenly, causing Luna to leap back. "What do you mean?"

Luna kept looking the way they had come and sniffed. "Ogre. Charlena."

Jace stared up the river and then down to the cat and back at the river. "Are you saying that the ogre took Charlena?"

"Yes," the cat said.

Jace felt like someone had blown his mind. He knew it was possible for monsters to take prisoners. In fact, some quests were rescue quests. In those quests, a player or group had to rescue someone who had been captured and usually punish the guilty party. They were difficult because it was often impossible to protect the NPC.

Charlena was a player character, not an NPC. He couldn't remember any instances where that had happened. But it was theoretically possible. Is that what had happened? Had the ogre kidnapped her?

If that were the case, Jace needed to find Charlena and rescue her. He had no idea how he would do that against a level 15 ogre but one step at a time. First, he needed to find her. Then he could worry about rescuing her.

Jace checked his stats. His health and mana were back to maximum and his *Stamina* was at 50%. He looked down to Luna. "Can you track where the ogre went?"

Luna sniffed the air again and looked back at him. "Yes."

"Let's go," he told her and she took off along the shore back the way they had come.

Jace jogged after her and had gone only dozen yards when he skidded to a stop. They had just past a large patch of what Jace thought were burned spider eggs, but something else had caught his eye.

"Wait up," he called out to his familiar and the little cat stopped and looked back.

Looking more closely, he saw he had been right. The fire had burned the eggs, but it had also burned cocoons around the nest that held the bodies of victims the spider had caught. Part of the cocoons had been burned away, revealing the glint of metal. He'd found the spider's treasure hoard.

Jace walked over and used his rapier to cut open the first cocoon. As he did, the mummified body inside fell to the ground and broke apart. Jace bending over, Jace saw what had caught his attention. Around the corpse's neck was a shiny golden amulet in the shape of a griffon. He took the amulet and examined it.

Griffon's Guard
Type: Necklace
Level: 5
Wt: .2 lb
Special: If wielding a shield, the wearer gains an additional +1 Defense
Description: Given to Knights of the Griffon who had distinguished themselves in a tournament, this amulet gives the wearer extra protection.
Restriction: Requires at least 1 rank in the Shield skill.

He took the amulet and slipped it into his inventory. The amulet was level 5 and Jace was one only one level from using it. When he gained another level, the extra point of Defense would be most welcome.

Quickly hacking open the remaining cocoons, he found 112 gold, a long sword, two daggers, and a potion of healing. He stashed all the items into his inventory and signaled Luna to go. It was time to find Charlena.

Chapter 50

Luna led him along the shoreline, occasionally stopping to sniff the air. Jace scanned the shoreline continuously, looking for ogre tracks, but could find none. Was the ogre too high a level for him to track or had the ogre walked up the river. If the creature had been pulling the raft, it would make sense for it to stay on the river.

But why was the ogre heading up the river? That didn't make any sense - unless it was heading back to its lair. That meant it had been tracking them. But they'd lost it. Hadn't they? Then Jace realized the truth.

They might have lost it, but there was no way that the ogre had missed the huge fire he'd created when he'd burned spider nest. The fire and associated smell must have attracted the ogre to them. Jace had done that. He was responsible for her being kidnapped.

Jace slowed as he felt what felt like an anxiety attack coming on. Had he killed Charlena like he had killed his family? It was his fault. Just like it was his fault his family was dead. If he'd just gone out to eat with him. They'd be alive. Charlena wouldn't be kidnapped. It was his fault.

"Okay?" Luna brushed up against his leg.

Jace looked down without really seeing her. The old guilt and pain was like a knife digging into his heart. His breath came in ragged gasps. No, not again. He'd done it again. And now he might never see Charlena again.

"Charlena?" the cat meowed, looking up at him.

He looked down at the orange tabby cat and they locked eyes. Luna was right. He hadn't been able to save his family, but maybe he could still save Charlena. He had to try.

He reached down and stroked her fur, eliciting some purrs. "Yes, little one, let's go save Charlena."

Pushing his guilt down so he could focus on what he needed to do now, Jace hurried after Luna. He wasn't sure exactly how much of a head start the ogre had on them. He'd gone down the river for a respectful distance before circling back. The ogre had to have at least an hour on them.

They followed the tracks for three hours before Luna came to a halt. Jace was afraid she might have lost the trail, but then he saw it too. Leading out of the water were enormous footprints. Ogre foot prints.

Jace bent down. He used his *Tracking* skill and examined the tracks.

Forest Ogre
Level: 15

That was his ogre all right, but he didn't see any prints from Charlena. Looking more closely, he saw something next to the tracks. It was a long straight track, like something that was being dragged. The raft! Charlena was still tied to the raft. And the ogre was dragging it along with him!

"Let's go," he told Luna and hurried up the shoreline toward the tracks. He didn't even have to look at the tracks as the path the ogre was following was well worn with many sets of tracks, but they all seemed to belong to the same ogre. He hoped they belonged to the same ogre.

The two of them ran on through the rest of the night and into morning. He found it odd that the ogre's lair was so far from where they had encountered it, but there were many things odd about this ogre. Then again, Jace had seen little of them in the wild. He'd usually just gotten a quest, found the ogre or ogres and killed them.

Was this what ogres did without players around? Went on a walkabout? Explored the countryside? He had to admit, if that were so, he had to hand it to the original developers for adding in some deeper, or at least more diverse, depth to the monsters. In a way, it almost made them like real people. But he guessed that was the point.

At midmorning, Jace received the *Hungry* debuff and quickly used up one of his rations to get rid of it. He hadn't had time to fish for food before they'd started after the ogre. Luckily, Luna had complained about food since she wouldn't eat the ration and he didn't have time to find something.

The morning turned into early afternoon, and still they followed the tracks. Jace wasn't sure, but if he had to guess, he thought they were traveling north. He tried to remember what was north of Charlena's map, but he couldn't remember her drawing much to the north. All he knew is that they were heading deeper into the Wild Lands. That meant more danger.

Jace continued their fast pace, trying to close the distance. Judging by the sun's position, he had an hour, maybe two, before Charlena logged in. He wasn't sure how she would react, but he didn't want her freaking out. Assuming she was still alive, if she freaked out, the ogre might kill her just to shut her up. Then all of this would be for nothing.

Another hour passed. They still followed the ogre's trail with no indication that they had gotten closer.

If Jace's *Tracking* skill had been as high as Mordred's, he would have been able to tell the age of the tracks. As it was, he had no clue.

Then the screaming started. It was distant, but Jace knew it instantly. It was Charlena. She must have logged in and realized her new predicament. He ground his teeth as he imagined what she must be thinking.

He had no idea where the screaming was coming from, his ears just weren't good enough. But luckily, he knew someone with excellent hearing. He looked down at Luna. "Can you find her?"

Luna's body was tense as her ears twitched and moved. Without looking at him, she took off down the trail and called back to him. "Yes."

Smiling at the spunky little cat, he raced after her. The screaming continued, but now Jace realized she was calling out a word. His name. She needed him, and he was on his way.

They ran on for fifteen minutes before Jace had to call them to a halt. He was dangerously low on *Stamina* and couldn't afford a repeat of his last encounter with the ogre. From this point, he needed to walk and regenerate. He just hoped Charlena could hold on.

As Jace followed the tracks, the screaming had stopped. The silence was ominous, and Jace hoped it wasn't because the ogre had killed her. He checked his system log but didn't see any messages. But he could be out of range. He just had to keep going and trust that she was okay.

A few minutes later, Jace came upon the raft. It was still intact, but she wasn't there.

The twine that had held her was broken. Charlena was gone. He guessed the ogre had gotten tired of carrying the entire raft and just pulled her off.

Jace dropped into *Stealth* and continued following the tracks until he reached a large clearing.   Scanning the clearing, he saw a cave in the far end with an enormous bonfire in front of it. The ogre sat near the fire, looking down at something.

Peering at what the ogre was looking at, Jace saw that it was a make-shift cage. Inside the cage was a very familiar red-headed elf. It was Charlena, and she was alive. Relief washed over him like rain on a warm summer day. She was alive, and he'd found her.

Yet, while it relieved him to see her alive, there was still the ogre to deal with. Going at the thing one on one was suicide. Even having recently gained another level in *Fighter*, he was no match for the creature. He had to think of some other way to deal with it.

He looked at his skills and abilities. Jace had nothing powerful enough to truly hurt the ogre. Nor did he have anything that could keep him alive long enough to kill the thing. That meant he had to outsmart it somehow. But how?

From his hiding spot, Jace looked over the entire clearing. It was barren except for the ogre, the bonfire and Charlena's cage. There was nothing he could use against the beast. He considered getting above the cage and seeing if he could drop something on the thing. But anything he hauled up to the top of the cave wouldn't do enough damage.

What did that leave? Nothing. The ogre was simply too tough to kill. It just wasn't possible given the weapons he possessed and the thing's thick hide. Was this it then? He'd tracked the ogre all the way to its layer only to fail?

At least if they both died, they'd wind up together. They'd be out there equipment but they might be able to do more quests in Sinking Springs to earn enough money to get the equipment and items they needed. Maybe.

It seemed like the only plausible solution and the only one that involved them being able to stay together. He just needed to let her know what he was planning. That he'd let the ogre kill him and then she'd need to figure out a way to get it to kill her too. Then they could try again. Who knows, maybe they'd even try another raft.

Jace stopped. The raft. Their raft was nearby, and it was intact. Suddenly a crazy idea came to mind. It would be a long shot - a very long shot - but it just might work. He slipped away from the clearing and made his way back to the raft. Jace examined the raft and realized his plan just might work. Maybe. If he were lucky.

First, he untied the logs from the raft. He ended up with ten logs and several pieces of rope. He used the long sword he'd recently acquired to sharpen one side of the logs. Next, he used the frying pan and his buckler to dig holes in the ground. Once the holes were dug, he set the logs into the holes with the pointy side facing up, slightly tilted towards the ogre's camp.

In essence, he'd created a large spike trap. The problem was how to get the ogre on the spikes. It couldn't run into the trap, it had to fall onto the trap for the spikes to do any real harm. That was where the second part of his plan came into play.

Jace took the pieces of rope and tied them together. He strung them across two trees as tightly as possible, making a tripwire in front of the spikes. Theoretically, if he could get the ogre to run into this area, it would trip over the rope and fall into the spikes. Theoretically.

He went over the trap again, making sure everything was right. When he was confident there was nothing more he could do to improve the trap, he put the next phase of his plan into action. It was time to get the ogre's attention.

Jace once again snuck up to the edge of the clearing. Remembering a very old vidstream his dad had made him watch, Jace yelled in his best Sloth voice. "Hey you guys!"

The ogre's head shot up, and its angry eyes fixed on Jace. The thing climbed to its feet and grabbed a nearby stone. With surprising speed, it hurled the small boulder directly at Jace, but he was ready.

Forest Ogre throws Draining Rock at YOU but you Evade.

Jace used his *Evade* ability to completely dodge the rock, which went sailing harmlessly past him to smash into a nearby tree. Making a chicken gesture, he yelled out at the ogre. "Chicken!"

The ogre roared and grabbed another small boulder and threw it at Jace. This time, Jace deflected the attack with his buckler using *Bastion.*

Forest Ogre throws Draining Rock at YOU but you Block.

"Jace?" came Charlena's familiar voice. "Is that you?"

"Can't catch me chicken!" he yelled. "Bock! Bock! Bock!"

Jace turned and ran towards his trap as the ogre grabbed its club and stood up. He didn't look back but could hear the thundering footsteps of the ogre as it ran after him in huge loping strides.

Running at full speed towards the trap, Jace could feel the ogre catching up to him. He turned the corner and then threw himself to the right just as he reached the tripwire. The ogre seemed to see the trap and skidded to a halt, its arms wind milling to keep its balance.

Jace stared in horror as it looked like the ogre would regain its balance and not fall into the trap. Then a familiar orange tabby cat, grown to giant size, slammed into the ogre's head and tipped it over. Its arms still wind milling, the thing cried out as its immense body toppled over into the spikes. "Kitty!"

Your familiar has been banished.
Your Spike Trap damages Forest Ogre for 19 damage.
Your Trapsetting skill has increased by 1.
Your Spike Trap damages Forest Ogre for 20 damage.
Your Trapsetting skill has increased by 1.
Your Spike Trap damages Forest Ogre for 21 damage.
Your Trapsetting skill has increased by 1.
Your Spike Trap damages Forest Ogre for 17 damage.
Your Trapsetting skill has increased by 1.
Your Spike Trap damages Forest Ogre for 16 damage.
Your Trapsetting skill has increased by 1.

Luna had transformed into her giant form and knocked the ogre onto the spikes! The ogre roared again, but this time it was in pain. Unfortunately, it had missed some of the spikes and was still alive.

Wasting no time, Jace leaped onto its back and stabbed it.

You backstab Forest Ogre for 11 damage.
You backstab Forest Ogre for 3 damage.
Forest Ogre is Poisoned.

You backstab Forest Ogre for 12 damage.
You backstab Forest Ogre for 3 damage.
Forest Ogre is Poisoned.

The thing roared against and pushed itself off the spikes, throwing Jace to the ground. It scrambled to its knees. It turned towards Jace with murderous intent.

Grabbing its club, it swung down at Jace who used another *Evade* and dodged the blow.

Poison hits Forest Ogre for 3 damage.

Turning his dodge into a roll, he came up behind the ogre again and struck out at the thing's back.

Poison hits Forest Ogre for 3 damage.

You backstab Forest Ogre for 9 damage.
You backstab Forest Ogre for 2 damage.
Forest Ogre is Poisoned.
Forest Ogre dies.
You gain 150 experience.

The ogre stiffened and then slumped over, falling back onto the spikes. He'd done it. He couldn't believe it, but his trap had actually worked. Jace had killed the ogre. He started to laugh at the absurdity of it and the fact that he wasn't dead.

Chapter 51

He was still staring down at the ogre when he heard Charlena call out his name. "Jace? Is that you? Hello?"

Running over to her cage, he stopped in front. "Hey there."

"Thank God it's you! Is the ogre dead?" she exclaimed. Almost immediately her voice hardened. "Wait?! What the heck happened?! Why did I log back in a cage?"

Jace was looking at the cage to see how to open it but had no door. The cage was just a bunch of saplings driven into the ground. The ogre probably set her down into it. He looked back at her. "The ogre sucker punched me with some special *Stamina* draining attack. By the time I could move, you were gone and I had no idea what happened to you. We eventually found the trail, followed it, and here I am."

She looked around. "We? Where's Luna?"

Jace sighed. "She did her giant cat thing and knocked the ogre into the spike trap I had created."

"Oh," she interrupted. "And how am I level 5 now?!"

"Well," he took a deep breath. "Did I mention the entire colony of giant spiders plus his huge spider queen

I killed? We were still grouped, so you got experience too.”

“Spider colony? Spider queen?” she asked in concern. “And you killed them all?”

“A few might have gotten away,” he admitted.

Charlena shook her head, but he saw the corners of her mouth turning up in a smile. “I can’t leave you alone for even a minute, can I?”

Jace smiled and shook his head. “Nope.”

“Can you get me out of here?” she asked, gesturing at the cage.

Jace looked up and down the cage. “Can’t you just climb out?”

She smirked. “I tried, and the ogre caught me and smeared fat or grease or something on the top of the bars. Once I get halfway up, I lose my grip.”

Jace brought out his axe. “I’m a lumberjack…”

“And you’re okay?” she ventured.

Jace grinned. “Exactly so.”

By his estimate, it took him fifteen minutes to cut through two of the “bars” so she could squeeze through. When she finally got out she threw her arms around him and kissed him. “I was so scared. I didn’t know where I was or where you were. I thought I’d have to figure out some way to kill myself and respawn.”

"I'm sorry," he told her. "I was in the same boat. I didn't know where you were until we finally found the ogre's trail."

She clung to him and he returned the embrace for long minutes before she finally pulled away and punched him hard in the arm. "Never do that again! I didn't know where you were or what I should do! I almost logged out a dozen times waiting for you!"

"Ow!" he said, rubbing his arm. "Full sensory input, remember?!"

She rolled her eyes. "You kill an ogre and an entire colony of giant spiders and you're complaining about a girl punching you?"

Jace looked sheepish. "Well, when you put it like that."

Her eyes suddenly brightened. "Do you think the ogre had loot?"

This time it was Jace's turn to roll his eyes. "Only one way to find out."

They searched the camp but found nothing. Then they searched the ogre's cave. It was smaller than he'd expected, by ogre standards. It had just enough room for some sleeping furs and a pile of "treasure" it had collected. Unfortunately, most of the treasures still had body parts attached, and most of it was worthless junk.

"This is disgusting," Charlena said, holding up a bracer. The bracer was still strapped to the previous owner's arm from the elbow down.

Most of the items were like that but they did find a jeweled ring, still on the finger, that while not magical, was probably worth a hundred gold.

Charlena scrunched up her nose. "You can carry that."

The most interesting find was what they thought was a helmet, still on the previous owner's head. When Jace removed it to examine it, the helmet transformed into a large floppy hat with a feather that looked like something one of the three musketeers might wear. At the same time, the shriveled face of the skull the hat had been on changed, morphing into that of a bearded dwarf.

"Did you see that?" he asked, nearly dropping the helmet turned hat.

Charlena looked up at him. "See what?"

Jace examined the hat in his HUD.

Infiltrator's Hat
Type: Helmet
Level: 5
Wt: 1 lb
Special: On command, this hat allows the wearer to assume the general appearance of any humanoid race of approximately the same size. This effect lasts until the hat is removed.
Description: Created for the daring cat-kin spy, Malyi Praukkir, this hat is responsible for her unparalleled success until the day she was required to remove her hat in the presence of the Queen.

Restriction: This cannot be used to emulate the appearance of a specific player or NPC. The hat does not grant racial specific abilities.

"Cool!" Jace said aloud.

Charlena perked up. "What's cool?"

Jace put the hat on his head and thought of an elf, focusing his thought at the hat. Almost immediately his body blurred. He didn't feel any different, but he felt… shorter.

Charlena's eyes went wide. "You turned into an elf! How did you do that?"

Jace removed the hat and felt his body returned to normal, including his height. "It's the hat. It allows you to change your form."

"That's so cool!" she said. "Let me try!"

He gave the hat to Charlena, who spent the next several minutes changing into various forms. Each time she changed, she checked out her reflection in a somewhat reflective metal shield they had found.

Smiling at her whimsicalness, Jace went back to sorting through the treasure pile. He hadn't gotten far before she called out to him. "Look at this!"

Jace turned to see Charlena in her normal body except with purple hair. "This is awesome! If you concentrate hard enough, you can change little things about your own body. And this…"

Charlena furrowed her brow in concentration and the hat changed into an ornamental hairpin, then it transformed into a tiara. "You can change the hat itself too!"

Remembering how the hat had originally been a helmet, Jace nodded. "Nice going. Do you want to keep it?"

She looked excited but then took off the tiara and watched it revert to the feathered hat. "No, you might need it more than me since you're on all the time." She brightened. "But I get to borrow it!"

Smiling, he took the offered hat and put it in his inventory. "Deal!"

Jace checked his mana and health levels and saw that he was back to normal. He sat down and re-summoned Luna.

"Ogre dead?" the cat asked when she appeared.

"Yes," he told her. "The ogre is dead and Charlena is safe."

The little cat went over to Charlena and rubbed back and forth against her leg while purring loudly. Charlena reached down and picked up the cat, hugging it to her. "I missed you too."

Luna allowed Charlena to hold and pet her for several minutes before starting to squirm and hopping down. The cat began walking around the cave, sniffing.

It took them another fifteen minutes before they'd gone through the rest of the treasure. They found a longbow and quiver, but it wasn't as good as the Crystalburrow bow Charlena carried. They also found another 103 gold in various pouches, a potion of mana and another potion of health. Since Jace already had a potion of healing, he told Charlena to keep it.

Once they were confident they'd found all the treasure there was to find, Jace led them back to the ogre's body.

"Wow," Charlena said. "You really did a number of it I can't believe you killed it."

Jace looked down at the huge body that lay impaled on the makeshift spikes. He could barely believe it he killed the ogre himself.

Idly, he wished he had access to the game forums to brag about it. Unfortunately, that wasn't an option now. Plus, he didn't have a recording of it happening. Without that, no one would believe him anyway.

Luna suddenly rubbed against his leg and looked up at him as if to remind him of the part she'd played. He bend down the stroke the cat.

"It was a team effort," he replied, scratching Luna behind the ears. "If it hadn't have been for Luna, I'd be dead."

Luna returned his look with a smug one of her own. "Yes."

Jace had almost forgotten he hadn't looted the ogre's corpse. He bent over and looted it.

You receive Bonk Stick.
You receive Necklace of Fangs.
You receive 97 gold.

Pulling up the items, he saw that they were both higher level items than they could use but they were powerful. Neither of them could use the Bonk Stick, but once Charlena reached level 11, the necklace would be very nice!

Bonk Stick
Type: Mace
Level: 15
Damage: 18
Wt: 20 lbs
Description: This oversized club, taken from a Forest Ogre, does twice the normal damage but also uses twice as much Stamina.
Restriction: Requires 12 Strength.

Necklace of Fangs
Type: Necklace
Level: 11
Wt: .2 lb
Special: Thrown or Missile attacks from the wearer of this necklace become Draining attacks, reducing the targets Stamina by twice the damage inflicted.
Description: This simple necklace of bear fangs was blessed by Ghazark, god of the hunt.

"What?! What did you find?" she asked. Jace held out both items so she could examine them. Her eyes went glassy as she read the descriptions, and then she whistled. "That necklace looks pretty nice. Too bad it's level 11."

"You're almost halfway there," he said. "And trust me, this is a very powerful item." He remembered the complete helplessness he'd felt when he was drained of *Stamina*. "You can literally reduce a monster's *Stamina* to nothing and they'll be completely unable to move. You can do it to players in PvP as well."

"PvP?" Charlena asked him quizzically.

"Player vs Player," he told her. "In certain areas in the game you can kill other players, especially players of other factions."

"That's right!" she said. "I remember reading that. It supposed to be tough."

Jace nodded, remembering his own experiences. "They have the same abilities we do but more strategy than a monster. Plus, PvP differs greatly from fighting monsters. People who do nothing but PvP get REALLY good at it."

"I think I want to avoid that for a while," she told him.

Nodding, he held out the necklace for her to take.

"For me?" she asked.

"You're the one with the bow," he told her.

"Thanks!" she said and took the offered necklace.

Charlena looked around and then up in the sky. The sun was sinking below the western horizon. "I'm going to have to go soon. I have to meet a study group for a test on Friday."

Jace tried not to look disappointed even though he had been looking forward to spending more time with her, given that just a few hours ago he had no idea if he would see her again. But he understood. Real world things were more important than game things. She had a life - a real life. "I understand."

"Well then, stop giving me those puppy dog eyes!" she teased.

"Sorry," he told her. "I wasn't sure I'd see you again. You'll have to forgive me if I'm sad to see you go."

Charlena moved in closer. "You can't get rid of me that easily. I'd find you, eventually. After all, I know where you're going! Remember, first pub from the main gate! Isn't that where you told the others to meet us?"

Jace smiled and kissed her for a long time until she pushed away. "No more of that," she said breathlessly. "Or I might just skip my study group."

He chuckled and her eyes went glassy for a moment. "Okay, I'm auto-following you again. Try not to lose me this time!"

She winked and then her eyes went glassy. She had logged out.

Jace smiled. Even though Charlena was gone, he felt better knowing he would see her again tomorrow. Still smiling, he motioned to Luna and began hiking back towards the river.

Chapter 52

The walk back took all night. When he finally reached the river, he could see the morning sun peaking over the mountains to his east through breaks in the forest canopy. With no raft, and frankly no desire to build another raft, he would walk next to the river.

First, he needed to eat. He brought out his fishing gear and took the time to catch several trout. He gave Luna one and then fried the others in a pan. It was a risk, but after what he had been through, he wanted an enjoyable meal.

When they finished eating, Jace and Luna set off down the road, giving the spider nest another look when they came to it. The smaller spiders hadn't been able to hurt him and he was hoping there might be some stragglers for him to kill and earn some additional experience. No such luck. They had either fled or died in the fire.

He kept walking through the day, encountering no monsters along the way. Part of him was happy about that. Another part of him wouldn't have minded the experience. He had that Griffon necklace that he wanted to use, but he needed to be level 5.

The forest thinned out around noon. By late afternoon, the forest had turned into rolling green hills. Even better, off in the distance, he spotted a large bridge that had to be the crossroads bridge. They'd made it.

Jace spun around on the lush hilltop with arms outstretched and bellowed, "The hills are alive with the sound of music!"

When he saw the odd expression on Luna's face, he stopped quickly. Dropping his hands to his sides, he pretended nothing had happened and continued on towards the bridge. After a moment, Luna followed but eyed him warily.

It was another hour before Charlena suddenly jumped onto his back, wrapping her arms and legs around him. "We're out of the forest!"

He laughed, and she giggled as he ran down the hill, giving her a piggyback ride. He reached the bottom of the hill with her still on his back. When he tried to go up the next hill, he lost his balance. One moment they were going up the hill and then his foot slipped and they were both tumbling on the ground laughing.

"That was fun!" she told him as she tried to control her laughing. "We should do that in real life."

"You haven't even met me in real life," he told her. "You may not even like the real me."

She turned over in the grass to face him. "This is the real you. I mean, the real you is your personality. When you wake up, you'll still be the same person."

Jace continued to smile, but inside he wasn't so sure. He had met other girls in the game and then met them in real life. It wasn't the same. Soon after meeting in the real world, they'd drifted apart in the game and then it was over. He hoped that wouldn't happen with Charlena.

Plus, there was the fact that he still wasn't even 100% sure he was alive. And if he was alive, what sort of shape was his real body in. There were so many factors.

She must have sensed his change in mood. "A penny for your thoughts. Or in game, I guess it would be a gold piece."

Jace chuckled but wasn't sure how to respond. He didn't want to lay out his fears to her. Not yet. There were just too many unknowns. Instead, he forced a smile. "Just hoping we find my body soon."

Charlena's face went serious too. "I know Jace. I made some more calls today, and I forgot to tell you, I made some yesterday. Still no luck. But we're about halfway down the list. We still have half to go!"

"Thanks!" he told her. "I can't tell you how much I appreciate you doing that."

She gave him another of her dazzling smiles. "You're welcome! I'm glad I can help!"

He got up and walked over to her. Offering his hand, he helped her up. He kept holding her hand as they walked and talked about her schoolwork and he related his fight with the spiders."

When his story was over, she shook her head. "So one fire bolt or whatever and the entire nest was on fire?"

"Yup," he replied. "It went up like tissue paper."

"Why would they make it so easy?" she asked.

"I don't know that they did," he told her. "The developers set certain rules that the overall Game AI abides by as it generates monsters and governs their behavior. Most of those rules are based on real life physics. This was one of those cases where the rules worked in our favor. Trust me, that's not always the case."

"I guess you were lucky," she said.

"I was," he agreed. "The little ones couldn't touch me but if that fire hadn't damaged the queen, she would have killed me before I could do enough damage to her."

"Let's hope you stay lucky," she said.

"I'm sorry, did you say you hope I get lucky?" he teased.

"Ugh!" she pulled her hand from his and slapped him playfully. "Is that really all you guys think about."

"I told you," he smirked. "We don't just think about virtual sex, we think about real sex."

Her eyes narrowed evilly. "Well, I guess you'll have to wait until you're back in your real body for that."

Jace realized his mouth was open and closed it. Had she just suggested that she would have sex with him in the real world. Or was she just teasing? The prospect both excited him and terrified him. Especially since he didn't even know where his body was at the moment.

He wasn't sure what expression was on his face, but she burst out laughing. "I see, you're all talk and no action."

"I… Ah…" he stammered.

Charlena turned serious. "Let's worry about finding your body first and then we can talk about what we're going to do in real life."

Jace nodded dumbly. He wasn't sure what she meant by that, but the possibilities excited him. He realized she was holding out her hand, and he quickly took it and resumed their walk.

Several hours after the sun had set, they stood at the top of a hill looking down on the crossroads. It wasn't what they were expecting. Crossroads wasn't a description of the place, it was the name of the small town that had grown up around the bridge.

It was dark and he couldn't make out all the details, but there were enough lights from various buildings that he could make out the general layout of the town.

"It's a town," Charlena stated, looking down the walled town.

"Apparently," he agreed.

"Well, this sucks!" she let out an exasperated breath. "I have to log out! I won't even get to see it!"

"I can spend the night up here and wait until tomorrow to go into town," Jace offered.

She returned the smile but gave a slight shake of her head. "No, go down there and get yourself a hot meal." He started to argue, but she held her hand up. "It's okay. Just do me a favor. Hang out there until I log back in tomorrow night!"

"Deal," he said. He would have waited up here in the hills overnight, but he had to admit that spending a night in town would be so much nicer. He wouldn't have to worry about being attacked.

"I'd better log then," she told him. "I have that test in my virtual design class tomorrow."

"Okay, I'll see you..." he started, but a sudden thought struck him. "Wait!"

She froze. "What is it?"

He turned and looked over the small town until he saw what he was looking for, just to the north of town. He pointed down at it. "Before anything happens, let's go down to the graveyard and change our bind point."

Charlena looked where he was pointing. "Good idea! That way we don't end up back in Sinking Springs."

They walked down the hill. The two of them skirted around to the north side of the town and found the graveyard. It was larger than the Sinking Springs graveyard, but that was typical. The larger the town, the larger the graveyard.

As they entered the graveyard Jace received a new system message.

New spawn point: Western Crossroads
Do you wish to set Western Crossroads as your bind point? (Yes or No)

Jace immediately chose Yes, and the prompt disappeared. He looked over to Charlena.

She tilted her head. "So, if you're staying here until tomorrow night, does that mean I can just log out without putting myself on auto-follow?"

Jace thought about it. There was no reason for her to be on auto-follow while they were in a town. When she logged back in, she'd appear here and could just come into the town and find him. But since Crossroads was larger than Sinking Springs, they needed a place to stay. "Sure. You can log off normally. When you log back in, look for me at the inn. Good luck with your test!"

Charlena bobbed her head. "Sounds like a plan. And thanks!"

She leaned in and kissed them, and then her body faded away.

Jace watched her disappear. It felt weird to not have her following him, if only in body. He'd gotten used to her being around.

He heard Luna sniffing and looked down at his familiar. She stopped sniffing and looked up at him. "Food?"

Grinning, he reached down and scratched her under the chin. "Oh yeah, food!"

The two of them walked back around to the front gates. He approached the gates and saw that there were seven guards hanging out at the entrance. Dressed in weathered tabards over dirty chain mail armor, each carried a sword on their hip. Five of the guards were male and the other two were female.

One of them noticed him approaching and signaled for him to stop. He was a large man, a good four or five inches taller than Jace with more muscle. He had a flat face that looked like someone had repeatedly hit him with a frying pad. "Who goes there?"

"Jac…" Jace started to answer with his real name but remembered his character name. Dedrurrurth."

The guard looked back at the other guards and snickered. "Dedr… what? What kind of name is that?"

"Old Aldorian," Jace said. He was lying, but he guessed this guy wouldn't know Kobold from Old Aldorian.

"Huh," said the man. "You don't say. Well, my name is Sergeant Foucher and I'll have what business brings you to Crossroads."

"We… I'm here on my way to Whitecliff," he told the sergeant. There was no reason to lie about his destination.

"Is that a fact?" the man asked. "And where are you coming from?"

"Sinking Springs," he told the guard. Again, no point in lying.

The guards exchanged looks with other and suddenly they were all looking at him.

"What do you know about the dragon attacks?" the man asked.

"I went through Skystead on my way here," he told them. "It's been completely destroyed."

There was more muttering until the sergeant hushed them. "What about Sinking Springs?"

Jace gave the man a confused look. "What about it?"

"We heard it was destroyed," he said. "Right before Skystead."

"What?!" Jace couldn't believe it. Sinking Springs had been destroyed? They'd just been there. He'd met all of those people. Now they were all gone. "I didn't know. Everything… Everyone… Was still alive when I left. Are you sure?"

The man nodded solemnly. "Sorry, we got confirmation today from a mage who was able to reach the town and then teleport back."

"You probably got out just in time," the man said. "You're lucky."

Jace nodded numbly.

"Did you have family there?" the sergeant asked him.

"No," Jace shook his head. "But I knew those people. They were my friends."

The man cleared his throat. "I'm sorry then. Go ahead inside. It's late so you'll be wanting to find the Wry Weasel. It's the better of the two inns in town."

Nodding, Jace walked into Crossroads in a daze. He couldn't believe Sinking Springs was gone.

Chapter 53

Jace and Luna walked through the rough, muddy streets of Crossroads in a daze. He was thinking of all the NPCs he'd met and did quests for in Sinking Springs.

"You lost?" a man's voice said and Jace blinked out of his stupor.

"What?" he asked.

"Are you lost?" the man asked. He was a little taller than Jace with greasy hair, a broken smile and mutton chops.

"I'm looking for the Wry Weasel," he told the man.

The man smiled, showing missing teeth. "You're not far. You make a right up there at that alley. Go two blocks and then turn left. Go four blocks and you're there. Good place."

Jace thanked the man and continued down the road for another two blocks. Following the man's instructions, he turned right down the alley. The alley would normally have been dark, but with his *Cat-Vision* allowed him to see far better than a normal person could. So, he saw the two men stepping out from behind some crates.

"Behind," said Luna in his mind and Jace glanced over his shoulder to see two men step in behind him, blocking his retreat.

Jace's instincts kicked in and he had his weapons equipped even as he scanned all four men in his HUD.

Brycen
Race: Human
Class: Thug
Level: 6

Darnell
Race: Human
Class: Thug
Level: 5

Leland
Race: Human
Class: Rogue
Level: 5

Trayen
Race: Human
Class: Rogue
Level: 5

Brycen, the man who'd given him directions, was the highest level of the NPCS and most likely the leader. He was a Thug, which was a watered-down version of fighter. Another of the men was a thug as well. The other two were rogues, which meant they'd have backstab. He'd need to keep them in front of him.

Leland and Trayen both brandished two daggers while Darnell held a sturdy looking mace. Brycen held a longsword. None of them posed a real danger to him alone, but together he wasn't sure.

"*Aeris Armatura!*" he spoke, casting his *Air Armor* spell. Everyone except for Brycen took a step back.

"You didn't say nothing about no mage," Trayen said, his voice shaky.

"Yeah," agreed Leland nervously. "Mage ain't good business!"

"Shut your holes," Brycen told them. "Look at those weapons. He ain't no mage. He probably knows a trick or two but that's it. Now stick him! Or you'll answer to me."

The leader's threat seemed to scare them more than Jace and the men closed in on him. Backing against a wall, he waited for them to approach.

Darnell was the first to stalk forward and drew back to a strike with his mace. Jace *Feinted* and stabbed the man with his rapier and spider fang dagger.

You critically stab Darnell for 12 damage.
You critically stab Darnell for 4 damage.
Darnell is Poisoned.

The strikes didn't do as much damage as he hoped, and Jace realized the man was wearing chain mail armor under his tunic. Darnell grunted but bought his mace down on Jace.

Darnell crushes YOU for 0 damage.

"His magic is protecting him!" Darnell snarled just as Trayen and Leland managed to get in a few strikes.

Leland stabs YOU for 0 damage.
Leland stabs YOU for 0 damage.

Trayen stabs YOU for 0 damage.

Trayen stabs YOU for 0 damage.

"This aint's worked," Trayen said. "I can't stick him!"

"Give me a shot," Brycen commanded and slashed across Jace's chest.

Brycen slashes YOU for 2 damage.

The slash hurt and took away a 2 health but Jace had felt worse. He steeled himself and focused on Brycen. Using another *Feint*, he stabbed out at the cutthroat.

You critically stab Brycen for 11 damage.
You critically stab Brycen for 3 damage.
Brycen is Poisoned.

Poison hits Darnell for 3 damage.

"Argh!" Darnell growled. "The knife wound burns! It's some type of poison."

"Poison?" stammered Leland. "This guy has poison too?!"

"Stop your belly-aching and stick this guy," Brycen yelled.

The three level 5 cutthroats struck again to no effect. With the *Air Armor* active, Jace was as protected as if he was wearing a suit of plate mail. Unfortunately, Brycen's long sword continued to get through his Defense, if only barely.

Brycen slashes YOU for 1 damage.

Jace continued his attacks on Brycen. He wanted to take out the leader, since only his weapon could hurt Jace.

You critically stab Brycen for 12 damage.
You critically stab Brycen for 2 damage.
Brycen is Poisoned.

Poison hits Darnell for 3 damage.
Poison hits Brycen for 3 damage.

Brycen grunted twice. Once when Jace hit him and then another when the poison kicked in. Jace could see the other men's courage was hanging by a thread. He just needed to cut that thread.

Jace once again shrugged off a flurry of attacks by the weaker thugs and took another slash from Brycen against his left arm.

Brycen slashes YOU for 1 damage.

He counter-struck back at Brycen, ignoring the other men.

You critically stab Brycen for 11 damage.
You critically stab Brycen for 4 damage.
Brycen is Poisoned.

Poison hits Darnell for 3 damage.
Poison hits Brycen for 3 damage.

This time Brycen staggered back, grasping the wounds in his chest. He had a surprised look on his face right up until the moment

Poison hits Brycen for 3 damage.

Brycen dies.
You gain 60 experience.
You gain -10 faction with Crossroads Thieves Guild
You gain +10 faction with Crossroads Guards

Brycen began foaming at the mouth as the long sword slipped from his lifeless fingers and he fell dead.

"He killed Brycen!" yelled Leland.

"Run for it!" Darnell growled.

The three remaining cutthroats ran off down the alley and Jace let them go. He walked over to Brycen's body and looted it.

You receive long sword.
You receive Crossroads Thieves Guild Medallion.
You receive 19 gold.

Jace examined the medallion, but it just said *quest item* so he stashed it in his inventory. He scrolled back up through the system messages and read the faction changes. It appeared he just lost faction with the local thieves' guild and gained faction with the guards. And now he had a quest item. Time to find out what it was for.

Jace stopped the first guard he came across and asked about the medallion. "A group of thugs just jumped me in the alley. I fought them off and killed one of them. They dropped this. Does it mean something?"

The guard gave him a hard look, but then shrugged. "There's a reward for killing thieves in this town. Go ask the sergeant at the gates, he'll tell you all about it."

Thanking the guard, he walked back to the main gain and found Sergeant Foucher. The man recognized him as he walked over. "You get lost?"

Jace held up the medallion. "I was jumped on my way there. Took this from one of the thugs. One of your guards said there might be a reward for killing a thief."

Sergeant Foucher nodded. "Aye! The mayor set a bounty on the thieves' guild. That's their symbol on the medallion. I'll pay you a 5 gold bounty for each one you bring."

You have completed the quest, "Crossroad Thief Bounty"
You gain 25 experience. Experience to next level 645.
You gain +10 faction with Crossroads Guards.
You gain +10 faction with Residents of Crossroads.
You receive 5 gold.

Sergeant Foucher has offered you the quest, "Crossroad Thief Bounty" (Repeatable)
Reward: +10 faction with Crossroads Guards, +10 faction with Residents of Crossroads.
Accept quest? (Yes or No)

Jace saw that he had been offered the quest again, and that it was a repeatable quest. He accepted. His plans just changed from a nice quiet night at the inn to hunting down thieves. After all, Charlena had hit level 5, and he needed to catch up to her.

He and Luna spent the rest of the night walking down alleys and trying to get mugged. He killed four more thieves before the world seemed to spread about him and he was no longer attacked. He was about to give up when he remembered the *infiltrator's hat*.

Using the hat to change his appearance from a human to a halfling, dwarf, elf and even gnome, he killed another five thieves who didn't realize they were trying to rob the same guy. By morning, he had earned level 5 in *Rogue*. Along with the extra health and mana, level 5 also meant he could use the *Griffon necklace*. Pulling it from his inventory, he slid the necklace around his neck and tucked it into his armor.

It also meant he now had access to find and disarm traps, which he'd found extremely useful in the past. It was actually one of the main reasons a party needed a rogue character on their missions. There were all sorts of traps that could wipe out the entire group if not disarmed.

He stopped then and went to the Wry Weasel and ordered a full halfling breakfast and a piece of salmon for Luna.

She ate enthusiastically, and she finished her fillet before he finished his breakfast.

Afterwards, he spent the rest of the day wandering around the town, looking in the various shops. He restocked some of his supplies, buying a new rope and more twine. He also bought additional rations and sold off some items he'd looted along the way.

Once he finished shopping, he checked with the guards and found out that a Caravan to Whitecliff was coming in tomorrow and it would only take a week to get to the capital. They wouldn't even need to go to Airedale. That was great news. It would shave a full week of their journey. He'd just need to secure passage on the caravan and they could follow it all the way there.

Feeling much more optimistic about their situation, Jace hung out at the Wry Weasel until Charlena showed up in late afternoon. He ordered her a mead and asked her how she did on her test.

"Okay," she told him sourly. "I think I missed a few questions on dynamic virtual lighting. Somehow I totally missed that when I was studying."

"I'm sure you did well," he told her.

She gave him an expression that told him she didn't believe it.

"I have some good news," he told her and she looked up from her mead. "There's a caravan arriving in Crossroads tomorrow morning. And it's headed for Whitecliff."

"That's great!" she said, a little enthusiasm bleeding into her voice. "So, we don't have to go to Airedale?"

"No, we can leave right from here and get there in a week."

"Awesome!" she said and held up her mug. "To Whitecliff."

He laughed and clinked mugs with her. "To Whitecliff."

After their ale, he took on a tour of the city and they visited shop after shop as she looked at the many virtual items she could purchase. She didn't actually buy anything but she really enjoyed looking at them.

Occasionally, she would make little comments like "I wonder if this was made in game or scanned in?" That plus the way she was analyzing some of the goods, he guessed she was looking at things as a future VR artist and not as a player. But he didn't mind.

They continued looking at stores until it was dark and nearly time for her to go and then headed back to the Wry Weasel. They had just turned down an alley to cut across to the next street when three men stepped out to block their progress. Jace looked back, Jace saw three more block their retreat.

Then a man in dark clothing dropped down from the roof above them and landed nimbly on his feet. He looked at Jace with cold eyes. "So, you're the one whose been killing my thieves."

Chapter 54

Jace spun to face the man while equipping his weapons. He scanned the man in his HUD and he grew concerned.

Guildmaster Dainard Drakkar
Race: Human
Class: Rogue
Level: 11

This guy was the guildmaster and he was level 11. Based on his class, he would have at least 88 health and half that mana. He'd be using higher tier weapons which would do a lot more damage and better armor than Jace had. In other words, Jace was outclassed in a one-on-one battle. Together, he and Charlena might be able to take the guildmaster, but not his men too.

"What? Nothing to say?" the man said casually. "That's fine. None of my men will care about last words."

Jace had to think quickly. They couldn't defeat this level 11 guild master and his men at the same time. He needed a way to at least get the guy one on one. But what? He didn't have anything that could help him.

If only he was Mordred, he might have some clout with this thieves guild. Mordred was a member of multiple thieves guilds in Visimar. He'd be able to drop some names and possibly get them out of the situation. He laughed inwardly. If he were Mordred, he'd challenge the guildmaster and wipe the floor with him.

That gave Jace an idea. It was risky but since the alternative was dying, he really had nothing to lose.

He wasn't Mordred but he did have Mordred's knowledge - and his own. Plus, from multiclassing, he did have some abilities the guildmaster wouldn't have.

"I'm here to challenge you," Jace said, mustering up as much confidence as he could. "For leadership of the Crossroads guild."

That took the guildmaster by surprise, but he recovered quickly. "Only a guild member can challenge a guildmaster. You're a nobody. You're not even a thief."

Who says I'm not a thief, Jace signed in Thieves Cant. Thieves Cant was a derivative of American sign language the developers had written into the game as a way for thieves guild members to communicate silently to each other. Only thieves could learn it or use it, unless the person was a player. Players could learn to actually sign it with enough time and Jace was geeky enough to have learned it.

The guildmaster looked at Jace and paled slightly, then looked at his men, who had obviously seen Jace sign. In their eyes, he'd just confirmed he was a thief.

"You claim to be a member. What chapter are you with?" Dainard Drakkar demanded.

This was the tricky part, Jace thought. As it so happened, he was still wearing the Infiltrator's hat. He thought of becoming a vampyre. His skinned pales to an ivory white and his features thinned. His eyes became red and his canines elongated into fangs.

"I am Modred Blacklock, a member of the Blightmourn chapter," Jace announced. Technically, Mordred was a member of the Blightmourn chapter back in Visimar, and several other chapters.

But he didn't expect to have been heard of here. Jace heard mutterings of "vampyre" and "Visimar" from the guildmaster's men.

The guildmaster himself had recovered and was looking over Jace. "Maybe you are and maybe you aren't. I happen to know who the guildmaster is in Blightmourn. Do you?"

"Alaric Dawnburn," Jace told him and the guildmaster blanched, and his men saw him.

"Challenge," one said.

"Challenge," agreed another, and then another until all six men were whispering it. They had accepted Jace as a challenger. The guildmaster had no choice but to fight him or he'd lose face with his men.

"Very well," Drakkar said. "Challenge made. Challenge accepted."

"Jace," Charlena whispered. "What are you doing?"

"Trust me," he whispered back. "It's either this or they kill us."

"You and I," he said. "No help from your little pet there."

At first, Jace thought he was referring to Luna but he realized the man was referring to Charlena. He nearly made an angry retort but stopped himself. No, he had to play it cool. "You mean my new Lieutenant? I don't need her help. She's just here to witness and report back to Alaric that I've assumed control."

He could see the guildmaster grinding his teeth. "Alaric sent you himself?"

"Of course," Jace told him matter of factly. "Why else would I have come to this dreadful country."

Jace had never really been one of those roleplay people who really got into their character but he was actually enjoying this part. There was a certain excitement and fear to it that made him feel alive.

"Very well," said the man, pulling two wicked looking daggers from his belt. "Let's begin."

"Oh," Jace said, gesturing. "I do have something to say before we start."

Drakkar snickered. "And what's that?"

"*Aeris Armatura!*" he incanted, and his *Air Armor* swirled around him.

"So," the guildmaster spat. "It's true. You are a mage. That won't save you."

The man disappeared and Jace knew he had used *Vanish*. He backed into the wall, so the guildmaster couldn't get a backstab in on him. A moment later, he felt two blades stab into his side but couldn't penetrate his *Defense*.

Dainard Drakkar critically stabs YOU for 0 damage.
Dainard Drakkar critically stabs YOU for 0 damage.

Jace smiled. He had hoped his calculations had been right and it looked like they were. The guildmaster's daggers couldn't damage him. But according to his calculations, his rapier should be able to penetrate the Drakkar' *Defense*.

You stab Dainard Drakkar for 1 damage.
You stab Dainard Drakkar for 0 damage.

As Jace thought, his rapier did enough damage to penetrate but the dagger didn't. It was going to be a very long fight if he could only do two points of damage at a time. He sheathed the dagger and switched the rapier to his left hand. Then grabbed the long sword that he'd taken from Brycen with his right hand. Luckily, as a *Fighter*, he could use slashing weapons.

As he was switching weapons, Drakkar darted in with a *Feint* and stabbed at Jace again without doing any damage.

Dainard Drakkar critically stabs YOU for 0 damage.
Dainard Drakkar critically stabs YOU for 0 damage.

Trying to get used to the balance of the new weapon, Jace struck out at the guildmaster again, this time with the rapier and long sword.

You slash Dainard Drakkar for 3 damage.
You stab Dainard Drakkar for 2 damage.

Well, that was a little better. But it was still going to be a long fight. He needed to shorten it and he had an idea of how. It was time to try out one of his abilities.

Drakkar used *Vanish* again and this time, Jace stepped away and allowed the guildmaster to backstab him.

Dainard Drakkar backstabs YOU for 0 damage.
Dainard Drakkar backstabs YOU for 0 damage.

"My turn," Jace said and used his Shield Bash ability.

You Shield Bash Dainard Drakkar for 0 damage.
Dainard Drakkar is stunned for 3 seconds.

Jace danced behind Drakkar and attacked him from behind.

You slash Dainard Drakkar for 3 damage.
You backstab Dainard Drakkar for 6 damage.

You slash Dainard Drakkar for 3 damage.
You backstab Dainard Drakkar for 6 damage.

He got two backstabs in before the stun wore off and the guildmaster spun away. Jace was disappointed that the long sword couldn't do a backstab but remembered it only worked with piercing weapons.

Before Drakkar could fully recover, Jace hit him with another *Shield Bash*, stunning him again. He ducked behind the man and got in two more backstabs.

Jace was low on mana but had enough for one more *Shield Bash* without tapping into Luna's mana.

They continued to dance around each other, both scoring hits, but only Jace actually doing any damage. The thieves were cheering now and Jace realized they were cheering for him. That seemed to unnerve the guildmaster.

After getting in a few more hits, Jace knew he must be getting close. It was time to use his last *Shield Bash* and finish Drakkar off.

Then the guildmaster used *Vanish* and disappeared. Jace waited for the inevitable attack but instead he heard a gasp of pain from a few feet away.

Dainard Drakkar backstabs Almedha Pressalor for 20 damage.
Dainard Drakkar backstabs Almedha Pressalor for 21 damage.
Almedha Pressalor dies.

"Consider her life as my severance package," grinned Drakkar as Charlena's lifeless body slid to the ground. Then the guildmaster *Vanished* again but did not reappear. Then one of the men guarding the alleyway was thrown to the ground by an invisible force.

"I will have my revenge," called a disembodied voice from the end of the alleyway. "I will have my revenge."

Jace realized what the guildmaster was doing. He was using up his mana to use one *Vanish* after another. Even at level 11, his mana wouldn't last long doing that but it had obviously lasted long enough to allow him to escape.

Looking down at Charlena's body, he was glad they changed their bind point earlier. That would have been terrible if they hadn't. With Sinking Springs destroyed, who knows where the game would have respawned her.

"Guildmaster," said one of the men from the alleyway, addressing Jace. "Do we go after him?"

Jace smirked as he realized Drakkar's former men had already accepted him as their new guildmaster. It was time to act like one.

"No," he told them. He pointed to four of the men. "Go back to the guildhouse and make sure he doesn't take anything or burn it to the ground."

The men nodded and ran off. Jace motioned to the remaining men. "Stay with me. We'll go to the guildhouse in a moment."

It took a few minutes, but an angry Charlena came stomping into the alley. The men with him gasped and made warding gestures. "Fate-touched! She is fate-touched!"

"Where is that son of a –" Charlena started to demand but Jace held up his hand.

"He's gone," he told her. "He'll probably flee the city since he'll know the entire guild, such as it is, will be out looking for him."

Muttering to herself, she bent down and looted her body. As soon as she had taken the last of her possessions, the body disappeared.

Once again, the men made a warding gesture, but this time kept quiet. No doubt they did not want to incur the wrath of the extremely angry elf woman who had apparently come back to life.

Jace always found it interesting when NPCs were forced to deal with the issue of players respawning.

Some of them just ignored it completely, as if it never happened. Some assumed it was the work of the gods. In this case, they thought fate had brought her back to exact revenge, like a revenant or avenging angel.

"I'm going to find that guy and I'm going to kill him," she told him, daring him to object.

"I doubt we'll ever see him again," Jace told her.

"If we do," she fumed. "I'm going to cut off his…"

"Maybe," he interjected. "We should go check out the guildhouse."

Charlena glared at him.

"He could have gone there," Jace said innocently. "If so, you'll have your chance to do… what you just said."

The elf brightened at that. "Let's go then."

"Take us to the guildhouse," he told the thieves.

Chapter 55

Jace, Charlena and Luna went to the guildhouse. The building was a dilapidated old house near the bridge side of town. Once there, he went to the guildmaster's office. The moment he sat down in the seat, he was offered the option to become guildmaster and he accepted. Doing so immediately lost him 200 faction points with the guards and gained him 200 faction with the Crossroads thieves guild.

As guildmaster, he had access to some new options in his HUD. He sent Charlena an invite to the guild and once she accepted, he immediately promoted Charlena to the position of Lieutenant.

"Cool," she said as she read her system messages. She puffed out her chest a bit. "I'm a Lieutenant."

Smiling, he also promoted a level 6 *Rogue* named Mikel as a Lieutenant. They were leaving and he needed to leave someone in charge. As the highest level member, he hoped Mikel would be able to do the best job. Or at least he hoped the guy would defend any attempts to wrest control away.

He then found the stash, the guild money. It seemed low and Jace guessed Drakkar had been skimming. Still, there were over 500 gold and he saw Charlena's eyes go wide.

"We need to leave this here to help the guild grow," he told her.

"What?" she asked in confusion.

"We're the leaders," he told her. "If the guild does better, they make more money. Since we get a percentage of the money each month, we'll make more money in the long run."

"Oh," she said smiling. "It's a profit deal!"

He nodded. "Yes, it's a profit deal."

He left the office and gathered the remaining rogues. "I've cleaned house here but now I need to go to Whitecliff to set up an alliance. I'm leaving Mikel in charge while I'm gone. If anyone steps out of line, I'll be back and I'll kill you all and start again. If anyone steals or tries to cheat the guild, I'll be back and kill you all."

The men in the room blanched and nodded.

"Mikel," he addressed his new Lieutenant. "You're in charge while I'm gone. I want you to use the guild funds we have to fix this place up. We need a proper guild house. Don't go overboard but we want it to look just like any other house in the area so we're less obvious to the guard. Start recruiting, but only take the best. Write everything in the guild journal and I'll find out about it and send you any further instructions."

Mikel nodded through his entire speech. When he was done talking, the man finally spoke. "Yes, guildmaster."

"Good," he told them. "We're leaving for the capital tomorrow, but I will be back to check on things periodically. And remember..." Jace willed the hat to change him from one race to another quickly. "I can be anyone, any time."

The men nodded.

"Good luck Mikel," he told his new Lieutenant as he and Charlena left.

They left then and headed back to the inn. Once they were out of earshot, Charlena turned to him with a look of admiration in her eyes. "Look at you, Mr. Gangster."

Jace smiled. He'd been playing the part for the benefit of the NPCs. They were programmed to react certain ways based on certain behavior. If he wanted them to treat him like a guildmaster, he had to act like one. In this case, all those gangster vids he'd watched paid off.

"I had to do a little roleplaying," he told her.

"Very take charge," she smiled.

They walked on to the inn where Charlena logged out for the night but not before she gave him a very passionate kiss that left him more than a little flustered.

Once she was gone, he went back to the inn and ate a meal of freshly caught trout and potatoes. The trout, he had to admit, was much tastier than what he prepared with his frying pan. He guessed he'd need to buy some spices if he wanted to experiment with cooking.

He hung out at the Wry Weasel until well after midnight when they closed down their common room and he was forced to leave or get a room. He chose the room and after paying the barmaid, he and Luna went upstairs to the tiny room he had rented.

It was tiny compared to modern standards, but it gave him a chance to relax on a comfortable bed and play around with the new thieves guild HUD options he had as well as think of ways of getting into the royal palace.

He briefly considered going down to the bridge side. He'd learned the White Run River here was so deep that boats and even some ships that came up it with trade goods and passengers. It only took them a day or two to make the journey down to the capital.

Unfortunately, upon asking around, he found that the cheapest cost for a passenger was 500 gold per person. While Mordred could afford things like that, Jace couldn't. They'd have to stick to the original plan and take the caravan tomorrow.

As his mind wandered with different ideas on how to get into the palace, Jace lost track of time. Before he knew it, morning had come. He and Luna went downstairs and ordered breakfast and was nearly done when Charlena appeared out of nothing and immediately yawned.

"Remind me again why I'm up at 5 a.m.," she said irritably.

"So, we can catch the caravan," he reminded her.

"Oh yeah," she said with no enthusiasm. "I can auto-follow and then logout and go back to bed, right?"

He smiled and nodded. "Yes, you can go back to bed once we book passage and you auto-follow the caravan master."

"Good," she said sleepily. "Let's go then."

They found the caravan stationed outside the main gate, getting ready to depart. Apparently, it had arrived earlier, dropped off some goods and picked up other goods and was getting ready to leave.

After asking around, they were pointed to the caravan master who was a dusky skinned female gnome who wore expensive leather travel clothes. She was attractive but her small stature and youthful appearance made her look too child-like for Jace's taste.

He walked over to the little gnome. "Caravan Master?"

The gnome stopped what she was doing and looked up at him, sizing him up with a critical eye and then looking over Charlena with the same professional appraisal. "Already have enough guards. Maybe next time."

The gnome started to turn but Jace cleared his throat. "Actually, we're looking to book passage."

Turning around, she eyed them again. "You got money?"

"How much is passage?" he asked.

"100 if you want to walk behind," she repeated in a practice, bored tone. "200 if you want to walk in the middle - more protection - or 300 if you want to ride in one of the carts. And that's each!"

Jace looked at Charlena, who was stifling a yawn. She gave him a questioning look.

He'd done so much walking, he would have loved to ride but they needed to conserve their money. From his time spent in other capitals, he knew everything would be more expensive once they reached Whitecliff. "Let's just walk behind."

Charlena nodded and he squared up with the caravan leader, whose name he learned was Jinklodez Fizzlechart, or Jin for short.

"Alright," she told them after she'd pocketed the money. "We pull out in fifteen minutes. Head to the back and follow the main caravan. Don't lag behind or we'll leave you, you'll get lost or you'll get killed. Got it?"

"Got it," Jace said and then turned to Charlena. "Target her, and then auto-follow. You should automatically find your spot and walk along."

She nodded tiredly and gave him a quick peck on the cheek. "See you later after I wake up and have some coffee and get my school work done." She yawned again. "And study for finals."

Before he could respond her eyes went glassy and she turned and started to the back of the caravan very mechanically. It was one thing to see her following him but watching her walk like a zombie on her own was a bit weird for him.

The long line of wagons stretched out over nearly one hundred horse drawn carts. All were backed with goods or livestock. By time they reached the end of the procession, they only had to wait a few minutes before a command was shouted down the line and carts began to move.

When the cart in front of them moved, Charlena robotically followed and Jace kept pace with her. He smiled. Finally, after all the things they'd been through, they were on their way to the capital.

He wondered if he'd find any of the players he'd met when he got to Whitecliff. He thought about Duglas, Diana and Mika whether they were okay. None of them were very experienced players - Diana had admitted she'd never played the game. Starting off naked and alone was not an easy start as he well knew. It would be tough for them but he hoped they'd be able to make it.

Realizing he was falling behind, he turned his mind to the walk and keeping pace with the caravan. They had a long way to go.

***

The next week passed excruciatingly slow for Jace. The trip was boring and tedious. He was literally just walking behind a bunch of carts for eight hours a day, watching while they set up camp for two hours, then they ate and then they all went to bed except for a few guards who weren't very talkative. In the morning, they ate and then took two hours to pack everything up before going again. He lost track of how many times he wished he could log out and come back in a week.

To make matters worse, it was finals week for Charlena. She had logged in a little bit over the weekend but once she realized how boring it was, had spent most of the weekend studying. When Monday came, she was barely on at all as she took finals and studied for finals. Friday, he hadn't seen her at all as she'd gone out celebrating with some of her classmates.

517

Part of him was excited to get to Whitecliff, he couldn't deny it. But the lack of time with Charlena was really weighing on him. With nothing to do but follow the caravan and think, he had quickly become bored. He also felt himself feeling a little anger and resentment towards Charlena, especially Friday night when she hadn't logged in at all.

He knew he had no right to. After all, she was a living, breathing person. He might be too, but he couldn't log out. He was stuck in the game. And maybe that was where the resentment focused. She could log out and he couldn't. She had a life. He didn't.

As Friday night dragged into Saturday morning, Jace was left with nothing but his dark thoughts.

Chapter 56

Early Saturday afternoon, the caravan pulled into Whitecliff and Jace's dark mood was momentarily brightened. Unlike the gothic cities of Visimar, where Mordred was from, which were dark and ancient, Whitecliff was a bright sprawling city larger than any he'd seen.

Thirty foot walls built from white stone surrounded the entire city and Jace could see siege engines mounted at various intervals along the wall. A moat thirty feet wide had been dug next to the walls to prevent any invaders from attacking the walls directly. The creators had definitely had defense in mind when they had built the city.

From his vantage point at the back of the caravan, he could see that part of the city was raised and surrounded by an inner wall. Jace guessed by the opulent houses he could see that it was the noble district. In the middle of the noble district, rising even higher, was a large fairy tale style castle with tall walls and towers. He sighed as he realized that the castle was his goal. It was the royal palace.

His ideas and plans all went up in smoke as he looked at the layout. The royal district was like a city within a city and then the pinnacle of that smaller city was a walled fortress. He needed to go back to the drawing board. He'd need to find out more information about the noble district and the castle itself.

He looked over at Charlena as she mechanically followed the caravan. Her auto-follow would automatically disengage when they reached the city and her body would stand there like a statue until she logged in. Jace had no idea when that would be.

They'd barely spoken on Thursday. She'd logged on really just long enough to tell him she wouldn't be tomorrow because she was going out to celebrate the end of finals.

Jace felt the bitterness rising up again and pushed it down. He looked down at Luna, who had been his only companion during the journey. "We're here."

"Here?" the cat asked and sniffed. "Food?"

Jace chuckled but also felt guilty. He had rations to eat but hadn't thought to pack anything for Luna. He'd had to barter with some of the caravan merchants and managed to find someone with pickled herrings. She hadn't been especially fond of those, but had eaten them once he'd explained that was all they had.

"Yes," he told her. "Food. Good food hopefully."

"Food!" she meowed happily.

He laughed again and looked around. There was no reason for him to stay with the caravan at this point. Breaking formation and going off to the side of the caravan, he broke into a jog and headed to the city gates.

Reaching them, he asked one of the guards at the gate where the graveyard was. The guard gave him directions and he ran along the wall to the north until he spotted it. To say it was large was an understatement. It was enormous. Based on the size of the graveyard, Whitecliff might be the largest city he'd ever been to.

As he reached the gates, he received the prompt he was expecting.

New spawn point: Whitecliff
Do you wish to set Whitecliff as your bind point? (Yes or No)

Jace set his bind point and then raced back to the gate with Luna trailing behind him. When he got to the gate, the guards stopped him.

"Business?" one of the guards demanded.

Jace thought for a moment before answering. He'd thought about trying to come up with some elaborate story but in the end, he was too impatient to explore the city. He fell back to the normal business of all players - adventuring. "Mercenary."

The guard made a sour face. Obviously, he didn't approve of mercenaries, and by extension, players. "Are you a member of the *Fighter's Guild*?"

"No, I'm in the Thi…" Jace stopped himself just in time. He'd almost told the guard he was in thieves' guild.

The guard raised a questioning eyebrow.

"I'm thinking about joining," Jace told the man.

"All mercenaries must be registered with either the *Adventurer's Guild* or the *Fighter's Guild*," the guard told him in a bored, official tone. "Acting in the capacity of a mercenary inside the walls of Whitecliff without being a part of a sanctioned guild is punished by a fine and/or imprisonment. Do you understand?"

"Yes," Jace told him.

"You may enter," the guard said and then added. "Stay out of trouble." The man caught his arm as he started to pass and looked him in the eye. "You disrespect the law, you disrespect me. Got it?"

Jace nodded and the guard released him. Jace shook his head as he walked through the gate. That was one guard who took his job way too seriously.

Once inside, Jace gawked at the huge city that stretched out before him. From here, the noble district on his left was even taller than it looked from the outside. The rest of the city was built on a downgrade that sloped down to the ocean. Even from far away, he could see the docks and the dozens of ships in port.

Between him and the docks were hundreds of houses, shops, inns and who knew what else. It was a fantasy metropolis, larger than any of the cities he'd visited in VEIL before. He couldn't wait to explore it.

The idea of exploring it made him think of Charlena and he realized how excited she could be to see it as well. That made him smile despite the fact that he hadn't seen much of her the last week. She was still his only friend right now and he still had feelings for her - even if he wasn't completely sure what those feelings were.

He waited near the gate for several hours, waiting for Charlena but she didn't log in. At one point, he walked back to where she would have disengaged from the caravan. Her body was still there, glassy eyed.

He walked back and went inside the gates again and looked around. He found the first inn he came to, a three story building called the Dwarvish Fork Inn. He found a seat at one of the tables and waited to be served.

Someone came over to his table and he turned to give the barmaid his order and froze. Standing in front of him was a stunning raven haired woman with amber eyes who looked familiar.

She was dressed in a skimpy white outfit decorated with runes that Jace recognized as mage robes but they'd been cut to reveal her ample cleavage and her long, shapely legs.

"Are you just going to drool," the woman said as she smiled seductively. "Or are you going to ask me to join you? I mean, you did ask me to join you here."

The pieces fell in place and he recognized her. "Diana!"

He rose from his chair and gave her a big hug and realized how much chestier she was than Charlena as her breast pressed against him. He released her quickly, heat rising to his cheeks.

Diana let loose a melodic giggle and slipped into the chair across from him. "Oh darling, you are such an innocent little thing aren't you." She looked around. "Where is that tasty girlfriend of yours? The elf with the fiery mane?"

"She… ah…" Jace stuttered. The woman oozed sexuality and Jace had a hard time concentrating. Finally, he pulled himself together. "She hasn't logged on yet."

"Oh," she said in a husky voice. "So, it's just the two of us."

Jace swallowed. "I… ah…"

"Jace Burton," came a soft voice near him.

He turned to see the attractive Asian girl in a patchwork of different color chainmail armor and a torn, dirtied tabard with the symbol of Faeshai, the goddess of sun and healing. Jace knew instantly who it was. "Mika!"

He got up to give her a hug but she bowed instead. "I owe you thanks I cannot repay, Jace Burton."

Jace stopped himself and did his best to emulate her bow. "You don't owe me anything. I'm glad you're human."

"Yes," she smiled. "Me too." Mika looked at the raven haired vixen across from him and made a little bow. "I am sorry to have disturbed you."

Jace looked between Mika and Diana, who was watching the exchange with amusement. He lowered his voice so the other patrons couldn't hear. "No, no… join us… This is Diana. She's like us." He gave her a meaningful look.

Mika's eyes opened wide. "You were a…" She lowered her voice. "You were a monster too?"

"Oh yes precious," the older woman replied. "When this young stud found me, I had eight legs and eight eyes. Quite ghastly, I can assure you."

Mika slid into the chair next to Diana. "I was a Yeti. Covered with fur."

Jace was overwhelmed. He hadn't expected to find Diana or Mika here so soon considering how long it had taken him to get here. It was good to see them and it was even better to see that they were human again.

"So, dear one," Diana looked at him. Her voice turned very suggestive. "Now that we're here, what do you intend to do with us? Because if you don't have any ideas, I'm sure I can come up with some."

Jace felt himself blush and saw a little color in Mika's face as well. He cleared his throat. "I need to get into the royal palace. Inside there is a hidden room called the *Help Desk*. It's an old method of contacting support, back when they tried to do everything in-game."

"And then what?" asked Diana.

"And then we explain our situation and they fix whatever bug caused this," he told her. "And we get to go back to our...lives. Or at least get your assets back."

Diane nodded. "I have to admit. As easy as the men around here are to manipulate, I would like to have my money. Out of principle, if nothing else."

Mika nodded. "I agree. The money from my grandmother's estate, it is mine now. She would want me to have it."

"Then all we have to do is figure out a way through the guarded and restricted noble district, get into the heavily guarded castle and then stay there long enough to find the secret room," he told them.

"Piece of cake," Diana told him and winked.

"Yes," Mika said. "We will help you Jace Burton. We will find this *Help Desk*."

Jace couldn't help but smile. They both seemed to have a lot of faith in him. It was more than he had. He'd thought this would be a formidable challenge, but from where he was now, it seemed impossible.

He looked across the table at the two beautiful women staring back at him and tried to look and sound confident. "Right, piece of cake."

Epilogue

Charlena groaned as she opened her eyes. Her head pounded and her stomach felt like she was going to be sick. It wasn't quite light out. Was it that early? Keeping eyes open made her feel like bombs were going off in her head. She closed her eyes again and tried to remember what had happened last night.

She remembered going out to eat with her friends after finals. They'd gone to Johnny's Bistro near campus that they loved. Her friends had wanted to hear the latest on her "virtual" boyfriend. She hadn't told them everything going on with Jace, just that she'd met a guy from Philadelphia online and they'd been hanging out a lot.

After dinner, they'd gone out to their favorite dance club, Pure Energy. She remembered dancing and doing shots. And then doing some more shots. And then… well, actually that's where things kind of ended. Had she passed out?

She forced herself to sit up and instantly regretted it as things swam and her stomach lurched. Charlena looked down and realized she was still in her clothes from last night. Obviously, she'd been too wasted to take her clothes off - assuming she'd been conscious at all.

Looking over at the bed on the other side of the dorm room, she saw that her roommate was still in her party clothes too. Good, the last thing she needed was Juliette ragging her about falling asleep in her clothes.

Charlena pushed herself up out of bed and instantly fell back as her head swam and the room seemed to move.

She didn't drink often and got drunk even less. Now she remembered why. It was fun while you were doing it, but the next morning was totally not worth it.

Her second attempt was more successful, and she stayed on her feet this time. Slowly, looking through slitted eyes, she went to their small kitchenette and started a cup of coffee. There was a really bad taste in her mouth, and she thought she must have gotten sick at some point last night.

She made her way to their shared bathroom and closed the door. She found her toothbrush and spent several minutes brushing her teeth until the acrid taste was gone. If it was still early, she could go back to bed and then log in to meet Jace. After all, they were arriving in the capital today, which should be exciting.

Charlena heard her phone ring but ignored it. The phone stopped ringing prematurely and she heard Juliette's rough morning voice. "Who? Luna Burton? You've got the wrong number…"

It took a moment to register but Charlena threw open the door. "It's for me! Juliette, it's for me."

Rushing over, she took her phone from her roommate and put it up to her ear. "Yes, this is Luna Burton. Sorry, we had a rough night and my roommate was trying to let me sleep in."

"Miss Burton," the voice said. "This Grace White from Thomas Jefferson University Hospital. We spoke earlier about your brother Jace Burton."

Charlena tried to make her voice as normal sounding as possible, even though her head was pounding and her stomach was making very non-feminine noises. "Yes, you said you didn't have my brother there, right?"

"That's true. There is no Jace Burton here." the woman's voice said. "But I checked, and we had a John Doe come in on the same day. The chart matches your description: automobile accident coma victim."

Could that be Jace? Is that why she couldn't find him? He was a John Doe? But that didn't make any sense. There was that report about him being pronounced dead at the scene. They must have revived him! That had to be it!

"Hello? Miss Burton?" the voice on the phone said.

"Yes," Charlena replied. "Sorry, your news was unexpected."

"I understand. We'd like you to come to us to identify him and let us know if it is your brother," Grace said.

"Yes," Charlena agreed. "Of course!"

"Good," the woman said. "I can put you in for next Friday at p.m.. Just come to the front desk and ask for me, Grace White."

"Do you have anything sooner?" Charlena asked. She didn't want to wait a week to find out whether this was Jace, though in her heart she knew it had to be. As it was, she'd have to take off work early to go check it out, but it would be totally worth it.

"I'm afraid not," Grace replied. "There's some authorizations that need to be done and one of the attending physicians must be able to attend. I'm sure you understand."

Charlena didn't really understand but she didn't want to press the issue, especially since she wasn't actually Jace's sister. "I'll see you on Friday. Thank you."

Charlena hung up. She couldn't believe it! She'd found him! It had to be him. What were the chances of another car accident victim in a coma coming on the same day? She couldn't wait to tell him! She'd been right the whole time! He was alive!

Then she looked down at the phone. It told her the time was 6:03 p.m.. She had slept the entire day away! She was supposed to have spent the day with Jace in game! Charlena needed to login right now and at least tell him the good news.

The FEVRE pods for the dorm were down the hall. She looked down at herself. It was fine. She could go into the pod in this - even if it might be a little ripe. Charlena really wanted to tell Jace and she wanted to tell him right now!

She started towards the door, ignoring the pounding in her head. Charlena needed to tell Jace right away. That John Doe had to be in. Jace was alive and she needed to tell him right now.

Join the Adventure

To learn more about the adventures of Jace, Charlena and Luna, or to learn of his other books and projects, visit the author's website at:

https://www.johncressman.com

Or visit him on Facebook

https://www.facebook.com/authorjohncressman/

About the Author

John E. Cressman is an author, magician, mentalist, hypnotist, programmer, and longtime lover of roleplaying games and fantasy/sci-fi books.

As a teen, he wasted long hours creating D&D fantasy campaigns for his friends to play. He has tried several pen and paper roleplaying games from the original Dungeons and Dragons, Traveler and Star Frontiers to the new Pathfinder games.

He still enjoys computer RPGs and MMORPGs, with his current favorite being Elder Scrolls Online. He used to play Skyrim, but then he took an arrow to the knee.

John has published two books on hypnosis and is now trying his hand at the fantasy LitRPG genre with his new LitRPG trilogy, VEIL Online.